*A burning romance that sweeps
from seething plantation intrigues
to the dangerous seductions
of old New Orleans*

It was at the great plantation of Cottonwood that Melanie first learned of the secret that tormented Roland Donavan—a secret that he refused to reveal even in the throes of passion as Melanie used every weapon in her arsenal of persuasion.

It was on the fashionable streets of New Orleans that Melanie first spied Roland in the company of the ravishingly lovely actress who clearly had first claim on his heart, despite the ardor with which he pursued and possessed Melanie as his wife.

Spurred by curiosity, lashed by jealousy, Melanie moved ever deeper into a maze of forbidden knowledge and shocking discovery . . .

. . . and ever closer to her moment of fearful decision about the man whom she told herself to despise—only to have her heart rebel. . . .

Also by Jennifer Blake and available
from Popular Library

LOVE'S WILD DESIRE
08616-5 $1.95

Tender
Betrayal

by Jennifer Blake

POPULAR LIBRARY • NEW YORK

TENDER BETRAYAL

Published by Popular Library, a unit of CBS Publications, the
Consumer Publishing Division of CBS Inc.

Copyright © 1979 by Patricia Maxwell

ISBN: 0-445-04429-2

Printed in the United States of America

10 9 8 7 6 5 4 3 2 1

For Jane Stone, a gentle critic and researcher extraordinary.

Part One

Chapter 1

MELANIE JOHNSTON lifted the front of her Maiden's Sigh Blue silk skirts, her lace-edged petticoat and crinoline, and set one satin-shod foot on the brass fender of the fireplace. As the warmth of the coal fire crept around her ankles and the calves of her legs, she shivered a little. It was bitterly cold outside. Though it was seldom that Natchez, Mississippi, felt the sting of sleet and snow, there was ice mixed with the rain pecking against the windows of the great house known as Monmouth. The inclement weather had not affected the ball given by Governor John Quitman, owner of that square, white-pillared mansion, however. Few wanted to miss the social event of the season or risk offending one of the most influential men in the state. Even from the seclusion of the ladies' upstairs retiring room, Melanie could hear the strains of a waltz and the buzz of excited voices.

It was surprising that she had this small bedchamber to herself, though not an unpleasant situation. She was tired of smiling and making polite conversation, of exchanging the same banal greetings with the same circle of friends and acquaintances that she had been seeing almost nightly for the past three months. The winter season had been a long one, made longer by her grandfather's stiff-necked determination to attend every affair to which he and his granddaughter were invited. He would allow no man an opportunity to say that he was sulking at home, afraid to

9

face his detractors, hiding from the ugly rumors which floated around the town.

Melanie sighed, lifting a hand to her temple. The vicious lies concerning her grandfather's conduct during the late conflict with Mexico were vexing; more vexing still was the question of how to convince her grandfather that there was no direct physical action he could take to quell them. He had always been a man of deeds, of quick, decisive campaigns of action. A veteran of the War of 1812, the Seminole Indian Wars, and the War of Texas Independence, it was hard for him to find his former bright honor inexplicably tarnished in his old age. Some men who had marched away at the head of their volunteer troops had returned with barrels full of Mexican silver dollars which they had melted down for tea services, cutlery, and mellow-toned plantations bells. Melanie's grandfather, Colonel Ezell Johnston, had returned broken in health, trailing not a cloud of glory, but a vague, disquieting suspicion.

So deep was Melanie's absorption that she turned, startled, as the bedchamber door opened behind her.

"Melanie Johnston! Here is where you have been hiding. I have looked this big house up and down for you. Dom declares his heart is broken because you missed the mazurka you promised him, and are at this very minute missing the next-to-last waltz before supper. You must be the most unnatural fiancée alive to prefer being up here toasting your toes instead of downstairs in the ballroom in the arms of the man you love!"

Melanie could, when she wished, appear most imposing. She was no more than average height, but her soft, auburn hair, worn in a plaited crown high upon her head, gave her a look of regal stature. The classically beautiful lines of her face could set in a stern mold; the soft, gentian blue of her eyes could take on a look of unbelievable chill. Only the generous curves of her mouth, with its hint of repressed passion, remained unchanged.

"If Dom wanted me," she said, a frown between her

10

brows, "he should have come after me himself, instead of sending his sister."

"Come himself? In here?" Chloe Clements asked with an inane giggle. "You must be mad. You know he would never dare! Besides, it is not at all the thing for a suitor, even a fiancé, to go about looking lovelorn, poking into empty rooms and searching behind the drapes for the girl who is to be his wife. It would make him a laughing stock."

"Something Dom would not like at all, would he?"

"Is that a slur upon my brother's character? Come now, Melanie, you know you would not like it if Dom began to play the passionate lover, trailing after you wherever you went, grabbing at you with hot hands, and breathing heavily down the neck of your gown. You would snub the poor dear unmercifully if he tried such a thing. Now I, on the other hand, get a thrill right down to the tips of my toes at the idea of a man staring at me with his soul in his eyes and doing his best to entice me into dark corners!"

An unwilling smile curved Melanie's mouth. "Yes, I'm sure you would."

"And if he was a forceful man, one who would sweep me up in his carriage and take me away with him, I know I would be too weak to resist. I would simply cling to him enthralled—Pray God I don't meet him tonight, however. Why is it that every time there is an important occasion I am afflicted with my monthly courses. It is maddening beyond endurance!"

Whisking to the dressing table in one corner of the bedchamber, Chloe leaned forward to peer anxiously at her reflection in the oval mirror which surmounted it. She frowned and from the reticule that hung at her wrist took out a rice-powder paper, pressing it to the dark circles beneath her eyes.

It was difficult to like or dislike Chloe. Her laugh was annoying, her view of life was colored by the lurid French novels brought to her by her brother from New Orleans on his frequent trips downriver, and yet, she was so frank in her speech and manner, so unself-consciously selfish in her outlook, that she evoked an odd form of admiration. She was not pretty, her features being too small, and her blond hair too fine and flyaway. Still, she attracted attention, especially the masculine variety, with her large, hazel eyes set in a slant in her face, like a cat, and the proportions of her form, which were generous for someone of her small size.

"Why it should be considered such a terrible thing to paint I can't begin to imagine," Chloe mused, turning her face this way and that. "A little color to distract from this pallid complexion would be marvelous. I heard Governor Quitman brought his wife some of the red papers used by the Mexican women to color their cheeks and lips, but if she has made use of them, I have yet to see it."

"I'm sure Eliza Quitman has better things to think about."

"Dear Melanie, don't be so stuffy. What is the harm in improving on nature, especially when nature plays such dastardly tricks on females?" Without pausing, Chloe went on. "Speaking of that Mexican business, do you remember Roland Donavan?"

Melanie turned her head sharply to stare at the other girl. "Yes, of course. He was second in command of Johnston's Volunteers under my grandfather."

"So he was," Chloe agreed. "Silly of me, though I had the idea that you were away at that fancy finishing school when the troop was formed and marched away. Before that, Roland Donavan was not precisely one of the *beaux sabres* around the ballrooms of Natchez."

That much was true. Roland Donavan had never been the type to be welcomed with open arms by the concerned mamas of Natchez society. This was, apparently, just as he wanted it, since he had preferred a different sort of entertainment from the stiff formality current in the big houses upon the bluff above the Mississippi River. Fast horses, high stakes, strong liquor, flashy women, a penchant for all these and more could be laid at the door of the man under discussion. Melanie had never met him,

12

but he was well known by reputation, and his name had come up often in her grandfather's reminiscences of the Mexican campaign.

"His father owns Cottonwood across the river on the Louisiana side, doesn't he?" Melanie inquired, clasping her hands at her waist as she straightened and turned from the fire. He not only owned it, he was in residence there, a damning circumstance. Many of Natchez's leading citizens held title to vast tracts of land in the Louisiana Delta country on the other side of the river; her own grandfather had owned a large tract before it had been sold to finance Johnston's Volunteers before the late war with Mexico. His home was in Natchez, however, since it was considered unfashionable and unhealthy to live on such holdings.

"That's the man," Chloe answered. "They say he has been in California for the two years since the war ended, making his fortune in the gold fields. Whether that is true or not, he is certainly home again now."

"Home? At Cottonwood?"

The other girl gave a quick shake of her head. "They say he doesn't get along with his father. He's staying here in Natchez at a hotel near the river. The River Rest, I think."

Near the river. That manner of giving the location was another way of saying the hotel was in the unsavory part of town, which lay between the foot of the high bluff on the bank of the river and the water's edge. Known as Natchez-Under-The-Hill, it was the province of river boatmen, cardsharps, drunkards, murderers, thieves, and women of easy virtue—the undesirables. It seemed fitting that the man they were speaking of should have taken up residence there.

"Why are you frowning so? Aren't you excited?" Chloe demanded.

"Why should I be?"

"Because there's a new bachelor on the scene, of course, and from all accounts, a rich one. He's a handsome devil of a man who has been to far places, done

13

fantastic things, had great adventures—I saw him on the street this afternoon talking to Governor Quitman and nearly swooned away. I was certain the governor, since he is also a veteran of the war, would have invited one of the last three survivors of Johnston's Volunteers to the ball this evening. If he doesn't put in an appearance, I'm not sure I won't go into a decline from sheer disappointment!"

"Don't be silly," Melanie said, her tone sharp. "You don't think he will come?"

"I can't be sure, naturally," Chloe said, slanting a quick glance at Melanie in the mirror, "but the night is young yet."

In a silken whirl of skirts, Melanie turned toward the door. Her grandfather and Roland Donavan must not meet, not here at the governor's house crowded with guests.

"Melanie, where are you going?" Chloe exclaimed.

Melanie, already hurrying down the wide hall with its turkey red carpet, did not answer.

At the top of the stairs she paused, clinging to the mahogany handrail. The great front doors were just opening in the entrance hall below her. A man in a dark green cape lined with beaver over his evening clothes was just handing his high-crowned beaver hat to the butler. The light of the brass chandelier overhead shone on the waves of his uncovered hair with a blue black gleam. His skin had the sun-bronzed look of an outdoorsman, and there were crinkled lines about his eyes, as though he were used to surveying great distances. He had the broad shoulders of a man who has known hard labor, and he was tall, topping the governor's butler, who was known to be six feet, by at least two inches.

Behind her Chloe, breathless from her pursuit, said, "I declare, Melanie, what came over you?"

At the sound of the other girl's voice, the man below them looked up, revealing eyes of a deep and startling green beneath craggy brows. In that instant, the name he had given the butler floated upward.

"Donavan, Roland Donavan."

"Yes, sir, Mr. Donavan," the butler said. "Come right in. We've been expecting you, sir."

With a determined lift of her chin, Melanie started down the stairs, leaving Chloe openmouthed behind her. "Mr. Donavan," she said, her voice raised in a tone that was both entreating and commanding. "May I speak to you for a moment?"

Roland Donavan paused in the act of unfastening his cape. A quizzical look tinged with appreciation leaped into his eyes as he watched her graceful descent. His surprise was understandable. Young ladies did not accost strange men, not even in the relative safety of a private home with scores of people within call. To do so left them open to the charge of being forward and pursuing, at the very least. He did not answer until she reached the level of his eyes, two steps above him.

"Certainly," he said, his deep voice pleasant, carefully noncommittal as he inclined his head in a slight bow. "Miss—?"

Melanie gave her name with a certain stiffness. If it meant anything to him, he gave no sign. A smile curved his firm mouth. "Is our conversation to be private?"

"If you please," Melanie answered. With some trepidation she took the arm he offered, then stood frowning in indecision. It was difficult to know where they could go to talk undisturbed. The parlor was filled with dancing couples, the library had been turned into a card room, where her grandfather, she hoped, was comfortably settled. In the dining room the servants were setting up the supper tables, putting the finishing touches to the evening repast. Upstairs was nothing but bedchambers, most strictly forbidden territory, even if Chloe was not barring the way, staring with fascinated horror at the two of them.

"Could—could we step outside?" Melanie asked, nervous apprehension making her voice abrupt.

Roland Donavan raised an eyebrow. "You will be chilled without a wrap."

"That doesn't matter. What I have to say will not take

15

long." And when she was done, Mr. Donavan would be out of the house, the first step in his swift departure from Monmouth.

Bowing in acquiescence, he led her toward the front doors. The butler swung them open, and Melanie passed through, ignoring the Negro servant's scandalized expression.

The iron lantern which hung above the door had been extinguished by the wind, leaving the portico, with its massive pillars, in darkness. The rain made a spattering sound as it was blown in upon the brick floor. Melanie's skirts fluttered about her ankles in the cold wind, and gooseflesh rose on her bare arms. Now that she was alone with Roland Donavan, she began to doubt the wisdom of what she was doing. She could not think how to put her request to him. The direct course seemed bald, even insulting, but there appeared no other.

"Mr. Donavan, I am afraid that if you go inside tonight there will be trouble with my grandfather, Colonel Ezell Johnston. The right or wrongness of what is between the two of you does not concern me. My first thought is for my grandfather's health and well-being. For this reason I must ask you to leave this house, and return at another, less public time."

It was a moment before he answered, and then his voice came strong and sure from the dimness beside her. "I have no quarrel with your grandfather."

"That may be; I wouldn't know. But I do know that he has a grievance against you that is deep and abiding. Will you go, or will you not?"

"I think," he said slowly, "that I require something more by way of explanation before I answer that."

Melanie made an impatient gesture. "There isn't time."

He shifted, moving nearer. It was an instant before she realized his purpose; he was blocking the cold wind from her with his wide shoulders. With swift, economical movements, he stripped off his cape and placed it about her as he answered. "I believe if you want me to do as you ask, there will have to be time."

16

"Really, Mr. Donavan," Melanie began, reaching up to push the cape away. But his hands closed warm and firm about her upper arms, holding it in place. For a brief instant she was aware of the heat of his body, the smell of starched linen, and the fresh aroma of some spice-scented soap. Her senses were assailed by the attraction of a strong male personality. It was ridiculous, yet she felt suddenly vulnerable and a little frightened. A tremor not caused entirely by the cold night ran over her, and she hurried into speech.

"Since my grandfather's return from Mexico he has been the victim of innuendos, of rumors hinting that he cooperated with the Mexican government during his imprisonment, that he promised to use his influence with men like Governor Quitman to persuade them to adopt a hands-off policy toward Mexican lands. In return, it is said, he was given lenient treatment and an early release from his confinement. My grandfather contends that you, Captain Roland Donavan, as the officer with whom he had had the most contention, the officer who had most often questioned his military strategy and his disciplinary methods, are the person responsible for these foul accusations."

"I see," the man beside her said as she came to an abrupt halt. The timbre of his voice was low, with a troubled sound. He let his hands slip from her shoulders.

"Do you deny it?" she asked. She tried to see his face in the black, windswept darkness but could discern no more than the grim outline of his features. She was surprised that he did not plead his absence of the past year and a half or more as proof of his innocence. It would not have weighed with her, of course. Though the rumors had been rife in Natchez during that time, they seemed to have originated in Mexico before the war ended.

"What difference would it make if I did deny it, since Colonel Johnston believes it?"

The bitterness of that statement was plain. Melanie wasted no time trying to decipher the meaning. "Then you will go?"

"I have waited a long time to be invited within the walls of Monmouth. It will take some persuasion out of the ordinary to make me give up the treat."

"You don't call the necessity of avoiding facing my grandfather over the barrel of a dueling pistol out of the ordinary?"

"It is, of course, and I would prefer not to do it. Still it might be easier than turning tail and leaving such lovely company."

"If you are trying to be complimentary—"

"No, at least that was not my whole meaning. What I was trying to do was suggest some form of—compensation for the sacrifice you are asking of me."

"Compensation? What do you mean?"

"My carriage is only a few steps from here. If you will go for a drive with me, I will gladly leave your grandfather to enjoy the governor's hospitality undisturbed."

"You must be mad!" To go with him, unchaperoned, in the darkness of midnight, would be enough to blacken her good name, brand her a loose woman for the rest of her life.

"I assure you I was never more sane."

Again that trace of bitterness, and yet, she had the impression that he was smiling, taking quiet pleasure in the dilemma in which he had placed her, waiting for her answer with confidence. Abruptly, the perfect reply came to her.

"I can't," she said. "If I went with you, it would be my fiancée you had to face instead of my grandfather."

"Your fiancé?"

"Dom—Dominic Clements."

He went still at the name. He knew it, of course. How could he help it when Dom, with her grandfather and himself, were all that was left of Johnston's Volunteers? At last he spoke, "I haven't seen Dom since my return; still I doubt that he would begrudge me a few minutes of your company—for old times' sake."

There was something in his voice, a tone, a shading of irony, that she did not understand. She did know that the

18

initiative had been taken out of her hands, however, and she did not like it. She was saved from the necessity of making a reply by the eruption of loud voices inside the house. Suddenly the tall, double front doors were thrown open.

"Melanie!"

That voice, trembling with rage and concern, was well known. To refuse to answer would be worse than useless. Melanie drew a deep breath, "Here, grandpa," she said.

Colonel Ezell Johnston, though in his late sixties, had retained the upright military bearing that had been his as a young man. The shock of hair that grew back from a broad forehead and the full goatee that he wore were both a silvery gray, as were his eyes under wiry white brows. His face was contorted in a frown as he strode from the house. In his hand he carried a slender malacca cane, and crowding at his heels was a number of other people, among them Chloe, her brother Dom, and their host, Governor Quitman.

"What is the meaning of this?" the Colonel demanded, his voice shaking with anger. "It isn't enough that you have ruined my good name, you scoundrel; must you ruin my granddaughter as well?!"

"No, grandpa, it was not like that at all," Melanie tried to explain. "Don't upset yourself. It's not worth it."

"Melanie is right," the governor said, stepping to the forefront of the crowd. "I'm not certain what the problem is, Colonel, but this is neither the time nor the place to settle it."

The colonel ignored both his granddaughter's plea and the governor's suggestion of caution before their fast-gathering audience. "Well, what have you to say for yourself, you misbegotten cur? That I should live to see the day when a man like you, Captain Roland Donavan, should be invited to a decent house! Will you answer to me for your conduct, both past and present, or shall I take my cane to you here and now."

"Grandpa!" Melanie cried, stepping forward to lay a restraining hand on his arm. It was promptly shaken off.

19

At that moment the butler appeared in the doorway carrying a branch of candles. In their wavering light, Roland Donavan looked a little pale under the deep bronze of his skin. He spoke with deliberation. "I was not aware that I had injured you in any way, at any time, sir."

"Weren't you? Damn your impudence! I take leave to doubt it, but regardless, you will give me satisfaction."

"I am sorry, sir, but I could not meet a man twice my age."

Even to Melanie's ears, there was a strange note in the younger man's voice. It was not fear, nor was it guilt precisely, and yet, it seemed to carry some consciousness of responsibility.

"You will either meet me on the field of honor or take your whipping here and now like the dirt-dealing dog that you are." Raising his cane, Colonel Johnston struck Roland Donavan a blow across the face.

As a gasp went up from the onlookers, blood began to trickle from a cut on the younger man's cheekbone made by the ferrule of the colonel's cane. Roland lifted a hand to his face, then stared down at the blood that came away on his fingers. His voice was quiet as he spoke. "I ask those present to bear witness that this quarrel was forced upon me."

"I'm sure they will be glad to do it for my sake," the colonel snapped. "Name your seconds."

"Oh, grandpa, no," Melanie whispered, all too aware of the trembling that shook the old man's frail frame.

Roland Donavan flicked his gaze over the crowd gathered in the doorway, coming to rest on Dominic. For a long moment it appeared he meant to ask his former comrade in arms to act for him. There was an intent look in his eyes as he stared at Melanie's fiancé.

Dom shifted, his face tightening as his gaze came to rest on the cape still hanging about Melanie's shoulders. It almost appeared he was reluctant to meet the hard stare of the other man.

A muscle grew taut in Roland Donavan's jaw. He gave

an abrupt nod in Colonel Johnston's direction. "My seconds will call upon you as soon as possible."

"Make it tonight," the colonel grunted. "I would like to get this over by breakfast in the morning. Dom, I know I can count on you to support me, and also you, John?"

Governor John Quitman frowned. "Dueling is illegal in this state; I would prefer to have nothing to do with it. However, I cannot refuse to see that the meeting is fair and equal."

"I knew I could count on you," the colonel stated with satisfaction before he turned back to Roland. "Have your friends meet with the governor and Clements as soon as you can arrange your business."

Once more the younger man inclined his head. "As you please." Without another word, he turned and strode toward the steps.

"Sir!" the butler called. "Your hat."

"And this," Melanie added, slipping his cape from her shoulders. She handed it to the butler to be passed over also.

Roland Donavan paused at the top of the steps, his cape on his arm and his hat in his hand. For a tense moment his eyes, as hard as emeralds, held Melanie's blue gaze. In their depths was self-censure, and something more, a hint of the pain of the outcast.

With a quick indrawn breath, Melanie turned away, stepping back to her grandfather's side. She did not look back as Roland Donavan plunged into the rainswept night. The sound of his footsteps on the gravel drive echoed long in the stillness under the portico.

The cold rain still fell when Colonel Johnston left his mansion known as Greenlea for the dueling field outside of town. Melanie was awake in that predawn hour to help her grandfather into his greatcoat, hand him the rosewood box containing his matched pistols, kiss his cheek, and watch as he bowled away down the drive. Dom, along with the governor and the best doctor in Natchez, had come to fetch him in a closed carriage. The presence of

21

the latter man, though a requirement under the Code Duello, did nothing to allay the fear that gripped Melanie.

Wrapped in a mantua cloak of gray velvet, she paced the veranda overlooking the river, stopping now and then to stare with unseeing eyes out over the mist- and rain-shrouded water. Her grandfather was all that she had. Her mother and father had been killed in a steamboat explosion when she was small—a tragedy of boiling steam and quick-spreading fire from which she had only escaped by the grace of God and the strong arms of her nurse. Her grandmother, the only gentle influence in her life that she could remember, had died when she was thirteen. If she lost the colonel, she would be alone.

Images of that proud old man lying bloodied on a sodden field passed across her mind's eye. She saw him maimed, crippled, reduced to living out his days as an invalid. How he would hate that! His fierce pride was such a burning thing that it would consume him; he would be dead in a matter of weeks.

There was another fear that haunted her, that her grandfather would not be satisfied by a mere show of blood from his opponent. If he should be fortunate enough to get off the first shot, he would aim to kill. If he succeeded, would his conscience allow him to rest? He had killed men before in the heat of battle, but never in cold blood, never on the so-called field of honor.

And what of Roland Donavan? Did he deserve to die? Had he committed the indiscretions of which he was accused? Even if he had, wasn't death too high a penalty to pay?

No, no, she must not think like that. She was being disloyal to her grandfather, and he deserved no less than her full allegiance. What did she care for the death of a man she scarcely knew? It was her grandfather who was in the most deadly danger, meeting a younger man, a hard, proven soldier. She must bear no thought for any other.

So vivid were her fears, so tightly drawn her nerves, that she felt little except numb apprehension when at last the closed carriage turned into the drive. Its approach was slow, the coachman carefully avoiding the water-filled potholes in the drive. By that time the rain had stopped and a watery sun began to show its face among the trees. Her grandfather should have been hanging out the window, urging the driver to greater speed, anxious for the breakfast that he had ordered for his seconds and himself from the Greenlea kitchen. He was not. The plodding progress of the carriage could mean only one thing.

Dom met her at the front steps. The light of the pale sun touched his blond hair and glinted gold on his unshaven cheeks. His hazel eyes, so like those of his sister, were somber as they searched her face. "Don't look so, Melanie, my darling. He is not dead. Donavan deloped, giving the colonel the first shot. You'll be glad to know that your grandfather drew blood."

Melanie gave a small shake of her head. "I don't understand," she said, her blue gaze going past him to where John Quitman and the doctor were lifting the limp form of her grandfather from the carriage.

"I am afraid your grandfather was not satisfied with the hole he put in Donavan. He grabbed my pistol and shot again. Fortunately, he missed, since there had been no agreement on a second round and it is a damning breach of the code to shoot an injured man, especially one who has deloped. It would have been no less than murder! At any rate, your grandfather was—not himself. When he was refused another pistol he was so enraged he had to be restrained. There was a scuffle. In his overwrought condition his heart failed him."

There was no time for more. From the house came the servants; the colonel's manservant and butler of thirty years, Cicero, Melanie's maid Glory, the parlor and upstairs maids, even the cook and the stablehands. The exclamations, the cries of grief, the efforts to help carry the sick man into the house created a confusion only Melanie could untangle.

Cicero and the other men put her grandfather to bed. Then while the doctor sat at his side, Dom and the gover-

23

nor settled their nerves in the colonel's study with a glass of his fine Napoleon brandy.

The minutes ticked past; one hour; two. The figure on the bed did not move, but neither did the faint rise and fall of his chest cease. At last the physician got to his feet. Melanie, rising from her seat on the opposite side of the tester bed, followed him to the door. Clasping her hands together tightly at her waist, she raised her blue eyes to his kindly gaze.

"Tell me, doctor, what must I do to make him well?"

"I'm sorry, my dear girl, there is little you can do. The human heart is a mysterious organ. It may fail once, then pick up its beat, heal itself, and continue for another twenty years, or it may fail once, twice, and stop altogether. Your grandfather is no longer young; this is something you must face. I understand he has been under great strain lately, then this insane duel—Well, no need to belabor the point. We must hope that in his weakened condition he does not contract pneumonia from his soaking while he lay on the field. That would be fatal. I'm sorry that I can't give you more hope, but I am paying you the compliment, my dear, of telling you the exact truth."

"Yes, I appreciate that," Melanie whispered. "Thank you." Her face like a pale mask, she turned back into the sick room.

The governor came to express his sympathy and make his adieus. Still shaking his head and apologizing for his part in the affair, he left the house with the doctor.

Dom stayed behind. He sat with Melanie at her grandfather's side for a time, though it soon became obvious that the figure lying so still upon the sheets made him uneasy. To ease the strain, Melanie spoke at last.

"So Donavan deloped. That means he admits his guilt, doesn't it?"

Dom frowned. "It might," he agreed. "On the other hand, it could also mean that he refused to pit his skill against a man of your grandfather's age."

24

"If he did not intend to fight, why did he accept the challenge?"

"It was that or be branded a coward, something that can certainly not be said of a man who stands rock still and lets another man take potshots at him."

"You don't think he was to blame for the rumors then?"

Dom looked away. "I couldn't say."

"Why can't you?" Melanie insisted. "You were a lieutenant in Johnston's Volunteers. You marched with Donavan; you were in the same prison with him and with my grandfather. You must have some idea of the cause of the stories."

"I—am afraid not," Dom said, though he still would not meet her eyes, staring at his interlaced fingers dangling between his knees. "I do know there was friction between the two of them from the time they left Mississippi. Captain Donavan was an admirer of General Zachary Taylor, our commanding officer for the Mexican campaign; the colonel was not. Your grandfather was a follower of the strict Prussian military school; he believed in forced marches, scant rations which forced the men to live off the land they were passing through, fighting in formation, and strict discipline. Captain Donavan, on the other hand, saw the men under his command as his friends and neighbors, fellow comrades in arms. The colonel accused him of encouraging them to treat the expedition like some kind of hunting trip, with a certain basic cooperation, but at the final showdown, every man for himself. They really went at it hammer and tongs a few times, though not before the men, of course. What really put the fat in the fire, I think, was Donavan's insistence that it was your grandfather's fault that the Volunteers were captured."

"What do you mean?" Melanie asked, a frown between her eyes.

"The colonel thought General Taylor was moving too slowly, failing to pursue the enemy when he had them on the run after a decisive battle. The old man thought that

25

if his troop went all out to chase down the retreating Mexicans, the rest of the regiment would follow, regardless of the general's orders. He was wrong. We were drawn into a trap and cut to pieces, except for the seven of us who were taken prisoners."

Melanie nodded. Only three men had come back, her grandfather, Dom, and Captain Roland Donavan. The others had died either of their wounds or of heat and dysentery and strange tropical fevers. There were only three who knew what had happened in that hot and squalid place. And of those three, one was dying, one was injured.

"The wound my grandfather gave Donavan, was it serious?"

Dom shook his head. "A flesh wound in the arm on the left side. Six inches over and he would have been a dead man."

Her gaze moving to her grandfather, who was lying like an image made of yellow wax, Melanie said suddenly, "I wish he had been."

Dom so obviously wanted to do the correct thing, to be the iron support and bulwark of comfort to the woman who was to be his wife. It was a pity that the atmosphere of the sick room made him so uncomfortable. His jittery attempts to hold her hand or to enfold her soothingly in his arms began to wear on Melanie's nerves. Every time she reached for a basin or a damp cloth, he was there before her, whisking the basin from her reach to hold it for her, squeezing the cloth and leaving it too wet. He anticipated her every move to the point where he only narrowly avoided colliding with her at every turn in his efforts to be of service. At last she could stand no more and sent him away.

His relief at being dismissed to return to his lawyer's office in Natchez was so transparent she was exasperated with him all over again. Not that she needed his help; she had Cicero and Glory to take over her vigil while she ate a few mouthfuls or bathed and changed her clothing. She

26

could not bear to be away more than a few minutes at a time, however.

The first long day passed and then another. On the morning of the third day came a rattling sound in her grandfather's chest that could mean only one thing. Pneumonia. By mid-afternoon he was tossing in the delirium of fever, complaining of the heat and of fleas. It was as if in some distant corner of his mind he was reliving his incarceration in a Mexican prison. Try as she might, Melanie could not quiet him, though she fought his flailing arms and twisting body until tears of exhaustion and sympathy rolled down her cheeks. There was nothing to be done. The doctor, when sent for, came, shook his head, and went away again.

Toward evening, he finally grew quiet. It was dinner time; Melanie was trying to spoon a little broth between his slack lips when he suddenly opened his eyes.

"Melanie," he whispered, focusing on her face with difficulty.

In her haste and numb weariness, Melanie slopped some of the broth from the bowl as she set it to one side. It did not matter. She ignored the greasy stain on her gown as she leaned over her grandfather. "Grandpa, I'm here," she said, picking up his hot, bony hand, holding it between both of hers.

"My sweet child," he began, then stopped to cough as fluid bubbled in his throat. Melanie supported him as best she could, her own lungs aching with the need to breathe for him. When the racking spasms had come to an end, he lay weakly upon his pillow, one hand pressed to his chest as though it pained him. "Melanie," he tried again. "You are—all I have left. Everything else—is gone. My son, my wife, my—honor."

"No, no, grandpa, don't talk so."

"Must—must tell you. I tried to wipe away the stain on my name—but I failed. If only my aim had been true."

Once more a fit of coughing cut off his words. When it was over there was a blue tinge to his lips and his eyes were filled with tears of effort.

"Don't try to talk, grandpa," Melanie pleaded. "You must rest."

"How can I rest—while Donavan lives to go on sullying my name, and yours, Melanie, and yours?"

"Oh, grandpa," Melanie whispered.

"Yes—yes, and yours. You are the last of the Johnstons. Soon, soon I will be gone—and you will be alone. You will need a man to take care of you, but how can you go to—to Dom? How can you ask him to take you when your family honor has been besmirched? It cannot be, it need not be."

"What are you saying, grandpa? I don't understand."

"You—you can cleanse the stain. I taught you to load a pistol, to shoot. You were—a good student. You are young. You will not fail as I did. You can rid the world of the man who destroyed my character. You can kill Donavan!"

Melanie shook her head. "Oh, no. I couldn't!"

"You could," her grandfather insisted, his watery eyes wild, imploring. He turned his hand to catch her wrist with a fevered grip. "You must—for me. How can I rest else?"

"Grandpa—"

"Promise me! Promise me you will—"

Again the coughing caught him, and he threw himself back and forth on the bed, struggling for breath. "Promise me," he wheezed, his face deathly pale. Tears trickled down his face, running slowly through the creases put there by age and stalwart, yet hard, living.

He had always been such a strong man. It was terrible to see him come to this, so ill and weak, obsessed by a single idea that robbed him of dignity and peace. He was dying, she knew that, and there was so little she could do to prevent it or ease his passing.

He gave her wrist a small shake, searching the pure lines of her face with wide, beseeching eyes. "Promise me, Melanie, promise," he breathed, his voice no more than a husky whistle in his throat.

The man who was the cause of her grandfather's illness

was strong and healthy. Did he deserve to live to see the contented old age he had denied her grandfather? Did he?

"I—I promise, grandpa," she whispered.

The old man gave a trembling sigh and fell back on his pillows. He lay with his eyes closed, breathing as though done with some desperate fight. Now and then a cough would shake his body and a froth appear on his lips. Before an hour had passed, a spasm so strong racked him that he sat up straight in bed clawing at his throat. Abruptly he clutched at his chest and fell back to lie still, his eyes wide and staring.

"Grandpa!" Melanie cried, leaning over him, but she knew there would not be an answer.

Chapter 2

MELANIE GOT slowly to her feet. Tears streamed down her face, but she did not notice. She stood staring down at her grandfather's body for a long moment, then moved stiffly to the bell pull at the side of the bed. The brass bell on the back veranda rang—a far-off, musical sound—as she gave the embroidered pull a hard tug.

It would be a few minutes before Cicero could reach the bedchamber. Melanie went to the wardrobe and took down the rosewood box that Dom had returned to her, the box holding the colonel's dueling pistols. With deft movements, she lifted one from its purple velvet bed. It was the one her grandfather had used; she knew that because it had been put away without being cleaned. Vestiges of burnt powder marred the chased silver barrel, and dirt was engrained in the walnut stock. Loading with the powder and ball included in their own compartment took no more than a moment. As a knock came on the door, she held the gun at arm's length at her side, letting the fullness of her skirt hide it from view.

"Come in," she called.

Her grandfather's manservant entered the room with a quick step and a look of both alarm and dread on his gray countenance. "You rang for me, Miss Melanie?"

"Yes, Cicero. He—my grandfather is gone."

For the first time he turned toward the bed. "I feared so, Miss Melanie. I feared so."

"I—I am not certain what I should do now," she said, a catch in her voice.

"You should rest, that's all. Rest now, and leave everything to Cicero."

"Yes," she answered, "I'll try. I think—I think his dress uniform. Don't you?"

"That's what he would have wanted, Miss Melanie. In spite of everything."

It was impossible to keep anything from the servants. They had their own highly efficient system of communication. "Yes," she agreed, wiping distractedly at the tears dripping onto the collar of her gown. "In spite of everything."

In her own bedchamber, Melanie stood in frowning thought, staring down at the pistol in her hand. It was a beautiful piece of workmanship, dependable, deadly. It did not occur to her, looking at it, to disregard the promise she had given the dying man. In the years she had lived with the colonel, she had taken on his values. Her word was her bond, as surely as that of any man. She had made a vow; she must keep it. That being decided, there seemed no better time than now, while her courage was high and she had the horror of her grandfather's last moments to keep in the forefront of her mind. If she waited, there would be the details of the funeral, the visits of condolence to detain her, and in the passing of the days she might lose this sense of purpose that buoyed her up.

How tired she was. She had not slept except in snatches for three days and nights, if the night before the duel was included, and yet, her mind was clear. She knew exactly what she must do. She would have to be careful, of course. If she were caught—but she would not be. Her mouth in a grim line, she began to unfasten the buttons down the front of her gown.

A half hour later, dressed in a riding habit of black velvet, her hair pulled back in a black mesh snood under a hat like a man's low-crowned beaver banded by a long, streaming veil, and wearing boots, she let herself out the

31

French window which gave onto the upper veranda of Greenlea. Behind her a lamp glowed with a low flame inside her locked room. If she were lucky, it would be morning before anyone sought to disturb her, time enough to ride into Natchez, and back.

It was a dark night and cold. The moon was hidden behind a solid mass of clouds, and there was a moist feeling in the night wind. Melanie was not too surprised to find a light rain falling by the time she led her saddled horse from the stables. She had encountered no trouble in taking the horse without being questioned. Her grandfather's groom, her groom now, as well as the coachman and other stable hands, was in the kitchen now with the gardeners and the house servants, holding their own wake for the passing of their master. Her maid, Glory, was there also, crying her eyes out, firmly convinced that her mistress had taken laudanum and was sound asleep.

The ride into town was not a long one, no more than three or four miles. Still Melanie was shivering with cold, and the long skirt of her habit was heavy with damp by the time she sighted the scattered lights shining in the wet night. Skirting the main streets, she picked her way around the edge of town before she reached the muddy thoroughfare which led down the face of the bluff.

The hotel called the River Rest was brightly lighted. A building of two stories, it appeared to have a saloon on its lower floor. The tinkling of a piano issued with a tinny sound through the steadily opening and closing entrance doors, along with loud voices and the sour smell of spilled liquor. Keeping to the darker alleys, Melanie made her way to the rear of the weathered structure.

The River Rest was no pleasant hostelry for overnight travelers. Even among the ladies of the big houses on the bluff, it was notorious for its back stairs, its unsavory clientele, and the frequency with which it figured in cases of scandal or sudden death. Melanie hesitated at the foot of the rickety stairs that led up to the second-story rooms. She was trembling as with an ague, and her heart beat so hard she could feel it pounding in her chest. Clutching the heavy pistol hidden in the pocket of her riding skirt, she looked around her. No one was in sight; her mount was well hidden in the deep shadows of a grove of willows and scrub oaks that grew behind the building, between it and the bluff at its back. A gust of wind sent rain pattering around her and set the branches of the trees to waving like walking shades.

Footsteps. They were coming along the side of the hotel, sloshing in the mud of the alley. Turning in haste, Melanie looped her skirt over her arm, set her booted foot on the stairs, and began her quiet, swift ascent.

The door at the top of the staircase opened beneath her hand with ease, swinging wide on well-oiled hinges. Melanie closed it without a sound, her gaze on the hallway that stretched dim and bare before her. It was lined with doors on either side, tall, narrow panels with painted numbers so worn they could barely be read. At each end burned a lamp hanging from a ceiling bracket, though their light was obscured by soot crusted in a thick layer inside their glass globes. A draft of cold air blew down the corridor, bringing with it the smell of mice, urine, and unwashed humanity. Breathing in shallow breaths, Melanie stood still. Which room belonged to Roland Donavan? She did now know and had not thought to find out. Stupid. What had she expected, his name on the door? From below came the roar of laughter with a rough edge, a mocking sound above the tortured shrilling of the piano.

Halfway down the hall, a door opened. A man shuffled out, closing the panel with a bang behind him. He was somewhat bald, and bearded, wearing baggy trousers held up by curling leather suspenders over a set of stained underwear. His gaze passed over Melanie as if she were not there. Without a blink or a word, he started down the corridor toward the inside stairwell almost lost in the dimness.

"I beg your pardon? Could you help me?"

The words springing to her lips surprised Melanie almost as much as they did the man. He jumped, swinging around so that Melanie could see the full chamber pot he carried by its bail in one gnarled hand, and the set of room keys that dangled from the other.

"You talking to me?" he asked in a voice made gravelly by years of hard drinking. Suspicion and a hint of familiarity lurked in his eyes.

"Could you tell me which room is occupied by Mr. Roland Donavan?" Melanie did not approach too close, preferring to keep her face in shadow. She held herself straight and tall, her grip on the handle of her pistol so tight her fingers were numb.

"Hoity-toity, ain't you?" the man sneered. "Putting on a show with your fancy clothes. Won't do you no good. Donavan ain't in his room."

From years of experience with serving people, Melanie knew that to hesitate at this point would be the end. "I will wait," she answered at once in her coldest tones. "Which room?"

The man pursed his lips, then gave a nod. "Across the hall there, though I tell you, you're wasting your time. The way he's been pouring down the drink, you'll be lucky if he can hold himself up, much less anything else!"

The leer in the man's voice sent a shiver of distaste over Melanie, but his words failed to pierce her determination. Moving swiftly to the door he indicated, she tried the handle. "It's locked," she said, swinging around.

"What did you expect? Didn't he give you no key? Maybe he'll not like finding you in his bed?"

Tight-lipped, Melanie drew her purse from her pocket and took out a silver dollar. "Open it, if you please," she said, nodding in the direction of the keys in his hand. Copying a gesture she had often seen her grandfather make, she flipped the coin at the man to keep him from coming too close.

He caught it, spat on it, rubbed it, then squinted at her in the uncertain light. "Gawd, you do be impatient, don't you? Enough to make a man wonder whether Donavan is paying you, or t'other way 'round."

Melanie made no reply. Her face cold, she stood back while the man inserted the correct key in the door, turned the lock, and then moved aside. Deliberately, she spun another coin just out of his reach. When he scrambled down the hall after it, she stepped inside the room and closed the door behind her. She heard the man curse. A moment later there came the sound of a key in the door once more. She whirled, grasping the doorknob, turning it, but it was too late. She was locked in!

In sudden panic, she shook the door. Then, as she opened her mouth to call, common sense returned. What did it matter? If Roland found the door unlocked, it might arouse his suspicions, cause him to be wary of who might be inside. Now, he would have to unlock the door to get in. He would be unsuspecting. Afterward, when she had finished what she had come to do, she would take the key from his body.

The room was as chill as the grave, and as dark and cheerless. She stood for a moment, letting her eyes adjust to the gloom. Across the side street on which the room faced, a door opened, throwing a glimmer of reflected light through the window on that wall. It revealed before her a scene approaching squalor. Nothing but caked ashes lay on the hearth; the bed was unmade, the covering tumbled and hanging over the side. An ancient carpet with the pattern worn away to the backing, where it was not obliterated by dirt, covered the floor. Yellowed, fly-specked muslin hung at the windows and was draped from a hook in the ceiling as a mosquito net over the bed, though looped high for winter at the moment. Other than the ramshackle four-poster, the room boasted a dressing table with the bottom doors missing, a wardrobe, and sitting beside the bed a bedraggled slipper chair with a split seat.

In that instant of time while the room was exposed, Melanie knew a feeling of perplexity. If Roland Donavan had returned from California a rich man, why was he living in such surroundings? Then, as the sound of breaking glass, followed by a drunken laugh and a high-pitched squeal came to her through the thin walls, she had her answer. No doubt it was the company he found congenial.

From the look of the room, it had been some time since the man she sought had left it. When would he return? The hour was already late, nearing midnight. Suppose he stayed away all night? What would she do then?

She would deal with that situation when it arose. For the moment, she would wait. Moving to the slipper chair, she sat down. She took the dueling pistol from her pocket, checked the cap to be sure it was not too damp to fire, and then placed it on the mattress of the bed within easy reach. Fastening her gaze on the dim shape of the door, she leaned back.

What would she say to Roland Donavan? Should she warn him of what she meant to do? It would be best; he should at least know why he was to die. If she were a man, she would have to give him a chance to defend himself. Perhaps she should anyway? Did he deserve that much? Could she afford it? He was a formidable opponent; he might defend himself too well. It was no part of her plans to be bested by him. Would he fire on a woman? She had no idea, but it would be better not to find out.

That awful little man. He had thought she had an entirely different reason for waiting in this room. It was not to be wondered at, of course. The kind of woman who slipped secretly into men's bedchambers was probably much more likely to be found in this place than a lady. Or was she? There had been rumors of bored wives who descended the hill while their husbands were downriver on business or visiting their plantations. Chloe had told her of one young matron who had had an affair with a gambler. And wasn't there a girl of good family, a few years back, who had run away with a soldier, been cast off by her wealthy family, then deserted, finally to turn up in a brothel Under-the-Hill? Melanie, who had spent seven years as her grandfather's housekeeper, seeing after his house slaves, arbitrating the quarrels that arose over their mating and marrying, and helping birth their babies, knew full well the act that made the difference between the status of the women who lived under the hill, and

36

those who lived above. It was disturbing to think that the hotel porter, if that was his proper title, could not tell to which group she belonged on sight, regardless of the circumstances.

She was so cold. Now that she was still, she could feel the clammy, bone-chilling dampness across the shoulders of the jacket of her riding habit. Her feet were numb, and her fingers without feeling. One shiver after another shook her, though she hugged herself, slapping her arms about her upper body. This would not do. Unless she could get warmer, she would not be able to stand on her feet when the time came, much less hold the pistol steady enough to pull the trigger.

There was a fairly thick quilt made of woolen squares on the bed. Melanie fingered its warmth-giving folds, then with sudden decision, pulled it free. Standing up, she swept off her hat, then unbuttoned her jacket and laid both to one side. The thin silk blouse she wore underneath her light jacket was relatively dry, though the linen stock which held it closed at the neck was not. She untied the stock, tossed it onto the jacket, then took the quilt, swung it about her shoulders, and sat down. That was a little better, though her feet felt like lumps of ice. Wriggling her toes, she found she could not even feel them moving. When she tried to pace, she stumbled, far more clumsy and unsteady than could possibly be acceptable if she were to succeed in what she had set out to do. The trouble was, her boots were wet. There had been that ditch behind the hotel she had not seen in time to avoid.

Outside, the rain fell with a monotonous sound. She was surprised it was not turning to snow; there was that kind of bitter chill in the air. What she needed was a fire, big and blazing, though she would settle for the next best thing.

Setting her lips in a tight line, she leaned to pull off first one riding boot and then the other. She shifted in the chair, tucking her icy feet underneath her, then huddled into the quilt once more. It would only be for a few minutes. If Roland Donavan had been gone this long, there was no reason to think he would put in an appearance any time soon. And if he did, she would be on her feet, the pistol in her hand at the first whisper of sound. By the time he came through the door she would be ready for him. Later, when he was no longer a threat, she would have time to step into her boots, pick up her jacket, and be gone.

Warmth crept over her by slow degrees. She sat staring at nothing; she did not allow herself to think, to consider what she was doing. Booted feet moved up and down the hall outside the room. Now and then a wagon or a carriage passed in the side street. The rain must be running down the chimney, wetting the wood ashes in the fireplace. Their acrid smell hung in the air, stinging her eyes. She let her eyelids fall for a few seconds. They felt as though there was cornmeal under them. She was not sleepy, certainly not, but it had been such a long time since she had been able to relax. In the next room, bed ropes were creaking, and a woman was moaning, a false, monotonous noise somehow. Far off, the piano still played. Somewhere outside a man yelled, a sudden outcry ending in a grunt. A woman began to scream, a sound that went on and on, dying away by slow degrees. Melanie shook her head, trying to block the intrusions upon her vigil. She must keep her mind on her purpose here. She must be careful, also, that her feet and legs did not go to sleep for lack of circulation. She could sit still only a few minutes more. Then she would have to leave her comfortable cocoon, put on her boots, and walk about a little. Only a few minutes more.

She came awake with a start, her eyes wide and staring in the darkness. The soft sound of footsteps on the worn rug sent a shiver of alarm like pain along her nerves. The shadowy form of a man moved between her and the blue black squares of the windows. He stopped, and there came a quiet rustle of clothing. From what she could see of his movements, it looked as if he were beginning to undress, without bothering to light a lamp.

38

Slowly, stealthily, Melanie moved her arms, groping for the opening in the quilt. She could not find it. She could not free her hands. Though she strained her eyes, she could not see her pistol in the blackness that filled the corner where she sat. Now the man was moving to the dressing table; she heard the clatter of his shirt studs as he dropped them on its surface, the quiet slap of his shirt followed them. He turned, moving toward the bed. She heard his breathed curse as he struck the rail with his shin. Then he sat down near the foot, drawing off his half-boots, dropping them on the floor.

Abruptly, Melanie found the edge of the quilt. Trying to slow her frantic breathing, she reached out toward the mattress. The pistol was not where she had put it. The man's weight on the end of the bed had caused the mattress to sag, sliding the weapon further from her reach, closer to him. Holding her breath, she strained after it.

Without warning, he exploded into action, coming off the bed. Before she could move, Melanie felt herself caught in an iron grip and thrown with a jouncing crash across the lumpy mattress. An instant later, the unyielding weight of the man's body fell across hers, pressing her into the bed. He drew back his fist to strike. Blindly, instinctively, she threw up her arm to block the blow, a gasping, indrawn breath catching in her throat.

The blow did not fall. He went still, dropping his hand. Melanie lay quiet for the brief flick of time it took her mind to accept the reprieve. Then she pushed with all her strength against his chest, arching her back, fighting the confining folds of the quilt as well as the hard restraint of the man who held her. She felt cool air where the covering parted. Before she could take advantage of that opening, the firm grip of a hand fell on her silk-clad shoulder, then moved lower to the soft round curve of her breast.

Immediately, the pressure across her chest lessened. The voice of Roland Donavan came from beside her ear. "I thought so! A nice surprise," he murmured as his hand

39

slid up to tilt her chin toward him, "a nice surprise indeed."

His mouth, warm, possessive, flavored with bourbon, came down on hers. Shock ran over her, holding her immobile for an instant before saving, strengthening outrage surged to her brain. She dragged her lips away.

"No," she cried. "No!" Reaching up, she tugged at his hand, digging her nails into the skin.

With a movement too quick to avoid, he twisted from her grip, catching her wrist in his strong fingers. Jerking it upward, he pinioned it above her head. "Don't fret," he told her, his voice husky. "You'll get your money."

Once more, his lips descended in a hard kiss. Demanding, probing, they forced hers open in an intimacy greater than any she had ever known. Her senses reeled under the burning pressure. A shiver of reaction rippled over the surface of her skin. Hard upon it, she began to writhe, pummeling him with her fists, but the weight of his body across her thighs held her immobile, and with the thickness of the quilt between them, her blows had little effect until she struck high upon his left shoulder. He flinched then, she thought. And a moment later, he eased his weight to that side to restrict her movement. At the same time, he passed his left forearm beneath her head so he could transfer her wrist to his left hand, freeing his right. Even pinioned by his superior strength, she recognized that the means he used to subdue her struggles could have been more vicious, more hurtful than they were. The knowledge served only to make her aware of the reserves of his strength and her own weakness. She felt the slide of his fingers as they moved over her breast once more, then fastened on the deep opening of her blouse. He gave a tug and the buttons were torn from the slippery material. She felt the cold night air on her naked flesh, and then his warm touch brushing across the sensitive surface in deliberate exploration.

She made a sound of protest deep in her throat, flailing her head from side to side while she kicked and squirmed,

40

trying to find purchase with her heels on the edge of the mattress.

"I told you I would pay," he said against her lips, the grate of impatience laced with anger in his tone.

This time the sense of his words penetrated. He thought she was a woman of the streets who had been waiting for him, offering to slake his lust in the hope that he would be generous. Like that other, bald little man, he had mistaken her for a whore! The fury that rushed in upon her was so powerful that she heaved upward, lunging against him. With grim satisfaction she felt her forehead strike his mouth, splitting his lip, heard his muffled curse as he was thrown off balance onto his side. He rolled back with a rush that drove the air from her lungs. His hold on her wrist tightened until her fingers went numb. There was something so grim, so purposeful in his manner that a shaft of fear struck through her anger.

"Wait," she said and was startled to find that her throat muscles were so tight the word came out as no more than a whisper. "Wait, I'm not—"

She got no further. The press of his mouth stopped the words she would have uttered. She felt his hand at her waist, and then the hooks at the band of her skirt gave beneath his hard tug. The tapes of the single petticoat she had donned in her haste snapped; the muscles of her abdomen contracted as she recognized his touch, slipping, pushing those impeding garments down her legs. In panic she twisted, trying to kick at him, but her movements only served to aid him. The feel of his hand on her thigh sent a shudder of revulsion over her. She strained away as his lips slid with a feeling of fire across her cheek to her hairline. He paused, brushing his lips across her earlobe before he said, "It doesn't have to be like this, damn it, if you would only be still."

"No, I can't. This is wrong! You are making—"

"All right." He cut across her words, his tones thick with exasperation and disappointed ardor. "I dance to nobody's tune. I like to know what I'm getting before I put my money down. Remember that you came to me. I didn't go looking for you."

There was a moment when she might have cried out her name. She did not dare. In his present mood, she was afraid of what his reaction might be if he should guess why she had come.

Once more his mouth captured hers, smothering protest. He smoothed the silken texture of her skin in a sensuous pleasure that ignored the twitchings of her muscles or the desperate kneading and clawing of her imprisoned hand. He shifted, divesting himself of his trousers in a swift, economical movement, before covering her once more, the hardness, the ridged muscles of his naked body pressing into hers. He forced her thighs open, his hand ravaging her tender flesh in a caress that set the blood to pounding in her head. And then came the probing, burning invasion. It was an inescapable thing, bringing with it a stabbing pain so intense Melanie's breath was trapped in her chest in a silent cry of pain. She went rigid, arching away from him.

For the space of a heartbeat, Roland did not move. Then his hold loosened, his touch became gentle. The thought grew in Melanie's mind that he was done with her, but she was wrong. As though driven by some primitive force, he molded her to the rhythm of his need, a need that spiraled, growing into a tumult of passion. The pain lessened. Still, tears of anguish overflowed Melanie's eyes. To her overwrought mind, his invasion seemed to go beyond the simple fitting of bodies together, to touch something deep within her being that had, until now, been private, inviolable. A prickling sensation moved over the surface of her skin. Her heart felt as if it were going to burst inside her chest, and in her despairing anger, she knew she would never be the same again.

At last Roland grew still. He lifted a hand to her cheek, smoothing aside loosened tendrils of her hair in a gesture that might have been taken for an apology. Melanie kept her eyes tightly closed as she felt the brush of his lips across her temple, remaining unmoving as he found the tracks of tears running into her hair.

With an abrupt movement, he released her, rolling to one side. "Who are you?"

The instant she felt herself free, Melanie lunged away from him, scrambling to the very edge of the bed. She could not trust herself to speak for fear her voice would shake, so she could not make herself understood. With trembling hands, she felt around her for her clothing, wanting one thing, and one only; to get away from Roland Donavan.

She encountered the soft silk of her blouse and petticoat and drew them toward her. With jerky movements, she struggled into them, knotting the ties of the petticoat in her haste.

"What are you doing?"

Still Melanie did not answer. She had found her riding skirt, its long folds hanging half off onto the floor. As she pulled it toward her, something cold and heavy came with it. Her pistol. The walnut stock slid cool and caressingly into her hand. Without conscious thought, her fingers tightened around it. She lifted the familiar weight, pointed the silver chased barrel at Roland, drew back the hammer, and fired.

It was the click of the hammer that alerted him. Even as the percussion of the shot exploded in the room, he came up off the bed, throwing himself to one side. Smoke roiled in the air, making Melanie's eyes water. Before she could blink them clear, the gun was wrenched from her grasp, and she heard Roland's angry shout.

"What in the name of hell do you think you are doing."

Sick frustration made her unwary. "I was trying to kill you," she snapped, "and I wish I had succeeded."

"For God's sake, why?"

"That must be obvious! For what you did to my grandfather—and to me!"

"For what I—"

It was as though it took a moment for what she had said to register. He lay motionless, though she could hear

43

the rasp of his breathing in the dark. "You—" he said at last. "You are Colonel Johnston's granddaughter."

"As I tried to tell you."

"Dear God," he said, a soft sound laced with wrath and disbelief. He shook his head as though trying to clear it. "First that insane old man, and now you."

Melanie leaned forward, her clenched fists resting on her knee. "That insane old man, as you call him, is dead—and you killed him as surely as if you had stuck a knife in his chest. Except you didn't even have the courage of a sneak thief or a paid assassin. You killed his pride and his soul, and finally broke his heart with words. You are a murderer, Roland Donavan, a murderer! And I wish I could torture you the way you tortured my grandfather!"

Her rising voice, the words she used, appeared to have little or no effect, until suddenly he surged to his feet. He swooped down upon her, dragging her to her feet. With swift, sure movements, he thrust her skirt and jacket into her arms, spun her around, and hustled her toward the door. He reached out, jerked the panel open, and pushed her out into the hallway. Before she could catch her breath to protest, before she could move, the door crashed to behind her.

Clutching her clothes to her breast, she stood for a moment in frozen horror. She felt naked, stripped of dignity, self-respect, and honor. How long she might have hesitated, trying numbly to decide what she must do, she could not have said. It was a small sound, like a smothered laugh, that penetrated her abstraction.

Swinging her head sharply around, she saw that she had an audience. Drawn by the sound of the shot, people, men and women in various stages of undress, were crowding out into the hall. More than one of the men was frankly enjoying the spectacle she presented with her wide vulnerable eyes and tremulous red lips, her hair falling from her snood down her back and the soft, white curves of her breasts visible where her shirtwaist had fallen open.

44

Among them was the hotel porter standing arms akimbo with a leer on his grinning face.

A heated flush rose to her hairline. The urge to scream or to succumb to tears gripped her. She did neither. With a hard look in her eyes, she lifted her chin and, swinging on the heel of one bare foot, walked away down the hall.

Chapter 3

THE FUNERAL of Colonel Ezell Johnston was well attended. There had been no difficulty in finding men to bear his coffin to the cemetery. In days gone by, he had been much respected, had many friends. Now that he was dead there was any number willing to come forward and insist that they had never doubted. It would have been much more to the point if they had made their protestations of faith to her grandfather while he was living.

Melanie, flanked on one side by Governor John Quitman and on the other by Dom, and dressed in bombazine, with a veil disguising the contempt she felt, accepted them with as much grace as she could muster. If once or twice she felt one of these gentlemen of her father's and grandfather's generation press her hand with more than ordinary fervor, she put it down to their sympathy for her plight as a young woman now alone in the world. If they seemed to be making more than usual effort to peer through the protecting layers of her veiling, she told herself it was no more than curiosity to see how she was taking her grandfather's tragic demise. Never for a moment would she let herself think there was any other explanation. Her grandfather's friends and neighbors were not the kind to frequent places like River Rest; they could not know of her humiliation there. They had no means of knowing.

It was Roland Donavan who disabused her of this notion. Early on the morning after the funeral, he presented

46

himself at her door. Melanie was in the colonel's study when Cicero brought the news to her. She was supposed to be going through his papers; instead she sat holding his malacca cane in her hands, smoothing the polished wood. Now she laid it carefully to one side. A hard light came into her deep blue eyes and her lips tightened.

"Tell Mr. Donavan, if you please, Cicero, that I do not wish to see him. Now, or ever."

The words were hardly out of her mouth before Cicero was shouldered aside and Roland stepped into the room. "Sorry," he said in a tone which held no regret. "I took the liberty of letting myself in, since I was fairly sure it was the only way I would cross the threshold."

Recovering his balance, Cicero drew himself up. "Do you want me to put him out, Miss Melanie?"

Melanie came to her feet behind her grandfather's desk, her face pale. She knew well that the elderly butler would try with all his might to eject this man, but she was not certain he could manage it alone. Summoning help would take time; before it could arrive, her grandfather's manservant might be harmed. Her every instinct cried out for her to give the order for Roland Donavan to be dragged none too gently from her sight, but she could not do it. Beyond the consideration for Cicero's welfare, there was the simple fact that she was a civilized person and a lady. The two men waited, each intent upon her.

"Thank you, Cicero. Since Mr. Donavan is so insistent, I will hear what he has to say."

Cicero bowed and withdrew, though she knew he would not go far. In all probability, he would ring for help from the stables. That being so, she had no reason to fear the man who stood so straight and tall before her, and yet, she could not prevent the faint trembling that possessed her as she found herself alone with him.

Silence grew thick between them. Roland stood staring at her, an intent look in his green eyes, his beaver hat that Cicero had failed to take from him, hanging forgotten in his hands. He surveyed the pure oval of her face and the soft waves of her hair drawn back into a knot low on the

47

nape of her neck. His gaze dropped to the lace collar of her black gown, lingering on the cameo which fastened it high at her throat, before dropping lower to the round thrust of her breasts against the material of her bodice and the slim indentation of her waist.

"Well?" Melanie asked, her tone sharp.

He dragged his eyes away as though with an effort. Looking around for a chair, he tossed his hat onto the seat and stepped closer to the desk. "Well, indeed," he said, leaning forward slightly to press one clenched fist on the polished mahogany top. "Tell me, Miss Melanie Johnston, were you in my room at the River Rest hotel five nights ago?"

The question took her aback. He must have been further gone in drink than she had imagined if he had to ask it. Here in the clear light of day, when she was rested and rational, no longer under the influence of her grandfather's last hours, it was incredible that she must answer in the affirmative. It was difficult to believe that she had set out deliberately to kill this man. If she tried, she could almost convince herself that she had not. The events at the River Rest, the long, cold ride home after she had struggled back into her riding habit while shivering on the backstairs landing, were like a dream. Coming back to Greenlea that night, she had stripped off her clothing and fallen into bed. The next morning, she had told Glory that she had gone riding because she could not sleep. The velvet habit, soaked by the rain, had been so beyond repair there had been nothing left except to dispose of it. Other than a certain tenderness between her thighs and a few bruises, there had been no reminders, no proof. Until now. How she wished she had not told him her name, had not made that last attempt to kill him. If she had gathered up her clothing and slipped away, he might never have known who she was, never have realized his mistake. There would have been no commotion to draw people to the scene. But how useless such thoughts were. If she was going to pursue that line, she might as well wish she had never gone at all.

"I have no idea what you are talking about, Mr. Donavan."

A grim smile moved over his mouth. "I would like to believe that, but I don't think my imagination is good enough to conjure up someone like you."

"You are making no sense whatever. I tell you I don't know what you are talking about."

"And I say you are lying," he told her, his voice soft. "Why, I don't know, unless it's pride—or guilt. I give you my word I don't intend to call in the sheriff."

As he spoke, he moved with a little step to the corner of the desk, rounding the side. Melanie hesitated, torn between an intense desire to retreat and her reluctance to appear frightened by his advance or nervous of his nearness. "Call in the sheriff?" she echoed.

"For trespassing, and attempted murder."

Anger darkened her eyes to a violet blue as she met his emerald gaze squarely for the first time. She wanted to counter his list of charges with one of her own, that of rape, but she could not bring herself to say the word. "That is ridiculous!" she snapped.

"Is it? Let's see."

In a single, smooth movement he reached for her, drawing her against the hard planes of his chest, holding her so close to him that she felt his shirt studs digging into her breasts and the metallic chill of his watch chain and fobs. Then as she drew in her breath to call for help, his mouth brushed across her parted lips in a fleeting kiss. An instant later, he caught her forearms in his hard hands and set her from him.

"No," he grated. "It isn't ridiculous. I may not have known exactly what I was doing the other night, but there are some things I remember with great clarity. The feel and smell and taste of you is branded on my brain beyond any woman I have ever known. What makes that so, I can't say, unless it was nearly getting myself killed for the pleasure, but I cannot be mistaken. Are you going to admit it, or would you like more evidence? If so, I have outside in my carriage your grandfather's dueling pistol plus a pair of small, ladies' riding boots. Shall we try them for fit, my shy Cinderella, or will you admit ownership?"

For an instant, Melanie swayed, then she drew herself up in a rigid stance. She might have known he would force the issue rather than simply dispose of her belongings. Glaring at his retreating back as he moved away from her, Melanie managed in a tight voice, "All right. I was there. I came to the River Rest, and I tried to kill you. What do you want of me, an apology?"

He swung around. "No, I came to offer you one."

His answer was so unexpected that she could only stare at him. His green gaze held hers without evasion. When she made no reply, he went on.

"I could plead the unusual circumstances, the amount of liquor I had taken before going upstairs, but that would not be an excuse. There is none, I know that. I can only say that for three days I had been looking for forgetfulness in a bottle and not finding it. Sometimes, for a man it can be diecovered, if only for a brief time, with a woman. You were there. You were warm and soft, and I thought—" He stopped with a quick, dismissing gesture.

He had wanted to forget the duel with her grandfather, the duel in which he had deloped, standing as a traget for the elderly man's rage. No doubt guilt played a part in his remorse.

"All right," Melanie said, her voice tight in her throat. "If you have said what you came to say, will you please go?"

"Not until I'm finished. You haven't been into town lately, have you? You have been so wrapped up with your grief you don't know what is going on."

"What of it?"

"Not a great deal," he answered, his tone edged with mockery that seemed to be directed as much at himself as at her. "Except that you were seen coming from my room that night, and recognized."

Melanie felt the blood recede from her face, then return with a rush as she recalled her unceremonious ejection from this man's room, and the crowd that had been gathered outside it. Though she had tried to deny it, she had always known the distance between Natchez-Under-The-Hill and the Bluffs was not great enough to offer protection. Her gaze moved to where the sun fell brightly through the window, while outside a crisp wind swayed the bare branches of the trees. Taking a deep breath, she looked once more to Roland Donavan.

"How do you know?"

"In the last few days, there have been a number of strange comments made to me. The gist of them seems to be that people suspect you are the direct reason for the meeting between your grandfather and myself."

Melanie felt a fleeting gratitude for the tact with which he had answered her question. No doubt the comments made to him had been more crude and to the point than he indicated. People were quick to seize on the worst, and they had long memories. They would not forget that she had been found by her grandfather alone in the dark with this man at Monmouth.

"I see," she said. "I suppose I must thank you for telling me."

"Thank me?" he said, a black frown drawing his brows together. "There has been more than enough politeness already. What we have to decide now is what we are going to do about it."

"Do? What is there to do? If you think there is a solution, you have little idea of the matter."

"Don't underestimate me. I was born and raised here, too, you will remember, even if it was on the other side of the river. I know the kind of things people are saying. For myself, it doesn't matter; I gave up caring what people say or think long ago. With you, the case is different. You will not like having them whisper behind your back—or the way they will act to your face. There is only one thing to be done."

"And that is?" she asked, her voice cold.

"You know it as well as I do. You will have to marry."

Nervous surprise at his words jerked a laugh from her.

"Are you offering yourself as a candidate for my husband, Mr. Donavan?"

"Yes, I am."

The expression in his emerald eyes was bleak, almost challenging. There could be little doubt that he was serious in his offer, and yet, it made no sense. A man of honor might have felt compelled to offer her his name, but what had such scruples to do with a man like this, the man who had slandered her grandfather and driven him to his death?

"Why?"

A muscle tightened under the bronze skin of his face. "That must be obvious."

"Not to me," Melanie answered. "I absolve you of gallantry as a motive, since I doubt, with good reason, that you know the meaning of the word. What does that leave? Marriage to me would make you master of Greenlea, since I am my grandfather's sole heir. It would also serve, when the furor over our irregular match has died away, to give you an entree into Natchez society. To my mind, these two things account nicely for your excess of concern for me."

"I could tell you that you are wrong, but I doubt you would listen."

"No," Melanie agreed with a proud lift of her chin. "So you would do well to save your breath, as well as your proposal. As I think you were informed at our first meeting, I already have a fiancé. That being so, I have no need whatever for the recompense you are offering. I am afraid the sacrifice you made in coming here was for nothing."

The irony in her tone was not lost on him. "Not quite," he said. "At least I was able to return your boots."

Bowing in the face of her speechless wrath, he strode from the room.

The riding boots were delivered into Cicero's hands, along with the dueling pistol. The manservant brought them to her and placed them on the desk before her. Avoiding his eyes, Melanie thanked him and nodded a dismissal. If he did not know already what had occurred, he would learn soon enough. He would be disappointed, incredulous, but she knew without question that she could depend upon his loyalty. Even if nothing was ever spoken between them, he would defend her in the other servants' quarters in town, for what good that might do.

Abruptly, her face twisted as though in pain. Taking up her grandfather's cane, she slashed it at the clean, freshly polished boots. They toppled to the floor with a muffled thud and lay sprawled apart, their soft leather gleaming in the chill winter sunlight.

Regardless of her feelings for Roland Donavan, Melanie realized that he was right. Her one chance of weathering the storm of gossip that was gathering was marriage. It would have to be a quiet, private ceremony due to her mourning, but that was all to the good. There would be fewer people present to gawk and whisper behind their hands. The sooner the business was arranged the better. Still, she hesitated. If the truth were to be admitted, she did not want to be married, had never wanted it. Even the possibility of pregnancy, remote but ever present, did not alter that fact. She could not quite remember how she had come to agree to be engaged to Dominic Clements. It had happened soon after the return of the soldiers of the victorious army from Mexico. Dom was often at Greenlea, talking to her grandfather, the only one of his old troop to return with him, at least at that time. The colonel had liked the young man, had enjoyed his air of deference and the respectful way he listened to an older man's opinions. The colonel had been an early riser, with that breed's habit of retiring early to bed. It had not been unusual for him to leave the two young people together when he said good-night. Of course, Glory was always somewhere about, sitting in the corner doing needlework, moving in and out of the parlor tending the fire or the lamps, offering refreshments, a thousand and one small tasks.

After some weeks, it had become understood that Dom

53

was coming to see Melanie rather than his old commanding officer. Her grandfather was pleased, rather than hurt, by the defection. He called Dominic Clements an up-and-coming young man, a knowing one who understood which way the wind was blowing. He thought his granddaughter could do worse than a steady fellow like that. At least he would stay put, build on the foundation of his father's and grandfather's estates. He would dress his wife in silks and satins and furs, treat her like a princess, take her to Europe every year. And he had ambition. It wouldn't be too surprising if one day he became a senator. At least he would if he had the good sense to keep a tight grip on John Quitman's coattails, and it looked like he had that all right.

Yes, that was how it had been. Her grandfather had expressed approval of the match to her, had given Dom permission to pay his addresses to Melanie, and made sure with a laugh and a joke that she knew it. There had, after that, been little necessity for a proposal in form. Her grandfather had begun to talk about his future great-grandchildren, and the deed was done.

Naturally, he was not too anxious to be rid of Melanie's company. There had never seemed to be a convenient time for the nuptials. Dom's every attempt to set a date had been brushed aside with an airy excuse. Winter was too cold, summer too hot, for wedding trips. The spring was a changeable time of year—a body could never tell what the weather would do; besides, his granddaughter did not want to join the rest of the herd rushing toward the altar. Fall, on the other hand, was a sad season. He had lost his loved ones in the fall and did not want to be reminded with banks of flowers and ceremonies. Melanie had sometimes wondered if Dom wasn't relieved at the indefinite postponement. He had never been an impatient suitor, or a particularly ardent one. He had never even tried to kiss her as Roland Donavan had done. A chaste salute upon the cheek or forehead was as far as he dared to go. That was certainly the prescribed form

54

between a couple enduring a long engagement. Still it did not argue for a strong attraction.

Melanie, seated at her writing desk in the parlor, stared into space, the ink on the nib of her pen drying as she held it poised over her writing paper. Against her will, she found herself thinking of the minutes she had lain in Roland Donavan's arms, and also of his ringing words of this morning. If there was one thing of which she could be certain, it was that he was not indifferent to her. A physical attraction, as degrading as that was, or was supposed to be, had certainly been there.

No, she would not allow herself to think such thoughts. The feelings of any man other than her fiancé could not matter. Dipping her pen in the inkwell once more, she sat biting her lip, still unable to write. Having convinced herself of the need for a hurried marriage, she could not think how to phrase the summons to Dom. Even less did she know what she would say to him when he arrived. She could not ask him to marry her on such short notice without telling him the reason for it, and yet, how was she to put such a thing in words? Moreover, how was she to do it without giving Dom cause to call out Roland Donavan? Much as it went against the grain, she would have to represent the episode as being entirely her own fault.

The fire beneath the white Carrara marble mantel fluttered and hissed, shedding a red light over the polished walnut furniture and the green brocade of the parlor set. It flared briefly, and Melanie put down her pen before rising to adjust the embroidered screen that protected her from the radiating heat. She stood frowning at the petit-point scene of a shepherd and his love disporting themselves in a field of clover when a knock came on the door.

It was Dom, punctilious as always, who followed Cicero into the room. Anyone who had been in and out of the house as much as he had could have saved the old manservant the trouble of announcing him, Melanie found herself thinking. Then an instant later she smiled and extended her hand in greeting as he crossed toward her over the Aubusson carpet.

Don did not return her smile. He held her hand for no longer than it took for him to incline his upper body over it. His face grim, he refrained from speaking until the door had closed behind Cicero.

"I turst I am not inconveniencing you?"

"Not at all, though I will own myself surprised. I thought you were promised for Mrs. Wesley's musicale."

"So I was," he answered, "but something more important has arisen."

There was a small worried frown between his blond brows. Melanie observed it, and the stiffness of his manner, with a sinking sensation in the pit of her stomach. Nevertheless, she strived for a normal tone. "Oh? Come, sit down and tell me about it."

As she spoke, she moved to the settee drawn up to the fire, indicating the place beside her for her fiancé.

"I would prefer to stand," he said. When she made no objection, he walked with deliberate steps to the fireplace and turned his back to the cheerful blaze.

The light from the brass chandelier overhead gleamed on his golden blond hair and cast shadows beneath his high cheekbones. It also made his mouth look thin, unformed. Odd that she had never noticed that before. Dom seemed to be having as much trouble broaching the subject that had brought him as she had been having penning her letter to him.

"May I offer you a cup of tea, or perhaps a glass of sherry?" she asked.

"What? Oh, no, nothing, thank you. Melanie, there is something I must say to you."

Melanie was astonished to discover, as she looked at her fiancé, that a dull red color had spread under the surface of his fair skin. This sign of his agitation seemed in some peculiar way to lessen her own.

"Yes, what is it?"

Dom glanced at her, then looked away. "I am not sure how I should put this. The matter is somewhat—delicate."

"But you are certain we must go into it?" Melanie asked.

"Yes—yes, I think you have a right to know what is being said, just as I have a right to be informed as to its truth or falsehood."

Melanie drew a deep breath. Clasping her hands tightly together in her lap, she raised her blue gaze to Dom's face. "Perhaps you had better say at once what is troubling you then?"

"Yes," Dom agreed, clearing his throat. "I only hope you will not be offended."

"I am certain I will not be," Melanie answered and earned a quick, almost accusing glance from Dom's hazel eyes. It was impossible not to contrast his hemming and hawing with Roland Donavan's straightforward approach to the situation. It might have been argued that Dom had more to lose, since he was in love with her. There was little anger in his face, however, anger that might have hinted at strong feelings in the matter. His expression, instead, held censure and the irritation that embarrassment often brings out in a man.

Now he cleared his throat once more. "I have had occasion in the last two days of hearing a most unbelievable tale. I would have put its circulation down to jealous spite, except that I had it from people I cannot regard as anything other than reliable. It is being told all over town, my dear Melanie, that you were seen coming from the hotel room of Roland Donavan."

He waited, his gaze narrowed upon her face, for her reply. The glow of the fire gave color to her pale cheeks and drew fiery sparks from the auburn waves of her hair. It revealed not a sign of shock or distress, though there might have been a flicker of disappointment mirrored in her eyes as she regarded him so steadily.

"Is that all?" she asked.

"All? Isn't it enough?"

"I hardly think so. From the little you have said, my meeting with Roland Donavan might have been nothing more than a social visit. Didn't your informants tell you,

57

for instance, that I was unchaperoned, that it was close on midnight when I left him, and that I was—let us say—in a state of undress?"

"Melanie!" he cried. "You don't mean what you are saying."

"You don't believe it? That is some consolation. Still, I assure you it is true."

"In God's name, why?"

"A mistake, more than one," she answered with a sigh. And staring into the fire, she told him what had taken place on the night her grandfather had died. As she spoke, Dom stood watching her, a look in his eyes as though he had never seen her before.

"You mean," he said when she fell silent at last, "you mean he actually made love to you?"

"He did. Actually."

"My God!" he said and swung around to clutch the white marble mantel. "How did he dare?"

"I told you. He mistook me for another type of woman—an understandable mistake, given the circumstances."

"How can you sit there and talk about it as if it was nothing? Don't you have any idea what people will make of this? They will have a field day! I will be a laughing stock in every saloon Under-The-Hill. And what a tale to pass with the brandy after dinner!"

"Would it help if I cried and screamed and swooned in your arms?" Melanie demanded. "I will be happy to oblige if you think it will, but I think we will be better occupied in deciding what is to be done." On the cold and wet ride back from Natchez to Greenlea that night she had not been able to see for the tears that blinded her. Still she could not tell him that, not now.

He swung slowly to face her. There was a look in his eyes that bordered on suspicion. "Do?" he asked, his gaze moving past her to rest upon the door. "I confess I see little that can be done, unless you had thought of going away? A few months in Europe, even a year or two? I'm

58

sure you could afford to stay as long as you liked. On your return, you may well find everything forgotten."

She wanted to ask him if he would have forgotten that another man had possessed her. That was another of the things it would be too indelicate for a lady to say to a gentleman. "That might be the very thing," she said with a light attempt at a laugh. "If I traveled slowly, I could be in Paris for the spring. Yes, I like that idea. It is much better than marrying, which is what Mr. Donavan suggested to me. Naturally, as a politician you could not have a wife with a tainted reputation. I quite understand that. Only think of poor President Jackson a few years ago with his Rachel. They were dragged through the mud, merely because of a mistaken idea that she was divorced from her first husband. There is no way of knowing what the public might make out of your marrying a woman so brazen as to—associate with—the man who was responsible for her grandfather's death."

"You have a point," he conceded, in his relief, entirely missing the scorn that laced her words. "Of course, if you would prefer marriage, if you think it would be the better course, I am perfectly willing."

This was so patently untrue that she could not sit still and watch the insincere smile that touched his narrow lips. She surged to her feet, turning away from him to stride down the room. "I could not permit you to make such a sacrifice," she said over her shoulder, a haunted look in her eyes as she recalled saying much the same thing to Roland Donavan so short a time ago. "It would be too much to ask of any man."

"No such thing. I protest," he said, taking a few hurried steps after her, so that when she turned they nearly collided. He stepped back away from her, as though he had touched a hot stove. His face flushing a dark red, he stammered, "I—I am just not sure it would serve. A marriage, so soon after your grandfather's death, would only convince the gossips that the story they are so busily circulating is true."

"That must be the prime consideration, of course, what

the gossips will say. What I think, and feel, doesn't matter!"

"If I thought you were genuinely upset, I would be concerned. But you are too sensible a girl, too much the colonel's granddaughter, to do anything foolish."

As he spoke, he reached out as if to put his arms around her. Melanie sidestepped him, moving with a swift stride to the bell pull which hung beside the fireplace.

"Am I?" she inquired, giving a vicious tug at the pull. "I am also too much the colonel's granddaughter to waste my time listening to your excuses. Cicero will see you out!"

The anger of chagrin supported her until Dom was out of the house. When the door had closed behind him, she dropped down upon the settee and covered her face with her hands. What was she going to do? Brazen the thing out, as her grandfather had tried to do after his fall from grace? Become an exile as Dom had suggested? Or simply extend her mourning, and the lack of amusement and circulation that went with it, into more than a year, two, even three—a lifetime of being a recluse? Until she became an object of awe and pity, that crazy old spinster who lived shut up alone at Greenlea? She would take her exercise at night, walking the streets, frightening the children in her old-fashioned clothes. No, oh, no!

There was one other possibility. It was such a desperate one, so remote from anything she could have dreamed of only a week earlier, that she approached it warily, circling about it in her mind. It would give her respectability, of a kind, once more. It would prove to Dom that she had no need of him or his halfhearted solution. More than anything else, it would serve as a means of repaying Roland Donavan for the injuries he had caused her in body and soul. For who could find the weaknesses of a man, who could exploit him better, than his wife?

She could, she would, marry Roland Donavan.

Chapter 4

THE CARRIAGE rolled sedately down the rutted road. Stiff upon his seat with disapproval, the coachman kept the gray and silver barouche moving at the proper pace for a lady driving out of an afternoon, despite its forward lurch as it descended the hill and the jar of potholes. His passenger inside clung to the hanging strap with one slender, gloved hand. As they swerved to avoid the carcass of a dead pig, Melanie held her handkerchief to her nose. The variety of stenches that crept into the closed carriage was incredible. Rotting fish vied with open drains coated with green scum, stable filth with shallow-dug privies. If it was this bad Under-The-Hill on a cloudy winter afternoon, what must it be like on a hot summer's day?

The River Rest was no more prepossessing by daylight than it had been in the dark. The sign which identified it hung askew, the paint was peeling from its clapboard sides, and several of the windowpanes in the top floor were missing. Even so, it was in better condition than many of the other buildings around it. Most were built of gray, unpainted boards and ventilated by square window openings that were covered by wooden shutters.

The coachman drew up beside the wooden planks laid in the mud that served as a sidewalk before the hotel. Climbing down, he came to stand at the carriage window. When Melanie had let down the glass, he took off his hat.

"We're here, Miss Melanie. Now what? You're not going inside, are you?"

"No, John. You will do that for me, if you please, and inquire for Mr. Roland Donavan. If he is in, you will ask him to step outside for a few words with me. If he is not, you will leave this note to be handed to him when he returns."

"Yes, Miss Melanie," John said, accepting the folded square of paper she passed out to him. He hesitated a moment, as though he meant to protest further. Then, ducking his head, he turned away.

Melanie leaned back, watching John disappear inside the River Rest. With fingers that trembled slightly, she smoothed her black kid gloves over the backs of her hands. They had come from the dressmaker only that morning, along with the bonnet she wore of black dyed straw trimmed with black lace and steel gray ribbons, her gown of black silk-faille, and her cape edged with fur. There had been other, more modest ensembles included in the delivery, but she had rejected them. This one gave her confidence, something of which she was sorely in need. It was one thing to consider accepting the proposal of a man like Roland Donavan; quite another to set out to commit the deed.

A chill wind laden with the dank feel of the river swirled about the carriage. Drawing her skirts aside, Melanie searched with her slippered feet for the clay pottery foot-warmer that had been placed in the carriage for her. If the man didn't hurry, the water inside would soon be stone cold. And so might her intentions.

No, that was not true, she told herself, sitting up straighter in her seat and folding her hands in her lap. She was determined that Donavan would not escape the consequences of his crimes, no matter what the cost to herself. She would see that he paid the full price.

Once more she smoothed her gloves, forcing the hand-sewn seams down between her fingers, drawing the cuffs firmly up her arms, checking to see that the tiny pearl buttons that closed them were still fastened beneath her wrists. It was so difficult, breaking in a new pair, making certain they were stretched enough, but not too much. Perhaps she should have used more talcum inside the palms; they were beginning to feel damp.

Abruptly she folded her hands in her lap, gripping them tightly together. Why was she worrying about gloves? She should be composing her thoughts, deciding what she was going to say. She had never asked a man to marry her before, and even if it was a question of merely accepting the proposal he had already made to her, it was bound to be difficult reminding him of it. Had his feelings been injured by her rejection? That seemed unlikely, and yet, it had to be considered. Their parting had not been an amicable one; her refusal had been so definite that he was bound to be suspicious of her reasons for reopening the subject. How was she to explain it?

Catching her bottom lip between her teeth, Melanie stared out the window. With unseeing eyes, she watched a Negro laundress saunter past, her hips swinging and a bundle of clothing wrapped in a sheet balanced upon her head. A pair of riverboatmen came staggering from the other direction. With unkempt hair, untrimmed beards, and shapeless, mud-colored clothing, they looked like nothing so much as a pair of drunken animals. Behind them came a massive woman dressed in a gown of bright purple brocade so tight the seams looked in danger of parting, and her bosom overflowed the neckline like cream melting over blackberry tart. Her hair was an unlikely shade of copper, and her black eyes were set like buttons in the rice-powder paleness of her face. As she came even with the carriage, she caught Melanie's eye and smiled, showing teeth yellowed by what could only have been either the dipping of snuff or the chewing of tobacco.

Melanie turned her head sharply. On the opposite side of the street, an elderly man stood in the doorway of what appeared to be a cheap roominghouse. It was a moment before she realized he wore nothing but a set of filthy red

63

underwear, and that he was in the process of relieving himself into the street.

A shouted order jerked her from her amazed disgust. By the time she could turn in her seat, John was climbing to his perch, and Roland Donavan had pulled the door open. He threw himself onto the velvet squabs beside her and slammed the laquered panel shut. Hard on the sound came John's shout to the horse, and the carriage started forward with a jounce that snapped Melanie's head back.

"What is the hurry?" she inquired in icy tones as she jerked her arm from under Roland's elbow, flouncing over on the seat to give him more room.

"Just trying to safeguard your reputation. This, as you know, is no place for a lady."

"Noble of you, but don't you think it is a little late!"

"Not for a young woman who is going to marry an upstanding gentleman like Dominic Clements. I understand he is not only a member of the Mississippi Bar, he is dabbling in politics. Caesar's wife, you will remember, must be above suspicion."

Melanie sent him a sharp glance. He could not possibly know her reason for wanting to see him, and yet, he had given her a perfect opening to introduce it. The only problem was, she was not quite ready. Her throat felt suddenly tight. She was intensely aware of the man beside her, of his size within the confinement of the closed carriage, of the way he sat at ease with his long legs stretched out before him, yet exuding an air of leashed strength, like a great swamp panther at rest. It was stupid of her to be so affected, of course. It had never happened before. No doubt it was the strength of her repugnance toward him that made her overly sensitive. There was something else to consider. By assuming the right to order her coachman, he had neatly turned the tables on her. Though he had come at her bidding, she was now being driven at his, and there was little she could do about it without putting her plan at risk.

"Where are we going?" she asked, striving for composure.

"No place in particular, just driving. I told your coachman to take one of the roads east out of town, but if you prefer another direction, I am perfectly willing to go where you please."

"No. North, south, east—any direction will do. It doesn't matter."

They rode along in silence. Melanie, noticing that she was smoothing at her gloves again, folded her hands in her lap and stared out the window as they climbed back up to the bluff and wound their way through the cobblestone streets of town. The road they were taking was a part of the Natchez Trace, a route which began in Kentucky and ran southwest across the state of Mississippi to Natchez. There it connected with another ancient trail, El Camino Real of the Spanish conquistadores. This road continued down beside the river, crossed into Louisiana, then marched across Texas and the provinces of Mexico to end in Mexico City. The Trace, originally an old Indian trail, had known so many countless feet over the centuries that its pathway had been worn deep into the soft soil. Now, great earthen banks loomed on either side of the road, banks matted with the roots of the trees that grew high overhead. Since the emigration of the southern Indian tribes more than twenty years before, escorted by the army to lands in the western territories, it was a rare thing to see an Indian upon it. It was used mainly by mail riders and by flatboatmen who had carried their produce downriver to New Orleans to sell, along with their floating crafts, and were making their way home with their profits. There were also a few wagonloads of people going to Texas and beyond. The lonely reaches of the trail, away from the settled communities, had a reputation for danger, for being infested with thieves and outlaws preying on anyone with money in their pockets. Here near Natchez, however, where winding dirt roads branched off from it to the magnificent homes of the planters, it was perfectly safe. Safe for travel, that is, though there was some danger of losing a wheel in the deep ruts or sliding into a ditch climbing and descending the steep hills.

Melanie, accommodating herself to their rattling, swaying progress, searched her mind for a subject of conversation without notable success. "It is a dreary day, isn't it?"

Roland nodded. The sky was overcast by a thickening mass of clouds. With the high embankment closing in on either side of the carriage, the light within was dim.

Suspecting a hint of sarcasm in his failure to take up the subject, Melanie glanced at him. She found him watching her, a disturbing look in his dark emerald eyes as they lingered on the curves of her mouth. At the lift of her eyebrow, he looked away and shifted, uncrossing his legs and then crossing them again in the opposite direction.

"They say you have just returned from California," Melanie ventured after a moment.

"Yes, I was there for more than a year."

"I suppose you found what you were looking for, or you would not have come home?"

"A logical deduction," he answered, which told her exactly nothing.

"It—it must have been exciting?"

"Some would say so."

"But not you," she said, her voice shaded with exasperation for the shortness of his answers.

"There were too many people, too much noise and confusion, too many men losing, and too few winning. It was a lot like being in an army at war that way. But then, some people call war exciting."

She stiffened, wondering with a frown between her eyes if he was referring to her grandfather. He had always claimed to enjoy the roar of the cannon, the whine of bullets. Bravado or not, he had certainly liked being on the march with his men. "I expect both war and life in a gold camp require something in the way of a tolerance for hardship."

If her barb struck home, he gave no indication. "They require more than that," he answered quietly. "One way or another, they require a stomach for watching men die."

"That is a subject that I have gained some knowledge

of recently." She had meant for her words to come out as a rebuke; instead, they were filled with pain.

"Yes," he agreed. "The time for saying it hasn't been right until now, but I am sorry about the colonel."

She could have sworn he was sincere. She must not let that affect her, however. There should be some way to make use of his supposed remorse. "Perhaps that was, in part, why you asked me to marry you?" she suggested and took careful note of the sudden stillness that came over him.

"It may have had something to do with it, though there were other reasons."

"I see," Melanie said quickly, too quickly, in fear that he was going to elaborate. "I—I am afraid my refusal that day may have been a trifle abrupt."

"Understandable, under the circumstances."

He was waiting for her to be more specific. He did not intend to help her until he was certain he knew what she wanted, if then. "Possibly," she agreed, staring straight ahead so that her bonnet shielded her expression. "Now that I have had time to think about it, I see that the arrangement has—would have had—merit."

She sent him a quick look from the corner of her eye. He was watching her, the beginning of a smile tugging at the corner of his mouth. She looked away again at once.

"Such as?" he inquired.

"As you pointed out to me, it would serve to scotch the rumors circulating about my visit to your rooms. It would also provide an acceptable reason for the duel; people can think, if they like, that my grandfather objected to the marriage. It would give them something to think about other than what may have happened in Mexico."

"It seems to me that it would make them wonder the more what the colonel had against me."

"And yet, if I was willing to give you my hand, they must assume, must they not, that I saw nothing so terrible? They will be forced to think that the problem was nothing more than an elderly man's irrational dislike."

For an instant Melanie was suffocated by a feeling of

disloyalty. It will be worth it in the end—she told herself—when Roland Donavan has paid his full atonement. It was possible that she would have cause to be thankful she had not killed him. A quick death was too easy. There were other, better forms of punishment, slower ones, more suitable as a recompense for the death of pride and happiness and honor that her grandfather had endured.

As if he could read something of her thoughts, he said, "I suppose it is safe to conclude you no longer feel the need to put a bullet through me?"

"Yes. I—was overwrought that night, so exhausted and—and disturbed from nursing my grandfather in his last hours that I was not myself. I hope you can understand and forgive me for that unfortunate incident." It was only words. What did they matter so long as he did what she wanted?

"You relieve my mind," he said in such an odd tone Melanie flung him a quick glance. He smiled into her eyes. "Where were we? You were enumerating the advantages of a match between us, I think. You must not forget the respectability you will bring me."

That had been one of the charges Melanie had flung at him. She chose to ignore the irony verging on sarcasm in his tone. "Yes, there is that."

"Tell me," he said, turning toward her, leaning to take up one of the ribbon streamers of her bonnet from where it lay on her breast. "Are you trying to say you have changed your mind?"

"It—it is possible," she replied with a catch in her voice as she felt him begin to draw upon the streamer, loosening the bow beneath her chin.

"Why? Was your fiancé so disobliging as to refuse a bride that is—less than pure?"

Melanie sent him a fulminating glance as a warm flush tinted her cheeks. It was infuriating that he should make such a suggestion to her. Worse still was the fact that she could not deny it.

"Not precisely," she snapped. "I could have been his
68

wife if I had been prepared to be eternally grateful for the favor, and to wait a year or two, kicking my heels in Europe, until the gossip died down."

"I see," he drawled, his thick lashes shielding the expression in his green eyes as he completed the destruction of her bow. "Gratitude is one thing your husband, whoever he may turn out to be, need not expect from you then?"

"I see no reason why the feeling should not be equal on each side. You realize, I believe, that if I restore you to respectability, you will also be doing the same for me, and so it is a fair exchange—what are you doing?"

He had tweaked her bonnet strings free and suddenly slipped that confection of straw, lace, and ribbon from her hair. She reached for it, but with a casual flip of his wrist, he tossed it to the other seat facing them.

"I never did like bonnets, makes it too hard to see a woman's face when you are talking to her."

"What you like is immaterial to me," she informed him as she reached across him, trying to catch the trailing ribbon of her bonnet.

"Even," he said, catching her arm in a firm grip and swinging her to face him, "if I am to be your husband?"

Melanie raised startled blue eyes to his, the frown of irritation fading from her face. "Are you?"

"I am, providing I am given some evidence that I will receive something, if not gratitude, in return."

As he drew her closer, slipping his arm around her waist, his meaning as well as his intention was plain. She had brought it upon herself. Why she should be surprised, why she should have expected anything different, she could not have said. To struggle, to refuse his embrace, might mean jeopardizing both the marriage and her scheme of revenge. Now was the time to decide; would she go through with it, or not? Could she steel herself to endure what she must from this man, or would a scream of refusal rise in her throat?

His mouth took hers with gentle strength, molding it to his own, moving with experimental slowness as he tasted the honeyed sweetness of her lips. Melanie stiffened at the first touch, caught for a moment in a memory of thrusting pain, and then as his hands moved slowly, firmly over her back, she felt herself begin to yield. A warm and tremulous feeling ran over her veins. In response to her compliance, his kiss deepened. He turned slightly, so that her head was resting against the velvet softness of the seat cushions. His hand moved to the slender indentation of her waist, smoothing upward over her ribs, barely cupping the round curve of her breast. Without violation, her hand crept upward to clutch at the lapel of his frock coat as she allowed her lips to part. Drowning in sensation, she was pressed closer against Roland, and then as the vehicle straightened once more, his hand moved on her silk-clad breast, brushing over the taut nipple. The pressure of his kiss lessened. His lips lingered at the moist, sensitive corner of her mouth. Then trailing fire, they moved to the curve of her cheek and along her hairline to the tender turn of her neck.

Without warning, the carriage started downhill. As they began to slide in the muddy road, Roland's hand tightened. At Melanie's soft, indrawn breath of protest and pain, he cursed and straightened, at the same time lifting her back from the edge of the seat. A black scowl on his face, he grated, "Dear God, yes, by all means let us be married—and soon."

The wedding was small, and as was fitting, considering Melanie's state of mourning, a quiet one. Glory, her maid, had wept a little as she laced Melanie into her stays and lifted the cream-colored brocade satin gown that had belonged to Melanie's mother over her head. The maidservant had come to Greenlea as a girl with that other young bride, Sarah Howell Johnston. She had been a wedding gift from Sarah's father. A great many sad events had taken place since that other wedding. The Howells, Melanie's maternal grandparents, had died in a yellow fever epidemic after taking in a traveler who had the disease. The Howell plantation, to the south of Natchez near Clin-

70

ton, Mississippi, had been divided among Melanie's uncles and aunts, cut up into so many little pieces that it was scarcely worthy of the name anymore. Then there had been the steamboat explosion that had taken Miss Sarah and her young husband. Glory had been on that boat. It had been she who had jumped into the water with the baby Melanie in her arms when it was certain the boat was going down; it had been she who had put the child on the chicken crate, tying her to it with her apron strings. She had not been able to swim and the crate would not hold both afloat, and so she had let the crate go with its precious cargo, as dear to her as any child of her own could ever have been. She had been nearly drowned when a barrel had floated past. Well, it didn't do to think on things like that. This was a happy day, or it should have been.

"Miss Melanie, honey, you sure you won't have something to eat?"

"Thank you, but no, I couldn't."

"Why? Is your stomach tied up in knots? It should be, marrying a man you hardly know at all, the man who killed the colonel. It's a shame and disgrace the way you acting."

"Please, Glory. I don't want to talk about it."

"Why not? You wouldn't be afraid I'm going to say something sensible? What's come over you? I don't understand you anymore, haven't since the night the colonel died, the night you went out in your best black riding habit and plumb ruined it, got it soaking wet. You know velvet can't take that. And it was tore clean to bits, like you rode right through a briar thicket. You never said what happened, and I haven't asked, but it don't seem right, a girl as white and hollow-eyed as you going to the altar with the man she was supposed to marry taking himself off to New Orleans as if the hounds of hell was after him."

The maid was standing behind Melanie at the dressing table, putting the finishing touches to her hair before the

71

donning of the veil. Melanie looked up, catching the maid's eyes in the mirror. "Dom?"

"Who else, unless there was some other man you promised to marry? They say he left days ago on the *Pride of Natchez,* the day before you announced as how you was marrying Mr. Roland. Folks are asking themselves why, just like they are asking themselves about this wedding. They know something happened, they just don't know what. And trying to find out has exercised their minds more in the last week than in the whole past year."

"It can't be helped," Melanie said.

"Maybe not, but I sure never expected to have my baby's name thrown around, pulled this way and that way, with people licking their lips over it like a piece of taffy candy."

"I will explain it all to you another time, Glory," Melanie said with a sigh. "Just now, I can't bear to talk about it."

"You don't want to talk about it because you think I won't like what you've done, and you are afraid if I say too much against you marrying Mr. Roland you won't have the strength to go through with it. Well, all right, if that's the way you want it. I won't say any more. I may not like the way things have been happening, but I'm bound to admit that even if Mr. Roland isn't the man that the colonel picked for you, even if they did have words, he has the look of being a man as well as a gentleman. There's a light in his eyes when he looks at you that's hard to mistake, like he knows how to treat a woman like a woman, as well as like a lady. Believe me, honey, that's important!"

Glory's assessment of Roland returned to Melanie as she stood beside him before the minister. She had reason to know that the maid was at least partially right; whether he knew how to treat a lady was another question entirely.

Her voice was low and steady as she made her responses, but her cool, slim fingers trembled in the warm clasp of Roland's hand. He was a tall and disturbing presence in his dark gray evening coat, gray and buff striped waistcoat, and buff trousers. A diamond stickpin gleamed in his silk cravat, and the white of his shirt collar made a striking contrast against his sun-darkened skin. Though Melanie thought he glanced at her once or twice, his gaze lingering on the aged Valenciennes lace of the veil that covered her hair and the Madonna-like severity of her profile, she could not bring herself to look at him after the first brief glance. The smell of myrtle wax candles hung in the air along with the fresh scent of the evergreen boughs and garlands used to decorate the long front parlor. The white camellias that quivered in her trembling hands had no scent to drift upon the air of the warm, close room. They were cool and perfect and pure.

At last the ordeal was over. The cold circle of the wedding band, like a miniature shackle, weighted her hand. Her lips burned from his light, almost chaste kiss. It was time to turn and face their guests and receive their congratulations. They were not many; Governor John Quitman, who had given her away, his wife Eliza, who had served as her matron of honor, her grandfather's lawyer and dearest friend, Mr. Jackson Turnbull, a friend of Roland's who had acted as best man and who, quite incidentally, was the owner of the River Rest, and then behind these, Glory, Cicero, the other house servants, stable hands, and gardeners of Greenlea.

Greeting those present, accepting their good wishes, did not take long. The servants retired to their own party in the kitchen, while Melanie and Roland presided over a small supper of turtle soup, grillade of beef, chicken in wine sauce, and assorted vegetables, all topped off by the white-iced bride's cake and also a dark fruitcake for the groom. To drink, there was wine, or the traditional syllabub, a drink of warm, sweetened cream mixed with cider and beaten to a froth.

Melanie sat pretending to eat, painfully aware of the solicitude of the governor and his wife for her, and also of their stiffness with Roland and his friend. Finally the last toast was made, the last drop of wine drained from the glasses, signaling the end of the wedding repast.

Although a newly married couple often set out on a wedding journey of several weeks visiting relatives, finally making their way to New Orleans, or if it was summer, to one of the watering places such as White Sulphur Springs or Saratoga, it was not the custom for them to depart directly from the ceremony. Often as much as five days to a week elapsed, while they lingered in the home of the bride, before the tiring and disruptive process of travel was undertaken. This occasion was to be no different. Melanie and Roland planned to spend at least their first night, and possibly several others, at Greenlea, before crossing to the Louisiana side of the river to make Melanie known to Roland's father. This fact was known, or at least surmised, by the assembled guests. Setting down their wineglasses, they looked at each other, then rose practically in a body, as though they had suddenly remembered they were preventing the bride and groom from retiring. Moving with them to the door, the bride and groom stood in the golden lamplight of the veranda lantern, waving good-bye. In the space of no more than a few minutes, Melanie found herself alone with her new husband.

She turned from the door as Roland closed it and bolted it shut. Stepping to the pier mirror that hung above a marquetry table on one wall of the entrance hall, she removed her veil and smoothed her hair carefully back into place. Becoming aware of Roland still standing beside the door, she flicked a glance at him. He was watching her. Her gaze fell, and she picked up her veil from where she had placed it, running her hands over the wrinkles that had been pressed into it as she sat at supper.

"You look tired," he said, "and that dress, beautiful though it is, must be damnably uncomfortable. Shall we go upstairs?"

The gown, the height of fashion when it was new in the year 1830, over twenty years before, had fifty-six tiny covered buttons down the back. The sleeves, full from the shoulder to the elbow, were held out in a bell shape by lightweight rattan forms. Beneath the elbow, they were tight-fitting to well past the wrist and were closed by twenty-four more tiny buttons down each forearm. The heart-shaped neckline, which revealed the uppermost curves of her creamy breasts, was echoed in the pointed basque. The full skirt swept backward into a demitrain. To hold out the countless yards of heavy satin, she had tied no less than ten petticoats about her waist and covered them with a crinoline stiffened with horsehair.

"Yes," Melanie agreed simply, turning toward the staircase. "If you will step into the parlor and ring for Glory she will help me with my gown."

"That will not be necessary," he drawled.

She turned slowly to face him. Her face was calm, her manner regal as she stood above him on the stairs. There was determination in the set of her shoulders, even if the hand that gripped the mahogany bannister was white at the fingertips. "I don't believe I understand you," she said.

"I mean," he answered as he sauntered toward her, "that I am fairly good with buttons."

"Indeed? But your skill is of very little use to me since we will not be sharing the same room." The decision to take this course had not been a hard one to make. Melanie was far from anxious to take on the duties of a wife. Still, the prime consideration had been the need to strike a blow at Roland Donavan. He quite obviously found her desirable. For the moment, this was the only weakness she could discern. Wasn't it reasonable to suppose he would suffer if he were denied what he wanted? She sincerely hoped so.

"Won't we?" he queried.

He did not seem upset, merely amused and curious. "No," Melanie said distinctly.

"Why?"

"I think you must agree ours is not the usual marriage; I fail to see why it should take the usual form. Also, what

75

passed between us has not altered the fact that I still consider you to blame for my grandfather's death."

"I am sorry about your grandfather, but his death does not lie on my conscience. If he had listened to reason he would still be alive. As for the other, we made a bargain that day a week ago in your carriage. I have fulfilled my part in it, and I intend to hold you to yours."

His words were so determined, so positive, they were galling. With ice in her blue eyes she said, "You took my acceptance of your terms for marrying me for granted. I made no bargain."

"I think you did—and sealed it with a kiss. So much more binding than a handshake, don't you agree?"

"I do not! In any case it doesn't matter. We are strangers who happen to be married to each other. Having satisfied the conventions, there is no need to carry the matter any further. So long as we make an occasional public appearance together, you can go your own way, and I can go mine."

"So cold-blooded," he said softly, an odd look in his green eyes as he surveyed the quick rise and fall of her breasts beneath the heavy shimmering satin of her bodice and the rose flush of temper that lay across her cheeks. It seemed to hold admiration, the gleam of desire, and something else that bordered on sympathy. "It sounds nothing like the kind of marriage I had in mind."

"I'm sure," she snapped, the color on her cheeks deepening.

"Are you?" he asked placing one foot on the bottom stair, his hand resting on the flat top of the newel post. "If you understood so well, I wonder what there is about it you are afraid of?"

"Afraid? Don't be ridiculous!"

"That touched your pride? I'm sorry, but that is the way it seems to me."

"I am not afraid of you," she said, promptly ruining the effect by taking a hasty step upward as he advanced a step.

"Aren't you? Why are you running away then? Why

76

don't you face me down, prove me wrong? Why are you so set on keeping your distance."

"I told you," she flung at him.

"So you did, but all that is past. We have the rest of our lives before us, lives tied together as husband and wife. If ours is not to be a true marriage I may as well have my freedom. I wonder what the chances are of an annulment—under the circumstances? It's possible a divorce will be necessary."

"You wouldn't," she said in stiffened tones. Whatever good might have been done by their marriage would be brought to naught. The vicious round of talk would begin again. And if it should come to divorce, she would never be free of the stigma. She might as well go to Europe and join the demimonde, for her isolation would be just as complete.

"I see no alternative," he said with a fatalistic movement of his shoulders. "It would be best, I think, if I left now. I bid you good-night—Mrs. Donavan."

His thick lashes came down to conceal the expression in his eyes. Inclining his dark head, he turned, descended the stairs, and began to walk toward the door.

With her hands crushing the veil she still held, Melanie watched him go. This should not be happening. She had expected him to shout and argue but ultimately to accept her terms and slam into the room she had made ready for him. She did not know what to do now. There seemed only one way to stop him, one way to bring him back.

He unbolted the door and drew it open. The cold night wind swept into the hallway, making the candle flames in the chandelier overhead sputter and dance on their wicks, and sweeping up under Melanie's skirts, so that she shivered in sudden chill.

"Roland," she called, a grim look about her mouth and the deep purple blue of despair in her eyes. "Very well. It—it shall be as you wish." She waited until he had closed the door and shut the bolt once more. Then she swung around and, lifting her skirts, began to climb the stairs.

A lamp had been left burning on the table beside the bed in Melanie's bedchamber. It revealed the mellow gleam of rosewood in a dressing table, wardrobe, and canopied bed, and the sheen of silk in hangings and draperies of peacock blue. Beneath the mantel a fire had also been provided for her comfort. Though it had shrunk to a bed of ash-covered embers, its warmth greeted them as they stepped into the room. Roland closed the door behind them, then, with an easy stride, crossed to the fireplace where he picked up a brass scuttle with a china handle and tipped more coal into the grate.

Melanie watched him for a moment, then turned away tight-lipped to place her veil upon the dressing table. The sight of him performing that small chore irritated her already strained nerves past bearing. He had not asked her if she would like the fire replenished. It was as if he were already assuming the right to order her life as he saw fit, to shape it according to his desires without reference to what she might prefer.

She was so aware of him behind her that when he straightened with an abrupt movement and began to shrug out of his coat, she turned to face him, barely suppressing a start. It was seldom that a gentleman ever appeared before a lady in his shirt sleeves, and then only on the most stifling of days during the summer. Her grandfather had never taken off his coat in public. For her to see a gentleman, as opposed to a laborer, do so, was not unlike a gentleman catching a prolonged glimpse of a lady's ankle. She would have averted her gaze, except that her attention was caught by the bulky shape of a bandage showing through the fine linen of his shirt sleeve. It was the injury given to him by her grandfather. Dom had said that terrible morning that the colonel had shot him in the arm. She had almost forgotten, though it seemed she could remember now that in their struggles on the bumpy mattress at the River Rest he had flinched when she struck him just there, that he had protected that left shoulder.

Suddenly, the enormity of what she was doing swept in upon her. She had been right; they were strangers. In the grip of reluctance that had nothing to do with her careful schemes of vengeance, she whirled around and made a dive for the door.

She had covered no more than half the distance when Roland, moving with long, swift strides, stepped in front of her. He made no attempt to touch her. Still she stopped as if she had reached a stone fence.

"Where are you going?" he asked, his voice carrying the unmistakable timbre of overstrained patience.

"I—I thought I would make sure Glory isn't waiting up for me. I would hate for her to worry."

As if reminded of his duty, he reached to take her arm now, preventing with ease her instinctive effort to jerk away. He turned her wrist over and frowning in concentration, began to release the buttons of her sleeve from their satin loops. "Tonight of all nights, you should forget about your maid. She won't expect it, and if she is awake still, it won't be because she thinks you have need of her."

"She is not a young woman, and she has been like a mother to me." Melanie kept her eyes lowered. She held her voice steady with great effort but could not prevent the trembling of her fingers as they brushed against the stiff material of his waistcoat.

"If she is that close, she will worry regardless. But are you quite certain it is not you who are worried—and just a little afraid?"

Her head came up. "Must you keep harping on that? I've told you I'm not afraid of you."

His attention was centered on what he was doing, his dark head bent over her wrist. His fingers, as they touched the smooth inner surface of her arm, were warm and unbearably intimate. She was wary of him, yes, and not at all eager to climb into bed with him at this moment, but she was not afraid of him. She was not.

"Then I wonder," he said, irony in his tone, "why you shudder when I come near you, why it takes every ounce of your willpower to make yourself smile at me, why just now you came near to bolting from this room."

Melanie struck back with the same weapon he had

used—words. "Has it occurred to you it may not be fear but disgust that makes me act as I do?"

His fingers were still. Melanie thought the color receded from under his skin, leaving it a shade paler, but when he looked up, his green eyes were steady, their expression almost reflective. "It's a possibility. Either way, something must be done about it."

"I fail to see what difference it makes," Melanie said, slanting a quick glance at him before looking away again.

"Do you?" he asked, dropping one wrist and reaching for the other.

"I was not aware my feelings weighed with you, any more than my reasons for keeping our marriage on a platonic footing."

A smile tugged at the corner of his mouth. "I assure you they do. Only, my reasons for entering into this marriage were not the same as yours, were they?"

"I certainly thought they were similar." Melanie said, frowning as she tried to follow his meaning.

"The reasons you pointed out to me were much the same. It was to be a fair exchange. We were to provide respectability for each other. At least, I believe that was what you said; I wasn't attending too well. I am afraid I was distracted by watching you—so earnest, determined, and altogether desirable—and remembering."

She did not need to ask the source of his memories. The glint deep in his eyes made that all too clear. Melanie felt the air leave her lungs in a rush. For the space of the moment that his gaze held hers, she could not think. It was a new experience, and not a pleasant one. When he returned his gaze to her sleeve once more, she drew a deep, seething breath. "I begin to see," she said.

"Do you? I wonder."

"It isn't difficult to understand. You made it plain from our first meeting."

"Made what plain?" he queried, dropping her arm and turning her with gentle firmness to begin on the buttons down her back.

"That—that you find me—attractive." She was just as

80

glad that she did not have to look at him as she brought out the words.

"Naturally I find you attractive. You are a beautiful woman."

She flung him a quick look over her shoulder. "You know very well that was not what I was trying to say."

"Yes," he agreed reflectively. "On the other hand, I don't think you know what I meant."

She did not reply. The sensation of being released from her gown by him was a distracting one. Tension gripped her, and whether from tiredness, the champagne, or sheer nerves, she could not seem to prevent herself from swaying slightly as she stood before him. She was on edge against the moment when he would take her in his arms.

"Is it so hard to believe," he asked, a stern note entering his voice, "that I could have some respectable reason for offering you the protection of my name, so impossible to think that I could feel some responsibility for you after your grandfather's death, and after what took place that night in my hotel room?"

For him to speak of those two things at this moment seemed deliberate cruelty. Still she was not so incautious as to answer with what she truly believed. "Does it matter?" she asked in stifled tones. "We are married now."

His hands were still. "So we are," he replied and, quickly stripping the last buttons free, stepped back.

Melanie, uncertain that she was actually free to move, stirred and then turned to face him, one hand holding her gaping bodice. He was already walking away. At the dressing table he paused with his back to her as he unfastened his cuffs. Leaving them dangling, he removed his stickpin, untied his cravat, and began to undo the buttons of his waistcoat with one hand.

Melanie ran her tongue over her dry lips. "I believe it is customary for the bridegroom to wait downstairs until the bride has retired to bed."

He swung slowly around. "As you pointed out, ours is not the usual marriage. I see no reason to pretend to be the usual bridegroom." His green eyes held hers, a smile

81

in their depths as he slipped the studs from his shirt and began to strip it from his trousers. "Besides, isn't it a little late for such modesty?"

"You enjoy reminding me of that, don't you?" she threw at him. "Why, I can't imagine!"

"I hadn't considered it," he answered, pausing to lift an eyebrow, "but I suppose I do. You turn such a charming shade of scarlet——and that makes you look like a woman, instead of a cold-blooded goddess."

"I suppose eventually I will cease to be affected by what you choose to say."

"In that case, then, I expect I will have to find other ways of bringing about the transformation."

Melanie swung away from him, depriving him, she hoped, of the pleasure of seeing the blush that mounted to her hairline. What was she to do? A few minutes before she had been dreading any movement he might make to take her in his arms. Now she saw that it would have been much easier to allow him to undress her than to take off her clothes under his watchful, yet sardonic, gaze. She would have liked to ask him to blow out the lamp, allowing them to complete their bedtime toilets under the cover of darkness. The certainty of his refusal prevented her. She was left with no choice except to follow his bold example. The longer she delayed, the more obvious it must become to him that she was reluctant; the more reason he would have for jeering at her reserve.

Moving with slow and unconscious grace, she crossed to the wardrobe, opened the mirrored door, and took down her nightgown. Draping it over a chair on the far side of the room from Roland, she began to release her arms from her gown, pushing the rattan forms which held the sleeves down over her wrists. Taking a deep breath, she caught the waist and drew the gown off over her head. The yards of aged satin joined her nightgown on the chair. Then she bent her head, working at the tapes of her petticoat. Behind her, she was aware of the thud of Roland's boots as he drew them off with the cricket boot-jack on the hearth. That left only his trousers. Bending her head lower, Melanie untied the laces of her stays and the ribbons of her camisole, then leaned hastily to take up her nightgown, pulling it on over her head. Under its protection, she slipped off her camisole and stepped from her other undergarments, leaving them in a pile on the floor as she settled the white batiste folds of her nightgown around her and pushed her arms into the long sleeves.

With a sense of triumph, she turned around. Roland stood staring into the fire, leaning with one arm braced against the mantel. There was a frown between his dark brows and a brooding look on his face. He glanced at her as she crossed to the dressing table, then looked again as she began to take the pins from her hair, letting it slide in a silken coil down her back. The expression in his face did not lighten. Watching him from the corner of her eye, Melanie wondered if his arm was paining him. Not that she felt any sympathy. He deserved everything that he might be suffering. Compressing her lips, she picked up her hairbrush and began to draw it through the long shimmering length of her hair, pulling it forward over her shoulder so she could reach the ends. When it was smooth and free of tangles, she divided it into three thick strands and began to make her usual bedtime plait.

"Don't."

"What?" Melanie asked, swinging halfway around.

"Don't braid your hair," he said, his even tone carrying an unmistakable rasp of authority.

"If I don't it will be full of tangles by morning," she answered, her fingers beginning to weave the silken sections once more.

"It will be easy enough to remedy that."

"Will it? And I suppose you will act as lady's maid again?"

"Possibly," he said, straightening, moving toward her with a determined stride. "At least I can promise to loosen any braid you insist on making. Anyway, we have dawdled long enough, it's time we were in bed."

Before she could guess his intentions, he scooped her into his arms. Swinging her high against his chest, he took

83

the few steps to the bed. He placed her in the center of the mattress on the turned-down coverlet, then dropped down beside her. Holding her startled eyes with his own, he reached to remove the white satin slippers which she still wore, then smoothing his hand up the calf of her leg, peeled off her silk stockings one after the other. Straightening, he stared down at her, indecision allied with what might have been self-mockery in his face as he surveyed the soft auburn waves of her hair spread around her and the tender curves of her body outlined by the thin material of her nightgown.

Abruptly, he pushed up off the bed. Melanie let her lashes fall as with a few swift movements he removed his trousers and stepped to extinguish the light. In that first moment of darkness, she slid beneath the covers, drawing them up over her as though she was chilled. For an instant, as he turned back toward the bed, he came between her and the red glow of the fireplace. The muscular planes of his body were outlined in the coppery light like some ancient statue of perfect manhood forged by the gods. It was a fleeting impression; still it left Melanie shaken. She did not move as she felt the feather mattress sag under his weight, but lay watching the dark form of the man who was her husband as he loomed above her.

Then he was beside her, his strong arms reaching to draw her against the naked length of his body. Stiff, unyielding, Melanie lay where he placed her with her eyes tightly closed. She thought he breathed deep of the yellow rose scent of her hair, thought she heard him sigh. His voice was low, without inflection as he spoke against her ear. "Go to sleep," he said. "Rest for tonight. There is always tomorrow."

Chapter 5

SHE WAS warm, deliciously warm. Despite the chill of the room she sensed hovering outside the bed covering, she was wrapped in comfort. Between waking and sleeping, she lay with her eyes closed, enjoying the sensation, aware also of the tingling race of blood in her veins and an inner glow of quiescent excitement. She stretched, then snuggled a little deeper into the covers and the feather bed. The movement brought her into closer contact with the source of the warmth that surrounded her. She was nestled in the curve of a hard male body. Roland. Her back was pressed against his chest. At some time during the night her turnings had worked her gown well above her thighs where she could feel the hard press of his knees against the backs of her legs. The batiste material was drawn tight across her breasts and his hand rested on one soft globe, gently caressing the nipple.

The temptation to lie still and see what would happen, what this man who was her husband would do, drifted across her mind. Hard upon it came a sense of shock at her own weakness that brought her eyes flickering open. She turned her head on the pillow to find Roland resting on one elbow, staring down at her in the predawn light. As she raised her violet blue eyes, clouded with confusion and vulnerability, to his, she saw dark desire mirrored in their depths. Before she could draw in her breath to speak, his mouth came down on hers, forcing her lips apart, moving, searching. His tongue touched hers with the feel of fire, and she stiffened in resistance to the spreading pleasure that moved over her. Roland took no notice. His hand slid down over the taut muscles of her stomach to where the hem of her gown rode across her thighs. His fingers slipped beneath the material, easing it, pushing it higher, baring the lower part of her body.

Melanie turned her head, dragging her lips away. "Roland—" she breathed in unconscious entreaty.

He shook his head, brushing his lips across the curve of her cheek below the ear. "Don't think," he whispered. "Just lie still."

She could not do it, not with his hands urging her nightgown higher and his mouth trailing across her throat to touch her uncovered breast with searing heat. She arched away from him, only to feel an arm underneath her, lifting as he stripped the gown off over her head. He gathered her close once more, the muscles in his arms rigid with his need. Beyond the turmoil in her mind and the mounting fire in her blood, she knew there was nothing she could do, no way she could stop him without destroying the style of living that was all she knew, all she had. Well, then, she would not try. But neither would she respond to him. Let him take what satisfaction he could, it was all he would get.

It was no easy resolve to keep. With her hands clenched into fists, she lay as he explored the curves and hollows of her body with infinite care, enjoying the silken texture of her skin, awakening a sweet ache in her loins that grew, demanding assuagement. His mouth ravished hers as his caresses grew bolder, more consummate in their understanding of what would give her uncontrollable pleasure. With a low sound deep in her throat, she moved her head from side to side. She reached out her hand to push him from her but instead clasped his shoulder, sliding her open palm along the corded muscles.

He shifted his weight, hovering above her as he eased his knee between her thighs. She felt the hard urgency of his desire, but his entry was gentle. Even so, the shaft of sensuous pleasure that radiated through her made her senses reel. She clutched his arms as he pushed deeper, penetrating remorselessly until he was a part of her. His heart pounded against her, an echo of the hard beat of her own. Then the wild rhythm of his passion caught them. They were hurled upward, mounting into realms of blackness. Striving together, they rose higher, the breath locked in their chests in the soaring wonder of their rapture. It was unbelievable, a wondrous, encompassing ravishment of the body and mind. Melanie gave herself to it, surging against Roland's thrusting ardor, coming ever nearer the tormenting edge of endurance.

With a bursting leap of ecstasy, they reached it, their bodies fused as they hurtled over and into the piercing, joyous downward plunge. Clasped tightly in panting content, they lay, until the chill reached their cooling bodies and awareness of themselves and who and what they were returned.

Roland eased from her. Melanie kept her eyes closed. For some reason she could not explain, tears hovered behind her eyelids, and she had no wish to look into the face of the man who was her husband. She felt betrayed, not so much by the man who lay beside her, as by her own body. She felt as though she no longer belonged to herself. She had not known that the act of love could be so overwhelming, that someone else could have such mastery over her emotions that they no longer answered to her will. Next time, she would know. Next time she would be better armed against this new and enthralling pleasure.

There came a rustling sound as he eased himself higher on the pillow beside her. His fingers, with their slight roughness at the tips, brushed a lustrous strand of her hair from her cheek, drawing it down across the smooth roundness of her shoulder. "Was that so great an ordeal?" he asked, a husky note in his low voice.

She refused to give him the satisfaction of an answer, turning her head away from him. Let him think what he pleased. If he was made to feel guilt for forcing himself upon her and, in the future, gratitude when she submitted to his need of her, that would be little enough in the way of punishment.

"I would like to make you forget that first time," he went on, his touch wandering to the blue-veined fullness of her breast that trembled with the beating of her heart. "It was no way to begin."

"No," she said with difficulty, "it was not." Of that much she was certain now. It crossed her mind that if she had behaved differently that night, if she had declared herself promptly—or at least fought him with less silent savagery—then he would also have acted differently. It was not a comforting discovery.

"We have made a fair start at correcting that bad impression, but I think it would be wrong to stop until every effort has been—exhausted." He leaned to press his lips between her breasts, moving with maddening, tantalizing slowness to taste the nearer rose-tinted nipple.

Amazement at her own reaction to his caress, and puzzlement at the mockery in his tone prevented Melanie from grasping his meaning for a long moment. Then as his hand slid lower over the flat surface of her belly, she realized his intention. With a gasp, she reached down to catch at his hand. "Roland," she gasped, "wait."

"What is it? It's not morning yet; it's too early to get up. They will not be expecting us to ring for breakfast for hours. It would be heartless to drag them out of bed just because we can't sleep. On the other hand, since we are awake, we must occupy ourselves in some way."

"Must we?"

"I believe," he said, his voice muffled, "it is essential."

They crossed the Mississippi River on the cable-drawn ferry. Since the afternoon was sunny and bright, they started out in Roland's open phaeton. Before they were halfway across the river, Melanie regreted the decision. For all the pale yellow brightness of the sun, the wind sweeping across the water had a cutting edge that made her fur-lined lap robe feel as thin as tissue silk. As long as Roland had been beside her, she had been fairly comfortable, basking in the heat of his body, but he had stepped down from the carriage to talk to the ferryman. Noticing they were moving against the wind, he had taken off his coat and set himself to giving the elderly man a hand in pulling the heavy ferry over the choppy waves. The sight of him in his shirt sleeves with wind flattening the soft linen material against his straining muscles made Melanie shiver with a sudden chill. He balanced so effortlessly on the heaving craft while the wind tore at his black hair and flapped the collar of his shirt against the side of his face. Fearless in his strength, he stood with his booted feet planted near the ferry's edge, where the waves lapped the planking, and never looked down. The hungry gurgle and splash of the river awoke no memories of childish terror for him. He was immune to the numbing, unreasoning fright that crept over Melanie as they inched farther and farther from shore. In an effort at control, she closed her eyes, forcing herself to think of other things.

Their destination was Cottonwood, Roland's home in the Louisiana Delta country. They had tarried a week at Greenlea before setting out. Even then, it seemed to Melanie, Roland was reluctant to start the traditional journey. From something Chloe Clements had said on that night of their first meeting, and a few things he had let fall in the course of their conversation, she had gathered he and his father were not on good terms with each other. He never spoke of his mother. From his reticence, Melanie assumed she was dead and, rightly or wrongly, attributed much of the friction between father and son to that fact. She would have liked to question him about it, but she could not quite find the words to broach the subject. Roland could be formidable at times. Just when it seemed they were coming to know each other, to be somewhat at ease in each other's company, he would withdraw, becoming distant. On those occasions in particular, he would stare at her with a sardonic light behind his green eyes. His mood might last an hour or an evening, ending with a sudden assault of hard kisses that left her breathless, or a swift ascent to their bedchamber with her in his arms for a brief tumble into bed. Such tactics left her on edge, uncertain of how to approach him at any given minute. It occurred to her once or twice that they might have been designed for that very effect, or worse still, they might be the results of the fact that he might have divined her motives for marrying him. Still, she could not bring herself to accept that explanation. If he had understood her so well, he would never have married her, would he? No. Regardless of how much she attracted him, and that attraction could not be denied, he would not have entered such a marriage with his eyes open. No man would tolerate such a blow to his ego, unless he had a reason.

What reason could there be? The same one that had caused him to slander her grandfather in the first place? Some grudge, some fancied wrong that had been done to him? What if he had recognized her that night at the River Rest before she had revealed her identity? What if he had seen her enter his room, had known that she was waiting? He had been quick to offer marriage, had seemed disappointed at her first refusal. And later, when she had changed her mind, hadn't his acceptance of her proposal been remarkably swift? What a fine jest it would be if Roland Donavan had his own diabolical reasons for what he was doing, reasons in some way similar to her own. Was it possible he held some hidden malice for her attempt to kill him and meant to punish her at his leisure? Or perhaps his reasons reached back farther into time, back to the Mexican campaign. It might be a fine jest, but she did not feel like laughing.

They were nearing the Louisiana bank of the river. Roland, with a quick word and a clap on the ferryman's back, shrugged into his coat. Vibrant with health and exercise, he swung back up into the carriage seat. As she drew away from him, he glanced at her pale face.

"What is it? Are you cold?"

"No," she answered, forcing a smile to her lips. "It's nothing."

"Come, you can do better than that. Does it offend

90

your fine sense of the conduct becoming in a gentleman to see me add my bit to that of old Jim there to get us across the river?"

She threw him a glance, surprised at the anger in his tone. "No, certainly not."

"No? I thought you were looking definitely horrified just now."

Melanie pressed her lips together at this unflattering description. He could, when he wished, be persistent as well as insulting; it would be best to give him at least a half-truth. "If you must know, I am not overly fond of boats of any kind," she replied and went on to tell him of the accident that had taken the lives of her parents.

"You bring yourself to ride the ferry, however," he said thoughtfully when she was done and when she had accepted his proper expression of regret.

"It isn't a steamboat. It has no engine to catch fire, and the end of the trip is always in sight. Besides, my grandfather insisted that I make the effort. He didn't think much of cowards, and he required me to go with him when he visited one of his old friends who lived just across the river. I always dreaded the time when he would ask me to go to New Orleans with him. I was spared because he did not particularly like the city."

"Would you have gone?" he asked, a curious note in his voice.

"I suppose I would have tried. I'm not sure I could have done it. I can't even bear to step on board a steamboat that is tied up at the landing. I begin to shake from head to foot and I am overcome by the feeling of something terrible about to happen."

"So you haven't been on a steamboat since you were a child?"

She shook her head. "My grandfather escorted me to school in Mobile. We rode a part of the way in the carriage and made the remainder of the trip by train." Her grandfather had not minded; he had wanted to retrace the trail he had taken during the Seminole Indian Wars. It had been great fun. She had returned by the same route

91

in the spring, traveling in easy stages from one to another of the homes of her school friends.

"We will have to see what can be done about that," he said.

Melanie turned to stare at him, but his attention was on the horses as the ferry grounded on the Louisiana shore. He gathered up the reins, slapped the horses' rumps, and guided the carriage up onto the rich black mud of the road.

They rattled along in silence for what seemed like miles. Unlike the rolling hills on the eastern side of the river, the western delta land was flat. Beginning at the banks of the river, the vast majority of it was under cultivation, though the fields lay fallow at this time of year. The plowed rows, with water standing between the furrows, stretched straight and darkly fecund as far as the eye could see. Here and there down straight dirt roads were the outbuildings that served some planter's property, the barns and storage sheds, the overseer's house of unpainted wood with its collection of slave cabins behind it.

The wind died away; the sun grew warmer. Melanie, since at Roland's wish she was not wearing a bonnet to shelter her face, put up a sunshade trimmed in lavender lace. It was a nuisance to be bothered with it, but though the sun felt good, fashion dictated a wan complexion.

Roland glanced at her, then looked back to the road ahead of them. "It isn't much farther," he said.

"You needn't worry about me. I am perfectly all right."

"I thought," he said, eyeing her sunshade, "that ladies never admitted to stamina, that they preferred to be thought of as weak creatures who easily succumbed to fatigue?"

"My grandfather had no patience with such nonsense. He was of the opinion that half the problems complained of by ladies could be attributed to tight lacing."

"Undoubtedly he was right, though you can have little idea of the problems most ladies face, since I never saw anyone with less need for lacing, tight or otherwise."

There was no point in arguing with him over the question, since he had been in charge of lacing her stays for the past week. In any case, she had learned life was more pleasant if they kept up at least an outward appearance of amicability. The strain of being at daggers drawn was too great to be maintained for any length of time. "Thank you kindly, sir," she said with every appearance of unruffled composure, though there was a suspicion of color across her cheekbones.

"You are welcome, Madame Donavan."

Afraid she might have unbent too much, Melanie hastened to turn the conversation into other channels. "Tell me, what is Cottonwood like?"

"It is a working plantation, nothing fancy. The house was nice enough, once, but it has been years since anything was done about upkeep, twenty years to be exact. I don't believe it has had so much as a coat of paint since I was twelve years old."

"You speak as if there was something significant about that year."

"There was. It was the year my mother left Cottonwood. She had left before, many times; once she even went back to Ireland for several months. But that year she didn't come back. Since then, my father has planted and worked the land, tended his fields, harvested his crops. In good years he bought more acreage, in bad years he hung on, but he never spent a cent on the house. It had been built for my mother, and she went away and left it, and him."

His voice was so hard it was as if he were speaking of a stranger instead of his own father. But neither had there been any pity for himself. Surely he had been left behind as well?

After a moment, he went on. "I didn't intend to play upon your sympathies, only to make you understand what you will find at Cottonwood. My father has become something of a recluse; he never leaves the plantation. All his business, the buying and selling of his yield at harvest time, the ordering of food and supplies, is done through his cotton broker in New Orleans. That is why he was not at the wedding."

"I'm glad you told me," Melanie said. "I will admit that I wondered."

"But you didn't ask, a remarkable example of self-control, or was it simply that the matter wasn't important enough to extend beyond mild curiosity?"

There it was again, that mocking inflection, following, as it so often did, after a compliment. It was as though he had no intention of letting her think he admired her too much, as though he were determined to find fault. She turned to look at him, her blue eyes clear and frank. "There was always the possibility that you had your own reasons for not wanting your father present. I did not feel that my position, at the time, gave me the right to inquire into them."

An unwilling smile crept into his eyes as he stared down at her. "From this day forward," he said, "I hereby give you the right to pry into anything that concerns me."

Before she could answer, indeed before he could change his mind, or so it seemed, he turned away and urged the horses to a faster pace.

Cottonwood was off the main road at the end of a long track that was little more than a pair of wagon ruts with last year's dried grass and twisted briar vines growing in the middle. Two great leafless cottonwood trees towered above the house, their white bark shining in the afternoon sun, the tips of the limbs brushing the unpainted boards of its western side. Unlike Greenlea, which had been built in the Georgian style, Cottonwood was a simple planter's home of two stories with a chimney on either end of the hipped roof and expansive double galleries built straight across the front of the house. Fanlights over the doors of both the upper and lower levels, turned balcony railings, round columns, and long shutters at the windows indicated that it might once have had charm and grace. That day was long past. Now the paint had weathered to a coating of scabrous gray, several balusters were missing from the railings, and the shutters, with their peeling

94

green paint, sagged this way and that against the walls. The outbuildings huddled in the rear looked more cared for, more habitable.

As Melanie stared, Roland got down from the phaeton, tied the team to the hitching post in front of the house, and came around to help her descend.

"Welcome to Cottonwood," he said, his smile grim.

With Roland's hand under her elbow, Melanie moved up the shaky wooden steps and crossed the lower gallery, passing through the front door as Roland threw it open without ceremony before her. Their entrance startled an elderly Negro man who was passing across the central hall. He rounded on them, staring, before a grin broke over his face. "Mister Roland! We didn't expect to see you again so soon."

"Good afternoon, Sutton. Melanie, this is Sutton, who taught me to fish and to swim, and also beat the few manners that I possess into me. Sutton, I would like to present my wife."

"Well, now. This is a fine day, a fine day indeed when you are bringing home a bride, and such a pretty lady, to Cottonwood. I'm mighty proud and happy for you, Mr. Roland."

"Thank you, Sutton. Is my father in the house?"

A shadow passed over the servant's face. "I'll have to see, Mr. Roland. If you and your new Missus would like to freshen up after your traveling, I'll set out something to drink in the parlor. When you are finished upstairs, perhaps you will wait in there."

"Like company, Sutton?"

"Why, no, sir. I just thought your lady might be more comfortable, for the time being."

"I see," Roland said, his eyes narrowing as he met those of the other man. "Whatever you think best, Sutton."

The house was in no better shape inside than out. The rugs were threadbare, the wallpaper stained, fly-specked, and peeling. The draperies and curtains at the windows hung limp and dull with dust under tarnished brass head-

95

ings. There was dampness in the air and a dank, closed-in smell, as though the rooms had not been aired for some time and had seldom, if ever, known the warmth of human voices and laughter. It occurred to Melanie as she washed away the stains of travel and dried her hands on a mildewed linen hand towel that there was little to choose between Roland's home and his billet at the River Rest. At least the hotel Under-The-Hill had some semblance of life about it, however sordid. Cottonwood seemed, if not dead, at least in the process of dying.

Roland was grimly quiet as they descended to the parlor. Taking a glass of the sherry which Sutton had left for them, he walked to the window and stood staring out. A fire had been kindled in the fireplace using wood instead of the coal so popular in Natchez. Melanie sat on the edge of a horsehair settee and watched the flames curl about the oak logs. She supposed this trip to present her to Roland's father was necessary, but it was easy to see that it gave her husband no pleasure. As for herself, she was growing more ill at ease with every passing minute. The sherry she held in her hand was sour, and she suspected the glasses had not been rinsed before the wine was poured, for above the vinegar odor of the wine could be detected the smell of ancient dust. Despite its drawbacks, she did not set her glass aside. It was better to have something to occupy her hands than to sit idle in the cold room, yearning toward a fire that was as yet too newly laid to give out heat.

The parlor door swung open with a jerk. A man stalked into the room. He wore the clothing of a working man, a jacket buttoned to the throat over worsted trousers thrust into mud-caked boots. His frame was tall and bony and so stooped at the shoulders that his head jutted forward, giving him the appearance of staring from under the ridges of his eyebrows. His thin brown hair, streaked with gray, grew back from a high forehead carved with undulating lines. Beneath a large nose, his lips were thin and set about with the down-curving marks of bitterness.

He halted in the center of the room, his dark gaze fixed

96

on Roland. "Well," he rasped, "I didn't expect to see you again for another year or two."

"Hello, father," Roland drawled in greeting. "You might not have seen me so soon if I had not married and, in a sudden excess of respectability, decided I owed you the filial gesture of presenting my wife to you."

"A wife. Some dance-hall harlot, I suppose?"

"Not at all," Roland corrected, moving toward Melanie, holding out his hand to take hers and draw her to her feet. "Melanie, my love, may I present my father, Robert Donavan, Esquire? Father, this is Melanie, the granddaughter of Colonel Ezell Johnston."

The older man looked confused as Melanie rose from behind the high back of the settee. He recovered quickly, however. "The colonel's granddaughter, eh? That was the man you fought, wasn't it, Roland? Died later, I hear. Oh, yes, I heard all about it. Not from you, though. I suppose the old man objected to the match. Shows he had good sense."

Melanie glanced uncertainly from Roland to his father. There had been something more than mere pique or irritation at a neglectful son in the elder man's voice. It had sounded like hate. Falling back on politeness, Melanie said, "How do you do?"

A wintry smile curved the thin lips of Roland's father. He opened his mouth to answer, but the words never came. They were snatched away by a sudden fit of coughing. The spasms racked him, doubling him over. Melanie started forward instinctively, only to be stopped by a touch on her arm. Roland shook his head as she glanced up at him. Releasing her, he drew a handkerchief from the tail pocket of his frock coat. This he passed to his father, placing a supportive arm across the older man's back. He was shaken off at once with a glare of anger. Within a few seconds, the older man was able to catch his breath, to conquer the impulse to cough. Straightening, he thrust his son's handkerchief into his sleeve, but not before Melanie had seen the blood which stained it.

"Well," he wheezed, "what are you two standing gawking at? I suppose since it's supper time you expect to be fed. Let's go and see what Sutton has scraped up for us to eat."

The fare set upon the table was plain—dried peas cooked with smoked ham, roasted yams, cornbread muffins, and a layer cake topped with a sauce made from dried apples. Roland's father ate in surly silence, putting away enormous quantities of food. It was only after his appetite had been appeased that he glanced across the table at his son, a crafty look in his deep-set brown eyes.

"I expect," he said, balancing his knife on the side of his plate, "that now you are married you will be thinking of settling down?"

"The idea had crossed my mind," Roland admitted, leaning back in his chair.

Melanie slanted a quick look at her husband. He had mentioned no such plans to her, though she had certainly wondered what he intended to do, how he meant to spend their future life together.

"Were you maybe thinking of settling down here? At Cottonwood?" the older man asked.

"If you mean to live, no," his son answered shortly. "Melanie has a house on the outskirts of Natchez that will come to her from her grandfather's estate. The thought had occurred to me, however, that you might need some help with the day to day operation of the plantation here. I will be glad to lend a hand when needed, of course."

A laugh shook his father's thin frame. "So you see yourself as a planter, do you? Living with the nobs on the bluffs of Natchez, crossing the river when the spirit moves you to check on the prosperity of the lands you hope to inherit one day and, just possibly, picking up a share of the proceeds from the sale of the crops at the end of the year? It's a pretty picture. Such a shame to spoil it, but it will be better if I tell you right now that this plantation is mine. I need nobody's help, nobody to share in the profits."

"Profits?" Roland asked with the lift of an eyebrow. "From what I see they can't be large. If I did take anything out at some future date, it appears to me it would have to be only after pouring in a lot of good money first."

"You talk like a fool pretending to have business sense."

"Do I? Look around at this place and then tell me, if you dare, that it shows any signs of prosperity. Where is the comfort and beauty these profits you keep talking about have brought you?"

"You know I don't give a damn for such things, never have." The elder man gave a short laugh. "Sutton sees to me all right, and I don't have to put up with a bunch of giggling maids underfoot or some busybody old woman from the quarters as housekeeper, fussing about a little honest dirt and trying to get me to spend my money to put on a show for guests that never come. I learned as a lad fresh off the boat from Dublin that the only thing that ever counts is keeping hard gold beside me and adding to it every year. Except for a few foolish months when I was a young man, that's what I've always done, and that's what I always will do to the day I die!"

"Will you indeed, with the price of cotton getting lower every year, and the cost of working the land higher? From what I've seen, your planting methods are as outdated as your ideas on what it means to be a rich man. Last year's cotton stalks are still standing in your fields, the ground isn't properly ditched for drainage, and I saw no sign of the green manures that should be growing now to be turned under to replenish the land. Cotton takes nourishment out of the soil like no other crop. You have been told that a hundred times, but you have done nothing but take from the land for thirty years here. It's a miracle that you can eke out any kind of a living."

"Fancy talk that you learned from that fancy military school, that Jefferson College. It's time you made up your mind whether you want to be a planter, a soldier, or just want to live on your wife's money." The older man turned toward Melanie. "You look like good stock, girl, that much I'll say for you. I may be an ignorant old Irish

99

farmer, but bloodlines are something I know about. So I'll tell you what I'll do. If Roland, here, gets a son on you, I promise to leave Cottonwood to that son."

The crude phrase brought a wave of color to Melanie's hairline. It was made no easier by the glance tinged with appraisal that Roland flung at her. Still, it was her husband who saved her from the necessity of forming an answer.

"As much as I hate to spoil your pretty picture for you," he told his father, "I have to point out to you that Louisiana law will not allow you to disinherit your only son."

"My son," the older man sneered. "And what of a bastard foisted off upon me by the bitch who was my wife?"

"You have no proof of that," Roland said softly. "In any case, the fact that you accepted me as your son, that I was baptized with your surname and allowed to use it, constitutes proof of parentage in the eyes of the law. Whoever's son you may think I am, you cannot deny me now."

It was obvious that what Roland was saying was no news to the man he called his father. "Maybe not," the older man wheezed, leaning across the table to stare at him with narrow, hate-filled eyes, "but I can keep you from getting a penny of mine as long as there is breath in my body."

The words had hardly left his mouth before he began to cough once more. His face turned purple with engorged blood as he hacked and whooped, gasping for breath. Sutton, entering the room with coffee, hastily set down the tarnished silver tray holding the pot and cups to go to his master's aid. Before the awful spasms finally ceased, two table napkins were red with blood, and their host had to be helped from the table. Roland's attempts to offer his support were fiercely rejected. Meeting his eyes, Sutton gave a sorrowful shake of his head and led Robert Donavan from the room.

There was little to do after that except retire to the

100

bedchamber that had been allotted to them. Though they had eaten early, the swift winter dusk was already closing in, and a lamp had to be lighted. After the long, stiff hours of sitting in the carriage, Melanie wanted nothing so much as a hot soak in a tub full of water. Such a luxury seemed unheard of at Cottonwood. She was offered a hat tub instead. Shaped exactly like a wide-brimmed hat sitting on its flat crown, it was something like four feet across and held, at the most, three or four gallons of water. The bather either knelt in the center or sat on a ledge for that purpose built into the side, soaped, then poured water over herself to rinse. The excess water was caught by the wide, spreading brim or lip of the tub and channeled back into the center receptable. In summer there might have been a certain amount of pleasure to be had from the cooling effect of the water trickling over the body and running, considerably cooler, back into the tub; in winter, with water that could only be called tepid to begin with, it was sheer torture. The pain was not lessened by the feeble excuse of a fire that burned under the plain wooden mantel, or the total lack of a bath screen to close off the drafts that whistled through the space between the bare floor and high ceiling.

Melanie had contrived a screen of sorts with chair backs and the wide skirts of her petticoats, but it was not high enough, even when she was kneeling in the tub, to afford much protection. Its greatest value was in shielding her from Roland's gaze as he lay stretched upon the bed. With great stoicism, he had already endured the rigors of the hat tub, rinsing himself with one thorough sluicing from a can of cold water, saving the heated water for her. She was grateful for the sacrifice, but she would be even more grateful if he would not lie watching her with such an intent look in his green eyes.

She raised her arms, holding the trailing strands of her hair with one hand while with the other she squeezed the fast-cooling water down her back. Behind her, the fire leaped higher, its light casting the shadow of her slender yet voluptuous form against the white material of her petticoats. From the opposite direction, the lamp at the bedside projected her shape like a magic lantern show against the far wall, giving her the majectic proportions of a goddess. With the cold water on one side and the growing heat of the fire on the other, she shivered, a movement exaggerated in shadow.

Flinging a glance at Roland over the low back of a slipper chair, Melanie discovered he was not watching her, but was staring at the wall beyond. Was he thinking of the harsh and hurtful things his father had said to him? Was tonight the first time he had heard them, or had he been forced to live with the accusation that had been made all his life, since his mother had left them? Had it occurred to him to wonder what incident in his mother's past might have caused his father to think he had been duped into claiming another man's child? Did he know whether it was true or not, or was he merely basing his legitimacy upon a legal technicality, a twist of the law which would not let a man disown a child he had previously acknowledged as his own? And if he knew, if he even guessed that he was in truth a bastard, what did it mean to him?

Watching his profile, the stern lines of his face, the wide-spaced eyes beneath heavy brows, the classical line of his nose and firm lips, the way his hair grew in a thick shock from his broad forehead, Melanie was aware of something she had never thought to feel in connection with Roland Donavan. It was compassion. She knew a sudden urge, overwhelming in its strength, to distract his thoughts, or at least to share them.

"What are you thinking?" she asked.

Reluctantly, or so it seemed, he turned to gaze toward her, then nodding at the wall, he said, "I was counting the goose bumps."

"What?" Melanie exclaimed, balancing precariously on one knee as she swung around. Behind her, she heard the rustle of bedclothes and the creak of ropes as Roland got to his feet. His shadow towered over hers on the wall. Crossing her arms uselessly over her chest, she swung

102

back to see him moving toward her, picking up a towel that hung over the back of a chair.

"It occurred to me," he said slowly, "that past a certain point, when the goose bumps were thick enough, you might appreciate whatever I had to offer in the way of a method of warming you."

Relief at finding him unaffected by what had happened at the dinner table clashed in Melanie's mind with alarm as she watched him skirt the edge of her improvised screen. He had undressed before her a number of times in the past few days, but never had she seen him in such glaring light, and never had he stalked her in such rampant nakedness. "You may be right," she said, committing herself recklessly. "If you will hand me the towel, I will get out."

"Nope," he said with a slow shake of his head. "If I am to do the job of warming you properly, I had better start now."

At the side of the tub he halted, slinging the towel over one shoulder. Reaching down he caught Melanie's arms and hauled her to her feet. "Wait!" she cried as he slipped one arm about her waist and lifted her free of the shallow tub to stand beside him on the hearth. She staggered against him, her breasts brushing against his chest before she regained her balance, but he did not seem to notice. His face intent with mock concentration, he flipped the towel around her and began to rub her dry. So brisk were his ministrations that she had little time to worry about modesty as she turned this way and that in his hold, trying to keep her skin from being scraped away by the rough towel. "Ouch! Roland, don't," she panted. "Stop!"

But little by little, his movements slowed as he reached the more tender sections of her anatomy. When at last he twined his fingers in her hair and drew her head back for his kiss, she was glowing with warmth and something more, a kindling flame of desire.

Roland let the towel fall. Melanie tried to catch it, but

the arms that held her were too strong, too quick, to allow her to retain that flimsy protection.

Roland savored her mouth with hard hunger, moving his hands over her back to her hips, pressing her close against the lower part of his body. In sudden ardor he released her and, bending, slipped one arm beneath her knees, lifting her against him. The bed was reached in a few steps. He placed one knee on the mattress, then fell with her, turning at the last moment to his back, so she sprawled across him. For a long instant their eyes met, in his a despairing demand, in hers the shock of awakened excitement and the residue of compassion, the feeling that is the other side of the coin of love.

In that brief space of time, Melanie knew that for all his pretense, he was not unmoved by his father's words, that he was not the same as on other nights when he had turned to her. She knew he wanted something from her he had looked for before in a woman, something he had needed on that cold and rainy night at the River Rest. Forgetfulness. Surprisingly, she did not mind. It seemed in the fever of the moment that she might even find the same thing in his arms.

With a heave, he rolled above her. She braced her hands on his chest, trying to subdue the raging in her blood and the soft female instinct that urged her to answer his need. Her victory was an uneven one. Though she lay passive in his arms, accepting the hard, insistent pressure of his mouth, the knowing touch of his hands for long enough to establish a token resistance, at last she could do so no longer. By slow degrees the strength left her restraining hands. She let them fall.

Roland took instant advantage of her weakness. His knee slid between her thighs as his arms tightened. They came together with clinging mouths and twisting, arching bodies, seeking mindlessly for the opiate of passion, the lulling peace of sleep-inducing exhaustion.

Later, basking in the animal heat of Roland's arms, Melanie roused from a dreamlike content to the sound of horse's hooves pounding up to the house. She lay still, tensing as at the approach of danger, staring into the darkness as the thud of footsteps came on the lower gallery, the thumping of a fist on the front door. A voice echoed up from below, a man's voice with a familiar ring, even through tones thick with anger and drunkenness, a voice demanding entry, a voice calling her name.

It was Dom.

Chapter 6

THE TENSION in Roland's arms increased, an indication that he was not asleep. When Melanie turned her head in wakeful listening, also, he released her and, rolling from the bed, began to pull on his trousers. By the time he reached the bedchamber door, Sutton, who slept in a small room next to that of his master, could already be heard descending the stairs. Melanie watched her husband step through the door and close it quietly behind him. The instant the latch clicked shut, she threw back the covers, searching for her nightgown and dressing gown of lavender, lace-edge challis that had been laid out across the foot of the bed. Dragging them on, she slipped from the bed, running in bare feet toward the door.

Out in the hall, she paused to straighten her clothing and tie the belt of her dressing gown before she crept toward the landing above the entrance hall. With her soft auburn hair swirling about her face and shoulders, she leaned to look over the bannister.

Below, Sutton was trying to close the front door on Dom, his face impassive as he ignored the loud, slurred demands to see Melanie. Dom, pushing on the panel with one hand, was trying to get his shoulder in the door.

"I know she is in the house," he insisted. "You can't fob me off by saying she's not at home, to vis—visitors. I won't stand for it! I—I've got to see her, you hear me? I've got to!" At the scrape of a footstep above him, he glanced up. "Roland!" he cried, catching sight of Mel-

106

anie's husband where he had stopped halfway down the stairs with his hands braced on the railing. "Roland, tell your man to let me come inside."

Sutton looked to Roland, who nodded. The butler stepped back, opening the door so suddenly Dom half fell into the entrance hall. In the light of the lamp burning smokily on the table in the center of the hallway, Dom appeared haggard. His cravat was twisted to one side, he had no hat or gloves, and his frock coat and trousers were sprinkled with soot as if he had not taken the time to change since he had stepped off the steamboat. Blown by the night wind, his fine blond hair was falling into his pale face, his eyes were red rimmed, and he had not shaved for at least two days, possibly longer. He showed no sign of gratitude for the permission granted him to enter but stood scowling up at Roland.

"Where is Melanie? What have you done with her?" he asked.

When Roland spoke, his voice was calm, the timbre even. "She has retired for the night, just as Sutton tried to tell you. As for what I've done with her, why nothing except bring her to my home like any other bridegroom."

"Bridegroom," Dom sneered. "I don't believe it. She would never have married you, not after what you did to her grandfather—"

"Which was—what, exactly?" Roland inquired.

Dom's eyelids flickered down, hiding his expression. "Never mind that now. I refuse to believe in this marriage until I hear it from Melanie herself. I refuse to believe she came here with you of your own will, free and open."

"Are you suggesting I abducted her?"

"If you want to put it that way," Dom said, striking a belligerent pose, staring up at Roland as he swayed on his feet.

"You are out of your mind. If you must have corroboration of our marriage, go to Governor Quitman; he was a witness."

"I don't want corr—corr—I don't want the governor to tell me about it. I want Melanie."

"I would refuse to allow you to disturb her at this hour even if you were in a fit condition to be received by a lady."

Melanie had not looked for such consideration from Roland. It was not, of course, the thing for a man to appear in the company of the fair sex in a drunken condition. She had never seen any man quite so far in his cups as Dom was at this moment. She had often smelled liquor on a gentleman's breath after dinner or sometimes, especially in the case of the older men who were her grandfather's friends, in the morning. And then, there had been Roland on that memorable night. Still, society in a body frowned heavily upon men who overindulged in public. If they must go to such lengths, they were expected to keep decently out of sight. Casting her mind back, it seemed to Melanie that Roland, at the River Rest that night, had not shown the effects of drink to nearly the same degree as Dom. There had been, in fact, little sign at all of his inebriation—an indication of his ability to hold his liquor, she supposed. That ability was considered one of the criteria of a gentleman; it was not, apparently, a reliable gauge.

If Dom felt the force of Roland's argument, he was not going to admit it. "You can't keep me from her, not from the woman I love."

"You should have thought of that before you went to New Orleans and left her alone," Roland told him, a forbidding look coming into his face.

Dom nodded, his features twisting as though with grief. "I know. I was a fool to go away. She had no one else, nowhere to turn. I never thought she would bring you to the point, never thought she hated you so much she would go to this length to repay you for what you had done to her."

Melanie drew in her breath, her hands clenching the railing as she waited for Roland's reply. When it came she let out a sigh of relief.

"No, Dom," he said, "you thought you had her safely set aside; you thought you could smuggle her off to Europe, let her languish there until she was desperate for

108

company. What then? Did you plan to visit the continent, introduce her into the demimonde, that group of beautiful young women who have also trespassed against the rules? What role did you have in mind for her then? If her name was so tarnished as to make her ineligible as a wife, there would always be the position as your mistress, wouldn't there? A woman with no one to protect her would, regardless of her birth, be fair game."

Melanie bit back a gasp of outrage, her attention centered so strongly on the two men that she was scarcely aware of the approach of Roland's father behind her.

"That's a foul thing to s—say," Dom cried.

"If you don't like hearing the truth, you can always call me out," Roland said, his voice hard with menace.

Dom's gaze wavered and fell. "You would like that, wouldn't you? I don't see why I should oblige you."

"Nor do I see any reason why I should grant your burning wish to see my wife."

"She may be your wife now, but she was my fiancée and I never released her, never! I only said we should wait. Doesn't that give me the right to say a few words to her, to discover if she is happy?"

There was a maudlin sound to Dom's words, a self-pitying tone embarrassing to hear. His moment of anger had passed, and now his eyes were filling with tears. Melanie stared down at him as if seeing a stranger. She was unmoved by his remorse, unconvinced of his concern. Roland had been right. Where had such deep feelings been when she had needed them? In a flash of uncharacteristic bitterness, she realized that once more Dom's greatest fear was of what people might think of him. Regardless of her conduct, or want of it, it could not add to his consequence to have her marry so quickly. It made it look as though he had not been able to hold her, gave credence to the rumors that she had preferred Roland Donavan to the man her grandfather had chosen for her.

"No, it doesn't," Roland was saying. "You lost any right you might have had when you refused to set your wedding date forward."

"You know why I couldn't do that, you know it was because of you."

"Yes," Roland grated, the single, hard word cutting across Dom's rising tones. "There is no need to go into it, no need to say anything more. You had better go before you place yourself in a position you will regret in the morning."

Dom flushed; then a bewildered expression formed on his tear-wet face. "We were friends once," he said, a quiver in his low voice.

"So we were," Roland replied, "once."

Melanie stared at the two men, a frown between her eyes, aware of an undercurrent in their words she could not understand. For a brief moment it was as if their quarrel, what they were saying, had nothing to do with her.

A hurt look appeared in Dom's eyes. When he opened his mouth to protest further, Roland gave an abrupt nod in the direction of the butler. Sutton stepped smartly to the door and swung it open, his face like a mask as he stared into space.

Dom hesitated, glancing from the butler to Roland. He took a step toward the darkness outside, then turned back. "Tell Melanie—" he began.

"My wife," Roland said deliberately, "needs neither your apologies nor your solicitude. The best thing you can do for her now is to leave her alone. I recommend that course."

In a drunken man's sudden shift of mood, Dom flung his head back, his fingers curling into fists as he stared up at Roland. From above, Melanie saw the tension that gripped him, the hauteur in the tilt of his head and the fixed stare of his hazel eyes. She thought in that instant that he meant to launch himself up the stairs at Roland. Swept by an abrupt, nameless fear, she started forward.

She was stopped by a touch on her arm. Roland's father, standing beside her, gave a warning shake of his head. When she looked down once more, Dom's shoulders had sagged. With slow steps, he swung toward the door. Roland did not move, made no attempt to stop him or to speed his departure, and yet Dom made a sudden dive out into the night.

Sutton shut the door, then moved unhurriedly to pick up his lamp. Roland pushed away from the stair rail and, with Sutton behind him, began to climb the stairs toward the landing. Melanie stood her ground. Her eyes crowded with doubt, she listened to the receding thud of hoofbeats on the drive.

Roland's father stepped out from behind Melanie to block the way of his son. Hands on his hips he demanded, "Since when have you taken upon yourself the right to deny guests my hospitality?"

"What would you have me do, stand by while a disappointed suitor forces his attention upon my wife in the middle of the night?"Roland's hard gaze flicked from his father to Melanie. A scowl in the back of his eyes, he reached out to catch her hand, drawing her to his side.

Changing his tack, the elder man said, "An odd business, that. From what I heard, it seems this marriage of yours is not exactly a love match. I'm not certain it's even respectable."

Melanie, watching the two men, was aware for the first time of the resemblance between them; the grim irony of their smiles were the same.

"No," Roland agreed, drawing Melanie with him down the hall toward their bedchamber. "That should make you happy. It is what you always expected, isn't it?"

Melanie did not sleep well. She lay staring up into the darkness for hours, her thoughts endlessly turning. The fact that she suspected Roland was not sleeping either did not help. She was afraid to move for fear of brushing against him. She had discovered already that such a touch, slight though it was, was often enough to arouse desire within him. When, long hours into the night, he turned and pulled her toward him across the sheets, fitting her into the curve of his body, she gave a despairing sigh. It was unwarranted. He did no more than hold her close

111

with his face buried in the scented softness of her hair. At last, with his regular breathing warm upon her neck, she let her own burning eyelids fall and slept.

She came awake slowly. Clearly sunlight was filtering into the room, though at an angle that suggested the morning was well advanced. Despite the brightness outside, the air was frigid. Her every breath rose above her head in small eddies of steam. Shivering a little, Melanie snuggled down into the covers. She met no warmth beside her, nothing but an expanse of cold sheet. Roland had gone, leaving her in sole possession of the bed. She must have been more tired than she realized for him to be able to get up, dress, and let himself out of the room without disturbing her.

She could brave the cold and get up, but then what? She had no idea what was expected of her. At Greenlea, she and Roland had breakfasted in their room, but if he meant to continue the practice here there was no sign of it. The friction between father and son, and especially the events of the night before, made it unlikely the two would take their morning meal together, unless it could not be avoided. Would they each eat alone, then, in solitary state? That would not endear them to the servants.

Sighing, Melanie drew back the covers enough to allow her to reach for the bell pull beside the bed. She would order a cup of hot chocolate and perhaps have a few words with the maid who brought it in the hope of finding out the habits of the household. With her hand on the cord, she stopped. There were no maids in this house, only Sutton. If she wanted chocolate, she would either have to get dressed first, or go downstairs after it herself. If she was going to brave the chill to put on her clothes, she might as well go in search of a fire where she could drink her morning stimulant in comfort.

In a gown of black merino trimmed in dull gray *cord du roi,* and a gray shawl around her shoulders, she descended to the lower floor. The taint of wood smoke greeted her in the cold atmosphere of the entrance hall, and she traced it unerringly to a small sitting room at the back of the house. With a light tap on the door, she turned the knob and stepped inside.

That this was the retreat of the master of the house during his solitary evenings was obvious. A rocking chair, its sagging seat filled with shapeless and dingy cushions, was drawn up to the fireplace on one side. On the other sat a velvet settee of no particular age or style with its upholstery worn in spots that indicated it was used more for lying upon than for sitting. News sheets and periodicals were piled on every table, along with a litter of pipes, cleaners, spilled tobacco, and saucers with dottle in them along with scraps of moldy food. A pair of boots lay sprawled on the hearth with a tin box of boot blacking beside them, while the blacking brush lay half hidden under the edge of the settee. Over all was a layer of dust of such long duration that it had furred the back of the settee, dulled the gleam of the china vases and figurines on the mantel, and captured the imprint of the dishes of many a meal upon the pie table near the fire.

The room had two occupants. One was Roland; the other was a man she had met once before, a man with sandy hair, twinkling blue eyes, and an engaging grin that masked a swift and thorough appraisal. Both men rose as she entered.

"Melanie," her husband greeted her with every appearance of cheerfulness, "we have a visitor this morning. You remember Jeremy?"

Jeremy Rogers had been best man at their wedding, a friend of Roland's from army days, and a companion during his California adventures. He was also the owner of the River Rest.

"Yes, of course," she said, extending her hand.

There was no fault to be found with his bow. He held her fingers in his long enough to indicate admiration, but not so long as to suggest familiarity. "I certainly remember you, ma'am," he said. "The most beautiful bride I ever saw."

"I don't believe I told you, Melanie, that Jeremy is a

113

near neighbor. His family owns a piece of property five or six miles down the road. We grew up together."

"I see," Melanie answered, giving them the pleasant, meaningless smile of a hostess. "And you went adventuring together, too, I think?"

"Not exactly," Roland replied, "though that was the idea when we set out. Jeremy, here, was with Governor Quitman. They wound up the heroes of Grasshopper Hill, conquerors of Mexico City."

"Some heroes, fighting schoolboys for a hill we promptly gave back to the enemy. But Mrs. Donavan doesn't want to hear about that expedition. As profitable as it was, it's over."

"Profitable, Mr. Rogers?" Melanie inquired, taking the place Roland had brushed clear for her on the settee.

"From the standpoint of the United States government, of course. I was thinking of the peace treaty that ceded the territories of New Mexico, Arizona, and California to this country. You realize that the late war in Mexico was little more than a filibustering expedition that happened to have the authorization of the government in Washington."

"Surely not, Mr. Rogers. It is my understanding that a filibuster is a civilian who intervenes in the internal affairs of another country with hired soldiers equipped at his own expense."

"True, but what difference does the uniform make when the motives are the same? The presence of regular army only indicates that the intervention has the approval of the top officials in the country. The point is that land and positions of power in the countries chosen for assault can be taken by force."

Roland had moved to stand with his back to the fireplace. "And the point of this political harangue you are enduring, Melanie," he said with dry humor, "is that Jeremy has grown tired of running his hotel already and is now flirting with the idea of joining a new filibustering campaign."

"You can laugh if you want, but being a hotel owner is no life for a man. Lord knows I never wanted it, never

114

would have had a thing to do with it if it hadn't been for holding a flush in an all-night poker game. You know that, Roland. If I can sell the River Rest, buy into Lopez's expedition, and maybe come out of the campaign with a nice piece of property in Cuba, why, I won't hesitate a minute."

"Lopez?" Melanie asked. "General Narciso Lopez?"

"That's the man. You've heard of him, ma'am?"

"I seem to recall my grandfather and the governor speaking of him and his ambitions in Cuba."

Jeremy Rogers gave an emphatic nod. "It's a worth-while cause. Cuba, being only a hundred miles off the coast of the United States, is too close for us to put up with its being held by a foreign power. The Spanish government in control there has used it to harass American shipping and American sea captains for the better part of two hundred years. Everybody knows there is hardly a one of our ships that leaves port without stopping there to take on water and fresh supplies. Think how much more convenient it would be if the port of Havana was under control of the United States government. That alone would make capturing the island a good plan, even if it wasn't for the rich land down there and the warm weather that lets a farmer keep crops in the field the year round."

"I know the governor is excited about the prospects of annexation, especially since he envisions Cuba as eventually coming into the union as a slave state, but my grandfather was more cautious. He seemed to think dealing with the might and cunning of a European country like Spain would be vastly different from fighting Mexican peasants."

Jeremy grinned. "According to General Lopez the might of Spain is a myth, and he should know, since he spent his youth rising to high rank in the Spanish army. The country has been in a decline for the last fifty years and more; it's as weak now as its interbred royal family. Besides, the Cuban people are tired of being ruled from a country two thousand miles away. A great many of the most influential people are ready to accept the benefits of being citizens of the United States. When we reach the island they will rise up and join us, overthrowing their Spanish masters from inside the country. More than that, Lopez knows the island like you know your own garden. I expect you know he was an official in the government there under Governor-General Don Geronimo Valdes?"

"Yes, before his ouster over some irregularity in his department."

"The general will tell you he was dismissed because of his sympathy with the Cuban party in favor of annexation. The truth is, he was relieved of his duties at the same time as Governor-General Valdes, but you can't blame a man for putting the best face on it. Lopez, being a Venezuelan by birth, decided to throw in his lot with the Cuban junta in the Americas instead of returning to Spain."

"It only remains to be seen if he made the right choice," Melanie said, smiling a little at the sandy-haired man's enthusiasm.

"I think he did, and I think everybody will know it before the summer's over."

"So soon?" Melanie tilted her head to one side. "You sound as if you expect to set sail before the week is out."

"So we would, if we could persuade men like Roland, here, to join us. There are few who can beat him at organizing men and supplies or turning raw recruits into soldiers overnight."

She glanced to her husband where he stood scowling at his friend, his mouth set in hard lines. "You have asked my—my husband to join you?" she queried.

"I know this is not the best time to bring up such a thing, you two being just married, but there's no time to waste. General Lopez is in New Orleans right now raising money, enlisting men, getting together the rifles and ammunition, the uniforms, and a thousand and one other things we are going to need. I wouldn't blame Roland if he was to tell me to go to hades; I know I would be hard put to leave a wife like you. But I thought, things being as

116

they are, that it wouldn't hurt to put the proposition to him."

"And what answer did he give you?" Melanie asked, lifting her chin a fraction at the suggestion that Jeremy Rogers was aware of the circumstances of her marriage. It was not surprising, considering his ownership of the hotel where it had all begun; and yet it was far from pleasant to have it brought into the open. No doubt it was Jeremy's frankness that was to blame for the dismay that settled over her, that and the unwelcome prospect of having her life disarranged once more. She was only just becoming used to the idea of herself as a married woman, beginning to think of the way life would be in the years ahead. Roland would be a planter, if not on his father's land, then on acreage he would purchase himself. She would preside over his dinner table, see to the smooth running of his household, and in due time, give birth to his children. And slowly, either in her present manner, or in a slightly different way she had been considering, she would exact retribution for what he had done to her grandfather and herself. If he joined Lopez, all that would be changed. He would take himself out of her life, beyond her influence as effectively as if he had walked out the door on their wedding night.

"No answer, as yet," Jeremy replied to Melanie's question. "I was still doing my best to make him see the advantages of the project when you joined us."

"You will have to admit," Roland drawled, his gaze barely touching his wife's face before he looked away, "that he is persuasive."

"Now that I have had time to think, Jeremy, I believe the answer is yes. I am with you."

After that, conversation was strained. The two men arranged to travel together to New Orleans in a week's time. There was some discussion of the gear they would take and the rank they could hope to be given under Lopez. Then Jeremy, his mission accomplished, took his leave.

The instant the door closed behind him, Melanie turned

117

to her husband. "Why? Why are you joining this expedition to Cuba?"

"That must be obvious," Roland answered.

"You mean because of our marriage? I didn't realize the loss of your freedom irked you so."

"It doesn't," he said shortly.

"Then why are you trying to regain it?"

"That is ridiculous. The truth of the matter is, my usefulness to you is over. If I stay, I will be a constant reminder to people of what happened. If I go, they will forget the sooner. By the time your year of mourning is over, some other scandal will have position of honor; you will be able to step back into your old place."

"Except that few hostesses will bother sending cards of invitation to a woman who is neither a widow nor a wife. I would be far too ineligible to be seated at dinner next to an unmarried man, and too dangerous to be placed beside one who is married."

"There is little I can do about that. You will just have to hope I get myself killed."

Melanie got to her feet. Moving to the pie table, she began to make patterns in the dust, circling the raised rings designed to hold plates in place (with the tip of one finger). Over her shoulder she asked, "Are you certain you are fit enough?"

"What?" The sound of amazement was strong in his voice.

"The wound in your arm," she replied, bringing out the words with difficulty. It was the first time the injury had been mentioned between them, though more than once Melanie had felt the urge to help him on or off with the sleeves of his shirts or coats. The bandage had been reduced to nothing more than a strip of sticking plaster. The changing of this covering over the furrow plowed by her grandfather's bullet had been an operation Roland had performed with Cicero's help, or completed when he was alone. It was as though he were embarrassed or ashamed, or else he wanted to keep the sight of it from her for the sake of the unpleasant memories it might recall. It was no part of her plans to cause him physical pain. Still she was often afraid she had hurt him by brushing against it, or rolling upon it in the night. If so, he never flinched, never protested.

"It was never anything more than a scratch and is nearly healed. In any case, though Jeremy managed to give the impression that the expedition would be leaving on the hour, it will probably be weeks, even months, before it gets underway."

"And in the meantime, what will you do?"

"If I am accepted as an officer, I will be given duties to perform, the kind of thing Jeremy suggested—drilling recruits, rounding up supplies, seeing the ships are loaded as they should be. There will be no lack of tasks to be done."

"And you want all that again? I thought—that is—you gave me to understand you despised war."

"Did I?" he queried. "I don't seem to remember."

That was so patently untrue Melanie was left with only one conclusion: his dislike of staying was greater than his distaste for the life of a soldier. She took a deep breath, then let it out slowly. "I hardly think your father will approve."

"You are wrong there. He has never disapproved of anything that would take me away from Cottonwood."

He had turned to face the fire, stretching his hand toward the blaze. Though she could not see his face, his voice was flat, without expression. He was a monster, devoid of feeling, she thought. A man who could take her in a moment of drunkenness, make her his wife, bring her to a state where she anticipated their nights together—though she refused to let him know—and then calmly tell her he was leaving. A man who could hear himself proclaimed a bastard without the flicker of an eyelid or a breath of explanation, one who could watch his father cough blood while he stood by unmoved. She should be glad he was going; she was glad, and yet already there was an empty feeling inside her.

119

Slowly her fingers curled until her nails cut into the palms of her hands. "And what am I to do?"

"Go back to Greenlea," he said, "and wait to collect my estate."

Chapter 7

ROLAND'S ESTATE. Though she would have scoffed at the idea less than a month before, it appeared she would have need of whatever he might be generous enough to allow her from it. Five days after their return to Greenlea, Melanie received a visit from Jackson Turnbull, her grandfather's attorney. When the elderly man had departed once more, she paced the floor of the library, her skirts swishing about her ankles in her agitation. It should not be, could not be, but it was. She was virtually penniless. Her grandfather had bequeathed to her the house, Greenlea, with its contents, the servants who staffed it, his personal possessions, and the sum of two hundred seventy-three dollars. There was also in his personal papers a note-of-hand outstanding to Governor John Quitman in the amount of six thousand dollars. The debt to the governor would have to be paid, though how, she did not know. She could not bear to sell the house servants, and even if she could, most were growing older, their value on the slave market declining.

Where had the money gone? Melanie could guess. There had been the expense of outfitting Johnston's Volunteers, and then, when so many had died, there had been the appeals from the widows, the aging parents left destitute. Though the troops had been from the best families of Natchez, they had not necessarily been from the most wealthy. Even her grandfather had been no more than comfortably well off. Why, then, had he beggared himself? Knowing that she would take a husband, thinking she would marry Dom in the near future, he had not been concerned with her welfare. He had felt free to deplete his capital and borrow more. Was it possible that this mad act of his had been an admission of guilt? Had he been to blame, as Roland thought, for the useless slaughter of his troops and the capture of the survivors?

No, she would not think such a thing. Doubtless, there had been investments and obligations she knew nothing about. Her own expenses must have been considerable. Her gowns and bonnets, fans and furbelows had not come cheap. Why could her grandfather not have told her the money was running low? She would have economized gladly. There was any number of things she had bought in the last few months that she could well have done without.

"Bad news, I take it?"

Melanie swung to face Roland who was just closing the library door behind him. He had been in town when Lawyer Turnbull had arrived. The elderly man had asked to speak to her husband, saying he had heard that Roland was leaving to join Lopez. It was only with the greatest difficulty that Melanie was able to persuade him to divulge his unpalatable news. In the course of the conversation, there had been a further revelation that, with its remembrance now, brought the stormy, violet hue of anger to Melanie's eyes.

When she did not speak, Roland went on. "I passed Jackson Turnbull's carriage on the drive. He looked as gloomy as a three-day rain, but then he never looks any other way."

He sauntered toward her with the careless, loose-limbed grace of a great cat. A smile curving his mouth, he encircled her waist and drawing her to him, dropped a light kiss of greeting on her lips. The action was so smooth, so swiftly casual, that she had no time to resist. Before she could form a scathing protest, he had released her and moved away again.

122

"Well?" he said, taking up a position leaning against the desk. "What did Turnbull want?"

"He came to tell me that I am a pauper," Melanie said baldly. "Worse than that, I owe six thousand dollars to Governor Quitman."

Roland frowned. "Why did he tell you that? There was no need to burden you with such things."

"I am afraid I insisted. He was so determined to have a word with you before you left for New Orleans, and I could not think that it concerned your finances."

"Couldn't you?" he queried. "Didn't it occur to you Turnbull might have been my father's lawyer as well as your grandfather's?"

"No, it didn't at the time. That was made plain to me only when Mr. Turnbull began to try to explain why he had been discussing my grandfather's affairs with you before our marriage."

"Gave the old man a rough time, did you? He was just trying to protect you. Our engagement, if you want to call it that, was a short one, but it did last nearly a week. During that period Mr. Turnbull needed someone to consult. I was the obvious choice. I believe I told him at the time I would clear the colonel's debt to the governor. I expect he wanted to be certain I still intended to do that before I left."

"You can't do that," she said sharply.

"Can't I? Why not?"

"The debt was made by my grandfather. It should be paid out of his estate."

"And how are you going to do that? Sell Greenlea? Put some of your people out to work for wages, or put them on the block? Don't be foolish. The debt may have been made by your grandfather, but it is now your responsibility as his heir, and since you are my wife, that makes it mine. The arrangements have already been made. My draft will be in the governor's hands in the morning."

Melanie stared at him. With a proud lift of her chin she said, "That puts me in your debt. Greenlea is worth a great deal more than that, but I will make the deed over to you as soon as possible in repayment."

"There is no need of that," he said, shaking his head with a smile. "When I married you, your property became mine. If you are still determined to repay me, however, I can think of a more pleasurable way of working out the debt."

Melanie searched his face warily as he eased from the desk and started toward her. What she saw shining in his eyes made her put out a hand to ward him off. "That— that is terrible," she said, stammering in outrage and chagrin that he could dismiss her offer so casually.

"Terrible? Considering the short time we have left, I thought it a munificent offer. There are not many women who can claim to be worth so much for a single night." The mockery and promise were so inextricably mixed in his vivid green eyes that Melanie could not be certain he was joking.

"I won't—" she began, but it was too late. His lips had captured hers once more in a kiss so thorough there could be no doubt that in at least one sense he meant every word he said.

A single night. That was all that remained until his departure. The steamboat that would take him downriver was already tied up at the dock below Natchez ready to stoke her furnaces, get up steam, and plow out into the Mississippi with the rising of the sun. His trunk had gone on board and been placed in his stateroom. It only remained to get through the night, gather his last personal belongings together, and wave him goodbye. Soon he would be gone from her life. Greenlea would return to her sole possession, as would her bed. She would be left in peace. Whether it would last a few weeks, a few months, or forever, was something she could not know, did not want to know.

A single night. The remainder of the morning vanished, melting into afternoon. Before it seemed possible, darkness was falling, dinner was over, and it was time for them to retire to their bedchamber.

Melanie stood at the window, staring out into the night as she drew her brush through her long tresses that spread over her shoulders like a shimmering cape shot with red gold highlights. With freedom drawing so near, she should have been happy, her spirits rising with the liveliest anticipation. Instead, her mood was somber. She recognized with a sense of incredulity that her feelings were much the same as when her grandfather had left to go to war, a numb desolation at being left behind.

Attacking her hair with the brush, she told herself that she was being childish. It was thinking of her grandfather that had brought the press of tears to her throat. The loss was so near, that was all, and so much had happened. It was not to be wondered at that she was not entirely mistress of her emotions. Her brush slowed. With the back of one hand, she wiped at the wetness spilling over her lashes.

Behind her, a fire burned brightly, its reflection dancing on the windowpanes with the blackness of night behind them. The paraphernalia of their baths had been removed; the long, deep julep tub, the hot-water cans, the soap, crumpled towels, and the Watteau bath screen which made bathing so pleasant here at Greenlea as compared to Cottonwood. All that was left was the basin of water Roland was using as he shaved. In the mirrorlike window glass, she could see him as he stood with a towel tucked about his waist, guiding the silver-handled straight razor over his face. His back was broad, tapering into slim hips. He leaned forward to peer into the mirror of his shaving stand as he rinsed his razor in the basin before him, and the muscles rippled smoothly under the skin. It was a long moment before Melanie realized she was as visible to him in the small mirror on the end of her marble-topped dressing table as he was to her in the window.

Abruptly she turned away, moving toward the bed. She laid her brush to one side on the nearby table, drew back the covers, and climbed in, settling between sheets that still held vestiges of heat from the bed warmer that had been passed between them. Roland slanted a glance in her direction, then flung down his razor, wiped the remaining soap from his face, and tossed the cloth to one side. Stepping to the lamp which occupied the other end of the dressing table, he blew it out. He removed his towel, dropping it on the floor as he turned toward the bed.

Melanie watched him move toward her through the flickering fire shadows. It may have been an effect of the uncertain light, but it seemed there was torment in his eyes, a look of suffering she knew he would never have allowed to be there if he had thought she could see. The sight affected her strangely, blending in some way with her sense of loss. She thought of his peculiar action in paying off her grandfather's debt. He had mentioned it neither before nor after the wedding, might never have told of it, if she had not prized the information from Lawyer Turnbull—just as he had known, but not mentioned, the fact that he knew she had no money, that she was completely dependent upon him. The situation was not unusual, of course, but she would have thought him much more likely to gloat, holding it over her, than to keep it hidden. In all justice, such generosity, not in the paying of the money, but in the manner of it, deserved something in return. She knew what method of payment he preferred; hadn't he made it plain to her? Lest her conscience tell her that she was betraying the memory of her grandfather, she assured herself that the gift of her favors did not have to be without benefit. It would be a good thing if in this their last night together for some time, Roland's undeniable desire for her could be heightened, if he could carry with him a memory of shared passion so strong it would make him long for her when he was far away.

The bed jounced on its ropes as he slid in beside her. He turned on his side, making a ridge between them in the soft feathers of the mattress. Reaching out, he touched her shoulder, his voice quiet and deep in the darkness. "What is it? Why are you crying?"

"I'm not crying," Melanie answered.

He gave a long sigh. "I suppose you have reason enough."

"I told you, I am not crying," she said, touched unexpectedly by his sympathy. Without conscious thought, she slipped her hand from beneath the covers to press his fingers.

He was still, even his breathing suspended. She had never made the least advance toward him before, had always endured his lovemaking without cooperation and with little sign of enjoyment. This small gesture, and the promise it seemed to convey, was therefore suspect.

With care, he smoothed downward from her shoulder to the tender, silk-clad fullness of her breast. She released his hand without hesitation, allowing him free access to her body. He took it, his movements bolder, his fingers making swift work of the buttons closing her nightgown. Drawing the material aside, he shifted to set his mouth to the warm globe he had uncovered.

Melanie drew in her breath at the fiery sensation that swept over her. Daring greatly, she lifted her hand to the crisp waves of his hair, trailing her fingers down the back of his neck to the hard muscles of his shoulder, feeling them ripple under the skin as he sought the slim curve of her waist. By slow degrees, his hand moved lower, smoothing over the soft roundness of her shape, gliding, grazing the delicate hollows. In sudden impatience, he drew back to drag the silken material of her nightgown from under her hips and strip it off over her head. For an instant she was entangled in its folds, and then she was naked, reveling in the freedom and the sense of abandon, despite the cool air of the room. Roland put the gown to one side and taking the coverlet, flipped it up over them. Under its enclosing tent, in the sweet anonymity of darkness, Melanie turned to him, her arms outstretched. He dragged her close, holding her with steely strength, so that her breasts were flattened against the unyielding hardness of his chest and she could feel the rigid heat of his desire. He took her mouth in a devouring kiss. Her lips burned as she pressed close. They twisted, turning, seeking to blend their bodies into one. All thought, all reason fled before the tumult of the senses that swept in upon Melanie. Deep in her loins was beginning to stir and grow a need more urgent than any she had ever known, a need fueled in vaulting measures by the sliding caress of his hand over her hips and along the sensitive inner surfaces of her thighs. With a small sound deep in her throat, she moved against him as the contact became more burningly intimate. She felt as though her senses were aflame, her skin fevered to the touch. She clutched his shoulders, wanting, needing to be closer, and closer still.

He levered himself to one elbow, drawing her beneath him. His penetration was slow and sure, filling her with intense, spreading pleasure. She caught her breath, her fingers biting into his forearms to steady her reeling world. It could not be done. The turbulence was inside, an ancient uncontrollable thing that thundered in her blood, rising, pulsing higher with every beat of his piercing rhythm. They were fused, inseparable, and still she wanted to take him deeper inside her that he might salve some ancient internal pain. As in a dream, she felt tears, so long repressed, start from her eyes, felt the tearing, inward explosion of rapture that subsided to a melting, giving, feeling of surcease, so that she pressed him to her, urging him to absorbing stillness, a stillness that touched her soul with peace.

They lay twined together for long moments while their panting, difficult breathing slowed and became even once more. After a time, Melanie felt his hands on her hair, felt him drawing it from where it lay taut under his elbow. Clasping her to him, he pressed his lips to her forehead, then dropped a light kiss on her eyelids. Drawing back slightly, he lowered his head to touch his lips, wet with her salt tears, to hers.

"And now, are you crying?" he murmured.

She gave a small shake of her head. "No," she said, "not now."

At last he was gone. Melanie saw him off on the steamboat *Crescent Moon*, steadfastly refusing to the last to go aboard for a final farewell. There was a moment when she thought he would not go, an endless time when he stared down at her with what seemed to be indecision, even reluctance, in his green eyes. And then Jeremy called to him from the deck of the steamboat. Roland's eyelids flickered down, shuttering his expression. A carefree smile curved his mouth before he caught her close for a bruising farewell kiss. Turning away with an abrupt swing, he strode across the gangplank without looking back. Melanie stood on the landing, watching until that floating white palace with its elaborate scrolls of jigsaw work passed out of sight around the bend of the river. Then she turned her face back toward Greenlea.

For the first few days she was too busy to think of Roland beyond a fleeting curiosity as to where he was and what he was doing. There was so much to be done around the old house. As often happened in the latter part of January and the first weeks of February, the weather turned warm. The opportunity to start the spring cleaning was too good to miss. The woolen rugs were rolled and taken out onto the galleries to be beaten. The floors were scrubbed and polished with fresh beeswax. The smell of lemon oil polish filled the air as every piece of furniture was wiped clean, then rubbed to a high gloss, adding to their patina of age. The veranda floor received a coat of fresh paint, as did the stables and carriage house.

It was only in watching the buildings take shape under their repairs and whitewash that Melanie realized how long it had been that such details had been attended to at Greenlea. She was forced to the conclusion that the funds for such things had not been available while her grandfather was alive. It was Roland who had suggested they be done now, his money that was paying for them. In this, as in all else, he had been amazingly generous, not only making her a household allowance for the duration of his absence, but a dress allowance as well. Not that she would need such a thing while she was in mourning, but she had been at something of a loss as to how she was to pay for the black clothing she had ordered before the wedding. The subject of money had not been mentioned between Roland and herself. It was Lawyer Turnbull who had explained the provisions that had been made for her, the amount she was empowered to draw each month, plus the enormous sum that had been left in her name for emergencies. Only by thinking of the money as compensation offered out of a sense of guilt could Melanie bring herself to use it.

News of the men who had joined Lopez was slow in coming. Once or twice, Eliza Quitman, whose husband made the trip a number of times in the passing weeks, was kind enough to send her some word of what was happening. Roland, it seemed, had been given the rank of lieutenant colonel and the responsibility of recruiting men for the cause. He had outfitted himself with a uniform and was fast becoming one of General Lopez's favorite officers. The city of New Orleans was bursting with enthusiasm for the Cuban expedition, and the general's headquarters at Bank's Arcade on Magazine Street clamored all day long with men, many of them, like Roland and Jeremy, veterans of the Mexican campaign. Of these, no small number had been officers. These men had now taken to squabbling among themselves for the honor of forming regiments to fight with Lopez. With the money provided by his backers in Mississippi and Louisiana, Lopez had purchased two ships, a steamer named the *Creole* and a bark, the *Georgina*. A brig with the name *Susan Loud* had also been donated to the expedition by one of its senior officers, Colonel Robert Wheat. Governor Quitman had been instrumental in obtaining financing for the effort in his home state, and it was rumored he was in contact with Washington concerning the possibility of the United States army, with himself at its head, intervening in Cuba when the faction there favoring annexation rose to join Lopez.

There had been no direct word from Roland. It did not matter, of course. She had not really expected it. Involved

130

in his new duties, he had little time for correspondence; this was something her grandfather had always impressed upon her when she had taxed him with not writing. Also, theirs was not a love match where each might die a little from dread if not reassured that all was well. Still, it did look as if he could have sent some kind of message, if only for form's sake.

News from Natchez was no more plentiful than from New Orleans. Other than an occasional missive from the governor's wife, Melanie had to depend on Cicero, who went into town for the marketing once a week, and the servants' grapevine for information on the day-to-day activities of her former friends and neighbors. She received no visits and so came to expect none. It was a surprise to hear carriage wheels on the drive one bright morning.

It was Chloe Clements, tooling a gig with scarlet leather seats and wheels picked out in red. As she drew up with a flourish and clambered down, it could be seen that she wore a gown of white muslin dotted with red which had a skirt comprised of at least twenty flounces. Perched upon her high-piled hair was a tiny hat of white chip straw banded with red ribbon and trimmed with a spray of cherries. Though the sun was shining, its lemon yellow light lacked the heat it would have within a few weeks. The outfit Chloe wore was not only unsuitable for driving oneself in a gig, it was more than a little in advance of the season. Chloe had always delighted in being the first to change from heavy winter fabrics; the lightweight materials of spring and summer were so much kinder to one of her pale coloring. On this occasion she had miscalculated, however. She fairly flew up the steps of Greenlea and, as Cicero swung the door open, ran shivering inside.

Melanie had watched her arrival from the parlor windows. Now she moved down the room and out into the entrance hall to greet Dom's sister. In her mourning gown of stiff bombazine she felt like a crow beside a cardinal.

"Melanie!" Chloe exclaimed, for all the world as though they had parted only an hour before and nothing

131

but everyday events had taken place in between. "Lead me to a fire, if you please. I declare I am frozen stiff. And if you could provide a cup of tea to revive me, I would rise up and call you blessed."

"Certainly," Melanie said, looking to Cicero who nodded, bowed, and went quietly away in the direction of the butler's pantry. Indicating the parlor door, she went on, "Come inside. I have a small blaze in the parlor that should serve the purpose."

Flounces fluttering, Chloe moved before her into the room, hurrying to hold her hands out to the coals that glowed in the fireplace. She gave an exaggerated shudder, then turned to face Melanie, her hazel eyes wide and searching. "What in the world have you been doing to yourself?" she inquired. "You look positively haggish."

"Thank you," Melanie replied. "It is always refreshing to hear the truth."

The other girl gave an inane laugh, spreading her hands. "That was unkind of me, wasn't it? I never meant to be. It's just that I was so shocked at the change in you."

"Were you? I would have thought it was just what you might have expected. One always assumes dissipation and notoriety to be wearing."

"Dear Melanie, please don't take that tone with me. I hope I have too much sense to hold it against you that you embarrassed my brother. If I have any ill will toward you at all, it's because you snatched the most intriguing man of the season before I had a chance at him. As to what went before the marriage, I refuse entirely to believe that you did anything really wrong. Despite what people may be saying, I know your principles would not allow it. Dom would not tell me what you said to him, but I suspect that if you were discovered without your clothes, they must have been forcibly removed. Am I right?"

The glitter of avid curiosity in Chloe's eyes was so obvious that Melanie was surprised the other girl did not blush for it. "I am sorry," she said. "I would rather not discuss it."

"Of course you wouldn't. How silly of me," Chloe said, the straw-colored wisps of thin, blond lashes sweeping down. "We will talk of something else, shall we? I understand your new husband has gone to New Orleans to join the filibuster, Lopez. You cannot imagine how relieved I was to hear it. I was so afraid he and Dom would meet here in town. That would be disastrous, for I am almost sure Dom means to call Roland Donavan out. He had been taking his pistol out daily to practice. You might warn Roland to be wary, if he should return anytime soon."

Unreasonably, Melanie found herself resenting this hint that Roland had more to fear from a meeting than Dom. "I would not worry. My husband and Dom have already come face to face with each other. Dom had the opportunity to call him out then and did not. I see no reason why he should do so at any other time."

"Oh? Well, perhaps not, though men are peculiar sometimes. They brood on things and then suddenly explode. Women are much more direct, or if they find direct action unwise, their revenge usually takes a devious turn."

The arrival of Cicero with the tea tray made it unnecessary for Melanie to answer. She sent the other girl a searching look, however, remembering that it had been Dom who had penetrated closest to an understanding of her motives.

In Natchez, tea was an old tradition brought directly from England. Though settled by the French in the early years of the eighteenth century, the Natchez country was, with the east bank of the Mississippi River, ceded to England at the time of the French and Indian War. The British Crown, in an effort to create a bastion of power along the river, had made available large tracts of rich land with the design of attracting men of substance and privilege as permanent settlers in the region. To these original colonists were added a large number of Tories, men and women loyal to England who were forced to retreat from the eastern seaboard states during the American Revolution. In later years, the section was taken by

133

the Spanish, who were then forced to give up their prize to the American government. Still, the English customs remained the same, afternoon tea, reels and cotillions at the balls, and in the clear, cool days of fall, shouts of "Tally-ho" and "View Hallo," as men in pink coats that were really red rode to hounds. Now, as Melanie prepared to serve tea from a Georgian silver service, she had first to brew it. To do this, she took a key from the chatelaine at her waist, that also held her embroidery scissors and an empty smelling-salts bottle, and moved down the room to a chest against one wall. Unlocking the chest, she released the scent not only of imported tea leaves, but also of cinnamon and nutmeg, coriander and ginger, for the chest held these spices and many more that, with the tea, were considered too valuable to be left open. Though the tea and spices were not so expensive as they had once been, the ritual still lingered from earlier days.

Relocking the chest, Melanie carried the tea packet to the table and carefully measured the leaves into the boiling water. While it steeped, the two women talked of fashions and of what this woman and that had worn to the last social events of the season.

As Chloe leaned to accept her teacup from Melanie's hands, she said, "You must be wondering why I came this morning. I am sure I must have been the last person you expected."

"Not at all," Melanie said politely as Chloe paused, waiting for her comment.

"Well, it was like this. I had a long talk with Eliza Quitman last evening. We decided between us that someone should speak to you and let you know that your friends will stand by you when your year of mourning is over and you begin to attempt to go around again."

"That was—very thoughtful." It seemed more likely that the suggestion had come from Eliza, though it was certain to have been much more delicately phrased. The governor's wife was a small, quiet woman, but strong-willed in her own way, and intensely loyal to those who earned her friendship or her love. The most prominent of

134

the latter was certainly her brash, sometimes overbearing husband.

"Not at all," Chloe said. "It is the least those of us who still believe in you can do."

Her words suggested the number who had remained loyal was not large; still Melanie was prepared to overlook that. "I am grateful."

With a brief smile and a shake of her head, Chloe went on. "You will never guess what Eliza is going to do. She declares that when the governor joins Lopez, she is going to leave the children at Monmouth with tutors and their nurses and go with him to New Orleans. That way, their parting will not seem so long. Isn't that sweet? They do love each other to distraction, don't they? I have never seen any man worship a woman quite like the governor does his Eliza."

Another veiled barb, this time the insinuation that Melanie did not care a great deal for her husband, or he for her, else they would have made some effort to be together. "Yes," she answered, forcing a smile. "Their devotion is touching."

Chloe nodded so that the cherries on her hat bobbed. "Of course Eliza will not be alone. You may not know it, but there has been at least one rally for the Cuban expedition here in Natchez. Dozens of men are joining, and more than one wife is making the move downriver with her man. With everyone in New Orleans, it will be sadly flat here. They say the city is entertaining them in grand style, with dozens of parties and balls. There is so much going on, so much excitement and gaiety, that it is almost like carnival time again. If it were not for being afraid Dom must inevitably run across Roland—or even seek him out—I would persuade my brother to take me, too, just for the festivities."

Melanie smiled with an effort. "You make it sound like so much fun that I am almost tempted to travel down to be with my husband myself."

"The very thing!" Chloe exclaimed. "That is, if you are serious. I did not want to upset you before, but I understand poor Roland is so at loose ends that he fairly haunts the theaters during his free time. The St. Charles is said to draw him particularly. There is a French-Irish actress there who calls herself Colleen Antoinette Dubois. She has been the toast of the season this past winter."

"I am sure there are a great many worse places in New Orleans he could be visiting," Melanie commented. Was Chloe actually trying to suggest that Roland had some interest in this actress? It was incredible, and yet, the sound of portent had been in her voice.

"Oh, many, and much worse." Chloe agreed with a giggle. "Still, Dom saw her when he was there a few weeks ago. He said though she is beautiful, she does not depend on a display of her charms to enthrall her audience. I suppose she must have some kind of talent, for she was just come from a successful engagement in California, at the opera house in San Francisco, in fact."

"Really," was all Melanie found to say.

"I told Dom it sounded as if he had some basis of comparison and begged him to tell me what other kind of women he had seen while he was in the city. He wouldn't, of course, any more than he would tell me whether he had visited the red light district." She sighed, setting down her teacup. "The closest I've ever come to such a thing is strolling in the Spanish Park near old Fort Panmure and catching a glimpse now and then of a man going into one of the shotgun houses that line the streets of Natchez-Under-The-Hill. I have been dying to go to the River Rest since you were there, but Dom absolutely refuses to take me. I am green with envy that you have been inside and I haven't. Dear, dear, Melanie, tell me what it was like!"

Melanie raised an arched eyebrow. "I have no idea what you mean."

"Come, Melanie, you must. I mean, did you see any of the women there? Did you see what they were like, or what the men were doing to them?"

"I think if you are really so anxious to know," Melanie said slowly, "you should go there without Dom."

"Really, Melanie, as if I would do anything so stupid! Oh, forgive me! I didn't mean that the way it sounds."

"Didn't you?" Melanie asked, her smile growing tight. "But you are quite right; it is a stupid thing to do. I don't recommend it, unless a woman is desperate."

As the meaning of the double-entendre struck Chloe, the blood rushed to her hairline, turning her face a dull, purplish red. "If that is meant as an insult," she began.

Opening her eyes wide, Melanie said, "How can you think such a thing. I meant no more harm than you by what you said just now."

Chloe stared at her though narrowed eyes. Then she gave an abrupt, high-pitched laugh. "I see. I must be more careful, mustn't I? You will forgive me if I don't stay longer. I have an appointment at the dressmaker to be fitted for a new gown. The name of the color is Swoon Blue. It has just a touch of mauve in a deep sky blue. It would be perfect with your eyes, my dear Melanie. I suppose if one weren't too particular it might do for semi-mourning. The sticklers still insist on lavender for the first return to colors, but I say it depends on the depth of your feelings."

Her smile stiff, Melanie ignored this parting shot. Stepping to the bell pull, she rang for Cicero and, when he came, allowed him to see her guest from the premises.

The suggestion Chloe had put forth, that she should follow Roland to New Orleans, was not such a bad one. After examining it for the space of three long days, Melanie decided it had considerable merit. In the first place, it would take her from Natchez, remove her from an area where her every move, from the buying of rose water to the attending of church, was noted and commented upon. In addition, it would give herself something to do besides mope about Greenlea looking for something to change or criticize and taking her crotchets out on the servants. The more she thought of the furor downriver, the more she wanted to be a part of it. She had always listened with awestruck attention to her grandfather's tales of military campaigns, had often wished when she was a child that she could become a man when she grew up and be a part of such an endeavor. It was not fair that men excluded women from such things.

Also, lately she had come to fear that if she remained apart from Roland for much longer she would lose her need for revenge. Already time was beginning to dull the sharp edge of her resolve. In their few days together she had achieved little, unless it was possible to credit Roland's abrupt decision to join the filibusters to her tactics. A sensitive man might have chosen to leave her rather than endure her reluctant embraces and constant coolness. Well, nearly always reluctant, almost always cool. The difficulty she had encountered in keeping to her cold manner had prompted her to consider a different approach. Even before Roland had left for New Orleans she had been turning over the idea of trying to make him fall in love with her. How devastating it would be if, when he succumbed, she could laugh and call him a fool. It would strike at his heart and his pride, those two most vulnerable points, the two where her grandfather had suffered the greatest hurt. She would have to be careful. Though the scheme was an intriguing one, it was not without an element of risk. But it could not be put into effect while she remained alone in Natchez.

What she would do when she reached New Orleans depended on her husband. Still it should be possible for them to take some sort of house for the time remaining before the expedition sailed. It would be a small place, no doubt; there would be no need to take anyone with her except Glory. They would not be going by steamboat for obvious reasons. The carriage would be slower by several days, but that could not be helped. The danger would be slight with her coachman and one or two of the stable hands in attendance as guards. If she did not send Roland a message, there could be no question of his refusing her permission to come. Even if he did not want her there, he would have to make the best of it when she arrived bag and baggage at his quarters. Once on the scene she would be hard indeed to remove.

"Glory!" Melanie cried, her eyes dark blue with excitement as she burst in upon the maid where she stood ironing bed linens in the laundry beside the outdoor kitchen. "Stop what you are doing at once and start packing. We are going to New Orleans."

Glory set the flat iron she held on its rest. "Miss Melanie," she said, giving her charge the same title she had always used out of habit, as did all the servants at Greenlea, "have you gone mad?"

"No," Melanie cried as she rounded the end of the ironing board and caught the elderly woman's arm to urge her forward. "We are going to join Roland and see the filibuster army."

"I knew it. I knew you was missing that man, missing him bad. It's easy to do without peaches if you never tasted one, but once you take a bite, why, you want to stay close to the tree."

"No such thing!" Melanie exclaimed with heat. "I just want to get away from here." There was not a particle of truth in what Glory said, not one. She would admit she had not disliked sharing her bed with Roland Donavan as much as she had expected, especially after that first time at the River Rest. She would even acknowledge that she had amazed herself at times by the strength of the ardor he aroused in her, but she did not miss him, certainly did not need anything about him. Glory just did not understand. It was not surprising, since Melanie had not confided in her.

"Have it your way," the plump, gray-haired maid said, eyeing Melanie with patent disbelief. Picking up the flat iron, she tested it for hotness by touching her finger to her tongue, and then quickly to the iron. As it sizzled, she murmured again, "Have it your own way."

Packing proved to be more of an ordeal than Melanie expected. It was not that her wardrobe was so extensive. The problem was in deciding the probable situation she would find, determining how long she could plan on being gone and to what extent she and Glory would be required to set up housekeeping. Bed linens would doubtless be necessary, as would table linens and toweling of several different kinds, but would she need china, crystal, and silverware? Cooking utensils and cleaning supplies?

Such mental agonizing proved useless. Before the carriage could be brought out, before the first parcel could be loaded, news came that the Lopez expedition had sailed.

All preparation for departure ceased. The prospect of visiting the city was, somehow, not nearly as bright now that the general and his men had gone. There was bound to be a feeling of letdown about being in New Orleans at this time, and in any case, Mardi Gras had come to an end in the past week. It was now the Lenten season. Entertainments would be few in that Catholic city until after Easter. Of course, it would be nice to be in residence when victory was announced, but that might be months away, and it was doubtful that it would signal the return of the men with the general from Cuba. The officers especially would be needed to establish a military government within the country. In addition, soldiers and officers alike had been promised land for their participation in the coup d'état. None would want to risk being absent when this division of the spoils of war was made.

With Natchez gradually catching the fire of the New Orleanians' enthusiasm for the venture, news became more readily available. Every steamboat from downriver brought a news sheet of some kind concerning the exploits of Lopez. It became Cicero's duty to make a trip to Natchez landing each day to collect these scraps of information. They did not make an encouraging picture. The expeditionary force, numbering some six hundred men, had rendezvoused off the coast of the Yucatan Peninsula on the islands of Mugeres and Contoy. There the ships had been unloaded, the recruits formed into companies along with a small band of Cuban patriots who joined them there, and arms and ammunition issued. Several weeks of drilling and conditioning followed, and then in the middle of May, the filibuster army embarked once more, taking the steamer *Creole*. The other two ships, the *Susan Loud* and the *Georgina*, were left behind, along with forty men who refused to continue.

If visions of disaster had prompted the decision of the forty, they were proven true prophets. Lopez planned to make a night attack on the Cuban port of Cárdenas, catching the Spanish garrison there by surprise. But in the darkness, while trying to enter the harbor without a pilot, the *Creole* went aground on shoals within a stone's throw of the Cárdenas wharf. After much delay and confusion, a landing was finally made, but the element of surprise had been lost. Though Lopez stormed the barracks and the railroad station, so many of his men were killed and wounded that it was impossible for him to regroup a large enough force to take advantage of his victory by pushing inland. If he stayed where he was, however, his men would be cut to pieces by Spanish reinforcements. He had no choice other than to retreat to the steamer. Getting his wounded on board, floating the ship free, he made all speed for the eastern shore of the island where he hoped to receive aid and additional men to flesh out his regiments from the native insurgents. He did not make it. During the morning, his path was crossed by the Spanish warship *Pizarro*, which gave pursuit. The *Creole*, with only one small bow-mounted gun, was forced to turn tail and run for the coast of Florida. She took refuge just in time in the harbor of Key West, gaining cover where the *Pizarro* could not bring her guns to bear.

The forty men left on Contoy Island did not fare quite so well. Learning of their presence by way of small fishing boats, the Spanish government sent warships to take them off. Though they had had the means at their disposal to return to New Orleans, they delayed their departure too long. At Havana, they were thrown into the dungeons of Morro Castle and sentenced to be hanged.

Lopez, when he finally made his way back to New Orleans, was given a hero's welcome. There was a torchlight parade and public speeches at which Lopez proclaimed that his first campaign had been solely for the purpose of reconnoitering, and that within a short time he would be ready to mount his main attack against the Spanish oppressors of the island of Cuba.

The celebrations were hardly over when the United States government, in a surprise move that shocked the citizens of Louisiana and Mississippi, indicted General Narciso Lopez, along with his most prominent backer, Governor John Quitman, for violating the Neutrality Laws of 1818.

It had been due entirely to Eliza Quitman that Melanie was able to learn that her husband had returned alive and uninjured with the general. The governor's wife had been too much of a friend in need for Melanie to ignore the disaster that had befallen Eliza now. Donning her best black silk-faille, Melanie had herself driven to Monmouth. She discovered the drive before the house so filled with carriages of all kinds that her courage nearly failed her. Then with a lift of her chin, she directed John to stop before the front walk. A yard boy, obviously delegated for the responsibility on this special occasion, came forward to open the door and help her to alight. Thanking him, Melanie stood a moment shaking the folds from her skirts; then she started for the front door.

She had taken no more than a half dozen steps when a maid came hurrying from around the side of the great white house. Motioning to Melanie, she said, "This way, if it pleases you, Mrs. Donavan. Come this way."

For an instant too brief to measure, Melanie wondered if she was being refused admission, if the maid would, perhaps, hand her a note requesting that she leave and return at another, less public time. An instant later, she shook her head. Eliza would not do that. She had never been one to bow and scrape to convention or to suffer gladly those who did.

Melanie was right. Following the maid around the house and through an arcade, she was shown up the back stairs and into the bedchamber of the governor's wife. As the door opened, a small, dark-haired woman turned from the window.

"My dear," Eliza Quitman said, coming forward with

142

outstretched hands. "When I saw your carriage I was so thrilled that you had ventured forth to see me that I had to send for you, though John just ordered me upstairs to rest."

"I should have known you would be swamped with visitors," Melanie replied. "I just didn't think. I promise I won't stay long."

"No, no, don't worry about it. It's been like this all morning and will continue until dark, I expect. John is still holding forth in the parlor—and enjoying himself immensely. Despite what he thinks, I need someone to talk to; someone I can depend upon to say something sensible instead of just exclaiming over and over how ghastly it all is, and what a terrible injustice."

There was a chaise longue covered in pink and gray striped silk drawn up before the high front windows. Near it was a secretary desk with a chair upholstered in the same fabric. Moving to the chair, Melanie drew it out, pushing it closer to the lounge. "Lie back down then," she answered, "and I will sit here and try to think of something intelligent to say. I feel I ought to warn you, however, that I know nothing of the laws concerning neutrality."

"Thank heaven you admit it," Eliza answered. "Half the men downstairs pretend they do, which makes for nothing but utter nonsense and confusion. Put simply, it means that during times of conflict between other nations, a country not involved is said to be in a state of neutrality. That being so, they may continue their normal trade relations with the countries at war, provided they do not aid either side by force of arms or by the contributions of implements of war. If they do so, their neutrality is considered to be violated, and their shipping, even their shores, can be attacked by the opposite faction. In the case of General Lopez and John, our government is, in effect, disavowing all connection between them and their unfortunate expedition in an effort to maintain their position of neutrality in the Cuban insurrection against Spain." Her tone dry, Eliza added, "It would have been quite otherwise if the attempt at a coup had been successful."

"The governor doesn't feel that he has done anything to warrant prosecution then?"

"Not at all. He compares it to the French intervention in the American Revolution. Where would we be now if France had decided at the first sign of defeat to withdraw its forces and arrest the Marquis de Lafayette for violation of neutrality?"

"What will happen now? What will they do to him?" Melanie asked.

A worried frown appeared on Eliza's face. "I don't know. John refuses to post bond. You know he has always been an advocate of states' rights. He declares that as the governor of the state of Mississippi he is, in reality, the head of a sovereign nation, and that the government of the United States has no authority to arrest him if he fails to appear at his trial. He says that even if he does appear, public opinion will sway the jury in the favor of the general and himself, especially as the trial is to be held in district court in New Orleans. Therefore, they are bound to be acquitted."

"What of the other men who are with Lopez? Will they be affected?"

"I think not," Eliza said with an understanding smile. "You need not worry about that handsome husband of yours. I suppose you are anxious to see him, aren't you? Although I understood Lopez is already planning his next invasion, for the time being his men are at loose ends, with plenty of time for—outside interests. In all probability, John and I will be going to New Orleans soon. We would be happy to have you travel downriver on the steam packet with us."

Melanie hesitated no more than a moment. "I appreciate your kind offer, but I have already made other arrangements for the journey." It did no harm to have people think she was anxious to see her husband. It was as good an excuse as any for going.

"And faster ones, I expect, though I do hope you are not planning to go alone?"

"Oh, no, my maid Glory will be with me, and John Coachman, of course, plus one or two of the stable hands as outriders."

"You don't mean to take your carriage? That is much too dangerous, my dear!"

"My servants will be armed, as I will myself. In any case, it can't be any more dangerous than the river, only more uncomfortable and tedious."

Eliza Quitman stared at her. "Yes, I was forgetting. I am sorry." The governor's wife was well aware of her fears. Melanie's mother had been her close friend; they had come out in the same season, received posies and proposals from many of the same young men. They had vied with each other for the honor of receiving the most offers of marriage, until both had suddenly been made one they could not bring themselves to refuse. "Still, you will be careful, won't you, and warn your servants to keep a close watch?"

"I will indeed," Melanie agreed and went on to speak of other things, filling in the remainder of the correct half hour until it was time for her to take her leave.

Chapter 8

THE DECISION to leave at once for New Orleans had been made on the spur of the moment, but Melanie began at once to act upon it. Before the week was out her trunk was packed again and strapped to the carriage. She began to have hopes she would be in the city in time to greet the governor and his wife when they arrived. It did not happen that way. Two days before the Greenlea cook had finished baking the cakes, breads, and hams, frying the chickens and dried apple and peach tarts she would take with her, John Quitman resigned his office and took the steamboat downriver, there to submit to the jurisdiction of the district court as a private citizen. The night before he left, a torchlight ceremony was held. From Greenlea, Melanie could hear the fifteen guns fired for Quitman, the fifteen for the southern states, and then the great salvo signaling the support of Natchez for its favorite son.

The carriage bearing Melanie toward the Crescent City rolled down the drive of Greenlea in the first light of dawn. The summer was well advanced, and it was best to take advantage of the cool hours of the morning for the sake of the horses, if not for the passengers. She settled her skirts about her and sat back against the blue velvet seats. Across from her, Glory propped herself in the corner and prepared to catch up on the sleep she had missed in the last few days of hectic activity. Melanie wished that she could follow her maid's example, but her nerves were

146

too tightly strung for her to relax. It would not be a short journey or an easy one. They could expect to be on the road the better part of a week, depending on the weather. By contrast, the steamboat trip would have taken no more than twenty-four hours. It was amazing to think that the Quitmans would be arriving in New Orleans before she had truly set out.

At the end of their first hot and dusty day, they broke their travels by accepting the hospitality of a planter whose great house overlooked the Mississippi River. In exchange for her night's rest, Melanie was able to impart the latest news concerning the Lopez incident and the governor's resignation, a fair exchange to the plantation family who spent the slow-moving summer month virtually out of touch with civilization. So reluctant were they to let her go, so insistent were they that she have one more biscuit, one more sliver of ham, one more cup of coffee or tea, glass of muscadine cordial, or slice of nice chilled melon, that the sun was well on its way to its zenith before the carriage rolled away down the oak-lined drive and back onto the road. The second night they did not fare quite so well. Still, though their room was cramped and spartanly furnished, it was clean. The widow who kept it was friendly, and her ample girth testified to the tastiness of the meals she provided.

They awoke on the third morning to pouring rain. In spite of the urgings of the widow, and of Glory, Melanie decided to push on. Summer storms were seldom of long duration, she pointed out. A little farther down the road they might leave it behind altogether. Glory, mumbling something about peach trees, finally gave in and ceased protesting. They set out.

The storm grew worse. Wind whipped the carriage, making it sway sickeningly on its springs. The rain pounded against the lacquered sides, seeping in around the windows. The sky grew so dark Melanie could hardly make out Glory's features in the dimness. Up on top, John was having trouble with the horses as windblown bits of tree limbs and clutches of leaves stung them, and

147

they shied at every streak of lightning and clap of thunder. In this particular stretch of road there seemed to be no plantations, no communities, no houses of any kind. The morning wore on. The road narrowed down to little more than a track. Melanie kept telling herself that turning back would be no better than going on, and would waste valuable time besides, that somewhere ahead there must be some sort of shelter for them all. But if there was, they passed it in the enveloping, rain-filled gloom.

By degrees the road became a quagmire, the ruts filled with water that covered the sinks and potholes through which they lurched. More than once Glory and Melanie, rattling around in the body of the carriage like two peas in a box, banged their heads and bruised their shoulders. Often they stuck in the mud, so that the stable hands, one riding guard, the other on horseback, had to get down and put their shoulders to the wheels. A tree, blown across the road, blocked their passage for a time. It had to be cut into sections with an axe before it could be removed. As the rain continued to slash down during the afternoon, there seemed only one explanation for the continued downpour. They were caught in the trailing tail of a gulf hurricane that had moved inland. Their progress was so slow they seemed to be crawling, and by the time night began to fall Melanie deemed it unlikely that they had come more than fifteen or twenty miles from where they had spent the night before. It crossed her mind more than once they had taken a wrong turn somewhere, though John swore they had not. As it began to look as if they would have to spend the night in the carriage, beside the road, the widow's unlamented accommodations began to seem, in retrospect, like palatial comfort.

"A light, Miss Melanie!" The shout came from John above them. "Yonder through the woods!"

"Praise the Lord," Glory said.

"They may not take us in," Melanie warned above the shouts of jubilation.

Her fears were groundless, though when the carriage rolled to a halt and she stepped down, she was not certain

that was a good thing. The building before her was a ram-
bling, unpainted shack with a sign nailed above the door
and illuminated by a pierced tin lantern that proclaimed it
to be the Real Inn. The name, with its suggestion that
they were still on El Camino Real, inspired satisfaction,
but that was the only thing. The yard before the place
was a sea of mud littered with bits and pieces of broken
wagons, staved-in barrels, cracked demijohns, and piles of
other unrecognizable rubbish, all soaking in the steady
rain. Her splashing progress to the entrance porch coated
the hem of Melanie's traveling gown with noisome filth
that was somewhat explained by the presence under the
rickety overhang of a cluster of pigs and roosting chickens. These fled squawking and squealing as John and the
stable hands in their flopping oilskins joined Melanie and
Glory, stepping to the far end of the porch.

At their approach, the front door swung open with a
powerful screech of rusty hinges. A man peered out.
Turning, he bawled back over his shoulder, "People out
here, Ma. Paying customers!"

The warm air that rushed from inside the room smelled
of stale woodsmoke, wet dogs, and the peculiar wild-ani-
mal-like odor of the man who held the door. Beyond him
could be seen a huge mud-daub fireplace, the hearth
liberally spattered with tobacco juice. A black pot hung
over the glowing coals, holding a simmering stew of some
wild meat, squirrel or rabbit from the smell. Beside it was
a haunch of venison on a spit. The fireplace was flanked
on either side by long, homemade benches, each using
half of an enormous split log. A number of chairs of
equally crude construction were drawn up to a makeshift
table in the center of the floor. At the table sat three
other men who might have been brothers to the one at the
door, though it was difficult to see their features for the
untrimmed beards that covered their faces and the fitful
light thrown by the lamp hanging from the rafters. Their
feet were caked with mud, as was every inch of the plank
floor not covered by the hides of deer, bear, or wolf. Beaver pelts with the paws still attached hung on the walls

rather than paintings, and the fur of raccoons had been used to upholster the seat of the only chair in the room that had come from a furniture maker, a rocking chair.

Melanie looked at Glory. For herself, she would much have preferred to go on than to even think of spending the night here, but the horses were exhausted and she could not ask her servants to endure their exposed positions in the wind and the rain any longer. There might be other shelter to be found further ahead, or there might be nothing but mud and rain. In a little while it would be pitch dark and almost impossible to see to keep to the road, even if the carriage lanterns would stay lit in the whipping wind.

Glory shook her head. "I don't know, Miss Melanie," she said under her breath. "John and the boys, they be glad to sleep under the carriage. Give them a quilt and they be snug enough."

At that moment a woman appeared in the door leading to the back regions of the house. Perhaps in her late forties, she had gray hair done up in a tight knot on top of her head, a lined face, and the stooped shoulders and worn red hands of one used to unceasing labor. Her deep-set eyes might have been pretty at one time, but now they held a shuttered watchfulness. Her smile was wary, with a placating quality painful to see.

"Why," she exclaimed, wiping her hands on her dingy apron, "it's a lady. She doesn't want to stay here."

"Yes, she does, Ma," the man who had opened the door said. "She most shorely does. You tell her we'll put her up. Tell her nice, so she'll stay."

One of the men at the table leaned back, tilting his chair onto its back legs, so that it groaned, threatening to overturn. "That's right, Ma. Invite her in real nice," he said, his eyes, above the bush of his beard, shining and overbright.

The woman flung a nervous look at the two men. Smoothing her hand distractedly over her apron, she started toward Melanie. "Good—good evening, ma'am,"

150

she ventured, ducking her head. "Were you wanting a bed for the night?"

"I don't know," Melanie answered, her tone abrupt. "Could you tell us how far it is to the next town?"

Licking her lips, the woman said, "Not far," then added at the sound of a grunt behind her, "on a fine day, that is. You would be hard put to make it before dawn in this weather. I—my name's Bascom, folks call me Ma, mostly. And this here is my son Buck who let you in. The others are Bart, Billy, and Burt. We—we would be pleased to have you stay with us. We're not used to—to bedding down the gentry, as I expect you've guessed, but you would be welcome to the best we have."

Beyond the woman, her son gave a nod, though whether in agreement or approval of his mother's speech it was impossible to say. To Melanie it felt as though some threat hung in the air, as if the poor woman standing so humbly before them might be made to suffer if her persuasion was unsuccessful.

"I'm not sure—" Melanie began.

"Don't say no," the woman begged, a hunted look coming into her eyes. "Let me show you where you'll sleep. It's clean, I promise you, as clean as lye soap will make it."

Taking up a tallow candle and lighting it from the lamp, the woman went before them into a bedchamber opening to one side of the main room. The door, Melanie noticed, had a stout wooden bolt on the inside, though there was a crack between it and its frame fully half an inch wide. The furnishings consisted of a homemade bed frame of rough poles with a cornshuck mattress piled high with patchwork quilts, and a washstand made from a tree stump with a plank nailed to the top. On the washstand was a tin pan with a towel hanging on a nail above it. An enameled tin chamberpot sat conspicuously in one corner, since the washstand had no shelf to accommodate it and the bed was too low to conceal it.

"What do you think?" the woman inquired hopefully. "Your maid could have a pallet on the floor. As for your

151

men slaves, they can sleep in the hay out in the barn; at least out there they'll be dry. And your horses, we can bait them, too. We don't have oats or grain, but there's plenty of clean hay."

The quilts did look clean, the towel sun-bleached and unused. That was no guarantee there would not be bedbugs or other inhuman occupants. Still, it was shelter, something they all had to have. Overhead could be heard the steady drumming of the rain on the cypress shake roof and the whistling of the wind through the trees. It had been a hard day and, even if the rain stopped during the night, would be just as hard tomorrow. Rest was a necessity. She did not like the place or the woman or her sons, but there could be little danger. John and the other menservants were armed; she had seen to that, and she had her own pistol. It was unlikely these people would try anything against such nearly equal numbers, even if they were inclined.

"Please don't say no," the woman whispered, clutching at Melanie's arm as her voice dropped into a whine. "Please. It will go bad with me if you do. My boys, they want to build up this place, make it an inn for fine folks like you. Only most go on the steamboats nowadays, except for them that's too poor to pay for the fast ride, or too saving. Just seems like we won't never get the chance to better ourselves."

"All right," Melanie said, freeing her arm, distaste warring with pity in her mind, "we will stay."

"Bless you," the woman cried. "I can't tell you how proud I am. Supper will be done in just a little while. I'll call you when it's ready, or I can bring it in here, if you would rather."

"Thank you," Melanie said, exchanging a look with Glory once more, "but we have our own provisions."

Glory spoke then. "That's right, but John and the boys might relish a hot meal."

"Yes, I'm sure you are right," Melanie agreed, looking with one lifted eyebrow to their hostess.

152

The woman gave a quick nod. "I can give it to them. Now if there's anything else you need, you just call me."

"A cup of hot coffee would go mighty good," Glory put in.

A frown clouded the woman's face. "I don't think we've got any," she began, then brightened. "But I can make you a nice hot toddy, both of you, to take out the damp."

Glory would be feeling the effect of the cool, wet weather and the shaking of the last three days deep in her bones. She should have thought of it sooner, Melanie chided herself. "The toddy sounds good, just what we need."

Since sheets were not among the luxuries provided by the Real Inn, Melanie and Glory retrieved their own from the carriage and remade the bed. At the same time, they brought in the things they would need for the night and what was left of the ham, bread, and apple tarts. Spreading their feast on Glory's pallet, they took their evening meal, washing it down with the toddy that had been brought to them in tin mugs.

The drink was potent. The wild honey that had been used to sweeten it instead of sugar had, to some extent, camouflaged the strength of the whiskey and hot water mixture. Before long, Melanie was yawning. She searched in her rattan box for her nightgown, but it was not to be found. Doubtless it had been put away that morning in another bag or trunk. It was not worth braving the rain again. She would make do with her camisole. Though a trifle short, coming just to the tops of her thighs, it would serve. There was only Glory to see her, and she had little use for modesty before the woman who had been her nursemaid. Glory, who had drunk every drop that was in her cup, plus the last inch of Melanie's toddy, tumbled on her pallet fully clothed and pulled a quilt up over her head as soon as she had helped Melanie to undress.

The least movement on the bed, even her breathing, set the cornshucks on which Melanie lay to rustling. The noise, slight though it was, kept her awake for a time.

The rain had begun to die away, she thought, though it still pattered overhead and dripped from the eaves. She concentrated on this sound, instead of the micelike rattling of the cornshucks and the slow rumble and growl of voices from beyond her bolted door, until her eyelids finally began to grow heavy. She was dragged back from the edge of slumber by the thud of hoofbeats, a muffled sound on the muddy road. They grew nearer, slowing as they approached the inn. She lay listening, troubled by the memory of another time she had heard hoofbeats in the night. She had not been alone then. With a shake of her head she banished such thoughts, wondering what business would keep a rider out on such a night as this. She expected to hear him pass on; he did not. With what seemed like caution, he drew closer, stopping in the yard before the porch. The horse whinnied. The front door of the inn creaked open on its reluctant hinges. It seemed the woman and her sons had another paying customer. Melanie turned over and slept.

The slamming of a door in the rear of the house roused her. Low voices and the pad of stealthy footsteps brought her wide awake. In the corner of the room, Glory's gentle snores could still be heard, though it was too dark to see her bulk beneath the quilt. Raising herself on one elbow, Melanie stared in the direction of the door, wondering if her imagination was at fault. She held her breath, listening, but could hear nothing except the whisper of the cornshucks in the mattress, shaken by the thudding of her heart against her ribs. And then there came a smothered laugh just outside her door. It was followed by a scratching sound. For an instant she thought it might be her hostess trying to attract her attention without waking the household, and then the wooden bolt shifted, rising a fraction before it fell with a thump back into its holder. A muffled curse came from the other side of the panel, and then a light bloomed, outlining the door in a faint glow, as if a lamp had been lit in the main room. Keeping her eyes on that streak of brightness, Melanie slid her hand beneath her pillow, drew out her pistol, and levered herself up straight in the bed, waiting.

Again the scratching sound came, and through the crack in the door slipped the silvery gleam of a knife blade. It passed under the wooden bar and began to inch slowly upward, lifting it free.

The instant the bar was clear, the door crashed open. Whooping, hollering, the Bascom brothers poured into the room. She did not trouble to aim. Steadying the pistol with both hands, she pulled the trigger, firing into them.

The gunshot roared around the room. The brothers came to a sudden halt as one of their number fell back screaming, the Bowie knife he held in his hand clanging to the floor. Glory sat up and began to shriek, her eyes wide and staring in the shaft of light striking through the door.

Then with a beastlike sound deep in his throat, Buck Bascom threw himself forward. He tore the smoking pistol Melanie still held from her hand and sent it spinning across the room. Melanie rolled, flinging herself headlong from the other side of the bed. Buck lunged to catch the trailing ends of her hair, jerking her back. She sprawled across the bed, clutching at the strands of her hair to relieve the intolerable tension as it felt like it was being torn from the roots. Tears of pain started from her eyes. Buck grabbed her arm, his horny nails biting into her soft skin. He hooked his free hand into the top of her camisole and pulled, tearing the fragile material, exposing one creamy, rose-tipped breast.

"Come on boys," he rasped. "Get her legs. Spread 'em wide and hold her down tight. Just remember, I'm first."

Stumbling over their fallen brother where he writhed on the floor, the others swarmed toward them. Their eyes glittered and their mouths were slack with lust as they stared at the white marble gleam of Melanie's bare thighs and hips as she twisted in the grasp of the man who held her and the silken glory of her hair swirling around her, shimmering in the lamplight, concealing, then revealing, the pearllike sheen of her shoulders above her torn bodice.

None noticed the last man who glided into the room, a tall, quiet-moving shadow. None, except Glory, who fell abruptly silent as the man turned to face the light.

"That will do. Let her go."

The voice was hard, carrying in its depths the whiplash of command and an echo of deadly danger. The Bascoms turned, the surprise on their faces making them look stupid, animalistic, as they blinked in the haze of powder smoke in the room, their eyes fastened on the gun pointed at them. Melanie gave a sobbing gasp, disbelief in her wide violet-blue eyes.

"The gun I am holding," Roland said quietly, "is not a muzzle-loading pistol but a Colt revolver capable of firing six times. If you don't want the Bascom line to die out here and now, you will do what I say. Let her go."

Buck Bascom, shielding as much of his bulk behind Melanie as he could, looked longingly to where his brother's Bowie knife with its long, cruel blade lay glinting in the wavering light. There was no possible way he could reach it. Taking a deep breath, he forced a smile. "Look friend," he said to Roland. "We'll make a deal with you, cut you in on a piece of this nice little thing we've got here. Them slaves we got tied up out in the barn, they're worth four, maybe five hundred apiece, quick sell, to a man we know across the river who won't ask no questions. Then there's the maid there, another three or four hundred. That's a nice bit of cash, even split five ways. As for this fine miss here, why, there's a market for her, too, after we get through with her. There's houses in New Orleans that would be glad to have her, once they teach her to keep her mouth shut and not go shooting at the nice gentlemen who come to her room. If you don't feel like having her, that's fine. You can sit and watch while me and the boys have our fun. Any time you feel like joining in, why you just up and at it."

"Thank you, no. I don't share what's mine. Take your hands off my wife."

"Wife!"

That instant of amazement, brief though it was, was

156

enough. Melanie jerked free of the hands that held her, diving to one side. As Buck stared after her a shot, harder, flatter than that of a muzzle-loading pistol rang out. The eldest of the Bascom brothers clutched his chest and reeled backward, falling to the floor with a crash that shook the house. He did not move again. With up-lifted hands, the other two backed away, shaking their heads as the unwavering barrel of Roland's revolver turned in their direction.

"Tie them up," Roland grated.

Melanie grabbed up her dressing gown, pushed her arms into the sleeves, before she hurried to obey. With Glory's help, she tore strips from the bedsheets and bound their arms behind their backs, knotting the linen with vicious jerks. The man Melanie had shot was not seriously hurt. He soon lay beside the others on the floor, the only concession to his injury a pad of linen pressed to the hole through the fat of his side.

When they were done, Roland inspected their handiwork, then gave a short nod. "All right. Now let's get out of here. Glory, go and release the men in the barn. Tell them to bring the horses around and hitch them to the carriage. By the time you get back, we should be ready to go."

Never in her life had Melanie dressed so quickly or with so little concern with what the results might look like. Though she turned her back on the men lying like trussed-up chickens on the floor, she could feel their eyes boring into her as she pulled on her stockings and garters, struggled into her petticoats and gown, and twisted her hair into a knot low on the nape of her neck. She was only glad that her traveling costume, made on the severe lines of a riding habit, buttoned up the front so that she needed no one's assistance, least of all that of the stranger who was her husband, to regain some appearance of decorum. As she threw her belongings together, her face flamed. What must she have looked like with her camisole rucked up to her waist? It did not bear thinking about. Though she sent Roland a fleeting look of gratitude as he

157

stepped between her and the prisoners, blocking their view, she was just as glad that keeping an eye on the men on the floor prevented him from giving her his whole attention.

When she was ready, he picked up her rattan box under one arm. Melanie, carrying the bundle which contained the pillows she and Glory had used plus what was left of the sheets, stepped shuddering over the body of Buck Bascom and preceded Roland out the door.

In the main room, they came to a halt as Ma Bascom ghosted toward them in a gray flannel nightgown and a faded wrapper that had shrunk so it flapped about her knees.

"I saw—I saw what you did," she whispered. "I don't blame you. I didn't want them to do that to the nice lady, I didn't want to help them, but they made me. They are unnatural sons, unnatural. If I don't do what they say, they will put me out in the cold. My fault, my fault for marrying their father."

On impulse, Melanie said, "Come with us to New Orleans. Maybe there you could find work."

"Nobody wants an old woman. This is my home; all I have is here. No! No! I'm too old. What could I do? But if you want to help me, tie me up, too. Tie me up, so they will know there was nothing I could do to help them."

Melanie tried once more, but it was useless. Miserable though she was, the Bascom woman could not bring herself to leave. With her teeth clenched tightly together, Melanie did as she asked, tying the woman in an upright position in the rocking chair. They left her there, rocking slightly, staring down into the gray ashes of the fireplace. She still had shed not a single tear for her dead son, nor offered to go to the aid of the one who was injured. Though Melanie pitied her sincerely, she was just as glad that her generous gesture had been refused, more than happy that she was not going to have to share her carriage with her for the rest of the weary miles they still had to go.

The rain had stopped. Though the trees still dripped,

the sky was clear enough to allow the glimpse of a silver sickle moon hanging low in the western sky. The carriage, glistening with wet in the light of its side lanterns, stood before the house, with the horses between the shafts. John and one of the hands were up on the box with the other stable man sitting his cob to one side. Another mount was tied to the back of the carriage. Melanie, letting her gaze travel from the horse to its saddle strapped in the baggage carrier with her trunks, felt her stomach muscles tighten. It appeared she would have company in the carriage after all.

Glory, inside the carriage, took the bundle of linens and the box Melanie and Roland passed up to her, setting them on the seat beside her. "Mr. Roland." she said, a fervent tone in her voice, "I was never so glad to see anybody in my whole life. I heard what that man said, and I hate to think what would have happened to us all if you hadn't come along when you did. The Lord sure must have sent you, and I just want to say it's thankful I am that he did!"

Roland, handing Melanie into the carriage, sent the maid a grim smile. "Actually, it was Governor Quitman who sent me, Glory, but it's pleasant to be appreciated, all the same."

Throwing himself down on the seat beside Melanie, he slammed the door. Immediately John shouted to his team, and the vehicle started forward with a jerk, rolling out into the mud of the road.

"You are that, Mr. Roland, you are that." Glory's wise old eyes searched Roland's set face in the dim light before looking to Melanie who sat staring out the window at nothing. Nodding a little to herself, she settled into the carriage seat. Her eyelids fell, and as the carriage rocked on, her body took on the boneless look of one who can fall instantly asleep.

Melanie sent her maid a suspicious look, then flicked a glance at her husband from the corner of her eyes. His anger was daunting. Still there was no reason why she

159

should allow it to affect her. Her manner as gracious as she could make it, she said, "Glory is right. We do owe you a debt of gratitude."

"Are you including yourself in this debt?"

"Yes, of course," she replied, determined not to be nettled by his scathing tone.

"Even though it pains you to admit it? Whatever possessed you to stop at such a place, or to set out from Natchez without a male escort."

"I had an escort," she said with a lift of her chin.

"John and the stable hands? And just what good did they do you tied up out in the barn. They are brave enough, I'm sure, but you must have known they would not be able to stay close enough to you at night to be of any use."

"Unfortunately, they were all that was available to me, since my husband was not at home and I have no male relatives."

He shot her a hard glance at the mention of his absence. "You could have had the company of Governor Quitman and his wife, but you refused it."

"They were going on the steam packet," she returned, angrily aware of the defensive note in her voice.

"So they were, and they made it safely and in good time, which is more than can be said for you and your overland route."

Melanie looked away. "I have tried to explain it to you, but you don't understand."

"I understand well enough what was about to happen to you, even if you don't."

"I know very well what they had in mind," she exclaimed.

"Then you will have to admit the danger is just as great this way."

"All right! I will admit it," she said, rounding on him. "But the danger was to me, so I don't see why you are in such a temper. I certainly didn't ask you to meet me!"

"No, you didn't, did you? You didn't even bother to in-

160

form me that you were on your way to New Orleans. If it hadn't been for the governor and his wife, I would not have known what you were planning until it was too late, and then where would you be now?"

Her violet blue eyes flashing, Melanie demanded, "Why should I bother to keep you informed of my activities when you never sent me so much as a line concerning yours these past few months? I would never have known you were alive if it weren't for our mutual informants, the Quitmans."

"How was I to know you cared one way or the other?" he demanded, a frown drawing his brows together. "From your silence I assumed the only message you cared to have of me was a death notice."

She stared at him for long seconds without speaking. It was no part of her plans to quarrel with him at this time. Moreover, she was indeed grateful for his timely arrival. "If you truly thought so," she said finally, "then I am sorry."

All expression fled from his face, leaving it masklike in the pale, wavering light. His eyes held hers, a probing look in their dark green, unfathomable depths. Abruptly he reached out and caught her to him, setting his mouth to hers in hungry passion, holding her closer and closer still, until she thought her ribs would break and her lips were bruised from the burning pressure of his kiss. Without conscious volition, she found her hands locked behind his head. Somewhere inside, she felt the dissolving of a close-held anguish. She had been more afraid than she had known, she thought. And now as she felt his arms around her, she knew she was safe. That must be it. She had no other explanation for the glow of warmth and well-being that crept in upon her.

His grip loosened, his lips moved to the corner of her mouth; then he pressed his cheek to hers. "When I think of you in the hands of men like that, like the Bascoms, I go a little mad. I keep telling myself I should have done something to keep them from so much as touching you, but I didn't realize in time what they meant to do. I am sorry, sweet Melanie."

She gave a small shake of her head. "It was enough that you came at all. It was like a miracle. I can't imagine how you found me."

"I left New Orleans in the midst of a tropical storm, taking the steamer as far as St. Francisville, since I didn't think you could have passed it in the length of time you had been on the road. Then I set out up El Camino Real. I was almost ready to give up, to admit you had made better time than I had expected, when I saw your carriage outside that thieves' den. You had already retired for the night. I decided not to disturb you, being none too sure what my welcome might be, though since you were coming to New Orleans presumably to be with me, I had hopes that you wouldn't refuse my protection for the rest of the journey."

"Oh, Roland," she said, drawing back slightly. But he would not release her, would not allow her to look into his face.

"You had been given the best the Real Inn had to offer, the only room not occupied," he went on, smoothing the open palm of his hand along her back. "I ate a bowl of stew for supper, shared a drink with my hosts, and made my bed on one of the benches beside the fireplace. I heard the Bascom brothers when they went out to see to your servants, but I had no idea they were intent on anything more than a visit to the privy. They came back, and three of them started drinking again while one, the youngest, took out his Bowie knife and went over to your door. By the time I recognized what he was doing and reached for my gun, he had it open."

"You weren't far behind the others," she said. "I might have hit you when I fired my pistol."

A small shiver ran over her at the thought. Sensing it, Roland allowed a smile to curve his mouth. "You might credit me with the good sense not to be the first through the door, knowing as I do your penchant for firearms. But what is this? No so long ago putting a bullet hole in me

162

was your most fervent wish. Have things changed so much that the idea no longer appeals to you?"

Despite the trace of humor in his tone, Melanie could feel the tension in his arms as he waited for her answer. "Yes, indeed," she said, forcing amusement into her own voice, "at least for the moment. You might credit *me* with the good sense to prefer you to any one—or all—of the Bascom brothers."

His breath left him in a soundless grunt. "I suppose that's something," he said. Removing his arms, he leaned back on the velvet squabs and stretched his legs out before him as far as the opposite seat would allow.

Melanie gave him a quick glance as she raised her hands to smooth her hair and reposition a few of the pins. The knot at the nape of her neck had never been the most secure arrangement, and the embrace she had just suffered had not helped matters. Roland did not look angry at her oblique answer to his question. Still, as she worked with her hair, she thought it would be best if he did not have time to dwell upon the subject.

"What about the Bascoms?" she asked, her head bent forward as she pushed the pins into the silken softness of her hair. "What will you do about them?"

"If you are worried about that crew starving to death in their bonds, don't bother. They are probably free already."

She paused to send him an indignant stare for this slur on her ability at knotting a strip of sheet. "I was thinking of the one you killed. Don't tell me he has slipped your mind?"

"No, no more than the man you left bleeding on the floor has faded from yours. I can't say I am sorry for his death. Still I suppose I will have to account for it to someone. The sheriff at St. Francisville should do. Buck Bascom was so knowledgeable about what he meant to do with your servants and, ultimately, with you that I suspect you were not their first victim. It is possible the sheriff will be more than a little interested in their activities. But if that is true, he will probably find an empty cabin when he rides out to question the Bascom brothers."

"Poor Mrs. Bascom."

"You needn't pity her. She raised that nest of vipers, she stays with them, and it wouldn't surprise me if she didn't abet them in their crimes at times. I wouldn't like to wager that her pretense of innocence isn't a screen, a carefully planned ploy, like the second escape route from a vixen's covert. Here," he said abruptly as he eyed her struggles with her hair, "let me help you."

Melanie let her arms fall. They were beginning to ache from trying to fasten her slippery tresses while the carriage jounced and swayed. She felt Roland's hands warm against the side of her neck, quick-moving as they pressed into the soft mass of her hair. The tension of first one ill-placed pin and then another eased, but there was no feeling of firmness to replace them.

"No," she cried, but it was too late. The knot slipped, tumbling down. Roland caught the heavy, coppery brown swath, drawing it forward over her shoulder, spreading it over her breast.

"Now, isn't that more comfortable?" he inquired, his jade green gaze shuttered as he lifted a curling lock and let it drift from his fingers in fine, shimmering strands.

His closeness had an odd effect upon her senses. She was intensely aware of the press of his shoulder against hers and the length of his hard, muscular thigh along her leg. By degrees, her annoyance faded to be replaced by a feeling of content. A slow smile curved her mouth and a whimsical, almost questioning expression rose in her eyes. "Yes," she said softly. "I believe it is better."

Roland drew in his breath, his gaze fastening on the pure, tantalizing lines of her mouth. Shifting, he enclosed her once more in the circle of his arms, his hand gripping her forearm with steely strength. At that moment Glory snuffled and began to snore with a quiet, even sound.

Roland gave a deep sigh, his hold relaxing as he gave Melanie's arm a gentle, almost brotherly pat. Fitting himself into the corner of the carriage, he drew her with him, pressing her head into the curve of his shoulder. "Go to sleep," he said, a ragged note in his voice as he rested his cheek against her hair.

It was difficult to tell if his words were for her or for himself. A smile flickered over Melanie's mouth once more before she closed her eyes.

Chapter 9

IT WAS mid-morning when they reached St. Francisville. Though a smaller town than Natchez, it had much the same character, being situated on rolling hills above the Mississippi River with the flat Louisiana shoreline in the distance. The homes of a number of planters graced the area, and their land, white with cotton under the August sun, stretched back from the river to the banks of Bayou Sara. St. Francisville owed its existence primarily to the steamboat landing which took the baled cotton downriver to New Orleans and from there to the mills of the northeastern seaboard states and Great Britain that were hungry for the long-stapled White Gold.

At some time during the miserable day before, they had crossed the boundary line of the state of Mississippi and were now in Louisiana. Though they were still less than a third of the way to New Orleans, they seemed closer due to this fact. Melanie would have liked to continue their journey after the briefest of pauses at the office of the sheriff; Roland decreed otherwise. They were all too exhausted, he said. They needed a good nourishing meal, a bath, and an uninterrupted night's sleep. There were the horses to be thought of. Moreover, he needed time to make himself presentable before calling on the sheriff, since he didn't care to be taken for a desperado himself. The matter of the Bascoms could not be hurried; it was doubtful he would be able to get away before the middle of the afternoon. No, it would be much better for them all if they put up at a hotel. The town had an excellent hostelry where the ravages of the past few days could be repaired. They could start out fresh the next morning. With Glory deserting her mistress to throw her considerable weight behind Roland's proposition, there was nothing Melanie could do except agree.

They had missed their breakfast. To make up for it, they had their heaviest meal of the day at noon, a meal that began with hot gumbo filet and continued through roasted squabs, braised beef in wine sauce, and side dishes of fresh corn oozing butter, golden-fried okra, butterbeans, and wedges of melon, finished off with caramel custard and steaming cups of coffee. The delicious fare helped convince Melanie that Roland was right; still, she fretted at the delay. Retiring to their room while he sallied forth to the office of the sheriff, she rang for a bath and lay lounging in the warm, scented water until it grew cool, then washed her hair and let it dry in the constant, humid breeze off the river. Despite the length of time she whiled away in this manner, Roland still had not returned. Sending Glory away to rest in her own quarters in the servants' wing, Melanie climbed beneath the mosquito netting draped over the bed. She would just take a short nap. She had slept a little in the early hours of the morning in Roland's arms, but not soundly.

It was growing warmer in the room as the sun leaned toward the west. A breath of wind still found its way through the window now and then to stir the gauze netting around her, but it had a furnacelike edge to it. Draping the mosquito netting on the headboard of the half-tester bed did no good. Perspiration still trickled along her hairline and formed a small runnel between her breasts. With an exasperated sigh, she finally sat up and cast off her dressing gown, flinging herself back down naked on top of the sheets. That was better, especially when she lifted the hot weight of her hair and let it trail over the edge of the bed.

The room Roland had hired was, she suspected, one of the nicer ones in the hotel. The furniture was the handiwork of the New Orleans cabinetmaker, Seignouret. The curtains and drapes at the windows, the rugs on the floors, the mirrors, lamps, and china appointments were as fine as any to be found in a private home. This was doubtless the hotel used by outlying planters and their families when they came into town to await the arrival of the steamboats to take them downriver. Before too long, the annual fall pilgrimage to the Creole city would begin, as those with the wealth to make the trip, and the pretensions that made it necessary, gathered for what was known as the *saison des visites*, the fashionable winter season. She would be there herself this year. She would, that is, if Lopez's second expedition did not leave before then, if Roland ever returned, and if she were ever permitted to leave St. Francisville!

She was awakened by a distant knocking. She opened her eyes, lying for a moment in confusion. She felt groggy with sleep, her body heavy and aching with weariness. It was only after the second knock that she came suddenly alert. Slipping from the bed, she grabbed up her dressing gown and padded toward the door.

"Glory?" she called with low-voiced caution.

"Roland," came the quiet answer.

Swirling her dressing gown around her, holding the front together at the waist, she turned the key in the lock and stepped back out of sight of passersby.

As he entered and closed the door behind him, she gave him a small smile. "I am sorry you had to wait. I must have fallen asleep."

His eyes rested with appreciation on the dew-fresh look of her skin, the heavy-lidded sultriness of her eyes, and the shining cascade of her hair falling past her waist. "I wish I had known," he said easily. "I would have tried to finish my business sooner."

"Is—is everything all right?" Melanie asked, turning away, disturbed by the expression in his eyes.

Behind her, Roland removed his high-crowned beaver and hung it on the walnut rack beside the door. "I am considered," he said, stripping off his coat and hanging it

168

beside the hat, "to have done a service to the community. As I suspected, the sheriff has had his eye on the Real Inn for some time. It is outside his jurisdiction, of course, and he had no evidence to place before a United States marshal, if he called one in. He promises to investigate, though he has no more hope of finding the Bascoms still in residence than I did."

"I see. At least there will be no trouble for you over it."

"No," he said, coming up behind her, placing his hands at the slender curve of her waist, "though I am touched by your concern, intrigued by it even. Is it, I wonder, another sign of your preference for me?"

"I would rather not see you hanged for something you did for my sake, if that is what you mean."

"That was not precisely what I had in mind," he answered, "though I appreciate it."

For a moment he was silent as his hands spanned her unlaced body, then slid upward to cup the ripe fullness of her breasts. "I was more interested in discovering if you were waiting for me when you fell asleep, and if you were wearing this modest garment."

He knew she was naked under her dressing gown. He was suggesting she had been anxiously anticipating his arrival. "Don't be ridiculous," she snapped.

"Not ridiculous," he murmured against the side of her neck as he gently, but firmly, removed her hands that held her dressing gown closed and slipped his fingers under the thin, lace-edged material, "merely hopeful. I thought you were glad to see me last night—or was it this morning?—but I will have to say that Glory did a better job of making me feel welcome—until now."

The trace of humor in his tone, the gentle insistence of his hands as they bared her warm flesh, coupled with the uncomfortable suspicion that he might be right, affected Melanie's will in strange ways. Her irritation at being left alone so long vanished. She no longer felt the least need to bandy words with him. Instead, she knew an awakening longing for something that could never be, a longing

169

to drop her guard, let down her reserve, and face him openly. She owed him a great debt for what he had done. That fact, combined with the effect upon her of his presence and his touch, made it difficult for her to hold to her design of revenge, or remember how much she hated him.

"I—I was glad to see you," she murmured.

His arms tightened, so she was pressed to him. Unconsciously, she yielded, leaning against his strength, her head resting on his shoulder. He moved his hand upward along the tender turn of her neck, tilting her chin. His mouth sought hers, molding her lips to his own in a deep, sweet quest without end. Their lips still clinging, he turned her pliant body to face him, drawing her close until the nipples of her firm breasts probed his chest and she could feel the studs of his shirt biting into her skin. Beneath her dressing gown, his hands moved over the slim lines of her back to her hips, compelling her to recognize the extent of his craving for her. As the heat of their bodies grew, the yellow rose fragrance of the soap she had used mounted around them, alluring in its wanton sweetness. The silken material of the dressing gown slipped, leaving her shoulders, falling to the floor.

There was something disconcerting about standing nude in his arms while he was still fully clothed. It was as though she were the supplicant, tempting him to come to her. Perhaps that could be turned to her advantage. For a man like Roland, wasn't satisfying his physical cravings a major part of winning his trust and love? When at last he allowed her to breathe, she bent her head so that her brow brushed his chin and, with trembling fingers, began to loosen his cravat. He went still, his breath caught in his throat, neither aiding nor restraining her as she left the ends of his tie dangling and dropped lower to the buttons of his waistcoat. When she had done, and his waistcoat hung open, there seemed no justifiable reason for calling a halt, though as his hands began once more to caress the small of her back, she wished she could find one. She had never intended to go so far as the studs of his shirt, but it

170

seemed he expected it, that his touch and the light kisses that he pressed along her hairline urged her to complete what she had begun.

She could not. As the last stud slipped from its bound hole, and his shirt revealed the shadow of the hair on his chest, she slipped her hand inside, spreading her fingers over firm planes and along the muscled wall of his ribs. Raising one arm, she curled it around his neck, and standing nearly on tiptoe, pressed her bare breasts against him.

With a smothered gasp, he crushed her to him, sinking his fingers into her hair to drag her head back for his bruising kiss. With dizzying suddenness, she felt herself released, then swept high and carried to the bed.

Roland shrugged out of his shirt and waistcoat, dropping them to the floor where they were quickly followed by his boots and trousers. In lithe and bronzed nakedness from weeks under a tropical sun, he joined her under the filmy white canopy of the mosquito netting.

His eyes burned with green fire as he reached for her. She had no thought of resistance. Her skin tingled with the need to be clasped to him, as though the nerves had been severed when they had drawn apart. The intensity of her yearning was frightening, but she pushed the fear to the back of her mind as she moved against him, a silent plea in the lavender twilight of her eyes.

Time ceased to exist. As in the slow and savoring magic of a trance they met, a singing in their blood and the liquid gold warmth of the summer afternoon jeweling their bodies with moisture. Tempered strength and scented softness, they forged the bond of enthralling pleasure, extending the tender agony, forestalling the final ecstasy with racing hearts, unwilling to rush toward the end when problems and personalities would crowd in upon them once more. And then, sensing the edge of his control, Melanie opened her thighs without urging, rising to meet his deep thrusts, her eyes wide and filled with sorrow overlaid with wonder, her mouth tremulous as she stared into his face. Theirs was an ageless surcease, man's

171

gifts from the immortals, more timeless than the rivers, more enduring than the reaching land, as ever renewing as the seasons. In its bursting fulfillment, it asked no commitment, promised nothing more than the moment. For that stretch of infinity, it came perilously close to being enough.

They were awakened at dawn the following morning by a cheerful manservant with a coffee tray and a can of hot water. While Roland shaved, Melanie lay watching for a time, sipping at the last of the coffee. She was aware of a feeling of well-being that made her stretch luxuriously, pushing her hands above her head as she held her empty cup, smiling to herself. The movement made the covers slip, exposing the creamy hills of her breasts. Roland, peering into his shaving mirror, gave a sudden exclamation and clamped his finger to a spot of red in the white lather on his face.

"Did you cut yourself?" she asked.

"A nick," he admitted, "You had better make a move if you mean to get out of that bed today."

"Oh?" she inquired, knitting her fingers together behind her head. "Do I detect the hint of a threat?"

"You do."

"Perhaps I don't intend to get up at all then."

"Whatever you say. It's all the same to me whether we leave today, tomorrow, or not at all."

"Certainly it is!" she jeered. "You know very well you can't wait to get back to New Orleans to see how the governor is faring at his trial and to see to Lopez who, I'm sure you think, can't get along without you."

"You may be right, but an hour, one way or another, will make little difference, so long as the time is spent in a good cause." With a few deft strokes, he completed the removal of his whiskers and, leaning over the basin, began to rinse the soap away.

"And just what would you consider a good cause?"

Picking up a towel, he wiped his face dry. Slinging the towel around his neck, he moved toward the bed, his stride as fluid and powerful as the swamp cat she had so

172

often compared him with in her mind. "Why, keeping my wife happy would qualify, I believe,"

Taking quick alarm at the effect of her bantering words, Melanie pushed up in bed, then hastily scrambled from the mattress on the other side. "I—I am happy enough," she said.

"Are you sure?" he asked, rounding the end of the bed.

"Fair—fairly sure," she said, measuring the distance between the footboard of the bed and the wall with her eyes, wondering if she could slip between them before he caught her.

She could not. His reach was as long as she had feared it would be. She was snatched into his arms.

"Oh, Roland," she breathed on a laughing protest.

"Oh, Melanie," he mimicked, smiling down at her, rocking her gently from side to side in his arms.

His skin had the fresh smell of Castile soap and water, and his square jaw was delightfully smooth as he pressed it to her forehead.

"Only fairly sure?" he whispered.

"Perhaps not quite that much," she murmured.

He heaved a great sigh. "If I wasn't so tired, and the hour so late, I would do something about that. But I had a strenuous night and expect to have an equally strenuous day ahead."

Her relief was not as great as she expected. "Yes," she said and released her breath in an unconscious sigh.

An odd light in his eyes, he released her and turned away to take up his shirt. He stood for a moment with it in his hands, his fingers so tight upon it that wrinkles were crushed into the fabric. Then he gave himself a small shake and began to push his arms into the sleeves. Though the muscles of his jaws were clamped tight and there was a rigid look to the back of his neck, he did not watch Melanie as she crossed with naked grace to the wardrobe.

Pulling the mirrored door open, she stared with disfavor at the gown that hung inside. Of dull black cotton pique, it had the short full sleeves suited to the warm

173

weather, but the scooped bodice, inset with white pique, with a high turned-over collar and a small black ribbon tie, was unbearably demure, bordering on coy. There was nothing to be done, however, except wear it. Knowing their stay at the hotel to be for the night only, Glory had pressed the one gown. Everything else was still packed away in her trunks that resided in one corner of the room. She could call Glory and have something else taken out, but she could think of nothing in her collection of mourning that she would rather wear.

"Tired of black already?" Roland asked.

It was an astute observation, so nearly correct that he gave Melanie the uncomfortable feeling that there was little about her he missed when they were together, that he was beginning to know her too well. "It has been eight months," she answered.

"Has it? It doesn't seem possible."

He was right, it didn't. Eight months since her grandfather had died, eight months, less a week, since they were married, eight months less three weeks since he had gone away. Without answering, Melanie reached into the wardrobe and dragged the gown from its hanger. Throwing it across the bed, she began to search for stockings and underclothing.

They had breakfast in the dining room of the hotel. While they were putting away a repast of ham and eggs, batter-fried French bread, baked apples in cream, and strong hot coffee, their trunks and bags were brought down and carted away to be loaded onto the carriage.

At last they were ready. Taking up her black net reticule hung with jet beads, Melanie preceded Roland from the dining room. She crossed the long, narrow lobby of the hotel and stepped through the imposing front doors. There she halted, looking up and down the street. There was an empty baggage wagon in front of the hotel and a dray trundling past in the early morning quiet, but there was no sign of the carriage, nor of John and the stable hands from Greenlea.

Glory, who had eaten earlier and seen to the packing

while they were at breakfast, rose from a bench beside the doors. She sent Melanie a searching look. Then as her gaze passed to Roland, just stepping from the hotel, an expression remarkably like an accusation came into her dark eyes. Moving with slow dignity, she came toward them.

"Glory," Melanie called, "why haven't they brought the carriage around?"

"They did, Miss Melanie," the maid said, flicking a glance at Roland once more before returning her gaze to her mistress.

"What?"

"They brought it around, all right. Then they left with it."

"Left with it? What are you saying?" Melanie wanted to smile at the portentous look on Glory's face, but something prevented her.

"They had orders to leave for Greenlea, taking the horses back to Natchez in easy stages, but to get away early, before you came down from your room."

It was a moment before Melanie could trust herself to speak. "Who gave those orders?"

"I did," Roland said.

She had known; she just could not make herself believe it. There was no one else who would, or could, have done this thing. And he had left their room before she had finished dressing. He had said he was going to order breakfast. There had obviously been a few more details to be attended to other than food.

"Why?" she demanded, swinging around with anger flashing in her deep blue eyes. "And just who gave you leave to order my servants?"

"I needed no leave from anyone," he answered softly, "since as we agreed once before, what you have is mine. As to why, we have no more need of the carriage."

"What are you saying? How do you think—?" She came to an abrupt halt, her face growing pale.

"Our baggage has been delivered to the landing. By now it should be in our stateroom on the *Delta Princess*

175

leaving for New Orleans in half an hour. I suggest we follow it on board."

"You must be mad!" she cried. "You know how I feel about steamboats. Besides, we have no tickets. How can we possibly have a stateroom?"

"The *Delta Princess* is the swiftest and least taxing means of reaching New Orleans. I made the decision to take her after I left the sheriff's office, when I learned she was due in yesterday afternoon. I bought the tickets then."

His words were nearly drowned out by the blast of a steam whistle at the landing less than two blocks away, below the hill at the end of the street on which the hotel stood. Melanie's nerves jerked, and her voice turned sharper. "If you want to travel on that deathtrap, go right ahead. But you will go alone. I am not about to set foot on it."

"Miss Melanie," Glory protested. "We got no clothes, no way to get home."

Melanie barely glanced at her. "Our things can be taken off the boat. We can stay here in the hotel until we hear of someone going either to New Orleans or back home to Natchez—or until we can send a message to John and the boys to return."

The triumph she felt as she laid these quick plans was shortlived. "No," Roland said. "That you will not. I have no intentions of letting you travel alone again, or of worrying about you taking up with the first presentable stranger who offers you a corner in his carriage."

"As if I would!" Melanie said, looking up and down in bitter contempt. "However, I don't see how you can stop me."

"Don't you?" he queried, a soft note of danger in his voice.

She chose to ignore the warning. "No, I don't. I have said I will not go, and I mean exactly what I say!"

"Miss Melanie—," Glory began.

"Even," Roland asked, "if sticking to your words proves embarrassing? I will grant you it may be a little

176

awkward carrying a woman in a crinoline, but I think it can be done."

"You wouldn't," she said, her eyes searching the lean lines of his face.

He did not answer, but neither did his gaze waver as he stood waiting for her decision.

Her tactics had been wrong, she knew that even without the apprehensive look on Glory's face. She had been foolish to let it come to a point where she must pit her strength against his. The contest would be far too unequal. Swallowing hard, she said, "I can't, Roland. I really can't! Only thinking of it makes me feel ill." As he seemed to hesitate, a gray cast appearing under his skin, she reached out to place her fingers on his arms. "I am not just being stubborn, truly I am not. Some people are afraid of high places or closed-in rooms. It makes them feel sick, panicky. With me, it's steamboats. I just can't bear the thought of setting foot on one."

"Fears can be conquered if you try," he said. "The one thing I never thought you lacked was courage."

"It isn't that easy," she cried, her fingers biting into his arm so tightly her nails bent, curling under.

"How do you know? You haven't tried since you were a child."

"I know," she insisted.

"Show me."

The moment of relenting was gone. He could not be moved by demands or pleas. She could do as he suggested, or she could defy him and take the consequences. That was the choice. Wisdom dictated one course, pride another. But what good was pride without the strength to hold it firm? What good was pride if it brought ridicule and humiliation? She recognized what she had to do, but she would not readily forgive Roland Donavan for forcing the choice upon her.

Releasing his arm, she stepped back. Then, with a lift of her chin, she turned and started down the wooden sidewalk that led to the landing.

Her footsteps slowed as she topped the hill. Before her

177

lay the *Delta Princess* with its white paint gleaming in the sun and its twin black stacks trailing blue smoke against the morning sky. Between the stacks was suspended something that glittered, a painted golden crown. The boat rocked gently on the river's current, while around her men bawled and shouted and a steady stream of steve-dores manhandled the last of a load of cotton bales. Great bales of burlap-wrapped cotton were piled high around the main deck, forming a bulwark that obscured the view of the steerage passengers who would ride there. On the upper deck, ladies strolled on the arms of their men, exchanging greetings in light, friendly voices and ex-claiming prettily as the breeze off the river billowed and fluttered their full skirts. A low thrumming sound came from the vessel's interior, like the warning growl of a watchdog. As Melanie watched, steam erupted in a white stream from somewhere beneath the smokestacks, and the ungainly white craft gave out a blast of its whistle like a scream of pain.

Melanie came to a halt. Roland touched her arm, urg-ing her forward, and she flung him a look of wide-eyed horror. "I can't," she whispered through stiff lips. "I can't."

"You braved the terrors of El Camino Real and went peacefully to sleep in a notorious thieves' den. Are you saying you can't brave a simple steamboat?" His mouth curved in a humoring smile, but there was a watchful look at the back of his eyes.

"I tried to tell you," she said, her fingers clenched on her reticule, her gaze slipping away past his shoulder.

"So you did. I think, however, that we will put it to the test."

Before she could take his meaning, before she could move her fright-stiffened limbs, he bent to place an arm beneath her knees and lifted her into his arms.

"No!" she cried in despair, dropping her reticule, her fingers gripping convulsively at his coat, twisting the material as she tried to lever herself out of his viselike grip. The urge to claw at him, to tear his face to ribbons

178

with her nails, flickered across the tumult in her mind. What restrained her she could not have said.

"It would be a shame if we both landed in the river," he murmured, his face set.

At the words she twisted to see the gangplank with its rope railings before them. She went still, the blood draining from her face as she felt the sway and give of that slanting, board entranceway under them, held in the numbing paralysis of a last effort at self-control. It seemed she could hear the exploding rush of live steam, the roar of fire sweeping through the tinder of the wooden vessel, screams, groans, pleas. Through a haze of remembered terror, she heard Roland speak to an officer in uniform, saw the amused or concerned faces of people turning toward them. Then they were making their way up a curving staircase and along the open companionway. A door giving onto the outside deck was pushed inward. They stepped inside, followed by Glory with an anxious look on her face and Melanie's net reticule in her hand. The door closed behind them, shutting out the noise, the faces, the sight of the shore.

Overhead, the whistle shrieked once more. They began to move, the steamboat shuddering through its flimsy woodwork as the engine fought to make way against the current, pushing the boat out into the river. Stepping to the bed, a fine piece of furniture in no way different from any to be found in a private home, Roland placed Melanie on the coverlet.

Melanie wrenched away from him, her eyes tightly closed, the trembling that possessed her so violent her teeth chattered. Holding her hand across her mouth in sickness, she drew her knees up, huddling within herself, turning her face into the pillows on which she lay.

"My poor baby," Glory moaned, standing in the middle of the floor, helplessly wringing her hands.

"Get a glass of wine, brandy, anything," Roland grated over his shoulder.

As if glad to be doing something, Glory scurried from the room. When the door had closed behind her, Roland sat down on the bed and with firm hands, pulled Melanie to him, forcing her to lie across his thighs. "I'm sorry, Melanie love," he whispered against the top of her head as he cradled her in his arms. "I am sorry."

Melanie heard him as if from a great distance. The shudders that ran over her in waves were painful, making her bones ache and the nerve endings of her body feel raw. In spite of the growing heat of the morning, she was cold, and clammy perspiration stood out on her forehead. It was the heat of his body that reached her, causing her to turn to him now as surely as she had pushed away from him moments before. Gathering her close, as though he recognized her need, he rocked her slowly back and forth.

The door opened. Glory sidled in with a glass balanced carefully on a tray. In it was dark gold liquid.

"Set it down," Roland said quietly, "here, within reach. Then step outside, if you will. I will call for you if I need you."

"Oh, but Mr. Roland—"

"I know, Glory, but there is nothing you can do. When there is something, I won't fail to call."

After a moment Glory's slow footsteps went out. The door closed.

"Drink this," Roland said, and Melanie felt the press of the rim of a glass against her lips. She shook her head, but it did no good, the glass remained, the fumes of strong liquor rising to her nose. "Drink," he insisted.

Taking a deep breath, Melanie allowed a little of the liquor wetting her lips to enter her mouth. Bourbon, potent, aromatic, burned its way down her throat as Roland tilted the glass.

She thought she would strangle or else be ill. Tears of effort rose to her eyes, squeezing from under her lids. Letting her eyes flutter open, she stared up at her husband with weak reproach and dislike. His arms tightened as he felt the force of the tremor that ran over her; still, he had the audacity to smile.

180

"That's better, love," he said. "It must be a good sign if you have the strength to hate me again."

She tried to draw away, but he would not permit it. Instead, he kicked off his boots and, lifting her back onto the pillows, stretched out beside her. Braced on his side, he pulled her to him once more, his hand moving gently over her back.

By slow degrees, her trembling died away. She began to relax. Her fingers uncurled, her lashes flickered and lay still, resting lightly on her cheeks, casting fan-shaped shadows onto their pearl paleness. Her breathing took on the steady rise and fall of sleep. She did not feel the light brush of Roland's lips across her forehead, or his sigh of relief that stirred the fine auburn curls escaping from her high-piled hair.

It was late afternoon when she awoke. Though it was warm in the stateroom, a pleasant current of air wafted over her, moving the bed curtains that had been drawn about her. Turning her head, moving the curtain aside, she saw Roland sitting near the open door, absorbed in a news sheet. Beyond him lay the yellow brown wash of the river and the green jungle of the shoreline slipping past with the speed of their passage.

Her movement brought his head up. He smiled. "It's about time you woke up. You have missed your luncheon, and I was beginning to think you were going to miss your dinner, too. That isn't done on the *Delta Princess*. She's famous for her chef."

Melanie made no answer. She was not hungry, but her throat was dry and raw. There was a pottery water carafe with an inverted cup over it on the table beside the bed. Raising herself on one elbow, she reached for it.

Roland was on his feet at once, taking the carafe, pouring the water, placing the cup in her hand.

"Thank you," she murmured without looking at him. She drank deep, returned the cup, and lay back once more. Through the mattress beneath her she could feel the throb of the steam engine, the rumbling turn of the paddle wheel. She was not frightened now, however, only tired.

Roland did not go back to his chair but stood towering over her, a considering look on his face. "Would you like to get up and go out on the deck? The fresh air will do you good."

"I suppose," she said in tones of quiet distaste, "that you consider yourself an authority on what is good for me now?"

"I think what I did was justified, if that's what you mean," he agreed.

"And do you think the cure will be permanent? It is a little—strenuous to go through every time I want to go on a journey."

"I can't say, but I see no reason why the next time shouldn't be easier, at the very least."

"If that is all you can promise, maybe I had better take advantage of this opportunity," she said disagreeably.

For an answer, he moved to the door and pushed it shut. At her look of inquiry he said simply, "You will want to attend to your appearance."

He was right, though recognition of the fact made Melanie long for nothing so much as a chance to slap his smiling face. "Yes," she agreed. "Will you send for Glory?"

She thought for a long moment he was going to refuse. Then, glancing at her rumpled gown, sadly in need of pressing again before it would be presentable, he gave a nod and let himself out of the room.

They strolled the decks, nodding to the men and women, the children and their nurses that they met. They came across no one from Natchez, for which small mercy Melanie was dutifully grateful. With the fear of yet another morsel of gossip to be added to that already attached to her name relieved, she began to look around her with greater interest.

The *Delta Princess* steamed past countless acres of waving sugar cane, an undulating sea of bluish green. Set among this lush foliage were the homes of the sugar planters, large houses with a French-Spanish influence and a look of the tropics in their spreading galleries on all sides and many wide-flung French windows.

They were not alone on the river. As they drew nearer to New Orleans, crafts of every shape and kind joined them on the great waterway. They passed flatboats with cabins and fenced areas for livestock, as well as barrels and bundles of produce to be sold at market. There were a few keelboats, though not nearly so many as in years past. These large arklike boats, moved up river by the muscles of men working with poles, or pulled by teams of horses or mules on towpaths beside the river, were gradually being driven off the water by the superior speed and economy of the steamboats. Near the settlements and towns, scows, rowboats, pirogues, and rafts crowded the water, though all gave way to the majestic steamboats. Of the latter, there was no small number, especially as they came closer to the end of their river trip. Trailing smoke and red orange sparks, they surged up from the city near the mouth of the river, making time before full night after their five o'clock departure from the New Orleans landing. From their decks, as the *Delta Princess* steamed past, could be heard the tuneful scrape and tinkle of music, the sound of voices raised in song, and laughter. As dusk began to fall, lamps were lighted, turning the tall crafts into palaces of light. Inside their sumptuous rooms, the passengers could be seen moving about, meeting, chatting, parting, taking the evening air before gathering for dinner. They seemed unreal, those people, dream figures, or the spirits of those who had died in the burned-out skeletons and rotting hulks of unlucky steamboats they passed grounded on sandbars or half-hidden along the banks beneath the overhanging limbs of trees. Exposed by the low water of late summer, they were also not few in number, these wrecks.

They were still at the dinner table in the long main cabin when they rounded a bend in the river and the lights of New Orleans came swimming toward them through the darkness. The town, curving with the crescent-shaped turn of the river, seemed to sparkle with life, though here and there were unlighted areas of mysterious blackness.

The landing for steamboats was along the river levee where the principal streets of the older section of the city, known as the *Vieux Carré*, met the river. There were three vessels already tied up for the night alongside the high, tree-planted bank of earth that held back the river. It took careful maneuvering by the pilot on the Texas deck to bring their packet to dock without letting the river's current push it into collision with the other boats.

Melanie watched the operation from the windows of the main cabin for as long as she could bear it. Then the tension, the rumble of conversation up and down the laden table, roaring under the ornate vaulted ceiling, the heat and suffocating smells of food and hot oil from the crystal and brass chandeliers overhead became too much. Pushing back her chair, she murmured an excuse and fled.

Out on the deck, she was greeted by the cool night air. Upon it came a rich medley of scents she could not recognize, overlaid by the muskiness of open drains that was the smell of the south. A snatch of piano music came on the breeze, along with the clatter of the glassy leaves of the orange trees on the levee and the far off sound of a church bell. Through the dimness she could make out the three sharp spires of St. Louis Cathedral, the up-lifted fronds of palm trees, and the scalloped edges of clay-tiled roofs.

The pilot, satisfied with their berth, gave the order to cut the engines. The steamboat shuddered and went silent. Men jumped from the deck to secure the mooring lines at bow and stern. The *Delta Princess* sat rocking gently, safely, at the port of New Orleans.

Footsteps on the planking of the deck signaled Roland's approach from the direction of the main cabin. He stopped close beside her, his arm brushing hers as he leaned against the railing. His voice low, he asked, "Are you all right?"

"Yes," she replied. "I am fine—now."

184

Chapter 10

THE HOUSE Roland had taken for their use was on Rampart Street on the outer edge of the French Quarter. Fronting directly on the street, it was a simple cottage over a raised brick basement. The hipped roof jutted out over a narrow gallery supported by slender, turned columns. The entrance stairs angled up from the banquette, or sidewalk, giving onto the gallery. Built with a facade of salmon pink stucco, it was fitted with green jalousied blinds on either side of the double entrance doors. The same type blinds flanked the French windows that lined the gallery.

Leaving their hackney carriage standing in the street, Melanie and Roland climbed the stairs, with Glory trailing behind them. Roland took a key from his pocket and let them into the house. Cursing softly in the gathering darkness, he found a lamp and set it aglow. As light filled the parlor, he turned to Melanie, watching her face.

Aware of his close scrutiny, though she could not understand the reason for it, Melanie looked around her. The room was well proportioned, done in shades of deep rose and wheat gold. It somehow managed to combine comfort with a surprising sense of luxury. The rug beneath their feet was soft, cushioned on mats of woven rattan. The chandelier tinkling overhead in the draft from the open door was of crystal with exquisitely etched hurricane globes. A satin-covered chaise with a scrolled back stood before one pair of French windows, and a white

Carrara marble fireplace mantel held an onyx and ormolu clock set which featured as end pieces, naked nymphs pursued by satyrs. Dragging her gaze from these odd figures, Melanie looked at her husband.

"It's a—lovely place," she said, "but are you certain you have the right address. It looks as if the owners just stepped out."

"They did, in a manner of speaking. The house belongs to a young Creole in my regiment. I understand it was a gift from his father on his twenty-first birthday. Since he preferred to join Lopez instead of keeping a household of his own, he let me have the use of it. From the appearance of things, I would say he must have had his people come in and make it ready for us."

"How kind of him, and thoughtful."

"Yes," he agreed. Swinging abruptly away, he made a swift inspection of the other rooms, then returned to the parlor. "Everything seems to be in order. If you and Glory would like to look around, I will see to the unloading of your trunks."

There was no hallway in the house. Each of the six rooms, the parlor, sitting room, dining room, butler's pantry, and two bedchambers, were interconnecting, each opening by way of the tall French windows out onto either the front gallery or the back gallery. These other rooms were done in much the same style as the first. Rich detailing was much in evidence. The butler's pantry gleamed with silver and the apricot sheen of Sevres china. In the sitting room was a settee of floral brocade outlined in gold thread. Everywhere the drapes, voluminous and folding onto the floor in the style used by many to show contempt for the exorbitant cost of the material, were draped with fringe and tassels, as were the royal purple hangings and the pale green mosquito netting about the full tester bed in the large bedchamber. The effect was one of opulence, a Sybaritic enjoyment of texture, color, and the play of light.

Glory lifted an eyebrow, her lips pursed, as she surveyed a statue of a perfectly formed, unclothed Cupid. "Miss Melanie," she began.

"Yes, I know," Melanie answered. "I suppose it must suit Creole tastes. I expect we will get used to it, given time."

In the rear of the house was a small, enclosed court-yard with a fountain and a brick-curbed cistern. The servants' quarters, kitchen, and laundry formed the back wall of this retreat. By the time Melanie and Glory returned from inspecting these amenities, the first of the trunks had been set down in the bedchambers. Removing clean sheets from its depths, they set about making up the bed. There was no use postponing the inevitable. The hour was growing late. Already, the houses up and down the street that were visible from the windows were dark. Parceling out bed linens to her maid, Melanie insisted they would wait until morning to unpack the growing collection of trunks. Bidding Glory a firm good-night, Melanie, in the process of smothering a yawn, pretended she did not see the elderly woman's knowing smile.

When the door had closed behind Glory, Melanie wandered about the bedchamber. The great wardrobe that took up the major portion of one wall stood empty, though in its depths there seemed to linger a trace of sweet verbena scent. The drawers of the dressing table were lined with scallop-edged paper, and in the back of one she found a whalebone corset stay. Here in this room there was a daybed as well as the high tester bed. Covered with lilac silk, it had high curving ends in the Empire style, and a round tube-shaped pillow on each end. Near the French windows which opened onto the back gallery and the quiet of the courtyard stood a marble pedestal. Upon this base was a statuette of a man and a woman clasped in a close embrace, an instant of ecstasy caught in glowing marble.

The opening of the door behind her brought Melanie around. Roland stepped into the room, carrying a cut glass decanter in one hand and a pair of balloon glasses in the other. He sent a swift glance about the room, then

187

with a quizzical look in his green eyes said, "You found the servants' quarters across the way?"

"Yes, I—hope you don't mind the trunks," she said, waving at the hide and leather bound boxes still in the middle of the floor. "I thought since it's so late, morning would do just as well for unpacking."

"I don't mind at all, as long as you have what you need." Stepping to the dressing table, he set down the glasses and began to work the stopper from the decanter in his hand.

"I am fine," Melanie answered. "But what of you?"

"Me?"

"There's nothing in the wardrobe, nothing of yours I mean."

He waved at the pair of saddle bags sitting on the floor beside one of the trunks. "The essentials are in there. Since I have been staying at the barracks set up for Lopez's men near the levee, the rest of my belongings are still there. I'll see to transferring them sometime tomorrow, after I report to the general. You needn't worry. You are not going to have to stay here alone."

He kept his eyes on what he was doing as he measured an inch of liquor into each of the glasses. Melanie, hearing the shading of irony in his tone, watching the play of lamplight over the masklike planes of his bronze face, was reminded abruptly of her purpose in coming to New Orleans. Taking a deep breath, she said, "Good. I am glad."

Roland slanted her a quick glance, then picking up the glasses, walked slowly toward her. "Does that mean," he asked, handing her one of the drinks, "that I am forgiven for this morning?"

She could not sustain his steady regard. In confusion she lowered her gaze to the liquid in the glass she held. "What is this?"

"It isn't bourbon, if that's what you are thinking. It's brandy, fresh from the stock in the butler's pantry. I thought it might be called for as a sedative. Apparently, I was wrong."

Melanie forced herself to smile. "Not entirely. Bourbon

188

and brandy in one day. I suppose you realize that I have never had anything stronger than a glass of wine before today?"

"You being a well brought up young lady, I suspected it."

"I'm not certain I can be responsible for what I do if I go on like this."

"I will take the responsibility," he said, a lower note in his quiet voice, "especially if it leads to a truthful answer to my first question."

Without conscious thought, Melanie raised her glass and drank. The liquor was so fiery it cut off her breath and brought tears to her eyes. With a tremendous effort of self-control she swallowed without coughing, though the deep gasp for air she took was a sign of her distress. As the fumes of the brandy rose to her head, she felt the rise of irrepressible humor. Lifting wet, laughing eyes to her husband, she said, "Steamboats and strong drink. What else must I brave to be with you?"

His gaze was watchful as he put the rim of his glass to his lips and tilted it, draining the last drop. Setting it down on the pedestal behind her, he took her glass from her fingers and placed it beside his. "This," he whispered and, taking her in his arms, set his mouth, burning with brandy, to hers.

He did not release her for a long time, and then only to push shut the French windows. He undressed her with slow care, the look on his face somber, absorbed. It was almost as though he were performing a ritual, an act of worship rehearsed in his mind a thousand times. He did not douse the light. The high white stretch of the bed as he placed her upon it and stood staring down at her pink and ivory nakedness had the feel of some pagan altar. Divesting himself of his clothing, joining her upon it, he was both neophyte and high priest. Meeting his strange green gaze, Melanie felt an instant of fear. The lamplight danced over her, shining with a tiny golden flame in the lavender blue of her eyes, gilding the curves of her body, leaving the hollows in secret shadow. As he stretched out

189

his hand to touch her, she knew the fatalistic acceptance that comes to those about to be sacrificed. It made no difference that she had arranged the thing herself, rushing toward it from the moment she left Natchez, or even longer, from the night she had climbed the steps at the back of the River Rest. He was taking from her with little thought of giving in return. As his body covered hers, she felt herself receding, becoming lost in him, and then as she took the swift, inward plunging of his ardor, a thought flashed across her mind. She had not given him her forgiveness. That much integrity, at least, she had retained. And though she allowed him the free use of her body, though she gave him her smiles, there was a portion of herself he could not touch, a portion no man could know until she so willed.

They lay side by side, the heat of their bodies in that closed room too intense to allow them to touch with comfort. The minutes slid past; their breathing slowed. Melanie, with her eyes closed, could not tell if there was actually a sense of estrangement growing between them, or if it was merely the result of her own feeling of withdrawal. To test it, she reached out and placed her hand on his. Immediately, he turned his palm upward, clasping her fingers. She gave a small sigh. After a moment, she spoke. "You know, Roland Donavan, despite the fact that you insist on being assured of your welcome, I have yet to hear you say you are glad I came."

"I thought I had shown you that well enough."

"Possibly," she admitted, "but it doesn't hurt to say the words. When I think of all those months of silence, of all the other men with Lopez sending after their wives and sweethearts—"

"All right," he said, rolling to his elbow so he could look down upon her face with its rose flush across the cheekbones, "I would rather you hadn't come during the cholera and yellow fever season, but as long as you are here, I'm glad, very glad." With his thumb he caressed the top of her hand with a slow, gentle movement.

"There are cholera and yellow fever in the city?"

"Always, this time of year, though it's not epidemic so far."

"I thought not, or we would have heard of it in Natchez," she said. "The town would have been full of refugees. No, I'm not at all sure I believe a word you say. It wouldn't surprise me to learn you were happy to have your wife safely in residence upriver. It left you free to dally as much as you liked with your actress friend."

"Actress?" His voice was steady enough, but the movement of his caressing thumb stopped abruptly, and the pressure on her fingers increased.

What had possessed her to bring up the subject, she did not know. It had not been a conscious decision. Having broached it, she had no choice but to continue. "Miss Dubois, I believe she is called. Chloe Clements was kind enough to tell me that you had been a regular patron at the theater where she was appearing last spring."

"Yes, a charming woman and an excellent actress. I did see her several times. She gave a benefit performance for the expedition, you know."

"No, I didn't," Melanie admitted.

"She did. It was quite a success; earned a large sum of money. I believe she means to do the same thing again, when the fall season begins."

"How—kind of her," was all that Melanie found to say.

"Isn't it? But what interests me is the timing of all this," Roland said in a reflective tone of voice. "Did Chloe's tidbit of information have anything to do with your sudden decision to join me?"

His use of the first name of Dom's sister should not have been surprising. After all, if he and Dom had been friends, he must have known Chloe also. In her consideration of this possibility, she very nearly missed the implication of what he was saying. Turning her head to stare at him, she asked, "Are you suggesting I was jealous?"

"The thought occurred to me."

"Well, you can dismiss it."

191

"Are you certain?" he asked. "It was such an intriguing idea."

"I don't see why," she said, her gaze flicking away, resting for an instant on the statuette beside the French doors, before slipping past it to the glow of the lamp on the dressing table. "I came to New Orleans because—"

"Yes? Because?"

"Because I was tired of moping at Greenlea, and because even without the company of your actress friend, it sounded as if you were having too much fun being a filibuster to want to come back to Natchez."

"Fun?" he queried, as if he had never heard of the word. "We lost nearly two hundred men in Cuba, and half that number were wounded."

"I didn't mean the fighting," Melanie said, lowering her lashes. "I know—that is, I wondered what it was like."

She thought for a moment he was not going to speak; then he let his breath out in a soft sigh. "It was an unlucky, ill-managed business from start to finish. As it turned out, the man who was supposed to guide us into Cárdenas harbor had only paddled around it in a rowboat. He had no idea of the draft a steamer the size of the *Creole* required, no knowledge of the shoals in the harbor, or the effect on them of the tides. We went aground. Most of the men who died were picked off in the water as they tried to reach shore. Not a few of the wounded drowned because no one could see to save the disabled in the darkness and confusion. There was never enough of us to begin with; after that, it was hopeless. Oh, we made a fine showing, took the railroad station and stormed the barracks, overwhelming victories, both, but there was no way we could hold the town against Spanish reinforcements from Havana. Back we went through the water to the *Creole*. We finally got her afloat. Lopez was certain we could join the Cuban insurgents on the other side of the island, but that was before the *Pizarro* hove into sight. If you have never been on a small, crowded ship under a hot summer sun, with the wounded moaning, their injuries festering in the heat, and the long guns of a

Spanish warship bearing down on you, then it's possible you might think being a filibuster could be fun."

Melanie's lips tightened. "But you are still with General Lopez; still a lieutenant colonel in his army?"

"I signed on for the Cuban campaign. I'll see it through to the end."

"Why? Why did you sign on, I mean. I never understood. Oh, I know what you said, but there must have been other things you could have done without resorting to war."

"Such as?" he inquired.

"I don't know," she said, disturbed by the irony in his tone. "You might have bought land and worked it, or—or made property investments; anything except returning to a profession as a soldier, something you so obviously dislike."

"Do you really want to know why?" he asked, reaching out to touch his finger to the frown between her brows, trailing it along the bridge of her small, straight nose, across her lips and chin and down the tender curve of her neck to the valley between her breasts.

"I asked you, didn't I?" she said, watching his progress with trepidation.

"So you did. To begin with, Jeremy was there dangling the prospect of a Cuban sugar plantation under my nose. Then there was one other reason that made the proposition quite irresistible; I had no money." His trailing finger had begun to circle the globe of the breast nearest him, spiraling higher with each turn.

"What?" she asked.

"I had no money," he repeated.

"But you must have! You paid my grandfather's debt to the governor and arranged for the repairs to Greenlea. Then there were my allowances."

He sighed. "Grand gestures, weren't they? They account for the last of my take from California."

Melanie sat up in bed, dislodging his finger just as he reached the crest of the hill of her breast. "Everyone said

193

you made your fortune in California; that was why you came back, because you were rich."

He looked ruefully from his fingertip to the rose red nipple just out of his reach. "Did you ever hear of anyone being rich enough, or leaving gold uncovered because of it? I had a small claim, but the vein ran out. I came back because I had heard my father was not well. I thought he might need help." Roland stopped, then with a shrug, went on. "Regardless, if you thought you married a wealthy man, I am afraid I must disappoint you."

"You—spent it all on Greenlea, and me?"

"Other than a small investment in the expedition, I am afraid so."

"But why?"

"It seemed the thing to do, at the time."

"Because of my grandfather?" she asked before she could stop herself.

His eyes met hers, a shadow in their green depths. "Partially, though not in the way you mean. There was also the matter of my responsibility as your husband."

"You—you told me to spend it on Greenlea, for up-keep. That was insane when you might have used it for living expenses these last months."

"My expenses have been paid."

Once he had advised her to wait at Greenlea, antici-pating the collection of his estate that would come to her if he were killed. He must have known even then there would be nothing to collect, just as he had known she would have nothing from her grandfather. What kind of macabre humor must this man she had married have for him to say such a thing? "You don't really think I mar-ried you for your money, do you? There were much more pressing reasons at the time."

It was his turn to look away. "Yes, I know," he an-swered. "Forget I said it. In fact, forget I mentioned money at all. We are not quite paupers, and I may yet win that sugar plantation. Just now there is another more important matter to be decided."

"Is there?" Melanie asked, made suddenly wary by

194

something in his voice and by the way he leaned to place his hand on her knee.

His fingers warm on the sensitive inner bend of her knee, he said, "I need to know whether you prefer to sleep now, or in the morning."

Melanie's mind was in turmoil. She hardly knew what to think or how she felt. With her bottom lip caught between her teeth, she eyed the sleek lines of his body stretched out before her, the rippling muscles of his shoulder as he kneaded her thigh, the powerful, sculptured strength of his long legs, the sharp demarcation line where his trousers kept the sun from his body. Though she might not know what to think, she was not unaffected either by his closeness, his touch, or the promise his words seemed to hold. For some peculiar reason, perhaps because they had come close to honesty with each other, she was more receptive now to the thought of being in his arms than she had been minutes before.

Taking a deep breath, she said, "I don't believe I am at all sleepy, now."

Roland slid from the bed in the murky, half-light of dawn. Melanie knew when he left her side, knew when he gathered up his clothing and padded from the room, opening and closing the door soundlessly. Hearing the splash of water in the courtyard a few minutes later, she threw back the sheet and went to the French windows to look. Roland was in the courtyard, washing himself under the pump above the cistern. He had donned his trousers and boots, but his shirt lay to one side. His dark hair, curling over his forehead and low on his neck, dripped water. His shoulders and torso gleamed with wet, giving him the look of newly molded bronze—except for a pale pink blotch high on the muscle of his right arm, the scar made by her grandfather's bullet. He had no towel with him. He flicked the water from himself in bright silver droplets and raked his hair back with his fingers. Taking up his shirt, he shrugged into it, doing up the buttons as he walked back to the house. He disappeared from sight beneath the overhang of the back gallery. There must have been a passageway leading through the raised basement onto the street. Roland did not return to the upper rooms of the house, nor did Melanie see him for the rest of the day.

Melanie returned to the purple-silk-draped bed for a time, but she was too restless to remain there. By the time the hot, subtropical sun struck the front of the house, she was up and dressed. Going in search of a cup of coffee, she found Glory in the kitchen on the other side of the court. The maid had started a fire in the fireplace, but that was as far as her preparations for breakfast had progressed.

Glory swung ponderously around as Melanie entered. "Miss Melanie, I found a keg of flour, a loaf of sugar harder than a rock, a peck of weevily corn meal, and a handful of dried-up raisins, but that's all there is in this here kitchen. I just don't know what we're going to give Mr. Roland for his breakfast."

"We won't have to worry about that. He's already gone."

"Without a bite to eat?"

"I suppose he will breakfast with his men. They must have some sort of arrangement for feeding so many."

Glory nodded. "You've still got to have something though, honey, and there will be supper to think about. Somehow or other, we got to find something to cook in this kitchen."

Melanie still had a goodly sum of money paid to her as an allowance in the last months. "You are right," she said. "We will go the the French Market."

The French Market was an institution visited by nearly every family in the French Quarter daily. Located near the Mississippi River levee, it was housed in long pavilions with fat masonry columns and slate roofs. Beneath this sturdy protection was sold almost everything that could be eaten. In the vegetable section at this time of year were long, plaited strings of onion, garlic, and peppers, enticingly displayed with large selections of yams,

196

greens, squash, and giant orange pumpkins. Further along, there were pears, freshly harvested pecans, persimmons, pomegranates, and bananas and other tropical fruits just off the ships whose masts even now towered behind the dirt-banked levee. From these ships had also come the bright birds with blue, yellow, green, and red plumage and raucous, unfamiliar calls, boxes of spices and tea, coffee and vanilla beans, and olive oil in clay jars shaped like snails. Live ducks and geese and turkeys were marketed along with the carcasses of beef, pork, and lamb. And then came the seafood: pompano, red snapper, oysters and shrimp, all spread on blocks of ice packed in sawdust. Ice that was fast melting in the growing heat of the day; ice that had been cut from frozen ponds and lakes in the northern states, stored, and then brought with all speed by steamboat down the river. Equally as fascinating as the enormous variety of food were the varied people attending the market. Melanie, with Glory behind her carrying a basket on her arm, moved in and out among expansive Creole gentlemen seeking squabs for their dinners, wizened old ladies in black lace covered to their eyes against the sun's rays, flamboyant quadroons in silks and satins with jeweled *tignons*, or turbans, wrapped about their heads, and here and there, an Indian woman in an odd costume of beaded leather combined with cotton cloth selling tightly woven baskets in earthen colors that were works of art.

Laden with their purchases, Melanie and Glory made their way back through the narrow streets to their new home. They were protected for most of the way by the overhanging balconies ornamented with graceful wrought iron. The protection from the sun was welcome, for as the day advanced the humid heat increased beyond belief. Few seemed to mind, however. The streets were busy with people. A priest in his flowing black cassock passed them, as did a nursemaid with her pale, large-eyed charges in tow. Creole gentlemen lifted their hats and stepped aside as she passed. Bonneted young girls with their mothers stared at the shining arrangement of Mel-

197

anie's uncovered hair, not even protected by a sunshade, since she had let it down to carry the bundles Glory could not manage. That in itself was an oddity, for most ladies never burdened themselves with anything heavier than a reticule and sunshade, or possibly, a sachet bottle. Also on the streets were sailors and soldiers, many of the latter in the red and blue uniforms of the Lopez expedition.

They had reached the house on Rampart and were ascending the stairs when from across the street a young Creole gentlemen in canary breeches and a bottle green tailcoat stopped and began to stare. Tucking the beribboned cane he carried under his arm, he whipped off his high, wide-crowned hat and held it over his heart as he trod across the cobbled thoroughfare toward them.

Melanie glanced at him, wondering at his rudeness in staring so unabashedly. At that moment he made her a sweeping bow.

"Ma belle!" he shouted up to her. "Never have I seen such a one as you. Your glorious hair, touched with fire, the purity of your complexion are beyond belief. Tell me what man has the good fortune to call you his own?"

Melanie had stopped instinctively as he spoke. Now, realizing his purpose, she turned her head sharply and continued on into the house. She had heard that men in New Orleans, like their European counterparts, did not stand on ceremony when they saw a woman they considered attractive, but this was too much, shouting at her from the street, making his overtures for all to see. It was especially amazing when he must have guessed that she was married. His words confirmed that much.

Once inside the house, she peeked through the blinds. The man had replaced his hat and was moving on down the street, but more than once he stopped to look back. The expression on his face was so intense she could not help wondering if he were memorizing where she lived.

The arrival of Roland's baggage a short time later swept the encounter from Melanie's mind, turning her thoughts toward the unpacking still to be done. She and Glory attacked the problem with concerted effort. By

198

mid-afternoon, not only had everything been put away and the trunks consigned to the extra bedchamber, but Glory had laundered every stitch of soiled clothing and hung it out to dry in the sun-filled back court. While the maid was busy with that task, Melanie had gone through the house dusting, sweeping away the trash they had tracked in on the rugs, putting away a figurine here, a statuette there. She even removed a painting or two that seemed, at least to her eye trained to English hunting prints, family portraits, and soft Turner landscapes, to be in questionable taste.

As evening began to fall and the smell of fresh baked bread, roasting meat, and seafood gumbo drifted from the direction of the kitchen, Melanie went out to rescue Glory's wash before the evening dew could dampen it again. Retrieving Roland's shirts from the line, she noticed buttons missing on one or two, a long rent in one sleeve, and a two-cornered tear in another. Depositing the other clothing in the laundry, she took his shirts with her as she returned to the house. Lighting a lamp in the parlor to ward off the encroaching blue-gray shadows of late evening, bringing out her sewing basket, she sat down to make the small repairs to her husband's linen, passing the time until he returned and dinner could be served.

Sewing was one of the few things Melanie had been taught by her grandmother before she died, setting the different types of stitches into a sampler with her name, age, and date of completion embroidered in one corner. Since then she had passed many a winter evening with her needle and thread. The steady in and out, the slow building of a design or a garment, or making whole something torn or split had a soothing effect upon her. It was easy for her to become so absorbed in what she was doing that she scarcely noticed what was happening around her.

The night drew in and blackness filled the unlighted street before the house. A moth floated around her, drawn to her lamp through the door that stood open to the cool evening air. When it lit upon her hand, she blew upon it, so that it flew away again. Though she knew moths laid eggs among clothing and that the eggs hatched into worms that could riddle the woolens with holes, she could not bear to kill the fragile, fluttering things.

The sound of an indrawn breath from the doorway drew her attention. A tall figure in a uniform of blue and red stood there. It was an instant before she recognized Roland in that strange garb, an instant more before she could make herself smile. How long he had been standing there she did not know, though she thought he could not have just arrived. The look in his eyes was intent, brooding, as his gaze moved from her face to the shirt she held in her hands. She had the uncomfortable feeling that she had done something wrong, that she had been caught prying into his belongings, meddling with things that did not concern her.

The impression lasted no more than a moment; then it was gone. With a smile tugging at his mouth, Roland lounged toward her and, leaning, tilted her lips for his kiss. "You are a marvel," he said. "Is that dinner I smell? I hope so, because I am starving."

The days which followed were little different from the first. Melanie spent them marketing, cleaning, stitching a little, and at times, helping Glory with the evening meal. With only the three of them to feed, she found that the money she had with her went quite a long way, so long as she was careful with her purchases and kept the menus simple but hearty.

She could not tell that she progressed with her effort to make Roland fall in love with her. His duties kept him away from her so much that there had been little opportunity. She had smiled at him across the dinner table, discovered his favorite foods, and made a point of seeing that they were served often. Afterward, when they had retired to their bedchamber, she had made herself accommodating. In return there had been light compliments and a certain friendliness from Roland, and in the soft, velvet warmth of the night, he turned to her, accepting her generosity as his due, slaking his passion again and again. But though he whispered tender endearments and held her, stroking the tumbled glory of her hair, she was never able to feel that his craving for her was beyond his control, or that he would be devastated if she went out of his life forever.

More than once in the passing days she heard the sound of crying from the house directly across the street. The only persons who went in and out there were a servant woman and a man, a Creole gentleman from the look of him, though not a young man. From her own front gallery Melanie had also caught a glimpse once or twice of a woman with a small child still in long gowns at a window or doorway. She supposed it was the youngster she heard, though the crying did not always sound childlike.

On this particular evening, Roland was later than usual. It was the dinner hour. Gradually the street outside the house emptied, and the peace of eventide descended. Melanie set her sewing aside and strolled from the parlor onto the gallery. On one end a moonflower vine grew up from the ground, its luxuriant green tendrils twisting around the corner column. Its great pure white flowers were opening in the cool of approaching night, waving gently in the breeze blowing over the city from Lake Pontchartrain. Though the purple dusk lay in the streets of the city, the sky still held the reflected light of the setting sun. In the west the horizon was streaked with mauve, pink, and gold. Leaning her head against the corner column, Melanie watched a flight of pigeons wheel across the sky, the afterglow staining the undersides of their wings with pink.

She had just reached out to break off one of the fragrant moonflowers when a scream tore across the quiet. This was no child's wail, but a woman's lung-bursting cry of terror. Before Melanie could move, the main doors on the top floor of the house across the street were thrown open and a woman with her loose hair streaming behind her ran shrieking out onto the gallery. At the far end she came up against the railing and turned, shrinking like an animal at bay. From inside the house a man appeared in his shirt sleeves. He stalked the woman with slow menace in every line of his paunchy, but powerful body; menace, and something more, the knowledge that the woman cowering before him neither could, nor would, run any further. As he closed in upon her, he reached out and caught her forearm, jerking her toward him. Drawing his hand back, he slapped her full in the face, then gave her the back of his hand. The woman caught her breath in a gasping sob. She tried to speak, but before the words could pass her lips, he struck her again, and yet again.

The cracking blows went on and on, echoing across the street with the pleas of the woman. In the doorway behind them, the child toddled from the darkened house, crying as it made its unsteady way toward its mother. At its appearance under the feet of the man, shifting and staggering as he beat the woman, Melanie could stand it no longer.

"You!" she shouted as she started toward the stairs. "Stop that at once!"

She nearly stumbled over her skirts in her haste to get down to the street. She crossed the muddy thoroughfare without so much as a glance in either direction. With her crinoline dipping and swaying around her, she came to a halt below the gallery of the house.

The man, as if amazed at her temerity, had halted his blows and swung to watch Melanie advance. Eyes blazing, Melanie shouted up at him, "I saw what you were doing to your poor wife, you beast. You should be horsewhipped, and if I had my way, that is exactly what would happen."

Throwing his head back, the man let out a roar of laughter. "Wife!" he cried. "You are a fool! You had best go back into your house and shut your door before your man returns and gives you the same thing I am giving this slut."

"My man, as you call him, has never touched me in anger. He is a gentleman, which is more than can be said of you!"

"This is true?" the man inquired with lazy insolence, though the veins in his forehead seemed to swell. "Then consider yourself lucky, for if you were mine, I would strip you and beat you until you screamed for mercy. I would tie you down and with my whip, make stripes across the white skin of your buttocks until you learned respect for the man who was your master. Oh, yes, I have seen you come and go. I know your beauty and your pale skin more nearly white than any I have seen. Where you came from, I do not know, but there are many other things I would like to do to you, when I put my whip aside."

Shock held Melanie speechless. Hard upon it came rage such as she had never felt in her life. What she might have said or done then, she could not tell, for the woman took a step toward the railing, gazing down at Melanie with one hand outstretched. "Don't, don't try him further. You cannot help me. No one can. Please go. Please, for you are only making things worse."

The woman's hair floated about her shoulders in a dark cloud of fine, tight curls. Her skin was creamy, with a yellow undertone; her eyes were large and black and liquid. It was an instant before Melanie, staring into her features, realized the truth. She was a quadroon, a woman three-quarters white, one-quarter Negro, the child of a mulatto woman and a white man, and the man who still held her in his cruel grasp thought Melanie was the same.

Tight-lipped, her blue eyes stormy, Melanie said, "All right. I will go. But this is not the end of it. I am the wife of Lieutenant Colonel Roland Donavan and a respectable woman, and I promise you this will not be the last you hear from me."

Nor was it. When Roland finally reached the house, Melanie was still so upset she could not sit still as she told him what had happened. Striding down the room, she came back again, stopping in front of him in a whirl of skirts.

"That man spoke to me in terms worse than I would

use to a slave. He thought I was a quadroon, Roland! Your quadroon mistress!"

"I understand that well enough. What I don't understand is what ever possessed you to interfere in someone else's quarrel."

"Quarrel? It was no quarrel, it was a beating. That woman just stood there and let him hit her without raising a hand to defend herself, and that beast knew she would not, that she didn't dare. All the time that baby was underfoot, and his father didn't give a tinker's dam if he trampled him."

"I still don't know what you thought you could do."

"Neither do I, but I couldn't just stand by and watch. But as bad as that is, it's far from the worst. That man assumed I was a quadroon for no reason that I could see, except that I live across the street. What kind of neighborhood is this, Roland? What kind of a house have you brought me to?"

He hesitated no more than a moment. "Exactly the kind you think it is," he answered.

She had known; she just could not make herself believe it. The fiery quadroons had been the traditional mistresses of Creole gentlemen, young and old, for nearly a century. They were usually, though not always, Free Women of Color, whose beauty and birth left them little choice except to become the kept woman of some man. Presented at the famous quadroon balls, sometimes by themselves, most often by their mothers who had come from the same life themselves, their security, and the security of any children they might have, was assured by the payment of what amounted to a dowry. Now and then the woman was the offspring of a white master and a slave, in which case, she was purchased directly from her owner who might also be her father. Often the alliances so contracted were for life and included large families of children, while the man might also have another legitimate family. The most common practice, however, was for a young man to set up his quadroon household for a year or two, then dissolve the relationship upon his marriage. The ladies of

Natchez had always congratulated themselves that the practice had never taken hold in that upright, English community the way it had in French-Spanish New Orleans.

That she could be mistaken for such a woman was incredible to Melanie, though casting her mind back, she realized tonight was not the first time. There had been that other young man who had accosted her from the street. The reason for his familiarity was now only too clear.

Lifting troubled blue eyes to her husband, she asked, "Why? Why did you bring me here?"

"Every hotel and rooming house in the city is crowded with soldiers and their families, and with the friends and neighbors of Governor Quitman. This house may not be ideal, but it is clean and comfortable and fairly convenient. I'm sorry, Melanie, there was just no other place for you to stay. If there had been a little more time, if I had had a bit more notice that you were coming, I might have done better. As it was, I felt lucky to find a place of any kind for you."

"I see." The tightness in her chest eased a fraction. It had been hurtful to think that Roland had cared so little for her feelings that he had placed her in this position for no good reason.

"I am sorry that you were insulted," Roland went on, "but I never dreamed you would have any contact with the other people in these houses. There seemed no reason for you to have anything to do with them."

Melanie glanced at the nymphs and satyrs upon the mantelpiece, then looked away again. The reason for certain furnishings in the house were now obvious. "Unfortunately, the contact has been made. As long as I am living here, I cannot bear the thought of that vicious man across the street mistreating that poor woman, whoever or whatever she may be. Something must be done about it."

"I agree."

Melanie looked at him with surprise in her eyes. She had not expected him to be so reasonable. "What did you say?"

"I said, I agree, though not for the sake of the quadroon so much as for yours."

"For my sake? I don't understand you."

"No man threatens my wife, regardless of the reason. As long as there is a misunderstanding, or a possibility that you may become involved again the next time you hear a scream, I will not be able to do what I must for thinking of you here alone.".

"He wouldn't dare touch me."

"Possibly, though if you interfere again in what he considers to be his right to treat his woman as he wishes, he may not remember your respectability in time."

"There is always my gun."

"Your pistol? Which you didn't happen to have with you tonight? As far as I have been able to see, on the two separate occasions when you used it, it made little impression."

That was too true to be denied. "What do you propose to do then?"

"This sort of thing, like public drunkenness and the severe mistreatment of slaves, is frowned upon by the Creoles. They have ways of dealing with it. If the man cares at all for his standing in the community, he will listen to reason. If not, there are other measures."

Other measures. The Creoles of New Orleans were well known for being quick to resort to the field of honor. "Not—not a duel? Not over a matter like this?"

"I can think of few things more worthy," he said shortly.

That was his last word on the subject. Though Melanie tried to persuade him to tell her exactly what he had in mind, he could not be drawn. Hearing a carriage stop in the street outside, the next evening, Melanie moved to the parlor window in time to see a delegation of men with the unmistakable stamp of men of substance, men also of French and Spanish heritage, get down and approach the house next door. Their stay was not a long one, lasting only a bare half hour. Whatever was said, it appeared to be effective. In the days that followed, no more screams issued forth from that shadowy house across the street. And yet, Melanie could not be easy. Often when she passed in and out with Glory on her way to the market or for a stroll about the streets in the direction of the Place d'Armes to take the air, she felt herself watched. So strong was this impression that she ceased to leave any of the French windows open along the front of the house unless the jalousied blinds were in place over them. If she felt the need to view the sunset or the twilight sky, she did so from the safe seclusion of the back gallery and the courtyard.

Chapter 11

By slow degrees the days grew cooler. The dark green foliage of palms and palmettos in the courtyard began to look tired and dejected, and the wide-leaved bananas torn and fretted by the wind. In one corner, the leaves on the fig bushes began to yellow and fall. Clouds boiled up from the southeast, and the autumn rains, cooling, drenching, and seemingly endless, came down.

The prediction made by Governor Quitman months before in Natchez became a fact. The jury in the trial of General Lopez and himself could not agree on a verdict. The government, despairing of obtaining a conviction, dropped the case. The former governor of Mississippi and the general were free men. The fate of the forty men from Contoy Island still at Morro Castle hung in the balance, however. Their imprisonment had become a *cause célèbre*, with the president of the United States intervening in their behalf. American and Spanish officials conferred; still nothing seemed to happen with any speed. The days crept past one by one.

Melanie was seated on the back gallery one morning, watching the rain pour in silver streams from the roof, when Glory stepped from the house. Her face was twisted with concern and a look of distress in her eyes.

"You've got a visitor, Miss Melanie."

With the clatter of rain all around her, Melanie had heard no carriage. "Who is it?" she asked.

"It is Mr. Dom. Should I let him in?"

Dom. In New Orleans. What was he thinking of, calling at this time of morning? He must know Roland would be absent, busy with his duties. Perhaps he was not only aware of that fact but had decided to make use of it. "Is he alone?"

"Yes, ma'am," Glory answered and folded her lips in disapproval.

The best thing to do would be to send him away. There could be little he had to say she cared to hear. On the other hand, it had been a long and dreary morning, and the afternoon looked to be the same. There was always the possibility that he brought news from Natchez, wasn't there? "Show him into the parlor, and offer him something to drink. I will join him there shortly."

"Miss Melanie, do you think you're doing the right thing? What will Mr. Roland say?"

"I doubt if he will care one way or another. If he spent more time here and less with his eternal soldiering, he might be at home now. In which case, he would have no cause for complaint."

Shaking her head, Glory went away to carry out Melanie's instructions. Rising, Melanie stepped from the back gallery into her bedchamber to check her appearance. She had spoken no less than the truth to Glory. Roland's excessive attention to duty was beginning to grate on her nerves. She realized she had invited herself to New Orleans, but she thought he might have made some effort to spend more time with her. She scarcely saw him before nightfall, and then he was so weary he seldom did more than eat his dinner and fall into bed. His physical need of her had not diminished, but she was growing tired of structuring her days solely for the appeasement of his appetites.

Dom was standing at the French window in the parlor when she entered. Melanie paused to look at him. He seemed thinner than when she had seen him last, and unless she was mistaken, there was a firmer set to his shoulders and a more determined jut to his chin. He had

209

adjusted the louvers of the blinds in order to look out. His attention caught by something in the street below, he did not notice as Melanie moved toward him, coming to a halt at his side. Following the direction of his gaze, Melanie saw the servant woman from the house across the street hurrying away toward town, her head bowed against the driving rain.

"Some people have no consideration," she said.

Dom swung around. "Melanie," he said and then repeated in a softer, warmer tone, "Melanie."

She gave him her hand, smiling a little, unexpectedly touched by the emotion in his voice. "How are you, Dom?"

Instead of replying, he said, "You are more lovely than ever."

"You are flattering a married lady," she said, a hint of warning in her smile.

"It doesn't matter, it's still true," he answered.

Removing her hand from his clasping fingers, she nodded in the direction of the settee. "Shall we sit down? I hope Glory offered you some refreshment?"

"She offered it, yes, but I want nothing except to see you; to find out how you are, and how Roland is treating you."

"I have no complaints on that score," Melanie replied, seating herself on a chair near the fireplace and indicating the settee to her left.

"You always hated to admit that you needed help from anyone. How can I be certain that you aren't just putting a brave face on it?"

She slanted him a quick look, surprised at his insight. "I don't suppose you can," she said after a moment. "You will have to accept my word. But you haven't told me how you have been."

"I've been fine."

"And Chloe, how is she?" Melanie wished he would not stare at her quite so fixedly. She had the feeling he was searching for words, trying to find a way to make

210

some statement he obviously considered important. She was by no means sure she wanted to hear it.

"My sister is well enough."

"Did she come to New Orleans with you?"

"Yes—yes, she did. As a matter of fact, it was her idea that we make the trip. She insists that everyone who is anyone is here."

"I suspected as much. She mentioned the possibility to me some time ago, before I left Natchez."

"Did she? I didn't know you two had met since—since before the wedding."

That was not surprising. "Chloe seemed to feel that you still hold a grudge against Roland. I trust that is no longer true, since you are here in his home?"

"I may no longer feel friendship with Roland," Dom said slowly, "but then, I have no quarrel with him either. I have sense enough to realize that though his conduct toward the woman who was my fiancée was something less than gentlemanly, he had provocation."

"Yes," Melanie answered, a strained note in her voice as she looked down at her hands clasped tightly in her lap. She was quite willing to grant the possibility of provocation herself, but she did not enjoy having it pointed out to her.

"I only hope Roland understands my position," Dom said.

It was a moment before Melanie recognized what he was asking. He wanted to know Roland's feelings toward him. He did not know, of course, that Melanie had witnessed the meeting between him and her husband at Cottonwood. For the sake of his pride, she was glad of that. It also made it easier for her to answer. "I know of no reason why he should not. I think you must be considered to have been the injured party, if anyone was."

"I'm glad," Dom answered, resting his bony wrist on the arm of the settee as he leaned toward her. "I would hate to think I was barred from seeing you, even in a social way. I don't think I deserve that much punishment."

"Dom, please," Melanie said.

It did no good. "I have been punished, you know," he went on. "For my sins of selfishness and pompousness, I lost you. It was a hard lesson, but I have learned a few things from it. I have learned that the opinion of other people matters very little. That people are all too prone to condemn the deeds they lack the courage to commit themselves. That in the end it doesn't matter which standard you use, so long as you follow your own heart and conscience." He looked away. "I wish I could go back and change the things I said to you; so many other things. But I can't. Sometimes I wonder if I can live with that knowledge. Not always, just sometimes."

"Dom, I—"

"No, you don't have to say anything. It was good of you to listen to me. I hope you will indulge me in one or two things more? The first of them concerns Chloe. She would like to visit you, if you will receive her. For some reason she thinks that you would not care to see her again."

It was, Melanie thought, loyalty to her brother that caused Chloe to be so offensive when last they met. Surely she could understand and forgive such family feeling. "Yes, of course. I would be glad to see her."

"I knew you would say that. One thing more, Eliza Quitman regrets you and Roland have accepted none of the invitations that have been extended to you. She asks that I give you her personal compliments and beg that you will attend a theater party she is giving within the week. If you will agree, she plans to hire a *loge grille,* one of the screened boxes used by Creole ladies to provide protection from the eyes of the curious during bereavement or the last months of waiting before childbirth. It is the accepted thing here. No one will think anything of it. Also, Eliza promises she will not depend on sending word of the date and time to the barracks but will have a card of invitation delivered to you here."

"That sounds delightful," Melanie said. "I cannot answer for Roland, but if Eliza will send the invitation, I will make certain that she receives a formal reply, one

212

way or the other." Was it possible that Roland had refused invitations to some of the gala affairs in the city without so much as informing her of them? She could not imagine why he would do such a thing, but she certainly intended to find out.

"I hope you will try to attend. Chloe and I will be there. The theater will be the St. Charles, the occasion the return of the French-Irish actress, Madame Dubois, to the city for the winter season, and her long-awaited second benefit performance for the expedition."

The name was that of the woman Chloe had hinted was so attractive to Roland. Suspicion flared in Melanie's mind, but her curiosity was just as burning. "How fascinating," she answered. "I shall certainly have to try."

"Try what?"

Those tones, laced with cold anger, came from her husband. With a gasp, Melanie swung around. Roland stood in the doorway with his sodden campaign hat in his hand and water dripping from his oilskins onto the floor. The clamor of the storm outside had masked his arrival. Melanie, in her startled surprise, could no more help wondering how much he had overheard than she could help the guilty flush that stained her cheeks.

"Roland!" she exclaimed with as much composure as she could manage. "Why are you here at this time of day? Is something wrong?"

"I'm not certain," he grated. "I received a message that my wife was entertaining a strange man."

The accusation in his voice, his pose of wronged husband, was completely uncalled for. Melanie got to her feet. Holding her head high, she said, "As you can see, that was a mistake. I am entertaining an old friend, both of mine and of yours. I was just going to ring for Glory to make us a cup of tea. Won't you sit down and join us?" As another thought occurred to her, she went on, "And while we are waiting, Dom can tell you of an invitation tendered to us by Eliza Quitman. I am astonished to hear that the message concerning my activities reached you so quickly, since it seems any number of cards soliciting our

213

presence at various affairs that were delivered to you at the barracks or offices of the Lopez expedition have gone astray."

"No, really," Dom said, rising to his feet also. "I don't believe I would care for tea. Another time, perhaps."

Roland, his green eyes on Melanie's face, said, "Yes, another time. Now that the misunderstanding has been cleared up, I have to get back to the barracks. If you are ready, Clements, I will walk with you to your carriage."

"That is not necessary," Melanie said. Any other time, Roland's determination to see Dom from the premises might have struck her as amusing, but not now.

"I believe it is," Roland said and, moving to the bell pull, rang for Glory. He stood waiting with tight patience until the maid brought Dom's hat and cane.

"Goodbye, Melanie," Dom said. "Or perhaps, since we are in New Orleans, I should say *au revoir*. Chloe will call on you in a day or two. It was kind of you to say you would see her."

"Not at all," Melanie answered.

Bowing, Dom took himself from the room. Roland, with a parting look at Melanie, stepped through the door and closed it behind himself. There had been the promise of a reckoning in his eyes. Very well. If he wanted to cross swords with her, then let him hurry back home. She was perfectly ready to oblige him.

The rain still fell with steady monotony when dusk came. Roland, returning at last, appeared to have been out in the weather the better part of the day, for he was wet to the skin and muddy to the eyebrows. With scarcely more than a grunted greeting, he went straight out to the kitchen to see about water for a bath. Since Glory was still busy with preparations for dinner, he made his own, carrying the cans of water up the back stairs to their bedchamber. Melanie heard no more from him until dinner was on the table. Then he emerged in a pair of buff trousers and a clean white shirt, his hair still wet and curling from the tub.

Both Melanie and Roland had been taught not to air

214

their differences before the servants. To Melanie, Glory was much more like family, on top of which she knew very well the elderly woman guessed something was wrong, and probably had a good idea of what it was. It made no difference. She knew Roland would have nothing to say as long as the maid was in and out of the room, serving the table. With a certain waspish humor, she told herself it was just as well. Of late, Glory had shown a lamentable tendency to side with Roland.

Dinner over, Melanie helped Glory clear the table. That done, she went in search of her husband, a militant look in her eye and a sinking sensation in the pit of her stomach. He was not in the parlor or the sitting room. Reluctantly, she turned toward the bedchamber.

The French windows stood open to the wet night. Through them came a mist-laden wind carrying the sounds of splashing rain and the clashing of the tough leaves on the palms and palmettos in the courtyard below. Roland stood leaning in the doorway, staring out. Behind him was the tub he had used, only now it contained cold and cloudy water. His wet clothing was piled on the rug beside it, and his damp towels draped over the footboard of the bed.

Melanie jerked the towel from the end of the bed, inspecting the wood for water damage. There appeared to be none. With a relieved and exasperated sigh, she turned toward his wet clothing.

"Leave that," he said over his shoulder. "Glory will take care of it, or I will."

"The rug—," she began.

"It won't disintegrate for some time yet. We have a few things to talk about."

There was a challenging sound in his hard tone. Melanie tossed the towel over the end of the tub and turned to face him. With one hand on her hip, she said, "I believe you are right. Shall we begin with why I wasn't informed of the invitations we have received?"

"To begin with, I have had little time to worry about that sort of thing—"

"The general must have time, since I am sure a large number of the entertainments were in his honor."

"—also," he went on as if she had not spoken, "you are still in mourning, or have you forgotten? I assumed you would have little interest in parties."

"Being in mourning doesn't mean I am dead!" she cried. "Even if I had no intention of accepting, I would like to know what is happening. Things have not been so exciting lately that I could not relish a little outside interest to enliven my days."

"I see. I am sorry you have been bored, Madame Donovan. For myself, I have enjoyed our quiet evenings."

"That is because you spend all day at Bank's Arcade, smacking your lips with the other filibusters over the pillage and rapine in store for you when you reach Cuba again, and planning just how you will persuade the Spaniards who have lived in Cuba for generations to leave their homes. Why shouldn't peace appeal to you?"

A muscle knotted in his jaw, and the green of his eyes took on the dark hardness of jade. "Is that what you think? Then I suggest you come down to the parade ground some day and watch. All you will see is a lot of hard work. On second thought, forget it. The sight will probably bore you."

"If what you say is true," Melanie retorted, flinging back her head, "then I expect it would!" She would have liked to retract her hasty words about the filibusters, but since that was impossible, she would not back down from them an inch.

The fingers of his right hand curling slowly into a fist, he said, "It seemed to me you were far from bored this morning. I wonder if you would have told me about the visit of your former fiancé if I hadn't received such an opportune warning?"

"I am not sure," Melanie said, pursing her lips thoughtfully. "It might have been more exciting to keep it secret."

"What did he mean by coming here while I was absent? What did he want?"

As he spoke, Roland took a long stride toward her. There was leashed anger in every line of his body. She refused to be intimidated. "To the best of my understanding, he wanted three things. First, he wanted to inquire after my health and happiness. Naturally, I reassured him on both counts. Secondly, he had been entrusted with the invitation from Eliza, which he delivered. Finally, he was most interested in learning whether you meant to call him out on sight, though why he should think you might, I am at a loss to understand."

"Are you?" he inquired with the lift of a brow. "That is a change."

Despite the sting of sarcasm in his reply, Melanie had the feeling his thoughts were elsewhere. "Possibly. Since you don't intend to answer, I am left to the conclusion it has nothing to do with me. If it does, Dom must be considered the injured party, must he not? Any challenge would come from him. As it is—"

"Don't worry about it. It isn't important. What matters now is why you entertained the man in my house."

Melanie swung away, answering over her shoulder, "I thought you had that figured out to your complete satisfaction."

His hand shot out to swing her back to face him. "So I did," he answered, "but it won't happen again. Do you understand me? If it is excitement you want, I will provide it."

He dragged her into his arms. For long moments his eyes held hers. The blank hardness had gone, and in their crystalline green depths she caught a glimpse of mingled rage and anguish. It struck her in that moment that it could well be jealousy that had moved him to such anger; fear of losing her that caused him the pain his eyes expressed. From their quarrel had come this much, the discovery that she was beginning to win, that her plan to make him love her was working. It would be a great pity if she did anything to jeopardize it now.

When his mouth took hers, she held nothing back. Lifting her arms, she twined them around his neck. With the blood pounding in their veins, they undressed each other and sought the bed. They moved together with savagery and tenderness, each seeking the most the other had to give, finding in sweet lust the substitute for the gentler emotion neither would nor could proclaim. Still, afterward, Melanie was also certain victory lay within her grasp. It was strange then that lying there, listening to the rain, she felt nothing more than weary desolation.

Chloe came. In a whirl of rust and green plaid taffeta flounces, she descended on the house on Rampart Street. Her tittering laugh echoed through the rooms, and she scarcely stopped talking from the time she entered the front door until the moment she exited from it. Her comments on New Orleans and the social life she had found there since her arrival were, as always, maliciously amusing. If she was curious about Melanie and Roland and about the house and the section of the city where they were living, she was at pains not to show it. She accepted a cup of tea, stayed the prescribed half hour, and took her leave.

That was by no means the end of it. Dom's sister was back again the next day, still smiling, still amusing, still talking as if she feared that if she stopped Melanie might ask questions she had no intention of answering, or introduce a subject she had no wish to pursue. As the visit passed off without her fears materializing, Chloe appeared to relax. The spate of words slowed finally. As she was standing at the door, smoothing on her gloves, making ready to leave, she said abruptly, "My dear Melanie, I can't help thinking that with your mourning and your duties as a wife that you do not get out enough. What would you say to a drive this afternoon? We could go shopping or, if you prefer, take a few turns around the Place d'Armes in front of the cathedral. It is quite the thing to do, or so I'm told. New Orleans still has some charmingly European customs, and the Place d'Armes is just like an old town square in a Spanish village. Eligible young ladies are promenaded by their mamas or their governess-duennas, and simply everyone who wants to see or be seen puts in an appearance of an afternoon."

"Yes, so I have heard," Melanie answered.

"Shall we go and view the natives, then? I had my gig brought down from Natchez. We will need neither coachman, escort, nor chaperone. My maid can visit with yours again while we girls lend each other propriety. If you are agreeable, I will come by and take you up. Shall we say around sunset?"

Hesitating no more than an instant, Melanie agreed. A drive to take the evening air was little enough in the way of amusement. Chloe could be an entertaining companion when she wished, and the girl was going to such lengths to repair their former friendship that it seemed petty not to meet her halfway. Besides, Melanie was not adverse to seeing something more of the life of the French-Creole city.

That Chloe considered herself an accomplished driver became obvious from the minute they set out. She perched upon the red leather seat of her gig in a driving costume of deep blue twill cut on military lines. The bodice fastened at the front with a double row of frogs formed of gold braid, and there were epaulets of gold fringe upon her shoulders. On her head, she wore an archer's cap of blue felt edged with gold braid. Flourishing her whip with its beribboned handle, she took the street corner heading toward the Place d'Armes on one of the gig's two red-trimmed wheels.

"I am so glad you decided to come with me," Chloe said, raising her voice. "There are not many single girls in New Orleans of my age, and there is a limit to how much I can impose on Dom for his company. Anyway, he doesn't like to drive with me."

Melanie sent the other girl a tight smile, releasing her firm grip on the side of the seat with difficulty. Ahead of them was a farmer's wagon piled high with the purple stalks of sugar cane. Seeing that its dawdling pace must slow their progress, she retrieved her reticule from the floor of the gig and straightened the skirts of her bombazine. "I am sure I can't imagine why," she replied.

Chloe sent her a quick glance. "Oh, you are teasing me," she said. "My, how I have missed your droll sense of humor. We really must plan things so we can get together more often."

"Yes, of course," Melanie answered. "I suppose you mean to go to Eliza Quitman's theater party?"

"I would not dream of missing it. You have had your invitation?"

"Governor Quitman's manservant brought it around this afternoon."

"I do hope you mean to come. It will be sadly flat if you don't," Chloe said.

"Since Eliza promises the privacy of a *loge grille,* I see no reason why I shouldn't."

"You must make sure Roland wears his uniform. After all, it is a benefit, and as many of the expedition uniforms should be in evidence as possible, don't you think?"

Melanie glanced at the other girl, but Chloe was concentrating then on passing the cane wagon. Deciding against a confession that Roland had not yet made his intentions known to her, she murmured an agreement.

"You are familiar with the Place d'Armes?" Chloe inquired.

"Yes, Glory and I walk through it often on our way to the French Market."

Chloe turned to stare at her in surprise. "You do your own marketing? How quaint. Dom and I are staying with family friends in the American section of the city, just a few blocks down from the house where the Quitmans are staying. I am enjoying it immensely, since being a guest relieves me of all household duties. Not that I have ever done anything more than plan the menus and inspect for dust after the parlor maids. But what was I saying? Oh, yes, the parade ground. If you know it, then you have seen the marvelous new apartment buildings in the French manner that the Baroness de Pontalba has erected on either side. They say they are the first of their kind in

220

the New World and should be ready for occupation by the first of the year, though a few are already completed. They will be one of the most elite addresses. Already some of the best families are preparing to move in. The baroness, to make certain of her investment, has offered rooms for the season to nearly every celebrity who will be visiting the city. I understand she has offered one of the best of those ready to Madame Dubois."

"Really," was all Melanie found to say.

Chloe nodded. "I would have given my right arm to have stayed there. They say the baroness is still in the city and that she goes every day to supervise the construction. I tried to persuade Dom to arrange a meeting with her to ask her if we could not be accommodated in one of the apartments, but he refused. They are magnificent buildings, don't you think?"

"They are indeed," Melanie agreed, hiding a smile. "I am becoming quite an admirer of wrought iron, especially against rose red brick. I understand from the newspapers that the baroness is determined to cut down the old cottonwoods in the Place d'Armes and construct a formal garden to be enclosed with a wrought iron fence and named after the hero of the Battle of New Orleans, Andrew Jackson."

"They certainly do need to do something after the mess caused by the construction on the apartments."

They went on in this vein until their destination was reached. Then Chloe swung down Chartres Street, passing before the government building from Spanish days known as the Cabildo, the towering spires of the St. Louis Cathedral, and beyond it, the Presbytere that had been built originally as a home for the officials of the church. She slowed her horse to a stately trot, holding her whip at an elegant angle.

"Unless you object," Dom's sister said, "we will just take a few turns around the streets that mark the boundaries of the parade ground."

"As you like," Melanie agreed. But Chloe, craning her neck to see the couples promenading up and down, and nodding to the people in the passing carriages, paid so little attention to her answer that Melanie was forced to conclude the suggestion had been one of politeness only.

The scene before them was interesting—that could not be denied. Gentlemen in frock coats and high beaver hats, most sporting the soft whiskers of youth, strolled along, twirling their canes or using them to mark each jaunty step. Middle-aged ladies on the arms of their husbands walked with such grace their full skirts scarcely swayed. Ahead of them marched their daughters, sometimes one, often as many as three or four, each in purest white, while behind came the other members of the family. The girls who moved ahead, without exception, had their hair up, indicating that they were of marriageable age. Those who walked behind still had their long tresses hanging down their backs. On the corners were the praline sellers, ancient Negro women in clean white aprons and *tignons,* or kerchiefs, around their heads. Beside them were the flower vendors with posies of daisies and chrysanthemums, the flowers of fall, in twists of silver paper. An evening breeze rustled the leaves of the cottonwoods. From the river came the wail of a steamboat. Pigeons, startled by the sound, wheeled about the steeple of the cathedral and settled back once more into the Place d'Armes, strutting about on their red legs, the afterglow of the setting sun, shining with purple and green iridescence, on their feathers.

"There is M'sieur de Marigny," Chloe said, "and over there I believe is James Gallier, the architect who designed the Pontalba apartments." She named others, giving brief histories, until Melanie was forced to wonder how the other girl had become so familiar with the population of New Orleans in such a short time. The phenomenon was the result of interest, she supposed. People and their activities were Chloe's main interest, indeed, her only interest.

They circled around by the levee and then turned to circumvent the square of the parade ground once more. "Would you like to get down and walk?" Chloe asked. "It

222

is so pleasant this time of day. It would be no trouble, I assure you. The instant I pull over to the banquette and stop, positively hordes of little Irish and Negro boys will appear to hold the horse."

"Whatever you prefer," Melanie replied.

"I see an opening yonder," Chloe said. Then she leaned forward, peering through the trees of the Place d'Armes. "Oh! Oh, Melanie! This is terrible. I never dreamed—"

"What is it?" Melanie followed the direction of the other girl's stare. What she expected, she could not have said, but by no stretch of the imagination could it have been what she saw. Roland, tall and straight in his uniform, was strolling beneath the cottonwoods. Clinging to his arm was a woman. Slender and poised, she was dark-haired. It was difficult to see her face for the distance, but she was dressed in a walking costume of leaf green trimmed with ruching and bidings of a darker shade. Upon her head was an enormous hat in the cavalier style, with a dark green ostrich plume curling around the brim.

"Oh," Chloe moaned, "I would not have had this happen for anything. I am so sorry, Melanie, so frightfully sorry. But who would have guessed he would appear with her in public, walking in broad daylight for all to see. We must only hope they did not notice us." Instead of pulling up, Dom's sister flicked her horse with the whip in her hand, and they sped away from the area of the Place d'Armes.

Looking back over her shoulder, Melanie said, "I don't think I understand. Who was that woman?"

"You mean you don't know? Why that was the actress I told you about last spring, the one we are to see at the St. Charles in two days' time. That was Colleen Antoinette Dubois."

Chloe, still mouthing apologies that somehow did not ring true, drove directly back to the house on Rampart Street. With determined politeness, Melanie invited her in for tea, but the girl declined. They said goodbye there on the street. Then Chloe, brandishing her whip in a salute

223

that bordered on being perky, drove away. Melanie stood watching her, a frown between her eyes, until the red-trimmed gig was out of sight.

She did not mention the incident to Roland when he returned that evening. She hesitated because she was uncertain how to proceed. It seemed the wisest course to decide first how this affected her relationship with her husband and her future plans. Examining her feelings with caution, she discovered she was angry, though mostly, she assured herself, because her husband had so little respect for their vows that he paraded his paramour for all to see. She was also aware of distress. The one thing she had thought she could depend on was Roland's physical attraction to her. So far as she could tell, that had not abated one whit, but surely it must eventually. And what of her grand schemes then? Her certainty that he was coming to care for her seemed premature. If he neither loved nor desired her, then she had lost. She must accept defeat or find some other means of exacting vengeance.

She must not be hasty. It was always possible there had been a mistake, that the meeting in the park had been no more than a chance encounter. Roland had admitted his admiration of the actress; it would not be surprising if he had stopped to say a few words concerning her performance for Lopez. No. That she and Chloe had happened upon such an accidental meeting was stretching coincidence too far. There was also Chloe's attitude to consider. It would not astonish Melanie to learn that Dom's sister had expected to come upon some such scene.

Upon reflection, it seemed the best thing she could do was to wait. The Quitmans' theater party would be soon. She would be able to have a closer look at Madame Dubois and, perhaps, come to a better understanding of where she stood. In the meantime, though she recognized it was unwise, she could not prevent coolness from creeping into her manner toward Roland. When they retired to bed, she lay rigid, as far from him as she could get without being in danger of falling off the mattress. Sensing his movement as he started to reach for her, she turned her back to him, stretching in a pretense of sleepy languor. He smoothed the slender curve of her waist, sliding his hand upward to cup her breast. She did not respond. After a moment he removed his hand and, sighing, settled on his back. Melanie gave a soundless sigh. It was not an expression of relief. Long after his breathing had fallen into a deep and even cadence, she lay sleepless, staring into the darkness with wide and burning eyes.

Melanie dressed with care for the theater party. It was a matter of pride that she look her best, she told herself; there was not the least question of competing with the French-Irish woman who would be on the stage. Beginning early in the day, she washed her hair and dried it in the sun, then brushed it until it shone with jewel-bright auburn highlights. After a leisurely bath, during which she used her yellow rose soap with a generous hand, Melanie sat while Glory arranged her hair. The maid, catching Melanie's mood, outdid herself, coaxing the gleaming tresses into a coronet of curls from which streamed three gently coiling lovelocks to lie softly on Melanie's shoulder.

Months before, in choosing her mourning wear, she had included one evening gown for those occasions when she might entertain guests quietly at home. It lay upon the bed now, its black silk taffeta folds shimmering in the lamplight. The style was simple, with a full skirt, a pointed bodice, and a round neckline. The neckline was edged with a falling bertha collar of black lace that hung to her elbows for a capelike effect. Lace also formed an overskirt a trifle shorter than the taffeta. With it went black silk stockings and black satin slippers. Frowning a little, Melanie touched a finger to the crisp folds of the taffeta. On this night, of all nights, she could have wished for a little color. Still, it could not be helped.

Putting aside her dressing gown before donning petticoats and stays over her camisole, Melanie allowed Glory to settle her gown over her head. Once it was fastened and she had pulled full-length gloves of black lace up her arms, she turned to view herself in the mirror over the dressing table. Against the shiny black material, her skin appeared milky white and as soft as a magnolia petal. The blue of her eyes and the auburn shading of her hair was intensified to incredible vividness. With the sheen of her grandmother's pearls at her throat and ears, she was forced to admit that even without the help of color she looked as well as she had in her life.

The dark of evening closed in. Melanie sat in the parlor with her mantua cloak of gray velvet ready to one side with her opera glasses and jet-beaded reticule beside it. The hour agreed upon for her and Roland to meet with the others at the theater drew nearer. Roland was supposed to return home early in order to bathe and have a bite to eat before changing into his dress uniform. The ormolu clock on the mantel ticked steadily. A carriage rattled past in the street. The appointed time came and went, and still Roland had not returned.

Jumping to her feet, Melanie paced up and down the rug. Where could he be? Surely he meant to attend; he must after allowing her to send their acceptance to Eliza. How galling it was to realize that though he could leave his duties to saunter in the Place d'Armes with an actress, he could not shake himself free in time to keep an engagement with his wife. It was some consolation to think it was unlikely Roland could be with the woman now, since she would already be at the St. Charles Theater.

What would Eliza think when they did not put in an appearance? Or Dom? And Chloe? How long would it be before everyone knew how little she meant to the man she had married?

The least her husband could have done was to send a message explaining the delay and giving her some idea of whether he intended to come at all. If only she had some means of transportation, she would go without him; but since they had none, Roland meant to hire a hackney, bringing it home with him when he came. It was possible to walk, of course. That was what she and Glory, as well as Roland, had been doing until now; but if she did so, she must arrive in such a windblown and breathless condition that she would seem more pitiable than if she did not manage to attend at all.

The unhappy trend of her thoughts was interrupted by the sound of a carriage drawing up outside. Swooping to the window, she saw a black and silver hooded victoria with a driver on the box. A man was just alighting from it, though with the onset of darkness, it was impossible to tell his identity. The sight of a high silk hat confirmed her instinctive knowledge that it was not Roland. The man passed under the gallery and began to ascend the stairs. Knowing Glory was in the kitchen across the court, Melanie moved to answer the knock herself.

It was Dom who stood in the doorway. Removing his hat, he smiled. "Your carriage awaits, milady."

"My carriage?"

"When you didn't put in an appearance, Eliza became worried. She saw General Lopez arrive and sent to inquire if he knew any reason why you and Roland should be late. The general informed her that Roland was in the process of unloading guns and ammunition. The shipment came in late this afternoon, and he cannot leave the job until it is done and the munitions are safely under lock and key in the arsenal."

"I see. It was kind of you to come and tell me."

"That isn't the only reason I am here. Eliza thought you might like to come to the theater now, and let Roland come on later when he has completed his duties. I volunteered to bear the message and to act as your escort."

"That was thoughtful of Eliza—and you," she said. Any other time she might have refused the offer, preferring to wait for Roland. She was not inclined to be so conventional now. He had apparently not considered her feelings lately; why should she consider his?

"It is not a kindness to do something that gives one great pleasure," Dom replied.

Melanie gave him her warmest smile. "Only wait until I tell Glory," she said, "and I will come with you."

The crowd gathered outside the St. Charles Theater was incredible. The gas lamps that burned before it re-

227

vealed a tangle of carriages and people on foot converging from every direction. Inside, the scene was one of splendor, made bright by the gaslights on wrought iron brackets placed at intervals about the semicircular interior. The theater had been built much like a European opera house, with a pit for the poorer classes, private boxes near the stage, and tiers of seats rising to the ceiling. The tiers were lined like an arcade with Corinthian columns and faced with ornate balustrades. There was much gilded wood carving, and in the center of the ceiling, an enormous medallion with its radiating sections filled with acanthus leaves formed in the shape of a lyre. The *loge grilles* were located in a special section in the center of the second tier. Divided into private boxes, they were screened from the view of the curious by an ornate, pierced wooden screen.

As Dom and Melanie entered the back of one such box, Eliza Quitman turned, smiling. "Melanie, my dear, how lovely to see you again. You have arrived in good time. The melodrama is over, but the drama has not yet begun, though the curtain will be going up at any moment."

Returning the smile, Melanie thanked her hostess for sending the carriage, then turned to greet the others. The governor, as they all continued to call him despite his resignation from that office, appeared to be in good spirits. With his luxuriant mustache, thick dark hair, and well-cut evening clothes, he was most distinguished, the epitome of confidence and good will. Chloe, seated on his left hand, opposite from Eliza, seemed by contrast to look dissatisfied with her situation. Her acknowledgment of Melanie's presence was so offhand as to be ungracious. Noting the pout the other girl wore and the magnificence of her costume of rose satin, Melanie wondered if the other girl did not resent having to hide her splendor behind a screen. Another factor might have been the lack of an appreciative audience. The man on her left was General Lopez, resplendent in his uniform, his silver white hair shining in the light that struck through the screen.

After rising to bow over Melanie's hand, he seated himself once more and took up his interrupted conversation with the governor, leaning to talk across Chloe.

The only other seats available were two directly in front of the grille, doubtless reserved for Melanie and Roland. Since the general did not appear to realize he was occupying Dom's seat, Dom handed Melanie into the front row, then with a small shrug, took the place beside her.

Eliza leaned forward to compliment Melanie on her appearance and to explain once more what had caused Roland to be delayed. Melanie had time for little more than a soft spoken word of thanks. The lights were lowered, the audience grew still, and the curtain on the stage parted.

The play to be enacted for their enjoyment was *Camille,* the English version of the play by Alexandre Dumas *fils,* originally titled *La Dame aux Camélias.* It was the story of a beautiful member of the demimonde of Paris who gives up her aristocratic young lover for his own sake, then dies of consumption and a broken heart. It was a perennial favorite with theatergoers in New Orleans. As Colleen Antoinette Dubois made her entrance upon the stage, she appeared ideally suited for the part. Dressed in a magnificent gown of white, with the white camellias from which the character she played took her name tucked into her dark hair, she looked both vital and ethereal, gay and vulnerable. Watching her, Melanie was aware of a tightness in her chest. The woman had poise and magnetism. Her every move was positive, and yet, natural. So great was her mastery of the craft she was employing that Melanie took out her opera glasses to study the woman closer. The discovery she made was an amazing one. Despite the stage makeup and her slender grace, the actress was older than she appeared. It was quite possible she was some few years older than Roland. The young man who played her lover was also outstanding. A conventionally handsome Frenchman whose name was given on the program as Jean-Claude Belmont, he brought such fire and emotion to his part Melanie could not help speculating as to his true feelings for the actress.

Melanie's scrutiny of those on the stage was interrupted by a slight noise from the back of the box. Turning, she saw her husband entering, closing the door behind him. The look he sent her was grimly smiling, before he turned to speak a few words to his hostess.

At that moment it must have dawned on the general that he was occupying one of the seats belonging to the party. He jumped up, beginning his apologies. Roland shook his head, waving the older man, his commanding officer, back into the chair. Folding his arms, he took up a leaning position against the back wall of the box. Melanie turned back to the play, but she could not concentrate on it now. It seemed she could feel her husband's eyes boring into her, and into the man who sat beside her.

The intermission, when it came at last, was more than welcome. Or so she thought until Roland came and leaned over her, taking her hand in a clasp that was none too gentle.

"Shall we stroll outside, my dear?" he asked in cool tones.

Something like alarm brushed Melanie. Slanting him a quick upward glance, she said, "Do you think I should? I thought the idea of taking this box in the first place was seclusion?"

"So it is, usually, but I think with your year of mourning drawing so close to an end, we can make an exception."

"Very well then." There was little else she could say with the pressure of his fingers compelling her to rise.

In the narrow hallway outside the boxes, Roland tucked her hand into the crook of his arm and began to stroll at a slow pace. Though the roar of voices echoed toward them along the curving corridors behind the tiered seats, in deference to those who might occupy the *loge grilles,* it was fairly quiet in this section.

"I can't imagine what Eliza thought of our leaving the box like this," Melanie said finally.

"She will think I wanted a word with my wife in private, and she will be correct."

"I can't think what you might have to say that couldn't have been said just as well inside."

"Can't you? I take leave to doubt it. You can't really have imagined I would say nothing after seeing you jaunting around all over town with Clements, and then coming here and finding him cozily settled in my chair beside my wife?"

Melanie swung her head sharply to stare at him. "You saw us?"

"You were just leaving the house as I arrived. I was treated to a most edifying spectacle of him pressing his lips to your hand before he put you into the carriage."

"Were you indeed? I hope you don't hold me responsible for the gallentries a gentleman may decide to pay me. I was taught that slapping a man's face is ill-bred, that it is always better to show him with quiet distaste that you don't approve of his actions. I did precisely that, though you did not see it."

"For some men a quiet protest is not enough. They are not discouraged by anything less than a slap in the face."

"Yes," she snapped, "I am well aware of that breed."

That she was referring to his conduct that night at the River Rest could not have been more plain. Melanie felt no compunction for making the remark. That he could take her to task for riding in a carriage the short distance to the theater with Dom, after his flagrant behavior with the actress, incensed her beyond reason.

"We were speaking of your indiscretion with Dominic Clements," Roland said, his features stern in the uncertain light.

"Were we? Well let me inform you that the carriage you saw me entering was sent by Eliza, and that Dom volunteered his services as an escort to see me safely to the theater."

"I am sure he did," Roland retorted.

"Yes, and I was glad. In a crowd it is sometimes useful to have a man at your side, and for some peculiar reason

231

my husband was not available and I had no idea when, or if, he would put in an appearance."

"I have duties and obligations more important than attending a theater performance."

"More important than squiring me to the theater, you mean! I am well aware of your duties and obligations, and I despise them, especially since I saw you carrying out at least one of them in the Place d'Armes two days ago."

"You what?"

"I saw you in the Place d'Armes with Madame Dubois on your arm. It was, I am sure, a most pleasant duty. You seemed to be enjoying it immensely."

He stopped to scowl down at her. "That can be easily explained."

"Good," she said, her blue eyes icy with contempt. "Then I invite you to do so."

The indecision that crossed his face was odd, totally uncharacteristic. When he spoke, his words had the stiff ring of a half-truth. "Madame Dubois had come in that morning by steamer. We did not know she was coming, and so there was no one to meet her. I wanted to warn her that the men of the expedition intended to stage an impromptu welcoming party that night outside her window, complete with a serenade and bouquets. If you saw the newspapers you must know what a near riot it caused."

"You will forgive me if I don't believe you?" she said with a bright smile.

"No, but I will call us even, because I certainly don't believe a word you have said."

"You have only to ask Eliza Quitman."

"And can she tell me how you behaved in the carriage between the house and the theater this evening, or how many times you have entertained Dominic Clements when I was from home, or what you do when the two of you are alone?"

White to the lips, Melanie jerked her hand from his arm. "You have a despicable, gutter-crawling mind. I will not stand here and be insulted."

"No," he said, "especially not with the truth, though why in the name of God you would want a man who refused to help you when you needed him I cannot imagine. But I will promise you one thing, as long as I am your husband, you will never be free to be his wife."

"If you think you are spiting me," she said, her voice trembling with the violence of her anger, "then you are wrong. But if I will never be free, then neither will you. Shall we see if hate makes a binding marriage?"

He stared down at her for long moments, a shadow behind his green eyes. Then with an abrupt turn, he walked away.

Melanie swung around. She would not watch him go. Lifting her chin, she walked a small distance along the hallway. She could not rejoin the others just now. She needed a few minutes to regain her temper, to let the color fade from her cheeks, and still the trembling of her hands.

She had taken no more than a half dozen steps when she heard the sound of a footfall, and a man overtook her from behind. She thought he would pass her by, but he fell into step with her. "Good evening, Madame Donavan," he said. "You are Madame Donavan?"

Melanie glanced up and down the corridor. For the moment it was deserted, except for a cluster of men at the far end absorbed in what was apparently a comical conversation. There was no one to notice or care that she was being accosted by this strange man. Surveying him, she saw an older gentleman with gray in his dark hair, a lined face, and a small, pointed beard. His evening wear was impeccably cut, and across his chest was slashed the ribbon of some order.

"Yes," she answered at last. "I am Madame Donavan. And who might you be?"

"Permit me to give you my card," he answered in strongly accented English. Taking a chased silver cardcase from the pocket of his tailcoat, he extracted a rectangle of engraved cardboard and slipped it deftly into her hand.

The name was not unknown to her from the daily news sheets. "The Spanish ambassador," she said blankly.

"Precisely, madame. I am taking something of a risk in speaking to you, am I not? But I am a man who believes in fate. To my mind, it was not mere happenstance that I overheard your disagreement with your husband just now."

"Indeed?" Melanie said stiffly.

"But yes, madame. It came to me that if you truly had no regard for the man to whom you are married, and if you had so little affection for what he is doing, then it might be to my advantage to make your acquaintance."

"I hardly think——," Melanie began.

"No, no. Do not be hasty. Only listen to me for one little minute, if you please. My government, that of Imperial Spain, has a great interest in the activities of the filibuster, Lopez, and his men. We would be grateful, most grateful, for any information we might receive concerning them. Any little thing, the number of men gathered under the banner, their plan of action once they reach Cuba, the time and day of their departure from here, the type and amount of munitions they have managed to secure, anything."

Melanie thrust the card back at him. "I have no such information, nor am I likely to have it."

Gently, the Spaniard pushed the card back at her. "One never knows when such facts may be learned. If you should discover something, you will find it profitable to contact me at this address. I beg you will consider it, Madame Donavan. Now I will bid you good-night."

In something like stupefaction Melanie watched him go. That she had actually been approached with such a suggestion defied belief.

"Melanie?"

It was Dom, stepping from the door of their box farther down the hall. He came toward her with concern in his hazel eyes. She looked at him, then back down at the card in her hand.

"It is almost time for the curtain," he said as he drew

234

near. "Where is Roland—My dear Melanie, is something wrong?"

"You will never guess what has happened," she said with a catch in her voice. "I have been invited to betray Roland and the expedition."

Giving him the card, she told him what had taken place. When she had finished, he handed it back by one corner.

"It is preposterous," he said. "You don't intend to comply?"

"No, of course not!" she said heatedly. She looked about her for a place to deposit the card, but seeing none, she pushed it into her reticule, her hands shaking as she drew the strings once more. "Still, it is extraordinary, isn't it?"

"I would put it out of my mind, if I were you," Dom said and, offering her his arm, led her back to the box. At the door, he excused himself, allowing her to enter alone. Whatever his purpose, he was gone no more than a few minutes. By the time the curtain parted once more, he had slipped back into the box and taken his chair, vacated by the general during intermission, at his sister's side.

Roland did not join them again until well into the final act. By then the champagne, the *pâté de foie gras,* the broiled oysters, and half a dozen other hot and cold delicacies had been served in honor of the occasion. He took a meager helping of the bounty while standing in the rear of the box chatting with Chloe, who had suddenly grown vivacious. As soon as the curtain closed, he bid the others good-night, pleading early duty in the morning, and ushered Melanie from the box.

They rode home in silence, mounted to the front doors of the house on Rampart Street in silence, and entered their bedchamber in silence. Melanie removed her mantua cloak and draped it over the daybed. With her back to Roland, she tugged her reticule open, intending to look once more at the card given to her by the Spanish ambassador. But though she searched in her jet beaded purse,

235

and even turned the contents out upon the lilac satin cover of the daybed, it did no good. She must have dropped the card as she tried to put it away, for it was gone.

Chapter 12

WITH THE trial behind them, the plans of Quitman and Lopez for the invasion of Cuba picked up momentum. Before the week following the theater party was over, the former governor of Mississippi, with Roland accompanying him as his aide, had departed the city for Texas and points beyond on a recruiting mission. Melanie was just as happy to have her husband gone. She had seen little of him since their quarrel, and no more than half a dozen words had passed between them. He had taken to using the house on Rampart Street as little more than a place to sleep, eating all meals with his men. He had returned later and later and arisen earlier. The last three days before he left, he had bedded down in the spare bedchamber among the boxes and trunks stored there. Melanie assumed he did so to keep from disturbing her, though she could not help wondering if it wasn't just as much to avoid her. Whether he saw the actress or not, she did not know and, she told herself, did not care.

Rather than staying alone, Melanie accepted Eliza Quitman's kind invitation to come stay with her during the absence of their men. The two of them enjoyed many long days of idle talk, leisurely shopping, and tea parties with the wives of the other officers and men congregated in New Orleans. John Quitman was an indefatigable correspondent, and Eliza, perhaps because letters from Melanie's husband were conspicuously absent, often shared the contents of her own. Without meaning to in the least,

Melanie began to understand something of the strategy of Lopez's second campaign.

The expeditionary force would be three-pronged, with each separate army numbering approximately five hundred men. Of the projected fifteen hundred, one third were currently in New Orleans; one third would be recruited in the Southwest by Governor Quitman and eventually become his command; the final third would be gathered together in the Southeast under General Ambrosio Gonzales. General Narciso Lopez would, of course, serve in the capacity of commander-in-chief of the armies, but it was not his intention on this occasion to take an active part. The honor of leading the spearhead of the attack was first offered to Jefferson Davis, a veteran of the war with Mexico and a United States senator from Mississippi. On his refusal, it was tendered to Major Robert E. Lee of the United States Army. When the major also declined, the post was finally given jointly to Robert Wheat, an officer who had been injured in the first campaign, and Colonel John Crittenden, whose uncle, John Jordon Crittenden, was attorney general of the United States. Once the army under Wheat and Crittenden was entrenched, the men with General Gonzales, leaving from the coast of Florida, were to make their beachhead on the northeastern shore of Cuba, then march inland to join the others, swelling their ranks with the revolutionary forces within the country. Governor Quitman was then to make a frontal assault upon Havana, taking Morro Castle, freeing the Contoy prisoners, making the governor-general of the island a prisoner, and sweeping Cuba clean of Spanish officialdom and oppression. The plan could not fail; certainly General Lopez was supremely confident that it could not. He not only issued bonds redeemable after Cuba had been secured, using the public lands and property of the island as collateral, but he also promised to pay each common soldier five thousand dollars when victory had been won and offered every officer double that, plus a confiscated sugar plantation. The only hitch in the grandiose plans concerned the Contoy prisoners. It would not be possible to rescue them after all. After months of anxious waiting and diplomatic maneuvering, they were finally released.

Christmas came. Though John Quitman managed to get away from his duties in order to return, Roland did not. Melanie spent the holiday in Natchez at Monmouth with the Quitman family. When the time for gift giving came, the governor presented her with the token from her husband, a mantilla of convent-made lace, black, of course. Melanie entrusted her own present for Roland to the governor in her turn, a small, portable writing case. Jovial, understanding, John Quitman promised to have her man back in New Orleans within a month's time. He kept his word, but by the time Eliza and Melanie had made the journey downriver once more, Roland had left again, this time to join General Gonzales in Alabama. It was, perhaps, a coincidence that the actress, Madame Dubois, also departed the city at this time for an engagement in Mobile.

While in Natchez, the anniversary of her grandfather's death had passed. When she stopped in at Greenlea to air the rooms and check on how the house was doing in her absence, Melanie packed her colored clothing and transported it to New Orleans. There she began quietly and by the slow-accepted degrees, to put off her mourning.

With the governor in residence once more with his wife, Melanie began to feel uncomfortable remaining as their guest, though the elderly widow with whom they were staying as boarders could not have been more friendly. With smiling stubbornness, she returned to the house on Rampart Street with Glory.

It was often frightening being in that house alone at night. More than once Melanie thought she heard someone prowling about in the street or along the courtyard wall. Sometimes when she peered out after extinguishing the lamp in the parlor, she could see the man across the street standing on his gallery watching the windows of her house, always watching. On one occasion in the night she

239

heard someone inside the courtyard. Sliding from her bed, she had reached the window in time to see the figure of a man as he crossed a patch of moonlight in the open court below. Her pistol was under her pillow. By the time she had reached it, checked it in the light of a sulphur match to be certain it was primed, and returned to the window, the man had climbed the back stairs and was easing along the gallery, angling toward the windows of the dining room. To open the French windows, possibly letting him have access to the house, took every ounce of courage Melanie possessed.

She did not have to fire. The snap of the door latch, the click of the hammer of her pistol brought the man up short. For an instant he froze, then he spun around, leaped for the stairs, and plunged down them. By the time Melanie reached the gallery railing, he had scaled the courtyard wall and dropped over the other side. The sound of his running footsteps faded into the night. There had been little time and less light to study him, but Melanie was almost certain of the man's identity. It had been her Creole neighbor from across the way.

Eliza, when Melanie told her of the incident, exclaimed in horror. She first did her utmost to persuade Melanie to return to John and herself, but finding her adamant on that score, declared that something must be done to afford Melanie protection in the absence of her husband on official business. The governor's wife must have gone directly to Lopez, for that night, and every night thereafter, a soldier appeared before Melanie's house. With rifle at the ready, the man in red and blue patrolled up and down until dawn.

That carnival spring was the gayest in memory. Balls, soirees, levees, routs—there was a score of such entertainments every evening, and every hostess wanted as her guest that daring adventurer and filibuster, Lopez. The newspapers waxed poetic over his courage and foresight, comparing him to heroes of bygone ages who had fought for the liberty of their people. The general was by no means dismayed by his popularity. He never missed an opportunity to expound before an audience. With the gentlemen, he was enthusiastic and confident, telling them of the great riches in store, helping them count the profits that would be theirs from the bonds they had bought from him. With the ladies, he was courtly and unfailingly polite. He soon came to be acknowledged as an asset at any reception, since he was quick with a compliment, accomplished on the dance floor, and so little conscious of his dignity that he never neglected to dance with the daughter of the house or a plain cousin.

Melanie, going out more and more as the weeks passed, danced with the general a number of times herself. She found his manner polished and engaging, and his excitement and pride at the prospect of the forthcoming venture contagious. Though most often she attended such events with Eliza and John, occasionally it was more convenient for them if she allowed herself to be escorted. Sometimes it was Jeremy Rogers who performed this service; more often, it was Dom. He had, so far, never stepped beyond the line of what was acceptable behavior toward a married woman. In addition, he was so persistent that it was difficult to keep refusing him. When troubled by her conscience, she asked herself, What could be the harm? He was an old friend, and since he knew the truth about her marriage, she need not pretend with him or feel that she must make some explanation for her husband's continued absence.

Mardi Gras, Fat Tuesday, was brought to a close by a grand ball. The next day would be Ash Wednesday, the beginning of Lent once more, the first day of a few weeks of quiet. For Melanie, that would be welcome. Dressed in her gown of Maiden's Sigh Blue silk, the same she had worn on that January night so long ago when she had first met Roland, Melanie attended the festivities, but long before the hour of midnight, when the winter season would officially end, she had had enough. Pleading a headache, she asked Dom to see her home.

The house was dark as the carriage drew up before it. That was unusual, since Glory was in the habit of waiting

241

up for her. More unusual still, was the fact that on this night no guard walked the banquette before the stairs. Dom stepped out of the carriage, then turned to hand her down. Staring at the house in perplexity, Melanie half expected to see the guard meterialize from the darkness of the stairwell. He did not. Gathering up her skirts, she accepted the arm Dom offered and went forward.

"It is certainly quiet tonight," Dom said as they climbed the stairs.

"Yes," Melanie agreed, her voice subdued.

"It's peaceful after the noise and constant coming and going. I suppose for some people it is already Lent; the day is over, they have retired, and when they wake it will be time to fast, to repent. Would you be offended, Melanie, if I said that I have been repenting for this year and more, that I will never be able to forgive myself for what I did to you, and to my own happiness?"

"Please, Dom. I am not offended, but it is pointless to say such things. They can change nothing." Lifting her hand, she knocked on the door, a quiet tap meant to summon Glory to let her in.

"Are you certain? You cannot pretend that everything is as it should be between you and Roland. It appears to me that his involvement in this expedition to Cuba, his failure to watch over and stay with you, proves that he has no intention of being a husband."

"You don't understand," Melanie said.

"I think it is you who doesn't understand, or won't. The man is a loner, an adventurer, with no use for family ties. He wants and needs no one except himself."

Once more Melanie knocked on the panel, reached for the knob to give it a shake. The doorknob turned under her hand. The door was not locked. That was strange, for Melanie was certain Glory had snapped the bolt behind her when she left that evening.

Her stillness alerted Dom. "Where is Glory tonight? She is not ill, is she?"

"She wasn't when I left."

"Better let me go first." Dom pushed into the darkened

242

parlor. Nothing stirred. All was silent. As he started forward, Melanie followed. The dining room was as empty as the parlor, and the only thing that moved in the butler's pantry was a mouse scurrying into a corner. But in this room there was no curtain over the French windows that let out onto the back gallery. Through the uncovered panes, Melanie caught sight of a light in the servants' quarters across the court. As she watched, she saw the familiar rotund shadow of her maid pass the window.

"It's all right," Melanie said. "There's Glory. I expect she just didn't think I would return so early."

"I suppose so," Dom replied, "though it is still strange about your guard. You had better report the fellow in the morning. Will you feel safe enough without him? I could stay, if you like."

"It is kind of you to offer, but there is no need of that," Melanie said.

"Are you certain?"

"Quite certain." Melanie was oddly aware of him there in the dark beside her. She wished that she had taken the time to light a lamp. She did not like the intimacy that seemed to stretch between them, and thinking back to the remarks he had been making earlier, she was suddenly uneasy. Dom had never tried to force himself upon her, but with her guard gone and Glory out of the way, she was alone with him as she had never been before.

"Perhaps I had better check the bedrooms," Dom was saying.

"I don't think that will be necessary," Melanie answered, her voice cool and firm as she turned back to the parlor. "You have done enough for me by seeing me home. Now, if you don't mind, I will say good-night. I am rather tired."

At the door, Dom tried once more. "Melanie," he began.

"Please, Dom, not this evening. Good night." Stepping back into the room, she closed the door upon him.

She stood still until she heard the rattle of his departing carriage; then sighing, she moved through the parlor in the dark, touching the now familiar objects, a table, the back of a chair, on her way to the door which led into the sitting room, and from it to her bedchamber. Stepping through, she crossed to the bed and put down the shawl she had used for a wrap and her evening reticule of silver mesh. A yawn caught her, and she smothered it, then glanced at the French windows. A long streak of light came in between the draperies. Attracted by it, she moved to draw back the heavy silk hangings, letting the glow of moonlight into the room.

Down below, the courtyard was drenched with silver. Nothing moved, not even the shadow of a leaf. Across the way, Glory's light went out. Melanie waited, thinking the elderly maid had heard her come in and was on her way to the back gallery. Glory did not come, however. Perhaps she had left the latch out on the front door because she was overly tired and meant to make an early night of it. It was not like her, but there had been a number of late nights for her lately. Melanie had urged her several times not to wait up. Doubtless Glory was finally taking her at her word. She was glad. She hated to feel she was depriving her elderly maid of sleep. There was actually very little she could not do for herself, few gowns she could not get in, and out of, without aid.

Reaching back, she began to unfasten the buttons of her gown with quick competence. With it undone to the waist, she pulled it off over her head and stepped to drape it over the coverlet chest at the foot of the bed. The tapes of her petticoats and crinoline gave at the first tug. They joined her dress, along with her knee-length pantaloons and her stays. Holding to a post of the bed, she kicked out of her slippers and stripped off her stockings.

Fingering the hem of her camisole, Melanie stood undecided. She was so tired she was tempted to climb into bed as she was, leaving her things to be put away in the morning. If she did, she would have to rise before Glory and do it, for if she didn't, Glory would begin scolding and picking up after her the minute she came into the door with the morning coffee. Peace in the morning might be better than rest now.

With a sigh, Melanie lifted her arms and began to take the pins from her hair, shaking her head so that it tumbled around her shoulders and down her back in wild abandon. Stepping to the dressing table, she put the pins down on the cold marble surface and felt for the chased silver box of sulphur matches. She found them and struck one, then reached for the globe of the lamp that sat beside the box. It was only as the wick caught flame and she was shaking the match out that she realized the globe in her other hand was still warm, as if the lamp had been extinguished for only a short time.

"A fine place to stop, as much as I enjoyed the show, and as fond as my memories are of the blue dress you were wearing. I have thought of you as you are at this moment a thousand times since that night at the Real Inn when the Bascoms broke in on you."

The glass globe fell from Melanie's nerveless fingers with a splintering crash. She whirled around. "Roland!" she cried.

He lounged against the head of the daybed with one booted foot propped on the lilac satin cover and a wrist resting on his knee. His eyes narrowed, he surveyed her brief costume, the white gleam of her limbs, and the ancient copper sheen of her hair in the lamplight. "Yes," he drawled, "the wandering husband has returned."

"What—what are you doing here?" she asked, meaning to question why he was sitting there in the dark, though it did not come out that way.

"I live here, if you will remember," he said tautly, coming to his feet in one easy motion. "I heard from the governor of your problems with prowlers; it seemed wise to put in a request to return and resume my rightful place as your guard and protector. Glory let me in some time ago, and a good thing, too, or so it appears."

"I suppose you mean something by that remark," Melanie said, the color returning to her face with a warm rush as she watched his slow advance. There was an ominous tightness about his mouth, and his eyes glittered with green fire.

"I mean it looks as if your need for a guard extends beyond the front doorstep. I heard Clements practically invite himself to stay the night."

"Then you also heard my refusal," she said with a lift of her chin.

"Yes, but when the situation arrives at the point where a man dares to ask, there is no way of knowing how long the lady will continue to say no."

"You should know all about that, I'm sure," Melanie threw at him, making as if to turn away.

He reached out and caught her arm to stop her, his fingers digging into the soft flesh. "Stand still," he said, a rough note in his voice. "You will cut your feet."

"Your concern overwhelms me. What can it matter to you?"

"It matters, just as it matters to me that you are given no chance to weaken toward your belated gallant, Dominic Clements."

"You—you heard that also, then?"

"Enough to make me interested in what you might answer. When I turned out the lamp, I didn't count on such a fascinating bedtime display. But I would not have missed it for anything." He stepped to her, his arms encircling her to hold her achingly close as he stared down at her. "Dear God, you are beautiful," he whispered. "I tried to forget, to pretend I did not need you, but it was no use. You haunt my waking hours and my dreams, and though I know that if I stay with you my soul will be lost and my life damned, I cannot stay away, nor can I put you from me. So come and let me drown in your bewitching angel's eyes. Some things bought dearly are worth the price."

His mouth claimed hers with a burning demand. He sank his fingers into the scented softness of her hair, confining movement. His other arm was like an iron band clamping her to him as if he meant never to let her go. His words were so strange, and it had been so long since she was close to him that her senses reeled. She clung to

246

him for long moments, long enough for him to feel the triumph of her surrender in his grasp. Reaching down, he swung her into his arms. As he moved with her toward the bed, his boots crushed broken glass into the carpet with a crackling, tinkling sound.

It was the breaking noise that dissolved the spell. "No," Melanie whispered, then cried louder, "No!"

The instant she felt the bed beneath her, she twisted from his hold, rolling to the far edge. He lunged after her, snagging his arm around her waist to jerk her back against the pillows. She struck out at him, catching him a blow on the side of the neck with her hand. Flinging himself across her pelvis, he snatched first one wrist, then the other, pinning them on either side of her face.

"What is this?" he grated, his face dark with frustration.

"Who do you think you are?" she panted. "Do you think you can flaunt your affair with another woman, follow her about like a tame dog, and then come back to take up where you left off? No, not as long as there is breath in my body."

"I had no affair. I tried to tell you that, but you will not believe it. Then be damned to what you think. You are my wife. You are the woman I want beyond all others, and I will have you. Make no mistake about that."

With a suffocating feeling in her chest, Melanie stared up at him, twin spots of color burning their way to her cheekbones under his steady and hot gaze. That he meant what he said was beyond doubting. She swallowed hard. "And will that content you?" she asked in a voice barely above a whisper.

"No," he answered, his eyes dark with pain, a smile twisting his mouth, "but it will be something. Once, for a brief time, you gave yourself to me. For whatever the reason, you came into my arms, you answered my touch and moved with me. I can always hope you will let down your guard and that miracle will happen again."

His words, the soft timbre of his voice, seemed to sap her will. In defiance of that weakness she warned him through clenched teeth, "It won't."

"Shall we see?" he inquired and lowered his lips to hers.

It was no gentle possession. His kiss was deep and ravaging. She tried to turn her head to be free of it, but he would not permit it. From deep inside there rose a sharp-edged resentment of his assumption of mastery and the right to order her life and her desire. Caution urged a careful resistance. Subterfuge could be matched against strength. When he released her wrist, dropping his hand to the round swell of her breast, brushing aside her camisole to expose its creamy contour, she made no sudden move. His mouth released hers to press liquid fire along her cheek, moving in measured progression to the trembling globe he held. Slowly, she let her fingers lift to touch the crisp vitality of his hair. The flick of his tongue was warm. Melanie allowed herself a small movement, a faint sound deep in her throat. His hand crept lower, passing under the hem of her short garment to brush the flat surface of her abdomen with sensitive persistence.

Her muscles tensed in reaction. In that convulsive moment, she sank her fingers into his hair and pulled, snapped his head back, heaving herself upward at the same time. He was thrown off balance. Before he could recover, she scrambled from under him, wriggling, sliding, pushing toward the edge of the bed, uncaring if she fell, so long as she escaped him.

With a catlike twist, he threw himself after her, pouncing, his hand fastening in the silk batiste of her camisole. The material parted in a jagged tear. Instantly he shifted his grip so that the straps cut into her shoulders, pulling her backward. Before she could recover, he caught her arm and wrenched himself forward to slide his hands over her hips, dragging her back toward him.

She came with ease, launching herself at him as she got a knee beneath herself. She entwined her legs with his, clasping his waist with her arms, and rolling with him so he was thrown to his back. She meant to fling herself free, but he saw her purpose. His arms tightened so she fell against his chest, strained to the length of his long, hard body. Raising herself on her elbow, flinging back her hair with a toss of her head, she stared down at him. She was aware of the press of his uniform buttons and the burgeoning strength of his need. Her blood pounded in her veins with her efforts and the acid rise of the ardor she would have denied. She felt the urge to claw at him, to sink her teeth into his lips, or else to bring her mouth down on his with hard fervor until the pain and its certain aftermath routed the hurt in her mind.

Roland's emerald eyes were watchful. He seemed to know her indecision, to recognize the moment when she determined to resist the urging of desire. Abruptly he pitched her up and over onto her back. For an instant she could not get her breath for rage and the press of his weight upon her chest. In that brief respite, he stripped off his uniform in a few swift moves, and then the rigid hardness of his male body was against her once more. Held fast in his steely grip, she suffered the taking of that pleasure she would not give. He finished the destruction of her camisole, ripping it from her, and sought the honey-eyed sweetness of her woman's form, leaving no tender area untouched. Though in the recesses of her mind she defied him, withholding her response, hiding it within herself, in her loins there was a tingling vulnerability. Suffused with the growing heat, she clenched her hands into fists, waiting with pent breath for the moment when he would fit himself to her. It came. He sank into her with rigid, pulsing fire. Tormented and enraptured, she felt the driving shock of his strength, knew the desperation that fueled his desire, and the fine edge he held to between savagery and impassioned tenderness. There came to her in that instant of transcending, clarifying exultation, a flash of truth. They were a paradox, she and the man who was her husband. For though inside she was hard and implacable against him, her body was soft and yielding; and though he ravaged her with rough strength, the emotions toward her that ruled his mind had no such firm defense. More poignant and important still was the recognition that there was no advantage in such insight. They were still evenly matched. For so long as neither saw victory in the other's grasp, then they each need not admit defeat. And so the battle could be joined again, and yet again, until at long last the Lopez expedition sailed once more.

It was a warm summer night, deep dark and velvety, when the final gala for Lopez and his men took place. It was held in the American section of the city known as the Garden District, a courtesy from one of the businessmen who hoped to increase his wealth by backing the Spanish general. Melanie, entering the ballroom of the magnificent Greek Revival mansion on Roland's arm, lovely and cool looking in a gown of aquamarine silk tulle, did not know it was to be the last affair. She only knew the gaslight in the enormous chandelier over the polished floor seemed extra bright, the smiles that turned toward her appeared friendly beyond the ordinary, and the lilting rhythm of Strauss's *Southern Roses* made her want to dance. For some reason she did not trouble to analyze, she knew a wonderful feeling of well-being. With surprise, she realized that she was happy. Instinctively, she turned to look at her husband, but at that instant they arrived beside Eliza and John Quitman. The two men shook hands and spoke together in low voices. Melanie and Eliza greeted each other with less reserve, exchanging compliments. Chatting easily, they stood watching the glittering throng, commenting on the costume of first one woman and then another, nodding to acquaintances, waving to friends, Dom and Chloe among them.

The governor did not shine on the dance floor, as he was the first to admit. Roland, after swinging Melanie through a lively cotillion, led Eliza out onto the waxed parquet. In his absence, Melanie accepted Jeremy Rogers's invitation to waltz.

"Roland is a lucky dog," Jeremy said as they circled the floor."

"In what way?" Melanie inquired.

"Because he has you, of course, but then I think he knows it well enough."

"I should hope so," Melanie parried in pretended conceit.

"I mean it. I never saw a man work himself so hard to get something for a woman."

"I wish he wouldn't."

"So do I, makes me look bad," Jeremy said with a droll grin. "I guess if I had somebody like you I would try harder, maybe even fight harder when we get to Cuba."

"I thought your sugar plantation was incentive enough," Melanie said, her eyes bright with laughter.

"I suppose so. Tell you what, I can't wait to see you in Havana. That will be something. Promise you will save me a dance at the first ball, when Lopez is installed as governor of Cuba?"

"I promise," Melanie agreed, affected in spite of herself by his enthusiasm.

"Yes, sir, that will really be something," Jeremy repeated, a faraway look in his guileless blue eyes.

The floor was becoming crowded. The August night was already warm. With the press of so many bodies, the warmth of the gaslights over head, plus her exertions, Melanie grew flushed with heat. Accepting Jeremy's offer of a glass of champagne punch with gratitude, she sank down onto a bench at the side of the room to wait for him to bring it. She did not realize she was near an alcove until she heard voices coming from behind a screen of potted palms and ferns.

"So you are determined to go through with it?"

"But yes, my friend. I see no reason to delay. My men are becoming impatient with waiting for the army you are gathering, and that of General Gonzales, to be ready. Where will I be if they desert? Besides, you must admit the climate of opinion is right. With the Cuban rising at Puerto Principe and in the province of Trinidad, if we are not careful the Spaniards will be driven into the sea before we can make a move."

With a start, Melanie realized the first speaker had been Governor Quitman, and the second, General Lopez. Though they had withdrawn into the alcove, she was not certain if their conversation was meant to be private, or if they had merely sought a quiet place away from the noise so they would not have to shout at each other. Catching sight of Jeremy on the other side of the room with two glasses held high as he began to make his way around the dance floor toward her, she stayed where she was.

· "I am afraid," the governor said slowly, "that I put little confidence in these reports of large revolutionary forces. It seems to me something of the same nature was said before, and yet you saw no such activity."

"You are correct, my dear Quitman," Lopez replied. "But it must be admitted that I was not on the island for any great length of time. Besides, I consider the source of this particular intelligence to be totally reliable."

The governor grunted something Melanie did not catch, and Lopez chuckled. "Ah, but I do not consider my judgment infallible. If I need reassurance, I have only to think of the mass meeting held last week. Everyone there was of the opinion that it is imperative to strike. Every newspaper editor in every journal one sees proclaims that the time is now. The Cubans are waiting, my men are waiting, and the businessmen who have given their money to my enterprise are waiting. I cannot disappoint them."

"I am not counseling an indefinite delay," the governor said. "What would another week, or even two, matter, if it increased the certainty of success, if it allowed the implementation of our plans for an attack on three fronts? Why in God's name, my dear sir, must you embark tomorrow with only a third of the forces we could put in the field in a few weeks' time?"

There was an audible snap in the Spaniard's voice as he answered. "For the reasons I have outlined to you, Governor Quitman, and because I have so informed my officers. I will not show uncertainty by countermanding that order at this late hour."

"It is possible that such a change in plans might be an act of wisdom."

"Possibly. Could it be, however, that this course you urge upon me would also allow you to finish gathering

252

your western army, and therefore insure that you share in what you fear will be the only glory that will come from this campaign?"

"That, sir, is an insult!"

"My apologies, sir," General Lopez said, "but I feel the matter to be too urgent to stand on ceremony."

It was a moment before the governor replied, and then he said slowly, "So do I, General. And I take leave to inform you that I would consider it foolish in the extreme for you to take at face value all the plaudits you have received in the news sheets these days. It will take more than one man, however great he may be, to win through in Cuba."

"I shall endeavor to keep that in mind," General Lopez said. The curt phrase was scarcely out of his mouth before he emerged from the alcove. He did not glance in Melanie's direction as he walked stiffly away.

The elation Melanie had felt vanished as if it had never been. She smiled at Jeremy, accepting the drink he brought her, but her heart was not in it. Why had Roland not told her the expedition would be leaving tomorrow? She would wager that the wives of the other officers present tonight had not been kept in the dark. Did Roland not trust her, or did he think that she simply would not care? He had not sent word before, at the beginning of that first abortive expedition, that he was leaving, but this time would be different. This time she would be here to say goodbye.

"Jeremy," she said suddenly, breaking in upon what he was saying. "Have you seen Roland?"

"I think he was over near the doors to the garden a few minutes ago, but what do you want with him when you have me?" he asked in mock complaint.

"I just thought of something I must ask him," she answered with a strained smile. "Will you take me to him?"

Melanie saw Roland from a distance, a tall, broad-shouldered figure in his well-cut uniform, with the gaslight gleaming blue on the waves of his dark hair. His head was bent as he spoke to the woman beside him, and his hand

253

was under her elbow in a curiously protective, almost intimate gesture. The dancers shifted, coming between them. When next Melanie looked up, the woman had turned. Her hair was done in a style of severe elegance, her gown of gold tissue silk came, without doubt, from Paris, and in her ears shone the green stars of emeralds. The woman beside her husband, the woman he was just leaning to kiss gently on the forehead, was Colleen Antoinette Dubois.

Melanie came to a halt. Jeremy, dragged to a standstill, tilted his head to look into her pale face. "What is it?" he asked.

At that moment Roland glanced in their direction. Smiling he spoke a few words to his companion, then with the actress on his arm, started toward them.

Melanie felt as if her heart were caught in a vise. It came to her in a rush of crippling jealous anguish that her husband had been making his farewells to Madame Dubois, comforting her, more than likely, for his forthcoming absence. Realizing Melanie had seen them together, he meant to pass his indiscretion off in fine style by presenting his mistress to his wife in public. She could not bear it; nor would she! Her blue eyes glittering and her lovely mouth compressed in a thin line, Melanie watched them approach.

"There you are, Melanie," Roland said, a look of quiet pleasure in his eyes. "I wondered what had become of you. Madame Dubois, I would like to present my wife——"

"I am sorry," Melanie said, her voice clear, cold, and ringing as it overrode his. "I have no wish to be presented to your *chère amie*. I do not acknowledge harlots, no matter where they are, nor what name they give themselves!"

Melanie did not wait to see what her husband might reply. Ignoring the startled faces of the bystanders, she picked up her skirts and pushed through the dancers on the floor, making for the entrance. She had no idea where she was going. She wanted only to get away from the intolerable scene she had created. In the tall and graceful entrance hall she paused. She would go home. The hired carriage could always return for Roland, if he meant to come home at all.

"Yes, madam?"

She turned to see the butler, stately in a black tailcoat, trodding toward her. Giving her name, she asked to have her carriage brought around, then added, "I—don't feel well. Is there somewhere I could sit down—somewhere away from the noise—while I am waiting?"

"Certainly, madam." Moving to a door on the far side of the wide hall, he opened it and stood to one side.

Murmuring a quiet thank-you, Melanie slipped into what appeared to be the morning room of the lady of the house. Bowing, the butler closed the door behind him. The latch had hardly clicked shut before the panel was thrown open again. She swung around to see Roland framed in the opening. With deliberate movements, he stepped inside and closed the door in the astonished face of the butler.

"Why did you run away and hide?" he asked with one hand still on the knob. "Why didn't you stay to see the results of your handiwork?"

"I am not hiding," she threw at him. "I left because I had no desire to be publicly humiliated any further."

"You humiliated? You? I have been trying for months to persuade Colleen to let me make her known to you, and that is all you can say? I never dreamed you were such a puritanical prig."

"A prig?" she cried. "Because I refused to be introduced to your mistress, your lady-love that you have flaunted all over New Orleans ever since I came last fall, and before?"

The rage that leaped into his face, burning in his green eyes was so great that Melanie fought the urge to recoil from him. "That was what I thought you said, but I could not believe it," he grated. "That woman is no mistress of mine, though she does have my love and my dearest honor. As I tried to tell you before you turned into a vicious-mouthed harridan, that woman, Colleen Antoinette Dubois, to give her her stage name, is my mother."

Melanie stared at him, the color draining from her face. "Your mother," she whispered.

"She was an actress before she met my father, and even then she used her mother's maiden name. Her father was an Irishman from a famous theater family. They were touring in the United States when she met my father."

"I didn't know."

"When she left my father, so many years ago, she became as one dead to him. For his sake, and for mine, she preferred to keep it that way. But you didn't wait to find that out. You didn't stop to think that even if what you thought was true, I would never have put you in such a position. You thought of no one but yourself, your own feelings, your own pride."

"Why not?" she blazed. "What else have I? I have no family. My character has been torn to shreds. For my livelihood I am dependent on a man who married me for duty and for lust, a man who has so little concern for me that he leaves me in ignorance of the fact that he will be leaving to go to war in the morning. What did you intend to do, leave me to find out when you did not return home tomorrow night?"

"I meant to tell you tonight, after the party. What I don't understand is how you discovered it."

"It doesn't matter, I did, and not from you."

"You are right, it doesn't matter. The most important thing now is to undo what you have done. We will go back into the ballroom. I will present you once more to Madame Dubois. You will extend your apologies for your outburst just now and be as charming as you know how."

"I am perfectly willing to express my regret for the misunderstanding if you will bring her here, but I am not going back in there."

"You will, if I have to carry you. You embarrassed her in public, you will make public amends. You owe her that much. Shall we go?"

Though one part of her mind acknowledged the justice of his stand, there was another part that hated him for it. He was arrogant and dictatorial. He had no concern or

256

understanding for her feelings, only for those of the woman who had borne him. The most unfortunate evening of her life had been at Monmouth at a ball such as this when she had first seen him.

With her head held high, she preceded him from the room. There was a feverish brightness in her eyes and a hectic wash of color across her cheekbones as she swept into the ballroom. The actress, Roland's mother, stood in a circle of admiring officers. Pinning a gracious smile to her lips, Melanie moved toward them. Holding out her hand, she said, "My dear Madame Dubois, you must forgive me. My husband has explained the matter to me, and I see it was nothing more than a stupid mistake. I cannot tell you how sorry I am for it."

If the woman was surprised, she did not show it. With superb aplomb, she gave a light laugh. "Think nothing of it, my dear. You were as magnificently honest before as you are gracious now. For myself, I hate so much to admit when I am wrong that I admire others who can do it with such a pleasant and ungrudging air. I am afraid I tend to sulk."

"You, Madame Dubois," one of the younger officers cried. "Never!" And they were off on a round of compliments that made it unnecessary for Melanie to pursue the subject further.

Roland, who had followed her, stepped to her side. "Well done," he said quietly. Melanie did not answer, but the look she sent him was laden with bitter contempt. Face impassive, he made her a small bow and moved away.

Melanie exchanged a few more words with his mother. Her manner as cordial as she could manage, she even invited her for tea and did not know whether to be glad or sorry when the actress accepted. It was still difficult for Melanie to think of her, with her brightness and gaiety and look of youth, as being of an age to have given birth to Roland.

Before many minutes had passed, Madame Dubois excused herself to take to the floor in the arms of one of the men around her and was thereafter claimed for a dance by none other than their host of the evening. With this proof of acceptance, Melanie considered her duty to be done. Glancing around for Roland, she saw him at the far end of the room. Deliberately, she turned in the opposite direction, her goal the doors which led from the ballroom.

The butler was nowhere in sight as she crossed the great hallway. Pulling open the heavy front door, she let herself out into the night. Since she had not canceled the order for her carriage, the hackney in which she and Roland had arrived stood on the drive with the driver on the box. Seeing it, she allowed herself a deep sigh of relief. Then with her skirts billowing around her, she hurried down the high front steps.

The sound of a door opening behind her and quick footsteps sent her heart into her throat, but she did not pause or look back. A shout that was also her name sent her into a near run.

"Melanie, wait!"

Noticing her approach, the coachman had climbed down to open the door and hand her in. With one foot on the let-down step, she turned to look back. The voice calling her name was not the one she had expected.

It was Dom who came toward her, a frown of concern between his eyes. "What is it?" he asked. "Where are you going in such a hurry?"

"Home," she answered curtly.

"Now? Alone?"

"Now. Alone," she replied and stepped inside, flouncing onto the seat. Dom had stepped in front of the coachman, taking the door from the man's grasp. Short of pulling it out of his hand, there was little she could do to speed her departure. She glanced back toward the house, expecting to see Roland emerging after her at any moment. An appeal in her shadowed eyes, she said, "I really am very tired."

"Even so, you shouldn't be abroad alone. I will come with you, if you don't mind. I have wanted to speak to

258

you for weeks, but Roland has been in such close attendance since his return there has been little opportunity."

Any other time, she would have taken careful note of the tension that gripped him and the portentous sound of his words. Now, she only wanted to get away, and if Roland should learn of her choice of escort, well enough. She didn't care. Her mouth set in firm lines, she moved to the far side of the seat, making room for Dom.

When the carriage was well away from the house, Dom turned to her. "You are beautiful tonight. It seems to me that you grow more gloriously lovely every time I see you. I have been amply punished for the things I said to you that day at Greenlea. I have wished a thousand times that I could go back and relive that afternoon again. If I could, I promise you, my answer would be different. We would be married now. We might even have a child."

Melanie flung a startled glance at him, then looked quickly away again. "All that is past," she said. "What has been done cannot be undone."

"Perhaps, but I wanted you to know that I love you. If anything should happen to Roland in the coming campaign, if you should ever decide to leave him, I will be proud and honored to have you as my wife."

"It—it is kind of you to say so," she murmured at a loss.

Reaching out, he placed his hand on her forearm, brushing along it until he clasped her hand. "I didn't say it to be kind. I said it because I meant it. Why else do you think I have waited here in New Orleans, neglecting my law practice, everything, except to be near you when the expedition sails?"

"So you know, too. It seems everyone knew but me."

"Knew what?" he asked.

"Why, that Lopez and his men are leaving tomorrow morning. You said—"

"No, I didn't know. There's hardly five hundred men here in the city now. I was under the impression they were planning to embark a much larger force."

"Lopez thinks his army is strong enough, given the unrest on the island."

"I see. Then I may not have so long to wait for my answer."

"What do you mean?" Melanie asked, withdrawing her hand from his grasp.

Dom frowned. "There is every possibility that Roland will not return. You must realize that. This is a dangerous game these men are playing. If they are defeated, the casualties will more than likely be heavy, and if they are caught, it is unlikely the United States government will intervene as they did in the matter of the Contoy prisoners. Knowing they have been forsaken by their country, knowing also that for many, if not most, this is their second attack on Cuba, the Spanish government there will not be forgiving."

"Yes," Melanie whispered, "I expect you are right."

"I don't mean to press you," Dom said, "but I want you to know that I will always be here, waiting. In the event that the worst happens, you will not have to be alone."

The carriage came to a halt before the house. Stifling a sigh of relief, Melanie turned to the man beside her. "I appreciate what you are trying to say, Dom, really I do. Knowing your past sentiments on the subject, I think it is noble of you. But I don't think you really want a divorced wife, with all the attendant scandal, and I very much fear that Roland Donavan, whether in war or as a private citizen, will be a hard man to kill."

Dom gave a stiff nod. "Still, you will remember?"

"I will remember," Melanie said.

Dom stepped from the carriage, then turned to hand Melanie out. There was a lamp burning in the house, an indication that Glory was awake. Refusing his offer to see her to her door, requesting that he return the hackney to the gala for Roland's use, Melanie turned away and began to climb the stairs. With every step she took, she could feel Dom's eyes upon her from where he stood on the banquette. He did not move until she had gone inside and closed the door.

Melanie, though she escaped Glory's questions by pleading a headache and going straight to bed, did not sleep. Her thoughts turned endlessly, disturbed by some emotion that hovered just below the surface of her consciousness. With straightforward courage, she thought back to the night when it had all begun. So much had happened since then, so many things large and small had changed. She had been so determined upon vengeance. Where had all that rage and thirst for blood gone? When Roland had not been there all those long, lonely months, she had missed him and denied it to herself. She had maintained that she wanted to be with him again only to make him pay for what he had done, and in the end, the pain and humiliation had been hers. Roland had accused her long months ago of jealousy, and he had been right. It had been jealous anger that had made her lash out at the actress this evening. The truth about the woman, that she was Roland's mother, had brought hurt and embarrassment: hurt that he had not confided in her earlier, and embarrassment for her terrible mistake. She had made amends as best she could, and then she had gone. Why? Why had she run away? The answer could not have been plainer. It was fear: fear that her reparation had not been enough; fear that Roland would not forgive her; fear that he would recognize the jealousy that consumed her; fear that he would question the cause, and questioning, find it.

She was in love with him. There could be no more complete a betrayal of her grandfather's memory and her own honor, no more ignominious an end to her ill-fated schemes of revenge; yet it could not be denied. What a pitiable creature she was. She had done nothing to gain his love, and everything to make him despise her. With her coldness and her disdain, she had even killed with a slow, strangling death the one thing he felt toward her, a desperate desire. Why had it taken her so long to see? Why was it that only now, when he was leaving her and the child she carried, going into danger, that she had been given the power to read her own heart?

She heard him come in, heard his slow footsteps cross the parlor. With her bottom lip caught between her teeth, she flung back the sheet that covered her. With her tossing and turning, her gown had worked itself to the tops of her thighs, pulling tight across the curve of her hip. She left it there. Spreading her hair around her in a tousled cascade, she lay back on the pillow, feigning a deep and even sleep that threatened to lift one swelling breast from the twisted neckline of her nightgown.

Beneath her slitted eyelids, she was aware of the bloom of lamplight in the room. Roland pushed the door open and stood there, holding the lamp from the sitting room in his hand. The seconds ticked past. If he moved, if he breathed, she could not tell. At last he gave a long sigh. The light was withdrawn as he stepped back, closing the door upon her.

Melanie's eyes flew open. Lifting one hand, she pressed the back of her fist to her mouth, drawing a deep, trembling breath. As she let it out slowly, the difficult salt tears flowed from the corners of her eyes and ran in wet tracks into her hair.

Exhausted from doing battle with her emotions, Melanie slept late. When she finally woke, the summer sun was shining with a bright, piercing light through the parting of the drapes, and heat was already beginning to grow in the room. Pushing back her tangled hair, she slid from the bed. With fingers that trembled a little, she searched out her dressing gown and pushed her arms into the sleeves. The house was quiet, too quiet, as she padded through the sitting room. The parlor and dining room were empty. At the door of the extra bedchamber, she paused with her hand on the knob. Then with a resolute lift of her chin, she pushed open the panel and stepped inside.

That Roland had spent the night here was evident from the unmade bed and the basin upon the dressing table with soap scum congealing in the fast-cooling water. That he had gone was also evident. The bed was empty, as were the drawers of the dressing table, and the wardrobe on the opposite wall. The extra uniform and shirts, his shaving equipment and other odds and ends he had gradually accumulated in this room were no longer there. On the end of the dressing table was a button, a brass button from one of his uniforms, printed with the insignia of the expedition. Melanie picked it up, slowly closing her hand on it until she could feel its imprint upon her palm.

"He's gone, Miss Melanie."

"Yes, I know, Glory," Melanie whispered, glancing at her maid, who had come to stand in the doorway. "He didn't even say goodbye."

"I told him I would wake you up, but he said no, that you wouldn't thank me for it. There might still be time to catch him, if you was to hurry."

Melanie glanced at her maid, then looked away again. A wry smile with a hint of a quiver in it curved her mouth. "No. No, he wouldn't thank me for it."

It was perhaps an hour later when the message came. Melanie had dressed, smoothing her hair back into a simple knot on the nape of her neck, and was just sitting down at the small table on the back gallery to a cup of coffee and a French-style fried *beignet* drenched in fine sugar. Glory opened the door to the light knock, then brought the folded missive to Melanie upon the back gallery.

"It was a boy, Miss Melanie. He said as how a gentleman on the street gave him a picayune for delivering this paper to you." As Melanie looked up to meet her eyes, the older woman gave a slow shake of her head. "It wasn't Mr. Roland. The boy said he was short and gray-haired and wore regular clothes, not a uniform."

Melanie took the sheet of sealed parchment envelope into her hand. For some reason she could not have explained, she was reluctant to open it. Chiding herself for silliness, she tore into it, then spread the folded page it contained upon the table.

"Mr dear Madame," she read.

"Your message of last evening was gratefully received. You will be happy to know a steamer of renowned swiftness left this city before midnight carrying the news of the expected arrival of the guests you mentioned. I see no reason why it should not be possible for my countrymen to prepare for these guests a welcome so overwhelming they will be unlikely to leave us, ever. I am enclosing my card. The symbol in the upper left hand corner will, should you present it at my office, secure an immediate and private interview for the discussion of a recompense commensurate with the value of the great service you have rendered.

It was not signed, but the card mentioned was there. Upon that small rectangle of cardboard was engraved the name of the Spanish ambassador.

She had sent no message to the Spanish consul. She had not thought of the ambassador since that night at the theater when he had spoken to her. What could he mean by addressing this letter to her—unless someone had sent the information he had wanted and had sent it in her name, someone who had never expected the gentleman in question to acknowledge the receipt of it. That person could only be someone who had known the Spanish official had contacted her, someone who had been with her that night. Someone who had noticed the card she had dropped in her fumbling haste to put it into her evening reticule. It could only have been Dom.

And the message, so short, so cryptic, could mean but one thing, that the ambassador had been told that the filibusters were leaving today, that he had sent a swift packet with the information to Cuba the night before. It meant, in fact, that General Lopez, and Roland, and the five hundred men who were with them, would be going into a trap.

Melanie surged to her feet so quickly she bumped the

table, sloshing coffee out into her saucer. Pushing back her chair, she started at a run for the door.

"Miss Melanie! What is it?"

"It's a trap, Glory. I've got to warn Roland!"

"What kind of trap do you mean? What kind of trap?"

Melanie, already through the dining room and crossing the parlor, did not answer. She hurried down the steps and into the street. It was deserted. There was no carriage or wagon anywhere that she might borrow or beg for a ride. Setting her mouth in a grim line, she began to run.

She had not gone more than three or four blocks when she heard the faint, far-off sound of cheering. Perhaps they were making speeches before they left. Let them be long-winded, she prayed. Why else would the general decide to embark in the middle of the day, unless he had wanted a crowd to gather to watch his glorious departure? A few blocks more. There were people coming toward her, groups of people smiling, talking, people of all races and occupations, coming from the direction of the levee. They stared at her strangely as she pushed through them. Once a man put out his hand to stop her, but she shook it off, a look of such despair and anguish in her eyes that he did not persist.

Ahead of her were the long arcades of the French Market, and behind them, the towering masts of ships. There was a catch in her side, and she had stepped in a mud puddle, wetting the hem of her dress and getting water and fine grit in her slipper, but she could not stop. The levee was high here, and there was no way to mount it. Behind it, the river was low, so that there was no way to determine what steamboats were on the water, which packet's tall smokestacks towered above the earthen dike. But ahead of her was the landing with its wooden steps and passenger waiting rooms, its docking posts and stevedores and long line of cotton warehouses. Melanie dragged herself wearily up the steps and ran a few feet out along the wide top of the levee. There she stopped and stood still, sucking air into her burning lungs with panting breaths. Perspiration gleamed on her face flushed with her exertions, and the hot summer sun shining down upon her turned her hair to a mass of flame.

Before her lay the river, broad and yellow brown with silt, glittering, sweeping wide in its great crescent shape as it rolled toward the gulf. Upon its curving expanse nothing moved, not a rowboat or a raft. There was no sign of the steamboat *Pampero* that had been tied for so long beside the levee. It was gone, and all that remained was a curling trail of black smoke, like a mourning veil, against the blue of the sky.

Part Two

Chapter 13

TOO LATE. Always too late. Determined that some warning must be given, Melanie had returned to the house on Rampart Street for the message and the Spanish ambassador's card. With them before her, she had sat down to write a letter of explanation to Governor Quitman. What he could do, she did not know, but if there was any possibility that a fast steamer could be sent after Lopez, or that the expedition intended to stop at some point close to the island of Cuba to rest and issue weapons as they had before the first assault, then she must not fail to take advantage of it. Having no proof of his guilt, she did not mention Dom, stating merely that some mistake had been made, that she feared for the safety of the men, and requesting his opinion of the missive and card she had received. As she wrote, she sent Glory to find a messenger, someone with transportation willing to take her letter to the house where the governor and Eliza were staying. She could have taken a hackney and gone herself, but it would have taken too long. Every minute counted.

When the maid returned and the packet of letters was on its way, Melanie began an anxious wait for acknowledgment or some sign from the governor that he had acted on the information given. Nothing came. Two days passed. Melanie could bear it no longer. Hiring a carriage, she had herself driven, with Glory in attendance, to the private home where the Quitmans had been staying.

The woman who had extended her hospitality, a pleasant older woman with a birdlike voice and quick movements, greeted Melanie cordially. She was extremely sorry, but the governor was no longer in residence with her, had not been for the better part of two days—or was it three? Yes, she believed she did remember a message arriving for John Quitman. Brought by a drayman, was it not? Most peculiar. The governor and his dear wife had been gone the better part of an hour before it came. They had packed their things early and sent them ahead to the steamboat, while they met with friends over luncheon. Her butler, such a conscientious fellow, had brought the note to her, but by the time she understood what it was all about, the man with the dray had gone. My goodness, she did hope it was nothing important. There had been one or two other letters for the Quitmans since then, cards of invitation she thought, and she had been meaning to send them on to Natchez, only she had not found the time.

Reassuring the elderly woman, Melanie indicated that she would be traveling up to Monmouth in a day or two herself and would deliver her message in person.

"Well, then, that's all right," the Quitmans' hostess said brightly. Going to the secretary, she searched out the letter Melanie had sent, brought it back, and placed it in her hand.

It was not all right, of course. With such a tremendous head start, there was no way now that a warning could reach Lopez and his men. There was nothing Melanie could do except wait for news of the disaster.

It had not been a lie that she meant to return to Natchez. Roland had made her promise weeks before that for safety's sake she would not remain in New Orleans many hours after he had departed. Already, she was behind schedule. She was not sorry to be going. The heat of the summer was nearly unbearable, made worse by frequent rainstorms that left the city steaming. A ship coming from the coast of Africa had brought yellow fever, and there were rumors that it was spreading like wildfire in the Irish section. At Greenlea the breezes would be blowing across the veranda, rustling the leaves of the trees that shaded the old house. The crepe myrtles would be sending forth their feathery pink flowers, and in the garden the daisies and lilies would be in bloom. If bad news was to come to her, then let her receive it at Greenlea where she would be better able to bear it.

The only thing that stopped Melanie from throwing herself in to full-scale preparations for departure upriver was the arrival of an epistle from the woman who was her mother-in-law. Madame Colleen Antoinette Dubois would give herself the pleasure of a visit the following afternoon to discuss matters that concerned them both. To see the other woman was the last thing Melanie wanted. Knowledge of her existence had brought Melanie nothing but grief and embarrassment. Though after their first meeting they had finally parted on terms of amiability, it was not an experience she wished to repeat, especially now, when she knew that indirectly she might be the cause of the death of Madame Dubois's son. There seemed to be no help for it, however. Her spirits grim, she began to prepare for the visit.

Without meaning to in the least, Melanie found herself taking special pains. She saw to it that the parlor was cleaned and dusted and set about with flowers, the gallery and stairs swept, and the doorsteps that led from the banquette sprinkled with brick dust. She would serve tea, of course, and Glory would bake a cake and make a few of her delicious fruit-filled pastries. Melanie must wash her hair, cream her hands, buff her nails, and see that her afternoon gown of white voile sprigged with blue forget-me-nots was pressed and laid out.

At the last minute, just as Melanie was beginning to dress, Glory came hurrying into the bedchamber to tell her that the tea caddy, the small wooden box where tea was kept here in New Orleans, was nearly empty.

Raising the lid, Melanie gave an exclamation of annoyance. There was scarcely enough left for one cup, much less a full pot. With the heat of the last week or so, she had left off her evening cup. She had not remembered the supply was so low. She must have something to offer her guest. There was nothing for it, except to send Glory after a quarter pound.

The maid was nearly out of the house when Melanie thought of something else. Holding her dressing gown around her, she ran from the room into the sitting room and through it onto the front gallery. "Glory!" she called, leaning over the railing. "See if there is a lemon to be had, will you?" Though she did not use it herself, there were many who did. It was probable that an actress, with her exposure to exotic new ways, would expect lemon to be served.

"Yes, Miss Melanie, I sure will," Glory said and turning, trotted off.

Melanie stared after the maid, wishing she wouldn't hurry so in the heat. She would have called after her, if she had thought it would do any good. Glory, since Melanie had told her the true identity of the woman who was coming, was as concerned as Melanie, if not more so, with making a good impression. At least the elderly woman would not have to go all the way to the French Market. There was a small store only a few blocks away that carried such delicacies.

Pushing away from the railing to turn back into the house, Melanie's attention was caught by movement at the house across the street. In the doorway of the upper level stood the man who was the keeper of the quadroon who was her neighbor. It had been some time since she had seen him; he had been conspicuously absent since Roland's return in the spring. She had begun to hope he had deserted his mistress and his child. It appeared now they had not been so fortunate.

The man was staring at her with fixed intentness, his fists propped on his hips and his legs wide spread. For an instant Melanie seemed to feel his malignant dislike emanating toward her with his lustful interest in her state of deshabille. His gaze seemed locked on her hair spilling around her and the thin dressing gown she wore that molded itself to her form as she moved. The sensation was so unpleasant that she shivered. With more haste than dignity, she turned on her bare heel and marched back into the house, slamming the blinds closed behind her.

In her bedchamber, she brushed her hair and began to form the lustrous auburn strands into a figure eight. She would have liked something less severe, but there would be no time when Glory returned. It was all too likely that even now she would be forced to make some excuse to her guest for not being able to serve refreshments immediately.

She had just picked up her hand mirror in its silver frame, swinging around to use it to view her handiwork at the back of her head in the dressing table mirror, when a sound caught her attention. It was too soon for Glory to be back, yet she could have sworn she had heard the creaking of the front stairs. Another noise came, this time a shuffling whisper of footsteps on the front gallery. With the mirror still in her hand, Melanie walked slowly from the bedchamber, passing through the sitting room into the parlor.

The blinds were closed, the room still and heavy with the somnolence of late afternoon. A fly buzzed about the walls. Nothing else moved. Through the slats of the blinds, she could see a section of the gallery with the long, slanting rays of the waning sun lying on the floor. That golden heat was motionless, silent. Still, Melanie caught her bottom lip between her teeth as she stared at the blinds. They were not locked, nor were any of the French windows along the front of the house. At Greenlea the doors had never been locked, not even at night. She had seen to that task while Roland was away, even before the incident of the prowler. But once he had returned, she had lost the habit. So long as he was there, or she knew he would be returning, she had felt safe. The urge to slam the bolts home now was strong. Why she should feel more

273

threatened than on any of the scores of nights when she had gone quietly to sleep with the doors flung wide for coolness, she could not have said, but there seemed to hover in the air a sense of menace so strong that the skin at the nape of her neck prickled, and gooseflesh moved along her arms.

Imagination, she told herself firmly. It would be a good thing when she was away from this house and its memories and back at Greenlea. With a brief shake of her head, she turned, moving back toward the bedchamber. As she walked, she lifted her mirror, examining the sides of her coiffure.

Abruptly she came to a halt. There had been a shadow of movement behind her, inside the extra bedchamber. She whirled to see the man from across the street standing in the doorway. Behind him, the French windows that led out onto the front gallery stood open. He wore a shirt without studs so that it fell open to his waist, and trousers of black stuff over half-boots. On his florid, darkly handsome face there was a cruel smile, and he carried a slender and pliable carriage whip.

"What are you doing here?" Melanie demanded.

"We have a score to settle, you and I. I have waited a long time for this moment; waited and watched you and imagined how it would be. And now with the precious soldier husband of yours gone, the waiting is over. It is only you and I."

His voice dropped to a low note. His eyes raked over her as he came slowly toward her. His gaze returning to her pale face, he slashed the whip in the air, making it whine.

Melanie compressed her lips. "We may be alone just now, but my maid will return soon, and I am expecting a guest."

"Your maid, I can deal with. As for your guest, since you are not yet dressed, there should be time enough for my purpose before he arrives."

Staring at him, Melanie realized that if he expected her guest to be a man, that was all to the good. "What makes you think I intended to dress?" she asked with a small smile.

"So that's the way it is?" the man sneered. "In that case, I will simply have to hurry—and your guest will find you a little less clothed than he expected."

He drew nearer with every word. Only a little more and he would be able to reach her with the vicious lash of the whip he held in his hand. Swiftly, Melanie drew back the mirror she held and let it fly at his head. He ducked and it fell harmlessly past him to shatter against the wall, but by that time, Melanie had dashed around the end of the settee, plunging for the blinds at the French windows.

Her hand was on the knob, dragging at it, when he caught her from behind. As he jerked her back, the louvered panel shuddered in its frame; then both halves swung slowly outward. A scream rose in her throat, vibrating in the air. She kicked and twisted, fighting to get to the opening. Drawing back his hand, he struck her a blow that made her head ring. In that instant of shock, he lifted her bodily and threw her across the room. She crashed into the settee with bruising force. He was upon her at once, his brutal hands ripping at her dressing gown, tearing it, dragging it from her shoulders.

Rage exploded in Melanie's mind, and she came up with a shriek, clawing for his face with blue fire in her eyes. His quick backward jerk saved his sight from her raking nails, but he could not prevent the ribbons of red that scored his cheeks. Wrenching from him in his instant of stunned surprise that she would strike back, Melanie whirled around the end of the settee, tugging her dressing gown back up to cover herself, her frantic gaze searching for a weapon.

"Why, you little bitch," the man growled, touching his face, staring at the blood that came away on his fingers. Taking a firmer grip on his whip, he lunged after her.

He was stopped by an onyx figure of a nymph and satyr hurling into his ribs. He grunted, clamping his hand to the bruise as the statuette clattered to the floor. Then with a murderous look in his yellow brown eyes, he leaped for her.

The slashing whip caught her as she threw the second statuette. Its red-hot lash burned through the material of her dressing gown, and she gasped with pain as her missile fell short. The fireplace poker was close to hand. Seizing it, she swung it with both hands in a vicious arc at his head. He threw up his arm, catching the blow on his wrist. Then as she drew back once more, he lashed out with the whip, flaying her arms. Despite the searing agony, she brought the poker around, knew the satisfaction of hearing it crack against his skull. Her strength was only enough to madden him, however, and with blood fury in his face, he moved in. He tore the poker from her grasp, sending the whip curling and crackling around her. Writhing, trying to protect her face, Melanie staggered back. Even through the material that covered her, her nerves screamed, flinching from the pain. There was no protection from the biting lash. In horror, she heard the ripping sound of her dressing gown over her shoulders parting in shreds, felt the wetness of blood start on her arms and across her back. Sickness rose in her throat. Convulsive shudders shook her, and her knees grew weak.

As through a haze she saw him loom above her, felt his hands as they fastened on the front of her dressing gown, wrenching it open to expose the proud upthrusts of her breasts with the rose-tinted nipples contracted in pain. He hauled the neckline down her shoulders, entrapping her arms in the sleeves. Then he dropped the whip and pulled her to him, his squeezing hands mauling her flesh as he bent her backward.

His sour breath was in her face. His slick lips slid over her cheek, searching for her mouth. But as the pain lessened, her brain cleared. His hold was lax in his confidence that she was cowed. Melanie let herself sag as though faint. Then as he gave an obscene chuckle of triumph, she erupted, bringing her knee up between his wide-spread legs. As his breath left him and he doubled over, she dragged herself free, spinning away from him, though she left her dressing gown in his clutching hands.

The poker lay on the floor behind him. She dived for it. Seeing her purpose, he plunged after her. They came together, scrambling for the weighted weapon. Melanie was thrown off balance. Leaving the poker, the man grappled with her, and hooking an arm around her waist, half pushed, half dragged her to the settee. Throwing her down, he put his knee in her chest, driving the air from her lungs. He snatched one wrist so she could not defend herself. Then he smashed her across the face. As she lay stunned, his hard fingers shifted to her forearm while his other hand passed between her legs. As she gasped for breath, he gave a grunt and heaved her over onto her belly. For a moment he stood gloating over her white nakedness stretched out before him. Then he bent to pick up his whip.

Dazedly Melanie watched him, saw him straighten, saw the cruel smile that twisted his lips as he chose the place on her prostrate body where he would deliver the first of the red stripes he had promised her months before. He tested the suppleness of his whip between his hands, then with slow anticipation, raised it above his head.

In Melanie's fevered mind there was no thought of submission. Never, not ever, would a man take or touch her against her will again. She came up off the settee with a rush, rolling, launching herself at the man's legs. She struck hard against his knees, and he came down with a crash. She surged up on her hands and knees, but before she could get away, he seized her hair, his fingers gripping the loosened mass that hung in a tangle down her back. He turned his hand, deliberately pulling, and with tears starting in her eyes, Melanie was hauled twisting and kicking to lie under him. One arm was bent behind her, while his sharp forearm pinned the other to the floor. His legs confined her movement, and the bulge of his manhood pressed into her side. Defiance still shining in her violet blue eyes, she stared up at him and watched as he lowered bared teeth to the trembling mound of her breast.

277

"Henri! No!"

The shout came from the open door. Hard upon it came the hurtling figure of a woman. The quadroon mistress of the man who held Melanie struck her lover with both hands, shoving him from her, knocking him to one side.

On one elbow, he glowered up at her. "Get out, you slut. I'll attend to you later."

"I won't! You shall not do this, Henri. You are my man, and I will not let you!" Running to him once more, she tugged at his arm.

Deliberately, the man balled his fist and slammed it into her belly. The quadroon was thrown back, crouching over, pressing her hands to her abdomen as she made harsh, gasping noises.

Melanie squirmed, trying to drag herself from under him, but he swung back to her, ignoring his mistress. Shifting his position to hold her flailing legs more rigid, he sneered and ran his hand downward in an intimate caress that made the blood rush to her head. Abruptly, his mouth flew open and air rushed out. With a strangled sound in his throat, he released Melanie, grabbing backward, trying to reach between his shoulder blades. The strength and vicious purpose ebbed from him, and his eyes set in a fixed, unbelieving stare. Slowly he toppled forward across Melanie. From his back protruded the hilt of a slender knife, a feminine thing set with sparkling paste jewels.

For an instant Melanie lay still. Then with a shudder of horror, she shoved at him, sliding from under him. On her knees, she looked at the quadroon who crouched on the other side of the man who had been her lover. The woman's eyes were dull with pain, and though she still held to her belly where the dead man had struck her, her anguish was not physical. Her face was waxen pale, and she seemed to have stopped breathing as surely as the man who lay face down between them.

Suddenly the quadroon gave a gasping sob and fell face downward, throwing herself across the body of her man.

278

Clutching at him, she gave way to deep and desperate grief. Melanie, watching her, sat as one stunned.

How long she might have sat there unmoving was beyond knowing. It was footsteps that roused her, footsteps on the stairs outside, coming nearer. Pushing herself to her feet, she stood swaying, looking around for the tatters of her dressing gown. By the time she saw it, it was too late. The doorway was filled with people. It was an instant before her vision cleared, before she recognized that the person standing against the light was Madame Dubois. Behind her was Glory, her face shocked and anxious as she stared into the shambles of the room.

It was the actress who recovered first. "Merciful heaven," she breathed, then turning, drew Glory into the room and reached to close the blind. With her skirts rustling around her, she moved quickly to where Melanie's dressing gown lay and stooped to pick it up and shake it out. Her face turned grimly pale as she saw the rents across the back and sides. Still she moved to Melanie and helped her into it.

Stepping back, the actress said, "I am not certain what happened here, but one or two things seem fairly obvious. Did you kill him, or did she?"

Melanie's whip marks were beginning to burn now as if she had been seared with a hot iron. The trembling of reaction shook her, and when she tried to speak her teeth chattered so she could make herself understood only with difficulty. Finally she whispered, "I didn't."

"Is he a prowler, or what?" Madame Dubois asked, indicating with a gentle touch that Melanie be seated on the settee.

"No. He—he lives across the street."

The narrowing gaze of the actress went to the still-sobbing quadroon. "I begin to see," she said. "Is there, by chance, any brandy in the house?"

Glory had moved to stand beside the settee, touching Melanie's snarled hair with gentle brown fingers. Now she looked up. "Yes, ma'am," she said. "I'll get it."

Madame Dubois stood staring down at Melanie. Then

with abrupt decision, she put aside her fan and her gloves and moved to sit down beside her. "This man," she said with a brief, telling gesture, "he seems to have been something of a beast."

"Y—yes," Melanie answered simply.

"Toward you only?"

Melanie shook her head. "Toward her, his mistress, also, and his child."

"It would be a great pity then if anyone had to suffer for the manner of his passing."

Slowly Melanie turned her deep blue gaze upon the actress. "What do you mean?"

"In your case the authorities would be lenient, even sympathetic. It is unlikely they will look upon the woman there, who I assume to have been his mistress, in the same light. If such women were allowed to kill the men who keep them at will when they are wronged, then the lives of half the men in the city would not be safe. It is almost certain that she will be hanged."

"Oh, no! But—but it wasn't her fault, and she has a child, little more than a baby. What will become of him?"

"It sometimes happens that the cause of justice can best be served by avoiding the law and the men who make it."

Melanie searched the face of the woman beside her. "What are you suggesting?"

"First, I believe we must do something for the girl there; then I, for one, intend to have a glass of brandy to steady my nerves. After that, when we are all calmer, perhaps we can decide what is to be done."

In the end, it was Glory who was most helpful. In the outdoor kitchen there was a large cotton basket of split white oak that she had been using to hold firewood. It could just as easily hold a man, if they acted quickly. It sounded difficult, but it was not. It was only grisly as they picked him up by the ankles and shoulders, trying to avoid getting in his blood, trying to get his flopping arms inside. The quadroon, whose name they discovered was Elena, wanted to help, but she could not, anymore than she could stop the tears that streamed down her face or her instinctive outcry (for them not to hurt him) as they pushed and shoved, curling the corpse into the basket.

The three women rested a few minutes, and then they dragged and pushed the basket from the parlor into the dining room and out onto the gallery, then down the stairs into the courtyard. There they piled it high with soiled linens, pushed it into the passageway that led through the raised basement to the street, and left it.

Madame Dubois inspected herself and her clothing for bloodstains. Taking up her belongings, she pulled on her gloves, at the same time going over the details of what must be done with Melanie. Satisfied that all was arranged, she descended to her carriage and waiting coachman with a tranquil smile upon her face, for all the world as though she had done nothing more than enjoy a quiet chat.

In her absence, Glory crossed with Elena to the house on the other side of the street. While they were seeing to the baby and packing the quadroon's things, Melanie pulled her own trunks from the extra bedchamber and began to fill them.

It was amazing how much could be done when it was necessary. By the time darkness descended and the wheels of Madame Dubois's carriage were heard once more, preparations for departure had not only been completed, but Melanie had found time to bathe her welts and let Glory spread a healing ointment upon them before she donned her traveling costume.

When Melanie let the actress into the house, however, Madame Dubois was not alone. With her was the actor who had played her lover upon the stage. Tall and quietly smiling, he stood back, waiting to be introduced.

"Melanie, my dear, don't look like that!" Madame Dubois exclaimed. "This is Jean-Claude Belmont, whom you may recognize from *Camille*. Being an actor, he has little respect for authority, and as a Frenchman, he has a great deal of sympathy for a pretty woman. Look upon him, if you will, as a strong back to lift those heavy things

281

which may be too burdensome for a woman, and as a means of safe conduct in dangerous places."

A look of communication passed between the two women. Melanie turned to the young man. "You are a most welcome addition to our number then," she said, extending her hand.

His smile was charming, if a trifle knowing, as he inclined his upper body in a bow. As he spoke, admiration lurked in the depths of his sherry brown eyes. "It is my pleasure. Ladies in distress have an irresistible appeal to me."

"Behave, Jean-Claude," the actress admonished him. "I believe I told you this lady is the wife of my son."

"So you did, though you look so young for such things as marriage-age sons that the fact keeps slipping my mind."

"I see that. Shall we get on with the job at hand? It is your brawn that is needed, not your blarney."

"Cruel Colleen," he murmured and, smiling at Melanie, gave a tiny shrug.

The passageway was a black tunnel that echoed eerily to their shuffling footsteps as they walked the basket through it. Outside, the street was empty, the houses that fronted upon it quiet and unlighted in the midnight stillness. The carriage in which Jean-Claude and Madame Dubois had arrived was a phaeton with low-slung lines that spoke of speed. It had been drawn up near the door of the passageway. With enormous effort they carried the basket to the carriage. Then the actor put his shoulder under it and heaved it up into the back. It tried to topple over, but Jean-Claude grabbed it, quickly stuffing the spilling sheets back inside.

Leaving Glory with Elena and the sleeping baby, the three of them, Melanie and Colleen, with Jean-Claude in the driver's seat, turned toward the outskirts of the city and the winding road that led alongside the Mississippi River.

It was morning before they returned, midday before the last of their things had been gathered together and delivered, with those of Madame Dubois and Jean-Claude, to one of the steamboats that sat beside the levee. Now that the filibusters had gone, there was any number of women leaving the city. No one evidenced the least interest in the going of a few more. They boarded the boat without incident and went directly to their staterooms. Elena, listed as the maid of the actress, was given a small room beside the stateroom of Madame Dubois for herself and her child. Melanie, since on this occasion she was traveling alone and with dwindling funds, took a much less luxurious room than the one Roland had engaged for their journey from St. Francisville to New Orleans. Instead of a tester bed, it was fitted with bunks, a much more satisfactory arrangement, since it meant that Glory could stay with her.

There was a time when it looked as if the steamboat would not depart until the next day—a matter of cargo, it seemed. Hearing the news, Madame Debois arrayed herself in a daring costume consisting of thirty yards of feminine, gracefully fluttering yellow muslin edged in apple green ribbon, then made her way to the Texas deck. The captain was not an unreasonable man, nor one impervious to beauty. He had seen and enjoyed Madame Dubois's *Camille,* he was flattered that she had chosen his packet for her upriver journey, and yes, he most definitely understood the importance of being on time for her theater engagements. If Madame Dubois would do him the honor of sitting on his right at the head of the table at dinner, he could promise her that the *Southern Belle* would be leaving the dock within the hour.

It was only after the steamboat was well out into the river, churning her way upstream against the sluggish current, that Melanie realized she had felt not the least tremor of fear. Too many things had happened, there had been too many other worries for her to succumb to such an outdated terror. She was cured. Would Roland be glad if he knew? Or would he shrug it off in cold unconcern?

Melanie stood in the stern of the boat, watching the revolving paddle wheel and their boiling, muddy gold

283

wake and listening to the rush of the water. The wind of their passage whipped her dress around her, showing the frothing lace of her petticoats. High overhead the black smoke flew like a flag, and now and then a down-draft sprinkled her with fine ash. Where was Roland now? she wondered. Did he stand on the deck of a ship, also? Did he think of her?

Her hand that gripped the railing tightened. With sudden violence she found herself wishing she had told Roland she was to have his child. Would that have moved him? Would he have been glad or sorry? Would it have made him stay, or simply increased his determination to wrest something of value from the island of Cuba?

The green shoreline drifted by. The sun began to set, its golden rays slanting across the water, giving it an opaline sheen. A white crane rose from its perch on a dead stump and, with a slow and stately flight, disappeared over the tops of the encroaching trees with their hanging rags of Spanish moss. Soon they would tie up for the night. By this time tomorrow evening they would be nearing Natchez. There she would occupy herself with what she did so well: waiting. She would wait for news of the expedition, wait for the birth of her child, wait for the time when the guilt and remorse she felt for her part in the Lopez affair began to fade. And what then? What if she were a widow? No, she did not want to think of that. Somehow she would survive, yes, and raise the babe she carried. Somehow she would forget—or did she want to do that? There had been times in the last months worth remembering, moments when she and Roland had seemed to draw close. Some of the things he had said came back to her now with a soft and tender cadence, and she could not help believing that his feelings toward her had, at least on those occasions, been the same as her own were now. What might have happened between them if they had met under different circumstances, without the tragedy of her grandfather's death to divide them, without the demands and duties of war, or her own willful misjudgment of his relationship with Madame Dubois to place strain on their days together? There were no answers. What had happened could not be changed, anymore than Lopez could be called back, and Dom's betrayal be undone.

Suspecting Dom as she did, how was she to comport herself when next they met, as surely they must? His guilt was not certain, that much was true; yes, the fact that she had not heard from him since the expedition had left served to help confirm it in her own mind. Even if he and Chloe had left New Orleans at the same time as the Quitmans, it seemed unlikely he would have gone without saying goodbye, unless there had been a reason. The evidence against him was overwhelming. He had been the only one who knew of her conversation with the Spanish official. He held a personal grudge against Roland, and on the night before the expedition sailed, he had mentioned to her the possibility that Roland would be killed. Still, she could have wished for some proof of her suspicions. It might be interesting to see how Dom would react if she faced him with accusations. Though what she would do if his guilt were indeed a fact, she did not know. Given the dubious legality of the expedition, he could hardly be charged with treason. Under the circumstances, the American government might even be tempted to present him with a citation. His action, if it were known, would not make him popular in the region where he lived. But could she expose him to the contempt of his friends and neighbors, knowing as she did that if she herself were not strictly to blame for what he had done, she at least lay at the heart of it?

Such thoughts were useless then. What she would do, what she would say, would have to wait upon the time when she saw Dom again.

Chapter 14

"So HERE is where you got off to! Your maid told me you were taking the air, but I never expected to find you at the noisiest part of the ship."

Melanie turned to smile at Madame Dubois as the woman came toward her with her yellow draperies flying in the wind. "I like it here. Is—is everything all right, Madame Dubois?"

"It would give me great pleasure to have you call me Colleen. As you know, I am sensitive about having a son, much less a daughter-in-law. And yes, everything is perfectly fine. Pray don't look so distressed. It may be too early to say so with any certainty, but I believe we have gotten away with our gamble."

Melanie could not suppress a shudder that ran over her. In her mind's eye, she could still see the cotton basket rolling, tumbling down the bank of the river, bubbling, making awful gurgling sounds as it sank beneath the water. It had been a terrible way to dispose of a human being, as if he had been no more than a dead cat, or a piece of offal. Despite what Henri had done to her, and what he had intended to do, she could not help feeling they should have treated his body with more ceremony. She had no feeling for him as a man. It was just that by their actions it seemed they had negated the dignity of all life.

Summoning a smile, Melanie said, "If we have won

free, it is due to your quick thinking. We all, Glory and myself, Elena and her baby, owe you a debt of gratitude."

"Please, you owe me nothing. I was glad that I was able to help you in some way, since I had injured you so."

"Injured me? Surely not."

"I am speaking of my insistence on keeping my identity secret. I thought it was for the best, not merely for the sake of my career, but for Roland's benefit, also. He has sworn a dozen times that it makes him no difference that his mother is on the stage, that I am one of those wicked women who deserted her husband, and, let it be admitted, her child. Nonetheless, I have lived long enough to know that such things matter. In certain circles, such as strait-laced Natchez, with its enthusiasm for the English upper class, its habit of aping London manners and mores, it matters greatly. Until he came to Mobile to tell me of the construction you had placed upon the attention he was paying me, and to beg me to change my mind, I thought it just possible you might prefer that your husband had a certain admiration for an actress to knowing that the grandmother of your children was a loose woman of the theater, and an adultress."

Melanie gave a shake of her head. "It would not have mattered."

"Possibly not, though I assure you, it would to some."

In all honesty, Melanie had to admit that was true. Only a year and a half before, it might have mattered to her. It seemed that making mistakes and finding oneself outside the bounds of acceptable behavior had a remarkable effect upon one's tolerance for the same thing in others.

"At any rate," Colleen Dubois went on, "I wanted to apologize for being the cause of dissension between you and Roland."

"We will forget it, if you please. I was stupidly jealous, and—and insulting to you. I cannot think of it without cringing inside with shame."

As if on impulse, the other woman reached out to

287

touch her arm as they leaned against the railing. "I would like to tell you how it came about, if you don't mind. For the sake of my grandchildren?"

Melanie looked at her, searching deep in the dark green eyes that were so like Roland's. "You know?" she asked.

"There is a bloom about you, a freshness and beauty that is hard to mistake. Also, yesterday, when I came upon you with that swine lying upon the floor, your face was bruised and your arms and shoulders covered with red weals, and yet you held your hand protectively, like so, over your abdomen. Such a gesture conveys much, especially to an actress who notices and remembers such small details. It is strange that Roland did not mention it. I cannot help wondering, does he know?"

"No," Melanie whispered with a shake of her head. "I didn't tell him."

"There are other ways of learning," Roland's mother said, a frown drawing her dark, winged brows together. "He is a fool if he inquired no more closely into the health and well-being of his wife. I must speak to him, I really must, though perhaps I should not be surprised. His father was much the same."

When she did not go on, Melanie said, "I met Roland's father when we were first married. He is not a well man."

"So Roland tells me. I wish I could care, but I cannot. Whatever was between us died long ago and cannot be brought back to life. I was going to tell you about it, wasn't I?"

Colleen Antoinette Dubois turned to look out over the fast-darkening water. It was so long before she spoke Melanie thought she had changed her mind. She did not move, but stood silent, waiting.

"Acting," the woman began at last, "was not a chance profession for me; my father's family had long been famous in the Irish theater. My father and his grandfather before him were well known on the stages of Dublin, London, Glasgow, Paris, and many others. My mother was also an actress of stature, though she had been cast off by her family for following such a disreputable calling. She met my father while he was playing in France, and they were married in a week's time. She died a year later, and my father was never the same. He took me with him wherever he went, however. By the time I was twelve I was treading the boards, using the surname that had been my mother's before her marriage. Then, when I was just turned seventeen, my father died. That same year, the company I was with was booked for an American tour. We played New Orleans, and in the audience was a lanky cotton farmer. He thought I was beautiful, an angelic being touched with stardust. To me he was handsome and virile. I was lonely without my father, and Robert Donavan represented security, something I had never had. There was, also, let it be admitted, the immediate leap of excitement between us. It is odd, is it not, how you feel that in some men, and not in others? How the touch of one man can be thrilling, while that of another brings forth no response, or else is actively distasteful?"

Melanie murmured something in agreement. Behind her, the lamps in the main cabin of the steamboat were being lighted. Soon the signal for dinner would be given.

The actress gave a sigh. "Robert and I were married and he took me to this tiny shack—it can be graced by no more exalted a name—on his plantation in the heart of the hot, pestilential delta land along the river. I was disappointed, and I am afraid I let him know it. I became pregnant at once, with all the ills and tempers usual to such a state. His fragile, lovely angel disintegrated into a querulous, quarrelsome young girl who was heartily sick of marriage and terribly homesick for Ireland. He, on the other hand, became a demanding husband who wanted a gentle and submissive wife who could cook and clean and sew and help him build his cotton empire while providing heirs for it. I left him, returning to Ireland to have my child." She shrugged. "It was, all in all, a wise move on my part. The stupidity was what I did afterward. Robert wanted his son and heir, and so he convinced himself he loved me. He came after me, and such was his conviction he convinced me of it, also. Everything would be different, he said. He would build me a house fit for a queen, and I would reign there. It was a pretty picture. The actuality was not. That time I lasted three years, until after the birth of another child, this time a girl, who died. At that time, we were neither quite sane, I think. When I announced that I was leaving, Robert went into a rage. He swore I would never leave with my child, that he would not be denied his heir because I craved the dissolute excitement of the theater. He called me names, hurtful dirty names that made me see what he thought of my mother and father and their way of life, and of me. In a towering temper I hit upon a means, or so I thought, to make him release my son to me. I told him that Roland was not his child, that I had been carrying him when we married."

Melanie made a small sound of shock and understanding. So this was the explanation for the bitter words Roland's father had thrown at him. It made sense now, tragic sense.

"I see what you are thinking and you are right," Colleen went on. "It was a mistake. He believed me, but his pride was so injured and his need to be revenged for what he thought to be the way I had used him was so great that he still was determined to keep Roland from me. I went to an attorney, but the law was on my husband's side. I had no right to the child I had borne. He would be raised by Negro nursemaids and menservants, and unless I returned to Robert, I would never see him again."

"What a terrible thing," Melanie breathed.

"Yes," Colleen said. "There was only one thing to be done, and I did it. I stole my own child. I went to the house while his father was in the fields. Roland was playing outside, and I picked him up, put him in my carriage, and drove away with him. I took him to Ireland where I returned to the stage. With him always near me, I played small towns and hamlets all over Great Britain and Europe. But gradually I began to be known. There were favorable reviews and newspaper notices. When Roland was eight, Robert's men caught up with me, and they took my son screaming from my dressing room at a Drury Lane theater in London. I returned to the United States, went to Robert, and begged him on my knees for my son. He refused. He had a court order which barred me from playing in the States until after Roland reached his majority. When I saw that it was useless, I tried to tell my husband that I had lied to him, that Roland was really his son. He would not believe me. He thought I was trying to ease the way of my misbegotten issue. He still thought Roland was the child of another man, and he had taken him from me not out of love but out of a need to punish. I had to go away and leave my son there. I did not see him again for ten years, until he was a young man away from home at military school. But he remembered me, and the days we had been together. He came to me with gladness and joy. And now, because we were torn apart, because we have both suffered at his father's hands, there is a closeness between us I cannot explain."

Melanie smiled, a sheen of moisture in her own violet blue eyes. "I think you have explained it," she said.

"I am glad, but can you also see why I am concerned that there is friction between you and my son? I know that hard and hurtful words can destroy, that misunderstandings can ruin lives, and I do so badly want Roland to be happy. He deserves that much, after all this time."

"Yes," Melanie replied. "It does seem so." What else was there to say? She could hardly tell Roland's mother her son would never be happy in his marriage because more than likely he would never live to continue it. And even if he did return, he was unlikely to discover contentment with a woman who was haunted by the knowledge that she may have helped cause the death of other men. The pain of such thoughts was private, hers alone.

"I am certain if Roland cannot find joy with a girl such as you, he can never fine it with anyone."

"It is—kind of you to say so, but then you have been kindness itself. I haven't yet thanked you enough for your intervention last evening. I am not certain what would

291

have become of us all if you had not appeared when you did."

"Nonsense," Colleen said. "I am only glad I was there. I would never have been able to forgive myself if you had been pulled into such a nasty business as that promised to be while I sat safely in my rooms, ignorant of it. Roland would never have forgiven me, nor would he have forgiven himself for leaving you to the mercy of such a man, and to the plight in which you found yourself. But enough. Let us erase such things from our minds. And if you will come with me to our cabin, we will see what can be done to erase the visible reminders of it, also. The art of camouflaging the years and other faults of the face with rouge and powders is a specialty of mine, and I believe I can do much to conceal your bruises, if you will let me."

Morning dawned bright and clear. Before the sun had burned its way through the river mists, the *Southern Belle* was plowing its way north against the current once more. Melanie, despite the gentle rocking of the boat against the bank, had not slept well. She was up and walking the decks in time to nod to the planters, drummers, and river-boat gamblers as they emerged from the smoking parlor after their all-night poker games. The men bowed and tipped their hats but made no overtures. There was about her an aloofness, a pensive reserve that defied familiarity by the simple expedient of refusing to recognize it.

Being without appetite, even a trifle nauseous, she did not go to breakfast. She spent that hour sitting on the foredeck in that area which had the look and feel of a second story gallery with its turned columns, balustrades, and comfortable rocking chairs. A watchful steward brought her a cup of coffee there, and she sat drinking it in small, difficult swallows, staring at the passing shore-line.

Footsteps approached. A man stopped beside her chair. "May I join you?"

Melanie glanced up to see Jean-Claude, the actor who was traveling with Colleen. As he inclined toward her, she

292

saw he was outfitted with elegance combined with flamboyance. His coat was buff, his trousers cream colored, and his blue and buff waistcoat was complemented by a flowing cream silk tie, the ends of which flapped in the breeze. His smile was frank, and his manner, though ingratiating, suggested that if she refused his request, he would take himself away at once. Melanie's thoughts were not so pleasant that she could not bear to be distracted from them.

"Yes, certainly," she replied.

"I did not mean to intrude," the actor said, drawing up a chair beside her, "but I cannot help myself. You fascinate me. Women, I do believe, are wonderful creatures. The more I see of them, the more obvious this becomes to me."

"I beg your pardon?"

"They seem fragile and helpless, is it not so? They must be protected, handed from carriages, helped through doorways, up and down stairs, and yet, when a man wants excitement or comfort, where does he turn? You absorb the passions and the wrath of men, you bring children into the world with great travail. Some, such as Colleen, take their livelihood from a world that thinks of them as helpless children. And still, you smile. If you will permit me to be personal, Madame Donavan, take yourself. If I did not know that only a short time ago you were beaten, saw murder done, helped to dispose of the corpse of the dead man, that you had been abandoned by your husband for the sake of a fool's quest, left alone with the knowledge that you will soon have his child, I would never suspect. You look calm and beautiful, untouched, and untouchable."

"Is that the way I seem to you? Then I must thank you for telling me, for it is far from the way I feel. I cannot help but believe that your appreciation for my sex must stem from your acquaintance with Colleen."

"Ah, yes. She is magnificent, is she not? A most marvelous woman. In ways that go beyond outward appearance, the two of you are much alike. She too has this great capacity for endurance."

"Have you known her long?" Melanie inquired, though more for something to say than from any curiosity concerning their relationship.

"A few months, no more. And in these last two days I have learned more of her than in all the other days and weeks together. I never knew she had a son, never realized she was of sufficient age to have one so mature. I still cannot comprehend that she is nearly of an age with my own mother. It is incredible. She is incredible!"

It was not a subject Melanie felt she ought to discuss in depth. She started to speak, to turn the subject into somewhat different channels, when her attention was caught by a steamboat fast overtaking them on the left. She was a side-wheeler with her paddle boxes on the sides, and from the looks of the smoke that poured from her stacks, she appeared to have a full head of steam. Melanie turned back. "I understand that you and Colleen have engagements upriver?" she said.

"Indeed, yes, St. Louis, Cincinnati, Baltimore, a dozen other cities. It is a hard schedule, but Colleen preferred to be busy to sitting in New Orleans waiting for news. Though you would not guess it to look at her, she fears for her son on that hot, sunbaked island. Not, I think, without reason."

Jean-Claude broke off as the steamboat drawing even with them gave a blast of its whistle. From their own boat came an answer to the challenge, and they began to pick up speed. From the main cabin people surged out to line the rail.

"You don't think—?" Melanie began.

"Indeed, yes, Madame Donavan," Jean-Claude answered, sitting forward, excitement rising in his voice. "It is a race!"

Above them, greasy black smoke began to boil from the stacks as the engine crew, in order to make a hotter fire under the boilers, threw boxes of rancid fat pork into the furnace. The stench of the putrid meat burning enveloped the boat, but few seemed to notice. White and proud, the other boat came on with her whistle screaming. The morning sun, inching higher in the sky, reflected off her windows and slid with a golden gleam along her brasswork. It also brought into startling clarity the jubilant faces of the boat's passengers as they beat the railings and thumped each other on the back in their enthusiasm.

As people flowed around them, lining their own railing, Melanie got to her feet. Deep inside her, she could feel a trembling. The color left her face, and the palms of her hands grew damp. It seemed she had stood where she was before, had heard the same cries of encouragement and the jovial placing of bets among the gentlemen, the same straining rumble of the engine, had felt the same vibration in the deck as shook the steam packet at this moment. The premonition of disaster came from within her, from deep in a childhood memory, and yet it was so strong she ached with it.

"No," she whispered, but in the noise of yelling and cheering, no one heard her. Jostled by the pushing for advantage by ladies who only a few moments before would have shuddered at the idea of a race, she was shoved along until she came up against the railing. Glancing wildly around her, she thought of Glory and of Colleen, of Elena and the baby. Where were they? Were they still in their cabins? She turned in that direction, driven by something she could not name.

A moaning sigh moved over the crowd as the other boat began to gain on the *Southern Belle*. It was quickly followed by a cheer as the *Southern Belle* began to nose forward again, picking up speed.

"They ought to tie the safety valves down," a man said at Melanie's elbow.

"You can bet they already have," another answered. "Captain Standish up on the Texas don't like to be beaten by any man."

At that instant Melanie caught sight of Colleen. She was standing further along the deck, almost directly amidships. Her eyes were bright with the thrill of the moment, and she clung to the arm of Elena. The quadroon, with her child on her hip, was also straining to see.

Overhead, the whistle of the *Southern Belle* shrieked. At the sound, something inside Melanie gave way, and with tears rising in her eyes, she started toward the other women, shoving, dragging people aside in her frantic hurry.

"Colleen!" she cried. "This way!"

The actress turned at the sound of her name, and a smile of greeting curved her mouth as she saw Melanie. The affectionate expression faded as Melanie's hand gripped her arm with desperate strength.

"This way," Melanie cried. "You have got to come this way, all of you!"

"What is it?" Colleen asked, her voice nearly lost in the outcry of those around her as the other boat drew ahead once more. The actress threw a helpless look at Elena as she was dragged along, and after a hesitant moment, the quadroon began to follow.

"You must not be in the middle of the ship," Melanie panted, dodging around an enormously fat man who stood pounding the deck with his cane. "That is where the boilers are. If they explode—"

It was doubtful the others heard her last words. At that moment the baby in Elena's arms began to wail. A growling shudder ran over the boat, and then with a mighty roar, the midsection where Colleen had stood only moments before spewed upward in a hissing cloud of boiling steam and splintering fragments of wood. Bodies were thrown high by the blast. Agonized screams tore across the morning as people were scalded alive. And then as the echoes of the explosion died away over the water, there came the ominous crackling of flames.

Melanie was hurtled forward by the concussion. She slammed hard into the deck and tumbled to a jarring halt against the balusters of the railing. Pain swept over her in a red hot wave, so that the crying, the screaming, and praying all around her seemed to come from a great distance. She lay still, huddled within herself with the breath stopped in her throat, waiting for the agony to cease.

The steamboat built almost entirely of wood would go up like tinder as the blast spread the furnace fires through its bowels. There was not a soul on board who did not know it, not one who had not heard a thousand horror tales of death on the river. The result was scrambling, shouting pandemonium. Men trampled women and children trying to get to the pair of skiffs the boat carried. On the lower deck, the poorer class of passengers, knowing there was no hope of rescue for them, began at once to abandon the boat. Flinging barrels, boxes, and crates—anything that might float—into the water, they threw themselves in after them. And the other large, white, majestic boat, with her passengers lining the rail in frozen, silent horror, steamed away from the burning wreckage and the survivors struggling in the water, continuing up-river.

Clenching her teeth together, Melanie pushed herself upright. Smoke swirled around her. A woman, still in her nightclothes, ran past clutching a velvet jewelry box. An elderly man with tears making tracks through the soot on his face wandered by, calling for a woman named Martha. There was no one else to be seen for long seconds, and then out of the rolling dark clouds of smoke and steam, there came a man with a woman in his arms. It was Jean-Claude. He was covered with grime from head to foot, and there was a graze on his forehead that dripped blood onto the cream silk of his flowing tie. At the sight of Melanie, he came to a halt.

"Madame Donavan," he shouted. "Can you rise?"

"I—think so."

"Come to the staircase then. There is no time to lose."

"Is—is Colleen—is she alive?"

A spasm flitted over his face. "I don't know," he said over his shoulder as he moved away, disappearing once more into the smoke.

Dragging herself erect, Melanie followed in the direction he had taken, clinging to the railing as she made her way around the foredeck to the staircase on the opposite side. Once she glanced toward the water. Once only. The surface was covered with debris, with floating cargo, smoldering timbers, bodies, and with struggling people who screamed and cried out for help. They were much closer than they should have been, a sign that the steamboat was settling, taking on water through the hole ripped in the underside. Like some wounded animal brought to its knees, it shuddered, its framework groaning.

At the stairs Melanie stopped, looking down. Already water had covered the bottom treads and was rising upward. The railings along the lower deck of the shallow draft boat were nearly covered, and the water sucked and gurgled as it crept up the inside walls. If she descended the remaining steps and launched herself into that hungry tide, it might pull her down with the boat.

Swinging around, she made her way back across the lurching deck to the railing. Without giving herself time to think, she climbed over the balustrade, held to one tilting column until she had gained her balance, then jumped.

The warm waters of the Mississippi closed around her like an embrace. Her skirts billowed, catching pockets of air, so that she floated for long moments entrapped in their inflated folds. A box nudged her shoulder, an empty fat-pork box from its rancid, salty smell. It did not matter. She clutched at it as the river threatened to pull her under. For an instant she could find no hold, and then her gripping, sliding fingers caught the rope handle. Pushing her hair out of her eyes, Melanie stared around her, trying to locate the shore through the billows of smoke lying upon the water. When she caught a glimpse of what she thought was the nearest bank, it looked so far away that her heart turned to lead inside her. Where Jean-Claude had gone, she did not know. Around her there was nothing that moved, nothing that lived. Through her mind flashed an old saying of the Negroes that lived near the river. A man floated face down, they claimed, a woman face up. It was always easy, therefore, to tell the difference in a corpse that had been overlong in the water.

They were wrong, Melanie saw, so wrong. And then as she splashed and kicked, trying desperately to stay afloat, she felt the burgeoning of pain deep in her belly. It grew, gripping, spreading, until she was consumed by it. A great darkness hung suspended above her, waiting to descend. Time was an endless twilight tainted with fire and blood, and the only real thing in it was the paralyzing clutch of her hand on the handle of the greasy wooden fat-pork box.

Hands, hurtful, tugging. She was so heavy. Her sodden skirts streamed water. The river had no hands. The sun, hot, bright, burning into her eyes. Soft, kind voices. A coarse muslin sheet. And overhead, the leaves of a tree moving in the breeze, breaking the sun into a thousand tiny sparkles that flared and winked out as night fell early.

Melanie opened her eyes. The gray blue shadows of evening surrounded her, standing deep in the room in which she lay. She was in a bed, propped high on pillows that smelled of starch and vetiver. The nightgown she wore, though beautifully detailed with embroidery and edged about the neck and sleeves with lace, was not her own. She felt strange, lightheaded, and her form beneath the sheet that came to her waist was thinner than she remembered. She was comfortable, without pain, and yet, there hovered just beyond the grasp of her mind the sense that wrenching anguish had not been long departed.

Turning her head slightly, she looked around her. None of the furnishings or colors in the bedchamber were familiar. She did not think she had ever set foot in it before.

A soft movement on the other side of the room drew her attention. There was a long, tall window covered with curtains of simple white muslin on that wall. In front of it stood a woman, a slim, straight-backed figure in the uncertain light, though Melanie was almost positive she knew her.

"Colleen?" Melanie said, the word no more than a husk of sound.

The actress swung around and came quickly toward the

bed. "Melanie? Did you say something? Here, let me light the lamp."'

As light bloomed from the table near the bed, Melanie winced a little at the brightness. Then her gaze fastened on the face of the woman who came to hover above her. It was Colleen Antoinette Dubois. In that much she had been correct, though one side of Colleen's face was seared and purplish with the thickened look of cooked flesh. "Colleen," she breathed again.

"You are awake, at last. Thank God," Roland's mother said.

"Have—have I been asleep long?"

"Not asleep. Ill. For the better part of two weeks, since the explosion of the steamboat. Do you remember that?"

The steamboat. Melanie closed her eyes. "Yes, I remember," she whispered. Her thick lashes swept upward. "Where—where are we now?"

"The survivors were picked up by a boat going downriver and returned to New Orleans where they could receive the medical attention that many, so many, needed. You are now at a small house I have hired. You were admitted for a time to the hospital here, but I did not agree with their treatment. To bleed a woman to reduce her fever after she has just had a miscarriage seemed the height of stupidity to me, and I did not scruple to tell the doctors so. They knew no more about the cause of this fever than I did, and so I had you moved here. Until last night, when the fever broke and you dropped into a natural slumber, you were delirious, quite unaware of anything or anyone around you."

"Miscarriage?" Melanie queried softly.

"I am sorry, so terribly sorry, but yes, you have lost your baby."

Melanie swallowed hard upon the swift rise of tears in the back of her throat. "I—I see. And you have nursed me all this time when—when you were injured yourself. I must thank you."

"It is Elena who deserves the credit. She took care of both of us during the first important hours."

300

Elena, the quadroon. Colleen had made it sound as though she had been alone with two sick females on her hands. But that should not have been, could not have been. Unless—"Glory?"

"I cannot say. She was not among those brought to the bank of the river. Jean-Claude swears that in his trips out to the boat in the skiff that belonged to the plantation, near where the boat went down, he kept a special watch for your maid. He did not see her. Nor was she to be found later, among those who had been brought to shore by the other boats. It was no easy task, making certain of that. You did not know, for you were mercifully unconscious, but many of those who were still alive were so badly burned and scalded, and in such pain, that barrels of flour from the plantation house were broken open and people were drenched with it to soothe their hurts and keep the blue-bottle flies from their injuries. I thank heaven that I was not in such distress that I could not refuse such treatment. That much, I owe to you, Melanie. If you had not pulled me from where I was standing I would almost certainly have died in agony or been so terribly disfigured that I would have wished that I had done so."

Melanie shook her head. There was still one other unaccounted for. "And Elena's child, little Henri?"

"Elena, perhaps because she was closer to the wall, or maybe for no other reason than a freak accident, was not touched by the steam. As a child growing up, she had learned to swim in the river, and so it held no terrors for her. With her baby in her arms, she jumped from the top deck. But as she began to swim away from the boat, someone threw a barrel into the water. She—she is not certain whether it actually hit the baby, or whether she lost him when it struck her shoulder on the side where she held him. At any rate, she never found him again."

"How horrible for her," Melanie said. To lose a beloved child that one had nurtured and bathed and taught to walk and kissed a thousand times must be far worse than losing a child that had never truly lived.

As tears of weakness and distress welled into Melanie's

301

eyes, Colleen gave a shake of her head. "I never meant to tell you all this. Not now, not so soon. I will never forgive myself if it makes you ill again."

"That's all right. I had to know. And—I am not certain not knowing wouldn't have been worse."

"I hope you are right. I do hope so," Colleen said. "But enough for now. We must see what we can do to make you well. You have eaten so little in the last days you are nothing more than skin and bones. Let me go and order a nourishing dinner for you. Some broth and a little chicken breast."

The other woman was halfway to the door when another thought occurred to Melanie. Struggling up on her elbow, she called, "Wait."

Roland's mother stopped, turning. "Yes, my dear? Was there something else you would rather have?"

"No, that is, if so much time has passed, there must be some news of the expedition."

Colleen's smile seemed to congeal upon her face, though her voice when she spoke was unchanged. "Yes, a little," she answerd. "Shall we talk about it later, after you have eaten?" Turning, she started once more toward the door.

"No, Colleen, please. I have to know."

The actress stopped with her hand on the doorknob. For long moments she stood still, her head bowed. At last she spoke. "A ship came from Havana this morning. According to all reports, Lopez engaged the Spanish troops there on the twelfth of August. He was defeated, and more than half of his men killed, including most of his officers. It seems the rumors of revolution were false, deliberately spread to entice Lopez to attack before the two other sections of his proposed army could be brought to the field. In addition, the Spaniards had been informed of his impending attack. They were waiting for him. It was little more than a massacre."

"And Roland?" Melanie whispered.

"There has been no news of him, no list of casualties. Lopez, it seems, refused to surrender. He and his remain-

302

ing men retreated, scattering into the hills. The Spaniards are tracking them down with dogs, and it seems they have little doubt of eventually seeing every man a prisoner in the dungeon of Morro Castle."

Chapter 15

MELANIE AND Colleen walked along the winding brick path shaded with ancient elm and sycamore trees. Around them lay the manicured, parklike perfection of White Sulphur Springs. In this autumn of 1851, the spa, located in the westernmost corner of Virginia in the foothills of the Allegheny Mountains, was one of the most popular watering places in the world. Modeled on the spas of Europe, notably Bath, England, it was famous for its steam baths, so efficacious for rheumatism and other bone disorders, for its pump room where visitors could congregate over glasses of warm, sulphur-tasting mineral water and exchange stories of each other's ailments, for its many strolling paths for the use of those to whom the morning and evening constitutionals were a ritual, and for its ballroom where the music and gaiety lasting far into the hours of the night could make the most infirm forget his aches and pains. The social life thus displayed was no small part of the attraction of the town. There were many who came for that above all else, though they stayed for the gracious and soothing atmosphere, and for the effortless way the days had of slipping past there.

The middle of September was not the peak of the season; that usually occurred in summer when so many of the cities of the south were plagued with fevers that made the cool and healthful climate of the mountains look inviting. Regardless, even though the sun was beginning to lose its strength and the leaves on the trees to show touches of yellow and orange, they did not have the town to themselves. Only the starting of the winter season in the larger cities and towns would have the power to shift the merriment away from White Sulphur Springs.

Melanie had been in residence with Colleen, in an entourage that included Elena and Jean-Claude, for the better part of a week. It had been Colleen's idea that they come. She would not hear of Melanie's returning to Natchez alone. They needed each other at this time, she said, and moreover, Melanie's health was not improving as the actress thought it should. A change of scene could not fail to be beneficial, as must the quiet and the salubrious waters of White Sulphur Springs. As for her own disfigurement, the waters were also said to be softening for such things, though the main thing was a period of rest. She had canceled all engagements and did not intend to appear on the stage until her face was presentable, at least under grease paint. The doctors, both in New Orleans and at the spa, had not been optimistic of that happening. Colleen had merely smiled and mixed a concoction of white goose fat, herbs, and oil of castor beans, which she applied nightly. As a consequence, her skin improved with every passing day. There were no longer any pits or abrasions on her face, and the injured area, though still red and mottled, was smooth, soft to the touch. Six weeks, the actress gave it, before she could resume playing *Camille*.

Another reason for the move was the fact that the watering place was not so very far from the capital city of Washington. Colleen had many friends there, and no few admirers. If it should happen that Roland's name appeared on the list of those who were captured and imprisoned in Havana, then she would be in a better position to harry the State Department until they did something about his release. Failing that, she could at least learn of his condition, or perhaps see that money and provisions were sent to relieve the rigors of his incarceration. Though they had made a stop in the nation's

305

capital before coming on to the spa, to date there had been no word.

"Elena said a strange thing to me this morning," Colleen mused as she strolled along, tapping the ferrule of her sunshade on the brick sidewalk with each step. "She said that she sometimes thought that the river had taken the life of her child, and of yours and your maid, in revenge for the insult we all had offered it by disposing of the dead in its waters."

"I would hate to think so," Melanie replied.

"So would I," Colleen admitted, a frown between her brows, "and yet, sometimes I wonder about such things. I wonder if I am not being punished by this terrible, maddening uncertainty over Roland's safety. If I had never left Robert, never fought him for my son, this might not have happened."

"Such thinking does no good," Melanie said. "If anyone is to blame, it is I." The effort it took to say those words was great, but not nearly so great as it would have been a month before. In the past weeks an understanding had grown between Roland's mother and herself. The things that had happened had drawn them close. They were more like sisters than mother-in-law and daughter-in-law.

"That is nonsense. You don't know what you are saying."

"Don't I?"

The path they were following had taken them over a wooden bridge that crossed a small stream and led at last to a secluded summerhouse. Indicating the benches that ringed the interior of the airy structure, Melanie said, "Come, sit down, and let me tell you."

When Melanie had finished the recital of the string of events, the duel, the night at the River Rest, her marriage to Roland, and all that came afterward, Colleen gave a long sigh. "I am so glad you trusted me with the story. I knew there was something troubling you, something to do with Roland, but I did not know what. When you were ill, you sometimes spoke in delirium or cried heartbrokenly."

306

"Did I? I guess it isn't surprising."

"No, not at all. I wished often that I could help you, but Roland was never forthcoming about his marriage or the reasons for it."

As much as Melanie liked and respected Colleen, it was good to know she had not been a subject of discussion between mother and son. "If only—," she began.

"Useless words, my dear. Pray don't torture yourself with them. Whatever has happened has happened and cannot now be changed. I am troubled most about this business of your grandfather. I realize I am prejudiced, but I would have said that for Roland to choose such an underhanded means to besmirch your grandfather's honor as spreading rumors is totally unlike him. He has ever preferred the quick way, the direct cut to the heart of a matter."

"Yes, so it seems to me now also. I have wondered if there wasn't some kind of misunderstanding; if Roland might not have seen my grandfather in a situation that looked damning, even though it was innocent; if he might not have spoken of it to someone, and then the tale grew as it spread, until it finally reached Natchez, carried by the men of the other regiments as they returned from the war. If Roland realized his hasty accusation might be the basis of the rumors, it would explain why he deloped as though acknowledging his guilt, letting my grandfather put a ball into his arm."

"All things are possible, I suppose," the actress admitted, "but I will not be satisfied until I hear it for myself."

Melanie looked away. "Nor will I," she said finally.

"Does that mean you no longer believe he could be guilty of deliberately harming your grandfather, or does it imply you feel he has paid enough for his mistakes; that you no longer feel the need to be revenged?"

Melanie turned her head sharply to stare at the other woman, but she was saved from the necessity of making a reply. Their privacy was at an end. Toward them over the bridge came a young couple pushing a sleeping babe in a carriage of woven rattan. Melanie got to her feet. At the door of the summerhouse, she and Colleen stood aside, smiling in greeting as the young couple entered. Averting their eyes quickly from the sleeping child in the carriage, they walked away, their footsteps echoing with a hollow sound on the wooden bridge.

It seemed callous to go dancing while Roland's life hung in the balance, but Colleen insisted. They needed to be distracted, she said. They must not mope and pine. Jean-Claude would partner them both. It was so gallant of Colleen to wish to appear in public in a ball gown with her face and shoulders still noticeably blemished that Melanie could not refuse.

Jean-Claude was an excellent dancer and a charming companion. He had done much to make the past weeks bearable. It had been good of him to stay with them; he could just as easily have left them stranded, pursuing his career. It was true, of course, that when Colleen had canceled her appearances, his own had automatically suffered the same fate. Still there were other shows, other parts and theaters, where he would have been welcomed. At first, Melanie had credited his loyalty to his attachment to Colleen, but as the days went by, that no longer seemed certain. His compliments to her were becoming more daring. His gaze often rested upon her with the warmth of a caress. And once, when she had gone walking with him while Colleen was resting, he had plucked a late-blooming rose and presented it to her with such a flourish and so pretty a speech that she would have had to be stupid not to understand that he admired her.

"You are *ravissante* tonight, *chérie*," he said as he led her into the slow revolutions of a waltz. "You grow more lovely every day, more blooming. The color of your gown is perfect, that shade of lavender blue as if made for you alone."

"Thank you, Jean-Claude," she said, her smile friendly and nothing more, as she tried for a mood of light banter. "You certainly should approve, since it was you who chose it for me." It was true enough. Jean-Claude, with the true Frenchman's lack of self-consciousness, had accompanied Colleen and Melanie on their rounds to replenish their wardrobes lost with the sinking of the *Southern Belle*. By silent consent, this buying spree had included no black, despite the fact that they lived in daily expectation of having to go into mourning.

"I am a genius, then, am I not? But the gown, as lovely as it is, would not be half so effective if it were not for the lady who is wearing it."

"Thank you again, kind sir. Now tell me what play that line came from. It has a familiar ring, but I cannot quite place it."

"You wound me, *chérie*. I mean every word."

"Yes, I am sure you do, every time you say it," Melanie assured him, a determined set to her mouth, though there was laughter in her eyes.

"You drive me mad! How am I to convince you that I find you attractive, that I feel for you something that I have never felt for any other woman. You bewitch me with your smiles and leave me in despair with your coolness."

"Oh, Jean-Claude! You know that isn't true. You are idle, at loose ends, and I am here at a time when Colleen has little time or thought for you in her preoccupation with her son and with regaining her looks. That is all there is to it."

"I tell you no! Oh, yes, I will admit our feelings, mine and Colleen's, have cooled since New Orleans. I did not enjoy being made mock of while she kept the truth about her past to herself. Her age, that is not so great a matter. Mature women are much admired in my country. But to keep it from me. Was she ashamed? Did she have so little belief in my understanding?" He shrugged. "It doesn't matter. As I started to tell you, it is what you are, what I see in you that makes me want you. It has nothing to do with anyone else."

"Please," she said. Over his shoulder she could see Colleen on the arm of the man who was acting as master of ceremonies for the ball. Though the actress was smiling, there was a shrewd look in her eyes, as though she understood perfectly what was happening between her daughter-in-law and the man who had been, and perhaps still was, her lover.

"Is that all you have to say when I make you a declaration? Please!"

She drew back to look at him, her violet blue eyes level. "Yes, it is," she answered.

He sighed. "Ah, conventional women. And if you knew you were a widow, would you hear me?"

A shadow moved over Melanie's face. "I don't think I need answer that," she said, her voice low, "because it will not happen."

It was late before they returned to their hotel. Melanie went straight to bed in her room. She did not expect to sleep after the disturbing things Jean-Claude had said to her, but she was apparently weaker and more easily tired than she realized. The instant she closed her eyes, she drifted into slumber.

She was awakened by the hotel maid with her breakfast tray, a daily luxury Colleen had prescribed for both Melanie and herself. Struggling up on her pillows, Melanie took the small table-tray across her lap. As always there was a fresh flower, this morning a red carnation, Jean-Claude's contribution to the morning ritual. Frowning, she leaned to breathe its spicy fragrance. Then, with a shake of her head, she handed the crystal vase to the maid to place on the dressing table out of the way. The maid, satisfied Melanie had everything she needed, picked up the coin Melanie had left out for her, curtsied, and whisked herself from the room.

The breakfast was substantial: light, golden, buttered biscuits, wafer-thin slices of Virginia-cured ham, an omelette, preserves, an apple, and a small silver pot of coffee. To one side, adding to the air of leisure, was the latest newspaper from the capital. This last Melanie laid to one side and gamely tackled the repast. Though she knew she probably needed the wholesome fare in order to continue gaining back the weight she had lost, it was just a little annoying to think that Colleen, who had ordered it, was

310

probably nibbling no more than a piece of toast with her coffee.

At last Melanie touched her napkin to her lips and dropped it on her plate, then reached for the newspaper. The front page was rather dull, though she perused a story of a theft in the home of a senator. Turning inside, she scanned the columns, then stopped, her attention caught by a name. The color draining from her face, she read the account of the capture on the last day of August, and the trial and execution, of the Cuban filibuster General Narciso Lopez. The method of death meted out to the one-time Spanish soldier had been the garrote, an iron collar which was fastened around his throat and slowly tightened with a screw until strangulation occurred. The British consul had persuaded the governor-general of Cuba to release to him those men who could prove themselves citizens of Great Britain. The remaining one hundred and fifty men had been put on a ship bound for Spain where they would be imprisoned. A list of these prisoners followed. Melanie scanned it with burning eyes again and again, but the name of Roland Donavan did not appear.

Letting the paper fall, she leaned back on her pillow and closed her eyes. Out of five hundred men, a hundred and fifty had survived to be hunted down with dogs, captured, and sent to Spain. Three hundred and fifty men must be dead then, and Roland was among them. While she had smiled and danced and enjoyed living these last weeks, he had lain lifeless on that tropical island. Had the victors in that uneven conflict buried him? Had they held a service? Had they thrown him in a trench and covered him with dirt? Or were his bones even now lying bleaching in the sun?

Stinging salt tears rose into her eyes and crept down her cheeks. Until this moment, she had not realized how much she had counted on his return, how much she had depended on their living together as man and wife once more. She had meant in some way to penetrate to the secret of what had occurred between Roland and her

311

grandfather, and if a mistake had been made, to try to understand and forgive. Now that could never be. She would never see his smile or the light in his green eyes again, never feel his touch or the warmth of his arms. She was a widow, and none of the warnings, none of the hints she had been given that it might happen had prepared her for that barren state. She was a widow, a childless widow, which in that moment seemed the greatest cruelty of all.

A tap sounded on the door. Wiping her face on her napkin, Melanie reached for her dressing gown and slid from the bed to answer it. Colleen stood outside in the hall. Her eyes were red-rimmed, but she was dressed in a traveling costume of lead gray, piped in green. Stepping forward with a rush, she enclosed Melanie in her arms for a brief, tearful moment, then stepped inside and closed the door.

"I see you have also read the news," the actress said, searching in her reticule for her handkerchief. "We must not despair. There is always the possibility of a mistake. I am taking the train this morning for Washington. I refuse to dissolve into grief until I have exhausted every avenue of information. The State Department will have some means of communication with the men who are prisoners. It is possible that someone among their number will have news of Roland, for good or ill. Some people might say it is foolish to cling to such hope, but I have never been one to turn loose of a thing unless I must. Sorrow will always come to us whether we wish for it or not; joy takes a little more effort."

"If you will wait, I will come with you," Melanie said.

Colleen looked up with a watery smile. "That is sweet of you, but no. My train leaves in less than half an hour. I will have to rush to make it myself. In any case, I have so many places to go, so many people to see, that I am not certain you could keep the pace. Waiting, I know, is the hardest task, but for now, it is all you can do."

She was gone in a whirl of skirts, the heels of her slippers tapping down the hall. Slowly Melanie turned back toward the bed, unfastening the pearl buttons of her

312

dressing gown. She had not yet begun to shrug from the voluminous folds of lace-edged pink silk when a knock sounded once more. She had not heard Colleen return, and yet, coming so soon upon her departure, Melanie thought the actress must have forgotten some instruction, some bit of information she had meant to give her.

It was Jean-Claude who stood in the opening. His dark eyes were soft with sympathy and the look on his face grave. "Melanie, *chérie*," he said, stepping into the room and pushing the door shut behind him, "I have come to comfort you."

With an air almost brotherly, he took her into his arms, brushing a chaste kiss across her cheek. His arms tightened as though with the strength of his pity for her, and his hands moved up and down her back a little, and then with a shake of his head, he touched his lips to hers, pulling her close. His kiss changed, deepening.

Melanie was still. In the arms that held her, in the warm human contact there was a modicum of the comfort he had offered, and also an affirmation that despite the many deaths, she still lived. One thing more held her unmoving. The distress of grief was so great that she felt the impulse to deny the love from which it sprang, to test its worth and abiding strength against the gauge of another man's caresses.

When she did not immediately fight him, Jean-Claude grew bolder. His hand moved to her breast and his tongue thrust into her mouth past her slack lips, seeking with skill and quick daring for some flutter of response.

He found it. Abrupt revulsion swept over Melanie. Her hands came up to grip the material of his coat sleeves, and she pushed him from her with such strength that he stumbled backward, a vacuous look on his face.

"No, don't touch me," she said. "I can't bear it!" Raising the back of her hand to her lips, she rubbed them as if to rid herself of something distasteful.

Recovering, Jean-Claude started forward again. "But Melanie, my love, *ma chérie*, come and let us talk."

"No!" Putting out her hand, she touched the tips of her

313

fingers to his shirt front to ward him off. "I have no need of your kind of comfort. I am sorry if I led you to think otherwise, but you must go and never come near me again."

"You don't mean that," he said, assuming a hurt expression that had in it a hint of little-boy petulance.

"I do mean it. I enjoy your company, and I will always owe you a great debt of gratitude for pulling me from the river, but I do not intend to be the third in your ménage à trois. You called me a conventional woman, and I am afraid that was an accurate description."

"But *chérie*, if I could have you, there would be no others."

"Do you mean that?" Melanie said curiously, then answered herself. "I suppose you do at this minute. It makes no difference. I feel nothing for you, nothing. If you sincerely love me, even a little, then I regret any hurt I may give you, but there is nothing you can do that will make me change my mind."

He stared at her a long moment. Then he inclined his head in a stiff bow. "It is not my habit to press my attentions where they are not wanted. I have never had to force myself on any woman. What I felt for you, Madame Donavan, I think, was not love so much as a fascinated desire to see if I could entice you from your shell. You are a beautiful woman, but cool, distant. I see in you the potential for a magnificent, glorious creature, if only she can be brought forth, freed from all frugality with love." He shrugged. "I am sorry it is not in my power. What a great pity it will be if it is never in the power of any man."

Before Melanie could speak, before she could even begin to frame a reply, he turned on his heel and left the room, closing the door quietly behind him.

It was three days before Colleen returned. During that time Melanie kept to herself, descending to the dining room for meals at odd hours, taking solitary walks. She did not see Jean-Claude again. It was only by accident that she passed his room and, seeing an elderly man with

314

mountains of baggage being installed in it, realized he had gone. An inquiry at the desk in the lobby revealed that he had left the hotel that morning and was not expected to return.

Melanie was out when Colleen arrived back at the hotel. She had visited the lending library and then taken her volume to sit and read beside the fountain in the garden behind the pump room. When she returned to her room, she found a message waiting for her, a message which requested that she step next door to the suite of rooms hired by the actress at her earliest convenience. Laying aside her book, she stepped to the mirror to see that her hair was smooth. Summoning a smile to her lips, Melanie prepared to comply.

Roland's mother had removed her traveling costume. She came to the door in a dressing gown of emerald moiré taffeta. Her wise gaze scanned Melanie's face, then dropped to the pale blue walking dress she was wearing. "Melanie, my dear, come in," she said. "I see you are not wearing black yet. Nor am I, despite everything. I have this superstitious fear that to go into mourning now would be to lessen Roland's chances of being alive. Ridiculous, but there it is."

Melanie advanced into the room. "Despite—everything?" she repeated.

"Everything, and nothing. The men in the bureaucratic offices in the nation's capital hem and haw and smooth their mustaches, but the truth of the matter is they know little more of this affair than can be read in the papers. I have gathered a half dozen promises of inquiries, but that is all. In short, my trip was endlessly frustrating, and absolutely useless. I know no more now than when I left here."

"I see," Melanie said, though her sigh was one of mingled disappointment and relief.

"Yes," Colleen said, echoing her sigh. "But that is not all I wanted to tell you. I have had news from another quarter. It seems, my dear, that although we may refuse to believe that you are a widow, it is certain that I am."

Her voice was so brittle, so hurried, that it was a moment before Melanie realized what she was saying. "You mean—"

"I mean that Robert Donavan, Roland's father, is dead. He was buried nine days ago at Cottonwood. I found the news awaiting me here when I returned."

"I am sorry," Melanie said.

"Are you? Then he must have been kinder to you than he ever was to me. Nonetheless, he has done me a great favor. It appears that Jean-Claude took it upon himself to collect my messages and read them, for I found them here in my room, opened. The instant he understood that I was free, Jean-Claude decamped."

Melanie stared at the straight back of the actress as the woman turned from her and moved with a nonchalant air to the secretary desk, flicking through the papers that lay upon its polished surface. Melanie swallowed hard. "I have been keeping rather close since you have been gone, but I thought it odd that I had not seen him. Are you saying you don't mind that he is gone?"

With her head bent, Colleen smiled. "Jean-Claude was a charming scoundrel with a rare appreciation for women, their minds and graces as well as their bodies. Still, he could be rather juvenile at times, and his certainty concerning his prowess with females was beginning to pall. It is a relief, at times, to have a relationship come to an end before one has to take on the difficult task of putting a period to it oneself. I trust you will not miss him unduly?"

Melanie's thoughts were so busy with the question of whether the other woman was giving an accurate account of her feelings or merely putting a good face on the situation that she very nearly missed that last hesitant question. "No," she answered. "No, I don't think I will miss him, though I will be grateful always to him for the aid he extended, not only in New Orleans, but later."

"I am glad," Colleen said. "He has been a little annoyed with me these last weeks for my lack of attention. It was not unnatural for him to turn his emotions elsewhere. I had feared he might upset you with his flirtation. But why are we standing? Come and sit down by the window. There are decisions to be made."

"Decisions?" Melanie inquired when she had taken her place on one of the lime velvet chairs on either side of a table under the windows of the room.

"Yes, indeed. You must understand that the death of Robert Donavan affects you also," Colleen said, gripping the arm of her chair and leaning forward.

"In what way? I am afraid I don't understand."

Colleen took a deep breath, her eyes clouding. "Since I was still Robert's legal wife at the time of his death, according to the succession laws of the state of Louisiana, I now inherit half of his estate. The other half goes to our children, in this case, to Roland. If by some chance he should not return from Cuba, then you, my dear, would become his heir jointly with me. You and I together would own Cottonwood."

"I think I understand what you are saying," Melanie said slowly, "but surely that doesn't call for any change in our plans?"

"I am afraid it does. You see, the cotton crop at the plantation is still in the field. Someone must go and supervise its harvest. Oh, we could write to the lawyers and have them manage it, but that isn't like seeing to the business oneself."

"You want to go to Natchez then?" Melanie asked.

"Not precisely. I feel that I should still pursue my inquiries in Washington, at least for a few more weeks. I had thought that you might return there, Melanie. You have a home there. You understand the situation and have some knowledge of the problems involved. You could make certain the job of harvesting is done thoroughly, with a minimum of waste, and follow the crop through until Robert's broker in New Orleans takes delivery."

"I have never done such a thing," Melanie protested. "I would not have the least idea how to go about it."

"Of course you would. It only requires common sense," Colleen said stoutly. "You will see, you will do fine. And if—if my efforts here prove fruitless, Elena and I will join you in a few weeks."

Chapter 16

MELANIE SLAPPED the reins against the rump of her horse and guided the gig off the Mississippi River ferry. Lifting her hand to the ferryman, she sent her vehicle at a swift pace toward Cottonwood. Intent on her driving, she spared not a thought for the fact that she had crossed the river without a tremor, or that, despite her second riverboat disaster, she had made the sea voyage alone from Virginia to New Orleans, and then up to Natchez with no more distress than the ferry crossing. Conquering her fear was not her only accomplishment. She had also learned to drive a gig, to make sense of the facts and figures Lawyer Turnbull placed before her, to recognize when a day in the fields had yielded a reasonable percentage of the harvest, and to arrange for the shipment and consignment of the crop she had come finally to think of as her own, at least in part.

At last the task was done. The baled cotton had disappeared around the bend in the river on its way to New Orleans. She had turned her thoughts lately to the living conditions of the slaves at Cottonwood. They were deplorable. Colleen had signed a power of attorney relinquishing the control of her portion of the estate to Melanie. With this in hand, Melanie had drawn on the funds available through years of Robert Donavan's miserliness to improve the cabins in the slave quarters. She had also arranged to have the doctor come out to treat the boils, scabies, and scurvy she found, along with a number of other diseases of malnutrition. She had purchased fencing to mark off small garden plots, and a few chickens and pigs for each family so they could raise a portion of their own food, as was the practice with most planters. If, after a time, the slaves had any excess produce or animals, they would be free to sell it for their own profit. She had also discussed the possibility of the men, if they wished, hiring themselves out as laborers during the rest of the harvest season and through the winter. The contentment that permeated Cottonwood these days was reward enough for her efforts.

Today she had with her in the back of the gig sacks of oranges, bags of seeds for greens, and barrels of molasses to add to the diet of those who were so dependent upon her. A little later in the year she intended to organize pecan thrashings and persimmon hunts in the woods.

So far, she had not turned her attention to the deficiencies of the big house. Unless someone was going to be in residence it would be a waste of money. She herself did not intend to leave Greenlea, and she doubted that Colleen had any attachment whatsoever to the place. The decision as to painting and repair would have to wait until the actress arrived.

Such plans for the future had come to seem natural to Melanie. As the weeks passed without news of Roland, she had begun slowly to accept the fact of his death. It had not been easy; she still could not bring herself to order her mourning clothes. Still, she was coming gradually to accept the fact that she must.

It was a warm day, but not too warm. The air was as dry and mellow and scented with dust as old wine brought up from the cellar. Along the roadsides, the goldenrod nodded its heavy yellow plumes, while bees crawled stickily over them and small orange butterflies hovered in the air. Black-eyed Susans and blue ageratum also grew in tangles along the fence rows. In the lowlands this far south, the trees had not yet begun to turn, but soon they would. The year was drawing to a close as surely as was the time she had spent as the wife of Roland Donavan.

At Cottonwood, the Negro children tumbled from the cabins to run laughing and cheering to greet her. She handed down her parcels, bags, and kegs with strict instructions to take them directly to the outdoor kitchen, along with permission for them each to have an orange, brought fresh off the boat from New Orleans, when they had done as she said. With a shake of her head for their boundless energy, she watched them scurry away. Then she turned back toward the gig. From the seat, she took a wreath of pink and white roses made of colored wax. The grave where Roland's father lay looked so bare. There had not been enough rain this autumn to make the grass grow on the raw earth. She did not know what words had been said over him when he was buried, but if anyone had laid so much as a wildflower at his headstone, there had been no sign. She had been meaning to make this small gesture of respect ever since she returned, but until now there had been too much else to do to think of it.

The small piece of ground set aside as the Donavan cemetery was some distance from the house. The path that reached it followed wagon ruts that led eventually to the fields down along a fence line, then veered off as it came to a rise near the woods that enclosed the back of the property. The high land was important, for the water table came so near to the surface of the earth here that it was difficult to dig a grave without water seeping into it. The presence of the small hill made it unnecessary to use an above-ground burial vault. Inside the white picket fence that encircled the summit of the small hill, there were only three graves. One was that of a man whom the Negroes claimed had died of pneumonia years before after he had wandered in off the road. Another was that of a child, a baby girl, born to Robert and Colleen Donavan. The last was the resting place of Roland's father.

The gate of white pickets squeaked as it swung shut behind Melanie. A grasshopper made a small clicking noise as it sprang from beneath her feet in the dry grass. From across the cotton fields, a crow sounded his harsh caw-caw, and overhead a lone buzzard floated, hanging motionless in the deep blue of the sky. The stillness of the morning was so intense that Melanie was aware of the rustle of her gown as she knelt to place her wreath upon the grave. Hesitating a moment, she reached to pull a pink rosebud from the arrangement, then leaned to lay it upon the grave of a little girl that would have been Roland's sister. She was still as she stared at the child's marker, aware of an ache of loneliness inside her that it seemed nothing could ever fill.

"What a touching picture. I might have known you would not neglect any of the expected observances for the dead."

Melanie turned her head toward the trees in the direction from which she thought the voice had come. She shaded her eyes against the dazzling brightness of the sun, still crouching, scarcely breathing, a portion of her mind suspended in disbelief. And then from the shadows came the tall figure of a man, swinging up the rise, stepping over the fence. The sun shone on his dark hair and picked up the satin sheen of perspiration on his forehead.

"Roland," she whispered, then said louder, "Roland!"

She surged to her feet. She took a step, and then she was running. She flung herself against him with stunning force. His arms closed around her, crushing her to him. She felt her feet leave the ground as he swung her around, and then his mouth found hers in the searching hunger of a kiss that seemed never to end. At last he lifted his head and hugged her to him once more. He breathed deep of her long-remembered yellow rose fragrance and the sweet essence of her body, and then as if he could not help himself, he leaned to scoop her into his arms carrying her quickly toward the cool and silent woods.

They came together without words or the need for them, touching, holding in an agony of well-remembered and necessary bliss. Lying on her wide-spread petticoat, they joined their naked bodies and, staring into each other's eyes, celebrated the joy of life. He swung above her, his arms trembling with the fierce exhilaration of his desire as he pressed into her with growing swiftness. She opened her thighs, wanting to take him deeper and deeper still inside her, until they were one, two parts of a whole. The wondrous magic of the moment burst upon them, a pulsing, splintering wonder, a thing of riotous beauty to make the senses expand, encompassing all living things, all beauty, all faith, denying only death.

Their breathing quieted. A breeze rustled through the leaves overhead, gliding over the moist skin of their bodies. Melanie stirred, sighing, and reached to gently twist a curl that had fallen forward over his forehead around her finger. He tilted his chin upward to brush her smooth, white knuckle with his lips.

"I could almost believe," he said tentatively, "that you were glad to see me."

"Could you? I suppose it comes from thinking I would never see you again. Do you know Colleen and I have feared you dead for these five weeks and more, have counted your spirit as shackled forever to the tropical island that fascinated you so?"

"And yet," he said sotfly, "you don't wear black."

"No. That will prove a great economy, will it not?"

"Does it also prove you would not give up hope?"

By now the shock of seeing him had receded, leaving Melanie with the memory of how they had parted, and of the many things that still lay unsettled between them. "I suppose it must," she admitted. "It also shows my confidence in your ability to emerge from prison. You have had more experience than most in that line."

"Yes," he agreed, the soft tone fading from his voice, leaving it bleak.

Melanie felt a small coldness around her heart. "You must tell me how you managed it," she went on, "since the trick was apparently not know to the State Department in Washington. So far as Colleen and I could learn, the only men to leave the island alive were the prisoners who were sent to Spain. Your name was not among them."

"There was one other group," he said. "The men of Great Britain. You may not be aware of it, but I was born in Ireland, which gives me dual citizenship, if I care to

323

claim it. With things going as they were, it seemed prudent to do just that."

"But it has been ages since the British prisoners were released."

"Yes, I know. We citizens of Britain, it was assumed, must naturally want to go home. We were transported to England and only then set free. The government of Great Britain, as personified by her majesty, Queen Victoria, declined to be responsible for the manner in which those of us who lived elsewhere made our way home again. As inconvenient as it was, we were lucky compared to most. Jeremy Rogers was shot when we were captured, hunted down in a field of sugar cane. He died in prison at Havana."

Poor Jeremy with his dreams of riches and a confiscated estate. "I saw his name was not listed with those sent to Spain either," she said, "I am sorry, so sorry."

"Yes, so am I," Roland said. "I suppose he is one of those shackled spirits you mentioned—somehow I wish you had not."

Melanie drew in her breath, then made a valiant effort to continue. "Then you have been in England all this time?"

"Yes, and in the Bahama Islands. From there I caught a ship bound for New Orleans, and so, here to Cottonwood."

Melanie sat up and begin to look around her for her underclothing. "Your mother will be happy. I will have to send word as soon as possible."

"Send word? Where?"

"White Sulphur Springs," Melanie answered and went on to tell him why they had been there, and why Colleen had stayed behind. There were a few details she omitted, among them the incident of Jean-Claude. It had been a minor thing, soon over. It would serve no purpose to drag it forth.

"I suppose," he said, when she had finished, "that you lost the baby?"

She went still, clutching her crinoline in her lap. The

324

pain of that loss had gradually faded, but at that moment she felt it as strongly as she had when she had first learned the news. She had not mentioned her loss in her tale, had seen no need to burden him with it. "You knew," she breathed.

"There are some things that are difficult to conceal from a man who lives close to you. I thought to the last you would tell me before I left, but you did not."

"If I had told you, would you still have gone?"

He looked away from her steady gaze. "Yes, I expect so."

"Then what was the use?" she asked, the acid of old bitterness etching her tone.

"You might have had some consideration for the way I felt."

"Why, when you had so little for my feelings?"

"I was trying to gain something for you, and for our child that you were carrying."

"Are you trying to say that is why you went to Cuba? If so, I don't believe it for one moment. You went for your own glory and enjoyment. If you must lie to me about it, at least don't lie to yourself!" Whipping her crinoline over her head, she tied the tapes, then reached for her petticoat, giving it a vicious yank, so that Roland, lying on his side, was rolled backward.

"Speaking of attitudes, I imagine yours would have undergone a dramatic change if we had won in Cuba. If I could lay the spoils of a rich estate at your feet, you would be all too ready to recognize the validity of Lopez's ambitions, and the essential correctness of what he was trying to do. You might even begin to support the expedition instead of holding it in such self-righteous contempt."

"I was never contemptuous of it," she exclaimed. "I was only doubtful of the outcome against the strength and cunning of the Spaniards, and I was right!"

"Yes, you were right," he growled, snatching up his trousers. "Someone saw to it very nicely that you were right by making sure the Spaniards were waiting for us with their guns cocked and ready."

"Are you accusing me?" she cried from the depths of the knowledge of her guilt.

He had pulled on his trousers and was shrugging into his shirt. With one sleeve on, he stopped. "No," he said, "though it occurs to me you were in possession of the necessary information early enough to have made use of it."

"But I didn't," Melanie could hear the strain in her own voice, though there was nothing she could do about it. "There were any number who knew as much as I did."

"Possibly, though the majority of them had loyalty to the expedition to persuade them not to be indiscreet." Pushing the tail of his shirt into his trousers, he did not look at her as he spoke.

"That is a despicable thing to say," she whispered.

"Is it? I wonder? I have had a great deal of time lately to think about this, and I don't particularly like where my thoughts have led me. Tell me, do you see much of Dom?"

The change of subjects was disconcerting and also revealing. "Why?" she demanded, her voice muffled as she ducked into her gown to conceal the dismay in her face.

"Because we still have a score to settle."

She struggled to her feet. The fact that he did not offer to help her added to her feeling of ill usage. "Why?" she said again in goaded tones. "Your father is dead now. Cottonwood is yours, as well as a large part of the money your father had been accumulating all these years. We can turn some of it back to the land, give it the care it needs, watch it grow prosperous again, as you spoke of months ago. Isn't that enough? Must you start out now on some terrible mission of revenge?"

"Don't tell me," he said softly, "that vengeance no longer holds its charm for you?"

With a lift of her chin she said, "I have learned that it is not as satisfactory as it is supposed to be, that often it brings grief in its wake."

"An affecting defense, but I think you will have to do better than that to protect Dominic Clements."

326

"To protect him?" she echoed.

"On the steamboat upriver I was fortunate enough to fall into conversation with a gentleman of Natchez. I was told that Dom has seldom been seen out of the company of a lovely young married woman named Melanie Johnston Donavan. That the pair of you seem, to all interested observers, to be anticipating your widowed state to a marked degree."

"Snooping, were you?" Melanie flashed. "I hope you weren't too surprised, considering the circumstances of our marriage."

"No," he answered, his green gaze moving over the clear, classical lines of her face, touching on the flush of anger across her cheekbones, and the stormy violet-blue of her eyes. A muscle flexed in the side of his jaw, and one hand slowly clenched into a fist. "No," he repeated, "just disappointed."

He swung from her, ducked under a tree limb, and began to walk away in the direction they had come. Suppressing an urge to stamp in a tearful rage, Melanie cried, "Where are you going?"

He stopped, turned. "To Cottonwood, my home, though it is not yours, apparently." His eyes raked her and the glade in which they had lain with unmistakable intent. "If you care to join me there, you may. I have no objection, though I promise nothing, especially as it concerns Dom." With a mocking bow, he walked on, disappearing among the trees.

It was impossible after that, of course. Melanie tidied her appearance as best she could, buttoning her gown, smoothing the wrinkles from her skirts, combing the bits of leaves from her hair with her fingers before coiling it once more on the nape of her neck. Then with troubled eyes and a thoughtful mien, she made her way back to the gig that sat before the front steps of Cottonwood, climbed into it, and drove away. It was not until she reached the Mississippi River ferry that she remembered the things in the kitchen at the plantation that she had intended to divide among the slaves.

327

Chapter 17

MELANIE COULD not deny her recent association with Dom. He had come to call when she first returned from Virginia. The need to discover if he had indeed been responsible for the message to the Spanish ambassador in her name had led her to receive him. Her questions had brought more than she expected. Dom had fortified himself for the meeting with liquor. At her accusing words, he had broken down and cried. He only wanted to secure her freedom from marriage to Roland, he said. He had never meant for so many to die.

There had been more in the same vein, but the most alarming revelation had come as he stood at the door, composed at last, supposedly sober. "We are in this together, Melanie, dearest, since it was you who gave me the information that sent Roland to his death. That secret is ours though, yours and mine. You don't have to fear I will tell a living soul. I will keep it safe while you put on your mourning, and when it is time to take it off, when we are man and wife at last, it will be buried in our hearts forever."

In that manner, Dom's plans had been made known to her. He had elaborated on them several times since, when he had come to escort her to various entertainments. Sometimes it required every bit of ingenuity Melanie possessed to keep him from speaking of them before others, especially when he was under the influence of drink, which was often. She had come to live in fear that he would say something that would betray them both, had almost begun to believe that she was as guilty as he.

Roland's return would be a shock to Dom; he had counted him dead too long for it to be otherwise. How he would take it, she did not know. Of late, it was impossible to guess what Dom would do.

She was not left long in doubt. Dom's carriage stood before the steps of Greenlea when she turned into the drive; his hat and cane reposed upon the table in the hallway. At the opening and closing of the front door, he sauntered from the direction of the parlor.

"Melanie, at last," he said, saluting her with a glass of brandy he held in his hand. "They told me you had gone to Cottonwood. I wish I had known you were going. I would have kept you company."

Melanie managed a tight smile as she drew off her gloves and dropped them beside his hat. "I expect it is a good thing you did not."

"What do you mean?" he asked, peering at her. "Is something wrong? You look a little flushed, and there are grass seeds on your skirt."

"Yes," she replied. "I think you could say something is wrong. Let us go into the parlor and I will tell you about it."

When she had finished her tale, Dom sank down into a chair. The brandy he held sloshed over onto his fingers, but he seemed not to notice. "Roland, alive. I can't believe it," he whispered.

"I assure you it is true."

"He always did have the luck of Satan himself."

Melanie made no reply. Moving to the window, she lifted the drape and stood looking out. Behind her, she heard the click of the glass against Dom's teeth as he had recourse to the brandy in his hand. The memory came stealing into her mind of the days before she had left New Orleans, when she had looked forward so anxiously to the quiet peace and the slow, tranquil movement of the days at Greenlea. It seemed now there was no peace to be found anywhere. The tranquility had gone forever.

Dom stirred. "What do you mean to do?" he asked.

"Nothing," she answered. "What is there to be done?"

"You know what I am asking," he said, a rough note entering his voice. "Do you mean to live with him?"

"Not for the present," she said, her hand gripping the folds of the drape, dragging on it so that the brass heading above her creaked from the pressure.

There came a rustle of clothing as Dom got to his feet. "So you don't love him? I confess, I have wondered once or twice. Do you think he knows that the expedition was betrayed."

"He knows."

"But he doesn't suspect me, does he? He has no reason."

"None, except the dislike and distrust that lies between you. That is something I have wondered about, Dom. Why did you and Roland cease to be friends after Mexico? Surely you can tell me, now that we are—allies?"

"It was a private thing," Dom said quickly. "Nothing that has any bearing on our present problem."

"Are you certain?" she inquired, turning slowly to face him. "Our present problem, as you call it, has deep roots. Are you positive that your quarrel with Roland did not have something to do with my grandfather and the rumors from Mexico?"

He stared at her for a long moment, then he shook his head, moving toward her. "Melanie, my dearest. How can you think such a thing. Your grandfather trusted me, don't you remember? I want you to trust me, too. I want us to go away together. There are places in the western territories where no one could ever find us, where no one need ever know that you had another husband besides me."

He caught her hands, holding them in front of her. The urge to twist free was strong, but she kept still with a great effort. "Are you asking me to become a bigamist, Dom? Or worse?"

"I am asking you to come and seek out a new life with me, leaving everything else behind."

330

"Everything?"

"Yes, everything."

"Your home, Chloe, all your friends, your law practice?"

"They don't matter," he said quickly.

"I think they do," Melanie said, gently disengaging her fingers. "I know Greenlea matters to me, and Natchez. I couldn't leave them for a strange place, strange people."

He drew back, his thin lips pressing into a line and his hazel eyes flaring wide. "Couldn't you? Even if people here would have nothing to do with you?"

She affected nonchalance. "They have very nearly come to that anyway, because we have been so frequently seen together while I had a husband at war, missing in Cuba. Now that he has returned, the gossips will be busier than ever."

"All the more reason for leaving. I love you Melanie, and I want to be with you. I promise you will never want for anything so long as there is breath in my body."

That speech might have been more affecting if the words had not been slurred. He tried once more to reach for her, but she eluded his outstretched hands, pretending not to see as she swung in the opposite direction. "I think we should wait," she said, "and see what Roland means to do before we make any hasty moves. For the moment, he is installed at Cottonwood, and I am here. If the town doesn't like that arrangement, it makes no difference to me."

Dom's face twisted as though he were going to cry. "Roland will be a hero. See if he isn't. A hero who can do no wrong. If he should start hinting that Lopez was betrayed, it just might set people to thinking."

"Nonsense," Melanie snapped. "People are not clairvoyant. They will see nothing unless you give it away while you are in your cups."

"Melanie, don't talk to me so," he pleaded.

But Melanie's tenuous control was at an end. "Dominic Clements, don't talk to me at all!" she cried and whirling, ran from the room.

331

Though Melanie had given Roland his mother's direction, she was not certain he meant to contact her, especially since she had mentioned doing so. Since she would feel that she was neglecting a duty if she did not, she sat down and wrote to Colleen, explaining the situation. She realized that the things she had omitted from her letter were telling; still it could not be helped. If Colleen came, when Colleen came, she would see for herself that the situation was far from normal between her son and his wife. There was no use pretending.

Pretending was, however, something she had discovered she did fairly well. Entering a cotillion ball on Dom's arm three days after Roland's return, she was aware of a sudden quiet, followed by the babble of voices. Heads turned in her direction, then turned away just as quickly again as she met the staring eyes of first one guest and then another. For an instant she was assailed by panic, pure and engulfing. It was the tremor of nerves in Dom's arms that banished her fear. Curving her lips into a smile, holding her head high, she advanced, very nearly dragging Dom with her by the pressure of her fingers on his arm. She greeted her hostess with a gracious word or two, though she could not later remember what she had said. She was even able to feel a touch of pity for the poor woman who had not realized the recent acceleration in notoriety of her guest. One or two of the more starchy older women turned their backs upon her; the others did not give her the cut direct but merely ignored her, refusing to meet her eyes.

Melanie had never been the type of woman who despised friends of her own sex. It was disconcerting now to find that male attention, covert, faintly leering, was all she attracted. More telling still was the fact that none of her husbands and beaux who took such an interest in her appearance dared to approach her beneath the disapproving eyes of their female companions.

Her most severe trial came when she made her way upstairs. The door to the bedchamber alloted to the ladies as a retiring room was not quite closed. As Melanie drew

332

near, she heard voices inside, and then as she touched the handle, the sound of her own name.

"It is disgraceful, that is what it is. I would never have dreamed that a granddaughter of Colonel Ezell Johnston could behave with such a complete lack of shame. The way she is carrying on with Dominic Clements is a disgrace. She has quite ruined him, you know. His sister says he gives no thought whatever to his practice for spending time with Melanie Donavan."

A softer voice made itself heard. "You must admit she had reason to think her husband was dead."

"That is no excuse," the first woman declared. "If she thought him dead, she should have gone into proper mourning and completely isolated herself from the company of men, not started sending out lures for another husband."

A third woman entered the conversation. "No doubt," she said, her voice smug with portent, "it comes from being so friendly with actresses. You know what they are? Well, I have it from a friend of mine that our dear Melanie was seen in White Sulphur Springs in the company of none other than Colleen Antoinette Dubois, the Thespian who made such an impression at the St. Charles in New Orleans last season. With them was also a handsome young actor who seemed to be on amazingly familiar terms with Lieutenant Colonel Donavan's wife."

"You don't say," the first lady exclaimed.

"Indeed I do. One can only suppose that Roland has good reason for living apart from her."

"As I remember it, Roland Donavan's conduct was never angelic before he went away to war in Mexico. Have you considered that Melanie's actions may be a case of sauce for the gander, sauce for the goose?" the quieter-voiced woman inquired.

"That may be, but if it is, I consider it extremely foolish of her. They say, you know, that Roland was left well off by his father. The elderly Mr. Donavan may have lived like a skinflint, but he went through quite a few prosperous years. The sum he left to his son and heir is said to be staggering, considering the conditions of his plantation." There was a note in the strident voice of the first woman that suggested neither Robert Donavan nor his son had any business with wealth.

"But Roland doesn't get it all," the second woman said. "The man had a wife."

"Dead long ago, surely?"

"No, I think not. Now what was it about her? I cannot quite recall—"

Melanie had heard enough. She pushed the door wide and stepped into the room. "Good evening ladies," she said cheerfully, sending a warm smile to the quieter-appearing member of the trio, a woman she recognized as being a friend of Eliza Quitman. "Are you all having a nice gossip? How lovely for you. Life would be so boring if we had no one to talk about, would it not?"

"My dear girl, I don't know what you are talking about," the woman with the carrying voice said. The puce satin she wore tightened alarmingly over her chest as her bosom swelled.

"Don't you?" Melanie inquired with an arch smile. Moving to the dressing table, she turned this way and that before the mirror. "Perhaps I misunderstood the matter," she said over her shoulder, "but I rather thought my husband and I were the subject of your conversation just before I came into the room."

"You were eavesdropping!" the second lady, a sour-faced individual dressed in an unfortunate shade of green, accused.

"Oh, no! How can you say so? I just had not entered your cozy little circle. But there, I expect you are annoyed because I interrupted just when things were going along so well. I am sorry! I just was not thinking. Being so well bred, such complete ladies, you cannot talk about me to my face, can you? Perhaps I should go away again, and then you can be quite comfortable, tearing my character to shreds behind my back."

Dropping them all a mocking curtsy, she suited her actions to her words by sweeping from the room. As she de-

334

scended the stairs, Dom was waiting for her at the newel post, but the high color of anger across her cheekbones and the militant look in her eyes was so daunting that he did not speak as he offered his arm.

Melanie had expected Roland to put in an appearance at the gathering. As the evening wore on and he still did not come, the ball began to seem dull beyond bearing. The fact that for the first time in her life she was short of partners for the dances might have had something to do with it. There was a limit to the number of times she could suffer herself to be led out onto the floor by Dom. Not only were his hands damp and his hold too possessive, but as the evening progressed, his steps became increasingly uncertain. She suspected he had a flask of whiskey secreted in his carriage, for on more than one occasion she had looked around to find him gone. When he reappeared, his breath had smelled of liquor overlaid with the scent of hastily chewed cloves.

Someone else who was not present was Dom's sister.

"Where is Chloe tonight?" Melanie asked.

Dom turned this way and that, staring around the room. "I don't know," he said slowly. "She said she was coming with a friend."

"Perhaps you misunderstood. This isn't the only party this evening."

Dom nodded his agreement, but there was a frown between his hazel eyes.

One couple who did arrive late upon the scene was Eliza and John Quitman. Catching the eye of the governor's wife, Melanie smiled and nodded, but she did not put herself forward as a crowd gathered around the couple. She was conscious of having neglected her old friend. Though she had called at Monmouth once, Eliza had been from home, and Melanie had not gone back again. There were many excuses that she gave herself. She had been too busy with the harvest at Cottonwood. She did not want to intrude at what must be a trying time for the governor, when his office had been lost and also his dreams of empire in Cuba. The truth of the matter was, though she did not want to admit it, she did not wish to be reminded of the events in New Orleans, even less did she feel inclined to discuss them.

She should have known such a state of affairs could not continue. A short time later, as she stood talking to Dom, playing with the fan-shaped dance program that hung from her wrist, Eliza Quitman skirted the dance floor and came up beside her.

"Melanie, my dear. How nice you look tonight in your apricot silk. It is most becoming."

Melanie murmured the proper acknowledgment and inquired after Eliza's health and that of her family.

"We are all perfectly well, though it is kind of you to ask. My concern, however, is with you." Looking across at Dom, the former governor's wife went on, "Dominic, I wonder if I could prevail upon you to allow me to speak to Melanie alone?"

"Of course," Dom replied, but his bow was stiff as he moved away. With more than a few misgivings, Melanie watched from the corner of her eye as he made his way to the library at the back of the house. The library, filled with card tables around which the men who were not dancing were congregated, led to an open area at the side of the house where the carriages stood waiting.

Giving her attention to the older woman, Melanie said with a wry smile, "Now, what is it you have to say to me that cannot be said in front of Dom?"

Eliza Quitman looked down at her hands in their lace mitts. "I am not certain how to begin," she said. "I have heard the most disquieting rumors. I am sure they are not true, but it makes me afraid for you, and for your future."

"If you are speaking of the fact that Roland has returned—"

"Not entirely, though it concerns him. But we cannot speak of it here. Will you come for a drive with me tomorrow?"

"Yes, naturally I will. But though I am gratified by your concern, I am sure you are worrying needlessly."

336

"I hope so, my dear," Eliza Quitman answered. "I certainly hope so."

The Quitman carriage rolled along at a sedate pace. For the purposes of quiet conversation, Eliza had directed the coachman to drive south out of town, in the direction of St. Francisville. Melanie, remembering the last time she had traveled in that direction, was not too enthusiastic about retracing her steps, even for a small portion of the way, but she said nothing. There was little question that it should be quiet enough, especially this time of year.

It was cool riding along the sandy road under the overhanging limbs of great oak and sweet gum trees with their hanging vines and saw briers dragging along the top of the carriage. It was even a bit too cool. The weather had changed during the night, and there had been a touch of frost this morning. It was a sign that autumn was coming closer, and the cassimere shawl Melanie wore felt good.

On stepping into the carriage, Melanie and Eliza had exchanged the usual pleasantries. Now they rode along in a silence that seemed, at least to Melanie, to be tainted with embarrassment.

Suddenly from above them came a thump on the roof of the carriage. Both women looked up, then smiled.

"A sweet gum ball," Eliza Quitman said. "It is hard to believe it is time for them to fall again. How the children hate them; they are so uncomfortable to step on with bare feet. For myself, I have always thought they looked like tiny medieval maces."

It was an accurate description, Melanie agreed.

With the constraint between them broken, Eliza went on. "It was sweet of you to come with me today when you must think I am an interfering busybody."

"I never thought any such thing," Melanie said warmly.

"I wouldn't blame you if you had, though mind you, if you call me one to my face, I will still have my say."

"I'm sure of it," Melanie murmured, a wicked light in her eyes as she slanted a glance at her companion.

"You needn't think you can get around me by agreeing

with me either. The matter is so serious that it must be broached."

Melanie managed to smile, despite the apprehension that assailed her. Could Eliza possibly have stumbled onto the truth concerning the defeat of Lopez? Or had she learned of the knifing death of Elena's lover at the house on Rampart Street? "By all means," she said.

"It is this business with Dom. I know the circumstances of your marriage were not ideal, but I thought things were beginning to work out for you and Roland while you were in New Orleans. It seemed to me then, at least at times, that you were very nearly perfect together, and I often thought how unfortunate it was that the two of you could not have met and married in the usual way. It saddens me to see you alone now, and I am afraid that if this arrangement of separate establishments continues, you will never resolve your differences. Oh, I know I am sentimental where marriage is concerned. Being so happy myself, I would like to see everyone so. But there are some couples who are so right for each other that it hurts to see them apart."

"It is kind of you to worry about me," Melanie said, lowering her lashes to veil her gaze, "particularly now, when you have so much else on your mind, your children, and the governor's senate campaign. But the matters that divide Roland and myself are not such that the rift can be mended with a word or two."

"I know, my dear, and I never meant to sound as if I thought it mere stubbornness that separated you. I must insist, however, that there are few problems that cannot be worked out, if two people care enough to try. That is the question. Do you want to work them out?"

"Even if I did, by your own admission it takes both of us wanting the same thing to accomplish this miracle."

"How do you know Roland does not want it? Have you asked him? That may sound impertinent, but so many people think they can understand others without words. Often, they are quite wrong in what they think the other feels, or else they arrive at only half the truth. Honesty and love can surmount many obstacles, but someone must first summon the courage to speak."

Honesty? There had been little enough of that between Roland and herself. Love? It would make a difference, if it were mutual. "What if," she said at last, "the feelings you mention are onesided? The results of honesty then would be nothing but pain."

"At least you would know."

"Knowing, it seems to me, is not always such a good thing," Melanie said slowly. "Sometimes it is better to leave for oneself some small hope."

"To barter hope for the possibility of happiness is what requires the courage," Eliza Quitman answered quietly.

Above them the coachman gave a yell to his team, and the heavy body of the carriage lurched to the side of the road. Eliza was thrown against Melanie who braced herself on the side wall.

Straightening, pulling her bonnet back into place, Eliza let down the window beside her. "Jackson!" she called up toward the box, "What is it?"

No answer was necessary. Before the words were out of her mouth, they heard the clatter and rattle of another carriage approaching at high speed. It careered past them with its horses wall-eyed and straining and their manes flying. It was an open phaeton. Upon its high seat was a woman in a rose red driving costume with a cape lined in white satin fluttering back from her shoulders. Her face was flushed with the wind and the excitement, and if it appeared she was something less than completely in control of her team, it was also evident that she had no such misgivings. Her attention was centered on the man beside her to the exclusion of all else, including the carriage that had prudently made way for passage.

Recognition brought the breathlessness of an unpleasant surprise to Melanie. The woman was Chloe Clements, and the man who shared the seat with her was none other than Roland. With one controlling hand on the reins, he sat laughing down at the blond girl, his shoulder against hers and her skirts spread in obvious intimacy over his legs.

They were gone in an instant. Melanie, realizing she had been leaning to stare after them, drew back. Folding her hands in her lap, she looked straight ahead as the Quitman carriage resumed its progress.

"I am sorry you had to see that," Eliza said at last.

"Are you? I am not," Melanie snapped, recalling with a sense of discovery that both Roland and Chloe had been conspicuously absent from the dance the night before.

"You are hurt and angry, and who can blame you? But you must stop and think that Roland may have felt the same way when he came home and learned of your encouragement of Dom."

Melanie made no reply, turning her gaze out the window, watching the tangled brier vines and sumac bushes with the hint of red on their leaves that grew at the edge of the forestlands they were passing.

Eliza went on undeterred. "I have cudgeled my brain to think why you do not send Dom about his business. It would be a great shock to me to hear that you feel anything for him—or ever did—unless it is pity. Your purpose is not to arouse the jealousy of your husband, since your close association with Dom began while Roland was away. I wondered if it was a question of—if I may be so indelicate—money. If, thinking Roland dead, you meant to wed Dom for security. But then, to confound my understanding, you were not reunited with Roland when he returned, and Dom continued as your cicisbeo, to give him the polite name for men who were wont to dance attendance upon married women in my youth."

"I wish I could explain to you, Eliza, really I do, but I cannot."

"That was not my purpose, I assure you; you owe me no explanation. The fact that you feel yourself unable to speak of it alarms me somewhat, but I will allow you to know what you are doing. No, I only wanted to caution you not to let yourself be pushed into something you do not truly want. Do not let other people, male or female,

340

influence the course of your life more than you do yourself. If you become a pawn, manipulated for their convenience, if you let them take from you those things that mean the most, you have only yourself to blame. All that is required to shape events to your own purpose is a little resolution."

"Resolution being another word for courage?" Melanie inquired, the look in her eyes mocking and yet fond.

"Yes, I suppose it is," Eliza admitted.

"I will try to remember what you have said, but I think there is one thing more that I might require."

"Oh?"

"A good-sized portion of luck," Melanie answered.

Chapter 18

WITH THE crops in from the fields and the nights growing cooler, the fox hunting season began. The roads and bypaths echoed to the thud of hooves, and the packs of dogs could be seen pouring over hills, across pastures, and scrambling through the stripped cotton stalks with the riders hard at their heels.

The news that Roland had taken up the sport, buying himself a pink coat and a pair of new hunters, spurred Melanie's interest. She had been considering the things that Eliza had said, and now with a sparkle in her eye she set out to act upon them.

Her first move was to visit the dressmaker. There she had a magnificent riding habit of royal blue velvet with satin lapels made to her specifications. She also ordered a white silk shirt and stock, and a tall silk hat which trailed a swath of powder blue veiling. When her habit was complete and she was ready to leave the shop with her purchases under her arm, she had everything put on a bill to be sent to her husband.

Enlisting the aid of Eliza Quitman not only secured a mount for her and invitation to join the hunt, but also gained her an escort in the person of Eliza's young male cousins. It had been some time since Melanie had ridden. She had not been on a horse since that dark and rainy night when she had visited the Rover Rest. The art of sitting a sidesaddle had been taught at the finishing school she had attended, but there had been little chance to use it. She did not make the mistake of plunging back into riding again all in one day. She rode out several times beforehand. Finally, at the end of a week's time, she not only felt herself dressed to take to the field, but also physically able to stand the pace.

A fine mist of rain drifted in the air on the morning she set out. It was perfect hunting weather, cool enough to make a habit jacket comfortable, damp enough to make the scent easy to follow for the hounds, and not so wet as to be daunting for the riders or dangerous for the horses. Turner, Eliza's cousin, a young man of eighteen years, was late in coming for Melanie. By the time they reached the plantation where the hunt was to begin, the others were gathered on the drive, partaking of the stirrup cups offered by Negro menservants. The hounds, black and tan, tan and white, red brown, and any number of shades and combinations in between, created an enormous din. They barked, bayed, growled, bit, and wriggled around their holders, entangling their leashes while they tried to pick fights with each other, until it looked impossible that they could ever be separated.

The scene abruptly came to order as the master of the hunt sounded his horn. The dogs were led forward out across the field. Those riders still on the ground sprang to their saddles, and the horses sidestepped and curvetted, or stood with their ears pricked forward.

There were a number of other women among the crowd. Melanie had time to do no more than nod and take note of their bare responses before the horn sounded once more, the dogs were let loose, and they were off.

Turner appeared to be a neck-or-nothing rider. He left her behind at once in his eagerness to be in the forefront of the action. Melanie kept to a steady, even gait, staying with the center of the riders, neither surging ahead nor falling behind. She had seen Roland at once, talking to the master of the hunt before they started, though she did not think he had noticed her arrival. He was riding just ahead of her now, sitting tall and straight in the saddle, his shoulders stretching the broadcloth of his pink coat, a black armband around his sleeve. He exchanged a word or two with the man on his left, but he seemed to have no particular companion. That Chloe did not ride was one of the things Melanie had taken into consideration when she had decided to begin her campaign on the hunting field.

The fox, a wily vixen, ran, circled, doubled back, but did not go to earth. They crossed water-filled ditches, thundered across fields, splashed through creeks, over soggy water meadows that spattered them all liberally with mud, circled up the side of one hill and down the other. Once Melanie thought Roland looked back, but if he recognized her, he gave no sign. The sky grew darker overhead, and the mist turned into rain. Gradually, as the morning advanced, one rider after another dropped out to blow their horses or else to turn back. As Roland angled away toward a stand of trees, Melanie reached out to pat her horse's neck, drew rein, and followed.

He glanced around as she drew up beside him. A shuttered look came over his face. He did not smile, but neither did he frown. His reply to her greeting was not enthusiastic, but it was civil.

"That is a beautiful animal you are riding," Melanie said. "A recent purchase, I think?"

"Yes," he answered. "I don't believe your mount is from the Greenlea stables."

"No. Hunters were never in my grandfather's line." She reached out to ruffle the mane of her horse. "This fine fellow here is borrowed."

"From the man you were with?"

So he had noticed her arrival with Turner. "Hardly a man," she said lightly. "He is a cousin of Eliza's. He is at loose ends, marking time until his mother decides he is old enough to go away to Jefferson College."

"She will be lucky if he doesn't break his neck first," he said with a glance in the direction of the riders just disappearing over the crest of a rise.

"He may be a trifle reckless, but he is a good rider," Melanie defended him.

"So are you," he replied. "I never knew you rode."

344

She sent him a direct look, the violet shading of her eyes dark in the gray light. "I believe there are many things we never knew about each other."

"That riding habit is becoming," he said after a long moment.

"I am glad you think so, since you will be getting a bill for it before much longer."

His eyes moved over her, taking careful note of the straight line of her back, flicking away from the soft curve of her breast beneath the blue velvet. "I suppose I will have to pay it, since I have had the pleasure of seeing you in it."

Melanie smiled, unaffected by the dry note in his voice. "Yes," she said, "I rather thought you deserved that much."

"You overwhelm me," he said.

"Not yet," Melanie answered and lifted a brow as she met his narrow green gaze.

The rain rattled in the drying leaves of the white oak, spattering through, dripping around them. A huge drop fell on the flank of Melanie's horse, and as he moved restively, she reached out to quiet him once more. As though she had not laid down a somewhat provocative challenge, she said, "I understand you have also purchased a new phaeton. It is a dashing vehicle, I must say. It very nearly ran Eliza and me off the road the other day."

"Did it?"

"Oh, I absolve you of poor driving. It was Chloe Clements who held the reins."

"Ah, yes, I believe I remember the occasion."

"I am sure you do," she said, a caustic note creeping into her voice despite herself. "I must say I was surprised to see you with her. I would not have thought she would suit your tastes."

"My tastes? Are you saying Chloe is above my old standard, which I think you were once certain was low? Or are you saying Chloe lacks your quality?"

"Neither," she answered, despite the heat of the blush

345

that rose to her face. "But I would have wagered you would have been driven to murder by her laugh within the hour."

"There is that," he admitted, looking away. A wry grin came and went across his face so quickly Melanie could not be certain she had seen it.

"Why then?" she asked. "Chloe is flighty and impressionable, and her loyalty sometimes leads her to be less than kind, but there is no great harm in her. She does not deserve to be hurt unnecessarily."

"And what," he asked quietly, "makes you think I have any such design?"

"I don't know. Perhaps that is simply what I prefer to believe. Or maybe it is just that I have seldom seen you do anything without a reason."

"There are such possibilities in that admission that I am confounded," he said slowly. "I am also forced to wonder what, precisely, you are trying to do."

Melanie tilted her head to one side, an innocent expression on her face. "I am only trying to discover why you are cultivating Chloe Clements."

"I could tell you, but I doubt you would believe it, or believing it, approve."

"You might try me and see."

He shook his head. "I might," he answered, "but I don't believe I will. I prefer, instead, to trace down the exact cause of your interest."

"Let me see," Melanie said, pretending to think. "Would you accept wifely concern?"

"I think not."

"Why, I wonder. I am still your wife."

"What you are is a scheming jade who is up to something—again. I am not the only one who has an interest in the Clements family. Does Dom, perhaps, object to my association with his sister? If so, then let him come and tell me himself."

"Is that what you really want?" Melanie inquired, a frown between her eyes.

"That is something I have no intention of telling you,

346

unless you would like to unburden your soul and tell me why you allow Dom to haunt Greenlea. Without going into the question of your tastes, I would have wagered he would have bored you into a screaming fit in a matter of hours."

At that moment there was the sound of a horn, the babble of voices, and a great baying and barking of dogs. "Dear me," Melanie said, growing a little pale, though she strove for a tone of mock annoyance. "It looks as if we have missed the kill. I hope you don't mind."

"No," he said slowly. "I don't mind at all."

"Shall we join the others? If we are quick they will never realize we were not there." Without waiting for his reply, she touched her heel to her horse and rode out from the shelter of the tree.

The hunt breakfast waiting for them back at the plantation was a sumptuous meal, though extremely informal. Wet coats were removed and sent to the laundry to be steamed before the fireplace to a condition at least approaching dryness. Gentlemen and ladies alike sat down in their shirt sleeves to a table loaded with ham, sausage, bacon, turkey, fried chicken, and beef steak, to be eaten with platters of golden hot biscuits hot from the oven, and mounds of molded butter with the figure of a running fox molded on the top. There were stacks of hotcakes, and eggs, scrambled, fried, boiled, and baked. There were fried fruit tarts and muffins, custard pies, and cakes heavy with butter and eggs. Crystal pots of jam and syrup lined the table. To drink there was champagne, but there was also ice cold milk and steaming hot coffee. The table was set with English bone china, Georgian coin silver, and Waterford crystal. In the center was an enormous papier-mâche cornucopia from which spilled a bounty of fruits and nuts, well-scrubbed vegetables and small, ornamental gourds.

The quiet little woman who was their hostess had the harried look of someone who has attempted something that is too much for her, and more than once she cast an accusing glance in Melanie's direction as if she felt she had the right to lay at least part of her troubles at Melanie's door. Uncertain where to seat a couple who were married, but not living together, she had finally compromised by placing them opposite each other midway down the long table with the great, high-piled cornucopia between them. If it had not been for Roland's height, they would not have been able to see each other. As it was, Melanie merely sent him an amused look before turning to the man on her left.

The number of ladies at the table was so small compared to the gentlemen that they had been placed seemingly at random up and down the board. They were put to the shift of leaning to talk across the men, or else stretching to converse behind their backs. As a result there were a great many raised voices and shouted comments from the hardy types that were attracted to the hunt. None of the spate of words was directed toward Melanie, however. For all the attention paid to her by the other women, she might as well have been invisible. A few of the women were older, sporty females with sun-toughened faces, but most were of an age with Melanie. They had played together as children at birthday parties, went to pink teas as budding young ladies, and later, to cotillions. Now the young women, matrons for the most part, stared through her and turned away. It had been the better part of two years since she had been one of their circle, it was true, but in a place like Natchez, the fact that she was returned should have been a point of abiding interest, calling forth innumerable questions and explanations. The lack of them was distressing. She was being shown, as Eliza had tried to warn her, that her apparent loose behavior would not be tolerated by good society. By contrast, the attention shown Roland was effusive. The ladies fussed over him, Melanie told herself heatedly, as if he were a poor little orphan boy who had been deprived of food and comfort.

Melanie, with no recourse except to talk to the gentlemen, did just that. With a bright light in her eyes, she set herself to charm and amuse. She succeeded so well that the end of the table where she sat became unusually animated, and more than one sour glance was thrown in her direction as the gentlemen craned their necks to hang on her words.

For Melanie to remain so oblivious of the censure being meted out did not endear her to the other women. When the meal was over at last and the men had moved away to gather in small groups, the women banded together and swept away in a frigid silence, leaving Melanie alone.

Such a thing had never happened to her before in her life. The fact that she understood it did not help. Ostracism was an ugly thing, a terrible feeling. Nonetheless, she would not be humiliated, nor would she follow after them, hoping some one of their number would relent. Holding her head high, she turned toward a pair of double doors that led out onto a brick-floored portico at the side of the house. Opening one panel, breathing deep of the fresh, damp air as though it were her only concern, she drew her riding skirt higher over her arm and stepped outside.

She had not realized quite how flushed she had become until she felt the cool air on her face. The tapping sound of the heels of her boots echoed under the high, white-column portico as she crossed to one side. Beyond the protection of the roof, the rain fell with a steady gray monotony. The leaves of the camellia shrubs that lined the side of the house sparkled with wet, and there were puddles pocked with raindrops in the drive that stretched away from the portico winding around to the front of the house.

Sighing, Melanie leaned her shoulder against one of the great white columns that supported the portico and folded her arms over her chest. She would wait a few minutes, and then she would go back inside. If the situation were the same, she would find young Turner and go home.

Behind her, the door opened once more. She was aware of Roland from the moment he stepped from the house, though she pretended not to be. He moved toward her with an easy stride. As he stopped beside her, she slanted him a small smile, then looked away again.

"I would say you brought it on yourself, except I know that is not the exact truth."

"No," Melanie said, without bothering to pretend ignorance of his meaning. "It isn't. It has been some time since I was full and staid enough to join the ranks of the women in there."

"That is their loss," he answered. "You don't have to be bitter."

"I'm not, only disappointed. But I appreciate the words of comfort anyway."

He stared down at her as if he felt the impulse to say something he might regret. After a moment, he looked away. "I have been meaning to speak to you about Cottonwood," he said, his words off hand, almost as though chosen at random. "You did an excellent job of getting in the harvest. I feel I owe you something for the labor you put into it, and I would like to repay you."

"There is no need for that."

"I think there is," he insisted. "However, if you would rather not discuss it, I will speak to the lawyer about resuming your allowance. I had forgotten how short of funds you must be, until you mentioned your riding habit."

"That was not the purpose," she said stiffly.

"I am certain of it. Regardless, I don't think you can deny that you need it."

She could not. "That is kind of you, under the circumstances."

"Under the circumstances," he grated, "it is the least I can do. I am well aware that if it were not for me, your circumstances would be different. You would be safely fixed as the wife of a rising attorney and politician, with a child or even two to dandle on your knee."

Melanie hunched her shoulder, turning quickly away from him. The silence stretched. Then he reached out to touch her arm. His fingers were warm and firm as he turned her to face him, brushing his other hand up the silk of her sleeve to her forearm.

"I didn't mean to hurt you, Melanie. I never meant to hurt you." His green gaze searched the oval of her face, coming to rest on her parted lips.

Melanie stared up at him, excitement caught like a tight knot in her chest. The grip of his fingers increased. The look on his face changed to one of longing. She swayed toward him.

"Mrs. Donavan? Oh, I'm glad I found you. I promised my father I wouldn't linger. He always likes to check the horses over when I bring them back. He thinks no other stable but his can cool one down properly or that I will lame one of his precious steeds."

At the first word, Roland's hands had dropped from her shoulders. "Yes," Melanie replied. "All right, Turner." She hesitated a moment, waiting for some sign that Roland did not want her to go. There was none. Her husband made no move to stop her as she stepped around him and walked away.

The rain still fell when Melanie retired to bed that evening. She lay for a time listening to it, absorbing its peace. She let her mind drift to the meeting with Roland. He felt something for her; she knew it. What was it that stood between them? Was she being willfully blind to think it was no outside influence, no other person or tragedy, but something within Roland himself? She had gone over their meeting near the cemetery at Cottonwood so many times. The more she considered it, the more certain she became that the last hurtful challenge he had thrown at her, that last mocking invitation to join him as his wife, had been meant to set her back up, to prevent her from living with him in that capacity rather than encouraging it. Why? After today, she could not think if was because of Chloe. Dom then? The thought raised frightening possibilities.

It was warm tonight inside the house. Melanie had opened her window for air. The rising wind billowed the curtains inward. Far off, she heard the rumble of thunder.

Strange. It seemed almost like the stormy weather of spring. Autumn rains were seldom warm, seldom noisy. They usually fell in a deep quiet, like the tears of old grief.

In the soft and fragile substance of a dream, Melanie turned and Roland was beside her, calling her name, his voice gentle, cherishing. His body was warm, throbbing with desire, and he held her in a windswept void brilliant with the flare of light. Melanie moved closer, lifted her lashes to gaze into his face.

She came awake with a start. Roland was beside her, real, his body hard against hers. In the blue white flash of lightning she stared into his eyes, saw the haunted helplessness of his longing. His hair was wet with rain, and there was a gray tinge to his skin. The hand that rested at her waist was clamped rigid with the force of his need and the certainty of her refusal to meet it.

"You came to me once out of the rain," he said, his voice soft and uneven, "now I come to you."

Thunder rumbled overhead. Melanie started. Then with a joyous smile, she moved against the man who was her husband, reaching to slide her arms around his neck, drawing his head down. From some inner wellspring rose the sweet tide of passion to engulf them. She flung off her nightgown and stretched to help him rid himself of his clothing. Then with rapture singing in her veins, she drew him within her open thighs and took him deep inside her. Surging against him as in bright and sweet fury, they rode the storm.

The tempest died slowly away. Rainfall drenchingly beyond the window, a full, sated sound. Melanie smoothed the open palm of her hand over the planes of his chest and down the muscled flatness of his belly.

"Why?" she whispered. "Why did you come?"

"Because," he said, a tremor in his voice, "I could not stay away. I never could."

Satisfied, Melanie pressed her face within the curve of his neck. With the feel of his hands on her hair, she slept.

"Miss Melanie! Miss Melanie, you got a visitor!"

Melanie came awake with a start. She began to stretch and discovered a long, lean body curled around her back. Smiling, she turned her head to meet Roland's alert green gaze.

"Miss Melanie?" The call was followed by a knocking. It was the upstairs maid, the girl who had been doing her best to take Glory's place since Melanie's return.

Melanie struggled to one elbow. "What is it?" she called.

"I said you got a visitor, Miss Melanie. It's Mr. Dom. He's waiting in the parlor."

"At this hour?"

"The morning's half gone, Miss Melanie. I told him you was still abed, but he said he would wait. And he's been waiting downstairs now for nigh on an hour."

"All right. I will be down in a few minutes."

"Don't you want no help with your gown?" the maid asked through the door.

"I can manage," Melanie called. "Tell Cicero to see that the gentleman has some refreshment."

"He's already had that, Miss Melanie. Ordered it himself."

Roland removed his hand from Melanie's hip, threw back the covers, and slid out of bed. Without a word, he began to pull on his trousers.

Melanie sat up, watching him stamp into his boots. The russet brown strands of her hair cascaded about her, veiling but not hiding the rosy fullness of her breasts. "Are you going?" she asked at last.

He glanced at her, then looked quickly away again. "If Clements has taken to making himself so much at home here, then it is no place for me."

"That isn't true!"

He did not stay to argue. Pulling on his shirt, he pushed it into the top of his trousers, leaned to kiss her hard upon the lips, and then crossed the room with swift strides. Melanie watched him step through the wide open window, then sat listening to his receding footsteps on the upper veranda. She could tell by the sound that he was making his way to the servants' stairs at the house, leaving as he must have come.

When the sound had died away, she swung out of bed, strode to her wardrobe, and jerked down the first gown that came to hand. Her mouth set in a grim line, she stepped into her underclothing, dragged on the blue muslin she had laid out, then twisted her hair high on her head in a neat coil. Leaving her room in a swirl of skirts, she marched down the stairs.

Dom stood at the window in the parlor staring out. He turned as she entered, a frown between his hazel eyes. Downing the drink he held in his hand, he set the glass on a side table before he spoke.

"I just saw a man on horseback come around the back of the house and trot down the drive. Who was he?"

"A visitor," Melanie said shortly.

"Oh? I understood you were still in bed."

"So I was."

"The man," Dom said slowly, his frown deepening, "looked amazingly like Roland."

"What of it?" Melanie asked with a lift of her chin. "He is my husband."

Dom stared at her, dull red color mounting to his face, "What are you saying? You can't mean to go back to him. What of our plans?"

"Your plans, Dom, not mine."

"What—what of what we did, you and I. We have to protect each other. There is no one else we can trust."

"What we did? I did nothing. My one mistake was to trust you. You betrayed that trust. You used what I told you to destroy a dream, to kill more than three hundred men and injure many others. And worst of all, you lacked the courage to do it on your own. You did it in my name, hiding behind my skirts."

Melanie listened to the bitter words that poured from her lips as if she were hearing a stranger. She had not planned to say such things. Dom's behavior in coming uninvited into her home and ordering her servants, putting her in a position difficult to defend before Roland, had snapped the last fine thread that held her self-control.

"Yes, I did," Dom answered her accusations. "I used your name, knowing that I was doing what you wanted, though you could not bring yourself to the point of going through with it. I did it for you."

"For me? Is that what you tell yourself to salve your conscience? Thank you, but I don't remember being consulted, and I refuse to take the blame for your deeds."

Dom stared at her. "You are in love with Roland, aren't you? That's what all this means. I wondered why you arranged to go hunting without telling me. I came to find out what you thought you were doing. I couldn't believe it when I heard you had been with him yesterday. Now I see. You were running after him like a bitch in heat, while I treated you like you were something precious, the woman I wanted to grace my home and have my children. You were panting after that stud who bedded you out of wedlock and who has used you as he pleased since then. I wonder what he would think if it came to his ears that it was you who trafficked with the Spanish ambassador, who was seen speaking to the man at the theater?"

Melanie stared at him, her blue eyes icy with contempt. "Why don't you tell him—if you can find a way to do so without implicating yourself? Or are rumors more your line? I would still advise care, for Roland is a tenacious man, and he is all too likely to want to hear the tale confirmed by the source. You would be hard put, I think, to explain how you know so much. And I can promise I will not be silent on the subject myself. I wonder who Roland is most likely to believe."

"I will wager that even if Roland believes you, no one else in this town will, especially now," he said, moving toward her with a sneer on his thin lips.

"You think not? You may be right, but for myself, I think they will be inclined to take the word of a woman whose husband is willing to fight to vindicate her honor. How would you answer such a challenge, Dom? Do you think the chance of blackening my name and driving a wedge between me and Roland is worth risking your life? No matter what happens, I will never turn to you. Never!" She was far from certain Roland could be depended on for such a gesture, but Dom did not know that.

A yellow gleam shone in his eyes. "Then perhaps I had better take what I have waited for so long now. I have often thought as we sat here chatting in this room of throwing you down on the settee and pushing your skirts above your head."

"Have you indeed?" Melanie inquired, her lips curling as she smelled the whiskey on his breath and sensed the drunken bravado in his voice. "You will not find it as easy as you think. I have a strong pair of lungs, and if you so much as lay a finger on me, I will scream the house down. Cicero may be slow, but he is waiting outside, and I believe I can undertake to foil any advances you might make until he can come to my rescue. If you want to be interrupted at a time very likely to be most inconvenient as well as embarrassing, then go ahead, but I would advise you to choose a better time and place before making such threats."

His eyes searched her face as if he could not understand her composed and scornful defiance. "You have become a hard and brazen hussy," he flung at her.

"There are things that can happen to a woman to make her so," Melanie returned, her blue eyes steady, "and I am not certain it is a bad thing if it allows me to hear what you have said without swooning, a helpless victim, at your feet."

"I think I prefer to remember you as you were when we were engaged—quiet, sweet, and gentle."

She lifted her chin. "No doubt, and you can look back upon that time with regret that you did not have me upon the settee then. It would more than likely have been an easy conquest for you at the time."

"Melanie," he began.

She made a quick gesture with one hand. "No more. I must ask you to leave. I would appreciate it if you would wait for my invitation before you return to Greenlea. From this day onward I will not be home to you when you are alone."

He sent her a glance that bordered on hate as she stepped back, allowing him free passage to the door. With reluctant steps, he moved to the panel that opened into the hall. He paused there, then swung back. "You—you don't know what you have done to me," he said, a wild look in his eyes. "You have ruined my life. You have taken from me my good name, my law practice, my ambition, hope, even my honor, and given nothing in return. What am I to do now? What is there for me to do?"

His words touched Melanie with compassion for an instant. Then with a tiny shake of the head, she said, "You can begin by placing the fault for the loss of the things you value where it belongs. I took nothing from you. You threw it away out of pride and fear and the guilt you feel for the wrongs you have done to others."

"You know," he whispered. "I was afraid you would find out, afraid you would turn against me." His face twisted, and a vacant look came into his eyes. Swinging around, Dom snatched the door open and threw himself out into the hall, bolting from the house.

Melanie stared after him in frowning perplexity. What had he meant? Of course she knew of his treachery to Lopez and his men. They had thrashed that out long ago. It made no sense for him to hark back to it now. Unless that was not the only wrong that could be laid at Dom's door. Abruptly the memory of that strange confrontation between Dom and Roland at Cottonwood so many months before returned to her. Dom, learning of her marriage, had sought to deaden the blow with drink and had then come riding up to Cottonwood in the night. Roland had talked to him, standing above him on the stairs. She could not recall now exactly what had been said, but something had passed from Roland to Dom, something that had caused Dom to forget his bluster and hurt pride, something that had made him turn tail and run. What had it been? She was left with no more than an impression, the tones of their voices, the way they had looked at each other. Whatever it was, there had been something of the same stricken look in Dom's face then as had been there just now, the same bleak and despairing fear.

Chapter 19

MADAME COLLEEN Antoinette Dubois stepped down from the carriage wearing unrelieved black. Melanie, calculating the approximate date the actress would arrive, had sent Jim Coachman to meet every steamboat from New Orleans for the past three days. Despite that, she had not hoped to see Colleen before the end of the week. She was sorting linens when the upstairs maid came running from the front of the house to tell her that Jim had passengers this time. Without so much as removing her apron, Melanie hurried down the stairs. She reached the front veranda in time to greet Roland's mother with a swift embrace as she came up the steps.

"Colleen, how lovely to see you again," she said. "And you too, Elena," she added, stretching out her hand to the dark-haired quadroon woman who followed behind the actress. "Come into the house, both of you."

Elena smiled and murmured a quiet greeting. Then, as if determined to make herself useful in her capacity as Colleen's maid, she turned to Cicero who stood beside the door and began to make arrangements for Colleen's trunks to be taken upstairs.

Melanie glanced quickly at the deep mourning the actress wore. "Colleen, you did get my letter?" she asked.

"Yes, my dear," Colleen said, moisture rising to her eyes. "I did indeed, and also Roland's message. There, I never meant to dissolve into tears on your shoulder, but I am so happy." Taking a handkerchief from her reticule,

359

she dabbed at her eyes, laughing a little, then looking at the black border on that scrap of linen and lace, she gave a sudden exclamation. "Oh, but you mean my black. They are widow's weeds, my dear. I hesitated before buying them, but remembering how conventional Natchez is, I thought so long as I was returning from the dead for the sake of the dead, I should at least look the part."

"Yes, of course," Melanie said. "I am sorry. I was so concerned that you might not know Roland is still alive, I forgot you have another reason for sorrow."

"I quite understand, and lest you should call me a hypocrite, I should tell you I do not consider myself in mourning for Robert so much as the death of the love we once shared; he and I."

Melanie signaled for refreshments to be served in the parlor, and they moved into that room, exchanging a few laughing comments concerning the long sea voyage from Virginia and up the river. As they took their places on the settee Colleen asked, "And where is my son? Why isn't the rascal here to welcome me?"

"He—he is at Cottonwood," Melanie answered.

"Well, I call that fine, running off to work when he should have known I would be arriving any day. I shall have a few words to say to him about that. I suppose I must call myself lucky to find you at home, Melanie. I debated whether to come here or go straight out to Cottonwood, until I remembered your note last month telling of the deplorable conditions there."

Melanie took a deep breath. "It is possible you may still want to go to Cottonwood. Roland is not working there. It is where he is living."

Colleen regarded her with discerning eyes. "Is it now? You know I respect your privacy, my dear, but I cannot let the matter rest there. You must tell me how this state of affairs comes about."

Explaining was extraordinarily difficult. Her excuses for their living apart seemed lame, even to her own ears.

Colleen heard her out. Then with a thoughtful look in her eyes, she said, "It seems as if I must have a talk with my son. As soon as I am settled in tomorrow, I will pay him a visit."

Melanie glanced down at her hands. "I understand it is quite comfortable at Cottonwood now. Roland has been making improvements since he returned. When he has finished, it should be a pleasant home again, except during the hottest weather."

"I appreciate what you are trying to say," Colleen answered smiling. "But I do not think, regardless of what has been done, that I could ever be easy there. No, unless you would rather not have me, I will be happier here with you."

"I hoped you would say that," Melanie said simply. As the door opened behind her, she turned. "Ah, here is Cicero. Now while I am brewing a pot of good hot tea for us, you can begin to tell me what you have been doing, and what you plan to do."

Colleen made her visit to Roland as planned. What passed between them, Melanie did not know, nor did she ask, but the actress returned in a thoughtful frame of mind, and her manner was distracted, even a trifle anxious, for the rest of the day.

To Melanie, it seemed natural to take Colleen to visit Eliza Quitman. Her explanation of her living arrangements had, of necessity, included her current standing in the community and the complete lack of any visitors to whom she might introduce Colleen in her funereal black. She was glad to be able to take Colleen to one house where she was certain she would be welcome. Eliza knew Colleen, naturally, had seen her on the stage in New Orleans, and the two of them had met briefly at the debacle of the last gala for the Lopez expedition. The two women, Eliza and Colleen, were wary of each other at first, but by the time the visit ended, they were chatting like old friends. Eliza, refusing to listen to any dissuasion, was busily planning a quiet dinner party she meant to give for Madame Dubois to introduce her to a few of her friends.

They had found Eliza in her garden at the rear of the house, overseeing the division and replanting of spring bulbs by her gardener. As Colleen wandered away to inspect the budding camellias that lined the black wall, Melanie seized the opportunity to put a question to her hostess. "Eliza," she said, "are you certain you want to do this, give the dinner party, I mean? I will certainly understand if, after speaking to your friends, you discover there are many who would rather not appear at a gathering where an actress and a woman separated from her husband are present. Also, there is the question of the governor's candidacy for the senate. He may not consider it helpful to his campaign to entertain two such women in his home."

"My dear, how black you paint yourself and Madame Dubois. It makes me feel deliciously Bohemian and all the more determined to go ahead as planned. I am only sorry that the death of your father-in-law prevents me from giving a more lavish party, say a soiree or a ball. More than that, I shall enjoy doing my bit to reestablish you here. I shall invite Roland, of course, and you will do me the kindness to show the same amiability toward one another as you presented at the hunt breakfast a few days ago."

"I can only try," Melanie answered. She had reported what had occurred that day to Eliza when she had called to thank her for good offices in securing the invitation to the hunt. She had not mentioned Roland's late visit nor the break with Dom. Still she had managed to convey the feeling that she was hopeful she and Roland might reach an understanding.

"Yes, and so can I," Eliza went on. "A number of people have commented favorably on his seeking you out. I think if you will cooperate just a little, you will see that I am not without influence of a social kind. There are few in Natchez who would dare disagree with my judgment on who is, and who is not, respectable. I have only been awaiting the opportunity, and I will admit, the prospect of a reconciliation between you and your husband, to do my bit for you in that direction. As for John, he also trusts my judgment. But I tell you frankly, if you should be the cause of his losing the senatorial election I will be inclined to bless you. I am weary of sharing my husband with public life, and I would be just as happy if he were a private man again."

After that, there was nothing for Melanie to do except express her gratitude and join in deciding the arrangements for the coming event.

Before it seemed possible, the evening of the dinner party was upon them. Colleen, superb in black lace and emeralds, emerged from her bedchamber at the same time as Melanie left hers. The actress frowned as she saw the apricot silk that Melanie was wearing, one of the gowns Colleen had purchased for her in White Sulpher Springs. She said nothing, though her attitude seemed to suggest that someone, probably Roland, had been remiss in not providing a new gown for the occasion.

They descended the stairs together, their skirts whispering over the treads. The Greenlea carriage with Jim on the box stood before the door. Cicero handed them inside. Alone, unescorted, they set out for Monmouth.

The great white house shone with lamplight. Stepping into the enormous hallway with its staircase mounting one wall, Melanie could not help thinking that it was here on a night much like this one, when the house was decorated for gaiety and the hum of voices filled the air, that it had all begun. She was not given long to reflect. No sooner had the butler taken their wraps than Eliza came hurrying toward them down the hallway. Her eyes were worried and her tone apologetic as she spoke.

"I am sorry, Melanie, but there was nothing I could do about it. John saw Dom and his sister on the street in Natchez. He has no patience with gossip, so he is quite above things of this sort. Knowing we had all been friendly in New Orleans, he invited the pair here this evening. When I learned of it, it seemed to me that the best thing to do was to increase the number of guests in hope they would be lost in the crowd."

Melanie hid her dismay with a smile. "Don't worry. It will be fine," she said.

"There will be forty-eight sitting down to dinner, and I have arranged for a trio of musicians to come in to play for dancing afterward. I could murder John with the greatest good cheer, but after he had invited them, there was nothing else I could do."

"There," Colleen said, coming forward with the correct answer. "Don't upset yourself. It doesn't matter in the least. I have been wanting to see this couple at close hand; if we were introduced in New Orleans, I have no recollection of it. As for the number of people, why they do not trouble me on any account. People in large numbers, approving or otherwise, are something of a specialty with me. Shall we go in and face them?"

Forty-eight for dinner was a great number, but by no means was it out of reason. There were more than a few hostesses in Natchez who could boast of a service of china sufficient to set a place before more than a hundred. The table in the dining room at Monmouth could seat eighteen without difficulty at its smallest size. With the addition of leaves and supports, it could expand to accommodate more than sixty.

The food was excellent, simple but plentiful and well cooked, as suited the tastes of the master and mistress of the house. It was placed before them and the plates taken away with the skillful lack of intrusion that spoke of well-trained servants. Though John Quitman drank water, the wine flowed freely, the chandeliers sparkled overhead, and the scent of flowers that were placed in silver bowls at intervals down the board vied with the perfumes of the ladies present.

The only thing wrong was with the guests. It was as though a pall hung over the table, stifling conversation, making people clumsy and self-conscious. Only John Quitman and Colleen appeared unperturbed. Roland sat aloof, his green eyes watchful as they rested upon Colleen and the way she was drawing out an elderly spinster placed near her at the table. Dom, on the opposite side, well down the table from Melanie, slouched in his chair, scowling, reaching too often for his wineglass. Chloe, near her brother, smiled at Roland with a secretive twist of her lips, slanting stares at him from under her lashes, as if trying to draw his attention. She was, for the most part, unsuccessful, but that did not deter her.

On the whole, it seemed to Melanie that the best idea was to ignore any discordant element in the gathering and behave as naturally as possible. Toward that end, she met her husband's gaze without evasion, spoke to him about the various courses that passed before them, and other small matters just like any other married couple. When she found herself at a loss, she turned to the gentleman on the other side of her. This, thanks to Eliza's thoughtfulness, was Turner, the young cousin who had taken her fox hunting. Horses, hounds, and hunting sufficed to hold his attention, and with his able and uncomplicated assistance, she made it through the meal.

A piano, a violin, and a French horn comprised the musical ensemble that Eliza had been able to summon on such short notice. They were thoroughly familiar with the airs suitable for a party made up primarily of older married couples, however. They began with a reel to get things off to a lively start. Colleen would not be dancing, of course, and Eliza, ever thoughtful, sat beside her at one end of the room with the governor standing behind his wife's chair. Chloe, her catlike hazel eyes sparkling, picked up her skirts and began to make her way across the floor toward Roland. If he saw her coming, he gave no sign. He turned his back full upon her and with an ironic inclination of his head, led Melanie out onto the floor.

They danced until they were breathless, whirling, side-stepping, holding hands as they went down the column of dancers. Melanie, warmed by the contagious excitement of the moment, laughed up into her husband's face, her cheeks flushed and a gleam in her eyes that bordered on being reckless.

Turner, with a hint of red under his fair skin for his daring, swung her through the next dance, a waltz. She waltzed also with Roland, drifting around the floor in his arms. And then as a polka was announced, her hand was solicited by John Quitman. Though he was the first to admit he was not at his best on the floor, at this quick-stepping dance he was surprisingly adept, due perhaps to his German heritage. He twirled Melanie with a will and seemed reluctant to give her up when a man she recognized as the master of the hunt from her sortie at fox hunting presented himself before her.

After that, she had no lack of partners. The gentlemen came forward, gruff in their whiskers and mustaches, diffident, sheepishly smiling. And their dowager wives, when they met her eyes, especially if they had been seen speaking with Eliza and Colleen, nodded with a twitch of their lips that might, if one were charitable, be taken for a smile.

Pleading breathlessness, Melanie left the floor at last and went to sit beside her hostess. "My dear," Eliza said, "I believe we have done it. You were magnificent, with just the correct air of sweet carelessness. I have always said society gravitates toward those who show they do not court it and shuns the ones who do."

Impulsively, Melanie reached to press the hand of the older woman. "Thank you, it's been a lovely evening," she whispered and turned to smile at Roland as he came to stand beside her chair.

One of the few men present she had not granted a dance was Dom. He had tried to approach her a number of times, but always she had slipped away, accepting another partner, retreating to Roland's side or making her way to Colleen to help keep her from growing bored with her sedentary role. Roland had not always been able to avoid Chloe, though Melanie could not be certain he had tried as diligently as he might. Watching them take the floor had been a trial for Melanie. The blond girl had clung to him in a ridiculous manner, practically hanging in his arms, fluttering her lashes at him, and pouting her mouth as though inviting him to kiss her. The sly glances she had given Melanie as she danced past in Roland's arms had not improved Melanie's temper. Once, when the opportunity was placed in her way, Melanie had to struggle with her conscience to keep from stepping on the hem of the other girl's dress and sending her for a nice long wait while a maid repaired it abovestairs.

The band struck up yet another of Strauss's waltzes. Eliza made some laughing comment. Melanie turned her head to catch it and at that instant saw Dom coming across the floor toward her. There was a look of frowning concentration in his eyes and a slight weave to his walk. Beside him, smiling like a cat about to pounce upon a mouse, was his sister. There was no place to go. Melanie could only sit and watch Chloe twine her small hands with their long nails around her husband's arm while Dom made his bow before her.

"May I have the pleasure of this dance?" Dom asked in formal invitation.

Melanie turned to stare at him, only half aware of what he said, though she realized well enough what he wanted. Before she could frame a reply, Roland spoke. "Sorry, old man, I just this moment promised to take Melanie out for a breath of fresh air. Another time—maybe."

Melanie sprang to her feet at once. As Roland disengaged his arm from Chloe's grasp, Melanie slipped her hand into the crook of his other elbow. With a nod for her hostess and a barely suppressed grin for Colleen, Melanie swept from the room at her husband's side.

In silence they strolled down the great hall. The welcome freshness of the cool air that wafted through the enormous open space was an indication of how stuffy it had grown in the room where they had been dancing. A few steps further along, Roland tried a door. It opened upon a small, unlighted sitting room. Drawing her inside, he pushed the panel to behind them.

"What is it?" Melanie asked as they were close together in the dark. "Why did you bring me here?"

"For this," he answered and took her in his arms. His lips found hers, and for an endless time they stood locked together, their mouths searching, turning in sensuous exploration. Their hearts pounded together. Her breasts

367

thrust against his chest, and his hands moved over the silk that covered her back and shoulders.

He lifted his head at last. "I hope you didn't want to dance with Dom. That was something I did not feel like seeing."

"No," she said. "No, I didn't. And I am glad you weren't ready to dance with Chloe again."

The grip of his fingers tightened. He turned, groping for the settee. Finding it, he seated himself, then pulled her down across his lap. His mouth sought hers once more, and his hand smoothed upward from the curve of her waist to lightly clasp the globe of her breast. She touched his face, trailing her fingers down the strong column of his neck, slipping them beneath the lapel of his coat and waistcoat, spreading her palm over his chest, moving it on the fine linen of his shirt in a gentle caress. Roland let his hand travel downward over her hip. He encountered the folds of her skirt. Dropping lower, he found more skirts and petticoats, and yet more.

Sighing, he drew back. "Melanie, love?" he whispered.

"Yes, Roland, yes. Let's go home to Greenlea."

The light in the great hall revealed Melanie's lips wine red from his kisses and her hair not so neatly arranged as it had been. Melanie turned from the glass of the hall-tree, a smile curving her mouth. "I think I had better wait in the carriage while you make our adieus to Eliza and tell Colleen we are ready to go. I expect your mother is more than ready. She has been wonderful, but it has not been a particularly exciting evening for her."

"Yes, all right. We won't be long." He swung away, then turned back. "Did you have a wrap?"

"Yes. Colleen can bring it with her own, if she doesn't mind. I am not the least bit cool now." There was a definite sparkle in the look she slanted him from under her lashes.

He made no reply, but the expression in his green eyes before he stepped back into the long, double parlor was enough to make her smile once more to herself.

The butler was nowhere in sight. Doubtless he was on

duty in the library, seeing to it that the gentlemen were supplied with refreshments. Melanie let herself out of the house, crossed the front portico, and started along the drive toward the dark huddle of carriages in the open space to one side of the house. Jim would probably be asleep on the box, she told herself. She would have to wake him. He might as well pull the Greenlea equipage out of line and drive it around to the front door. There was no need for Colleen to walk this distance in the dark. For herself, it did not matter. She had been here at this house so many times she really did not need the glow of the lantern from the portico. There was a moon tonight, also. A full moon riding high and golden overhead.

Looking upward as she walked, she did not see the dark shape of the man who stepped in front of her until she was nearly upon him. With a sharp indrawn breath, she recoiled. "Dom!" she exclaimed.

"Yes, it is I," he said and laughed, a peculiar, mocking sound. "For once, luck is with me. When you walked away from me with Roland I followed you. Yes, I did, I was that jealous. At first, I couldn't find where you had gone. I walked up and down the hall, then outside. I decided to see if your carriage was gone, and what do I find? You, alone. No servants, no friends, no relatives, no husband. Just you." Again, he laughed. "Well, Melanie, what did you expect? You were the one who told me to try again."

"You are drunk!" Melanie flung at him.

He shook his head. "Not this time, not unless I am drunk with your beauty and my need for you. It is really too bad I did not know you would be so accommodating as to leave the house alone. I could have done the deed myself, without the need of hiring help. Such a pity, but I suppose they may as well earn their wages. All right, boys, this is the one."

From out of the darkness appeared three hulking shapes. Melanie watched them come toward her in frozen disbelief, three men with squat frames and long, swinging arms. She looked to Dom once more, but he only smiled, devouring the slender lines of her body with anticipation in his eyes.

Abruptly she whirled and began to run. Before she had taken three steps, she was caught from behind. At the feel of a hand on her arm, she screamed, a full-throated sound of rage and fear.

It was Dom who held her. She jerked her arm from his grasp, swinging with her hand for his face. He caught the blow with the side of his arm, then snaked an arm about her waist, reaching to clamp his hand over her mouth. She twisted and squirmed, trying to bite the soft skin of his palm. "Here," she heard him pant, "get her legs." An instant later, she felt the clutch of hard, groping hands, felt herself lifted in the air, carried with scuffling footsteps toward a closed carriage in the shadow of the trees. One man opened the door, then sprang to the box. She was swung high and half pushed, half thrown inside. Her ribs struck the seat, and she fell, tangled in her skirts, to the floor of the carriage. Before she could move, a man fell on top of her, forcing the air from her lungs, and another put a foot on her hip. The door swung shut. With a jerk, the carriage started off.

Melanie lay still, trying to get her breath, trying to think, while at the back of her mind there grew a fearful knowledge that sent a sick horror creeping along her nerves. The men with Dom had been familiar. How he had come upon them she did not know, but the bestial, bearded faces, the fetid breath and cruel grasping hands belonged to men she had thought left behind long ago in a wayside inn on El Camino Real. They belonged to the Bascom brothers.

The carriage flashed past the house, swayed around a curve, and went pounding down the straight stretch of the drive away from Monmouth. Melanie thought she heard a shout behind them, but she could not be sure. The strains of a waltz, mockingly sweet, grew faint and faded away, and all that was left was the night and the jouncing, rattling carriage, and the hands of the men who held her.

"Dom" she gasped, scrambling to a sitting position as

370

she felt rough, hot fingers feeling along her leg beneath her skirts. The hard edge of the seat was behind her shoulders, and she pressed against it, shuddering as she tucked her skirts around her feet. From the darkness nearby came an obscene chuckle, and a hand crept around her neck and plunged into the bodice of her gown, grabbing for her breast.

Abruptly it was snatched away. "That will do, boys," Dom said. "There is plenty of time and plenty of places a damned sight more convenient," he added as the carriage swung from the drive into the road, throwing him across Melanie's lap. Straightening, he slipped an arm about her shoulder and drew her against him.

"We been waiting a mighty long time," one of the men sitting on the seat above Melanie growled.

"You can wait a little longer," Dom snapped.

"Just so it ain't too long," the man returned, a shading of menace in his tone.

As her eyes adjusted to the moonlight dimness, Melanie could make out the Bascoms hovering over her, one on the forward seat, the other opposite. In their crouching shapes there was the look of animals about to attack. They were ready to fight over her like dogs over a tasty bone. There must be some way to use that antagonism.

Drawing a trembling breath, she fastened her hand on the sleeve of Dom's coat. "Where—where are you taking me?" she asked.

"Does it matter?" he inquired.

In the hard irony that colored his words there was little that offered hope; still she had to go on.

"Who are these other men? What are they doing here?"

"Don't you recognize them? They were sure you would, since you were responsible for getting their brother killed. They have a grudge against you for their mother's sake, too. It seems she drowned herself, all on account of you. An unfortunate effect you have on people's lives, my dear Melanie."

"No," she whispered, "Oh, no!"

"Oh, yes," Dom answered, satisfaction in his voice.

"As for why they are here, it is because I hired them. I heard they were down Under-The-Hill asking questions about you, saying what they would like to do if they could get their hands on you. Their ideas coincided so exactly with mine that I thought Providence must have meant for us to join forces. As I said before, I never dreamed you would walk right into my arms. I fully expected to have to ambush your carriage and get rid of your driver. There was even the possibility that I might have to deal with Roland, too. I am sorry in a way that it didn't turn out like that. I could have enjoyed what is going to happen so much more if I knew he was in no shape ever to do the same."

"You mean—"

"I do indeed. First it will be my turn, and when I am finished, the Bascoms can have theirs."

"It—it seems you are easily satisfied," she said, striving for a wistful note. "Once, a whole lifetime was not going to be enough."

"You cured me of that."

"If I did, then what you felt could not have been very strong." She could feel the agitation that gripped him, but she could not tell whether it was caused by wrath or anticipation.

"Maybe it wasn't," he said with a tight laugh. "Anyway, when I'm through, I'll have you out of my system. There will be no regrets when you are gone. I won't even miss you."

"When I'm gone?" she queried, a faint quiver in her voice.

"The Bascom boys have some ideas about that. The red light district in New Orleans has swallowed up quite a few women, though they think the best price for someone like you could be had from a sea captain, heading for the coast of North Africa."

"You can't do that. Your conscience would never let you rest."

He gave a strained laugh. "What conscience? I don't have one, didn't you know?"

"I don't believe that. No matter what you have done, you are a gentlemen."

He drew a deep breath, staring down at her in the darkness. "A gentleman, protector of helpless females?" he asked softly. "Would you appeal to my better instincts, sly Melanie? It won't work, you know. I have none of those either. All I have are the trappings, the name, and the empty promise. No, I am no gentleman, though I might have been one, if you had been a lady."

Melanie tilted her chin. "Whatever I may seem in your eyes, Dom, in my own I have never been anything else."

The Bascom on the seat above her cursed. "Enough talk," he snarled. "You better get busy, Clements. I don't mean to wait all night. This here is fine for me, I've jumped plenty of women in worse places. The feel I got just now has made me as horny as a goat. If you don't take her down and get after it, I will."

"That you will not," Dom said flatly. He shifted his position slightly, taking something from the pocket of his waistcoat in the dark.

"You don't say," the man sneered and shot out his arm, grabbing the shoulder of Melanie's gown. The silk tore with the sound of a small scream, exposing the creamy curves of her breasts. The man's fingers bit into that soft flesh as he caught her shoulder with the other hand, dragging her up onto the seat beside him. On the opposite seat his brother gave a snuffling laugh and began to cheer him on.

Melanie brought her hands up, clawing at the face of the man who held her, suffocating in the vile smell of his body. He kneaded her breast, sending waves of pain to her head, and his arm was at her waist in a bear squeeze so tight she thought her back would break. With blackness before her eyes, she twisted and turned, trying to avoid the rubbery wetness of his lips that slid along her neck and shoulders.

The body of the carriage shifted as Dom got to his feet, looming tall in the swaying vehicle. He reached out his fist and pressed it to the head of the man who held her. Mel-

373

anie heard a sharp click, and then the blast of a gunshot came so close beside her that she was nearly deafened by the sound.

Across from them, the other Bascom brother surged to his feet, grappling with Dom, trying to see what had happened. As he caught sight of his brother slumped across Melanie with blood streaming from a great hole in his head, he gave out a roar, reaching for Dom's throat. Dom twisted the barrel of the small gun, a derringer, that he held in his hand. It exploded again, and the other man sagged. Dom let him fall to the seat; then he turned to Melanie. His breathing ragged, he stared down at her as she lay with the blood of the dead man seeping into her gown. Then he stretched out his hand to draw her from under the body. She accepted his help, but there was a look of horror in her eyes. The moment she was free she released his hand and sank down onto the floor of the carriage. With trembling fingers, she covered herself, then took up the hem of her gown to wipe with shuddering distaste at the blood that stained her shoulders.

Above them they could hear the third Bascom yelling at the horses, feel the vehicle slowing as he applied the brake. He called out to his brothers and, when he received no answer, braked still more.

Suddenly the carriage was rolling free again, picking up speed. Hard on the realization, Melanie heard the mad clatter of another carriage coming fast. Dom heard it also. Muttering under his breath, he dragged the dead man aside, threw himself onto the seat, and let down the window to look back.

The sound of the oncoming carriage was louder now. An instant later, a phaeton flashed past. The man on the seat was Roland. His black hair fluttered in the swift wind of his passage, and his horses were wild-eyed and straining. With precision, he guided the wheel of his phaeton against the heavier wheel of the closed carriage. The man on the box was no expert at tooling such a cumbersome vehicle. It left the road. The off wheel dropped into the ditch, and the coach body leaned to scrape alongside the

374

high dirt bank of the road. There was a rending sound as a tree root caught it. A wheel cracked and broke in half, and the carriage pitched forward. The horses screamed as the shafts dug into the bank, splintering. The high-pitched cry of a man echoed the sound. The carriage jerked forward a few times more, then was still, lying against the bank.

Clean night air and the clear light of the moon swept in upon Melanie as the door was pulled open. "Dear God," she heard Roland breathe, and he stood still, his gaze fastened on the blood-covered bodies that had bounced into the space between the seats, with the apricot gleam of Melanie's silk skirts among them.

"Happily," Dom drawled, "your wife is not dead, only a little shaken up." Rising from his seat, he brushed past Roland to step down into the road.

Melanie pushed her way to a sitting position and, holding her torn bodice in place, reached out to Roland. He pulled her upright, his hand warm and strong, then pushing her skirts aside, guided her over the tilted step and lifted her down.

"Are you all right?" he asked, his voice quiet as he surveyed her face in the moonlight.

She nodded. Before she could speak, Dom gave a muffled exclamation. Toward them around a curve came another carriage, with yet another behind it. The first was the equipage from Greenlea with Jim on the box and Colleen hanging out the window. John Quitman drew the other to a halt and climbed down. The governor spared no more than a quick reassuring glance for Melanie before going to the heads of the rearing, plunging horses, still trying to drag the damaged vehicle from the ditch. A moment later he gave a shout. Beneath the hooves of the fear-crazed beasts lay the body of the last of the Bascoms.

"Melanie, oh, my dear," Colleen said, as she came hurrying forward. "What would have happened to you if your Jim had not seen those men take you, I cannot bear to think." Ever thoughtful, she had Melanie's wrap in her hand. This, Roland's mother draped around her, then put an arm around her.

Roland released Melanie. "Go with Colleen," he said quietly. "Go on home to Greenlea."

Melanie took a step, then looked back. "What about you?"

"There is much to be done here," he answered, glancing at Dom who stood to one side, his back to them all. "Part of it is business for the sheriff. The rest is just something that should have been finished long ago."

Melanie looked from one man to the other, a terrible fear rising in her mind. She wanted to speak, to question, to plead, but the words would not come. Colleen, beside her, urged her toward the carriage. With a deep, trembling breath, she lifted her bloodstained skirts and walked away over the dusty road toward the Greenlea carriage where Jim was waiting, with whip raised, upon the box.

Chapter 20

COLLEEN, CONCERNED by what Melanie told her on the drive home of the events of the night, made certain Melanie had a bath and something strong to drink as soon as they reached Greenlea. Clad in their dressing gowns, they sat for a time talking. At last the actress, assured that Melanie would have no ill effects from her treatment at the hands of Dom and the Bascoms, stated her intention of retiring for the night. At the parlor door, she turned and looked back, her green eyes wise as she surveyed Melanie, arrayed in her soft dressing gown with her hair rippling with a russet sheen around her shoulders. Though it had not been mentioned between them, Colleen was well aware that Melanie hoped Roland would come to Greenlea before the night was done. With a smile and a small gesture of encouragement, the actress went out, closing the door quietly behind her.

Once she was alone, Melanie thought of going up and waiting for Roland in their bedchamber. She decided against it. There was so much she wanted to say to him, so much she had to tell him. She would not stoop to appealing to his senses as a means of distracting him from the unpalatable truth.

Feeling chilled, she kindled a fire. The coals were glowing red before she heard the sound of a carriage on the drive. She had sent Cicero to bed. Rather than have the sound of the bell disturb him, she hurried to the front door and pulled it open.

It was not Roland who climbed down from the vehicle that stood before the steps. It was Chloe Clements. She was still dressed in the gown she had worn to the Quitmans' dinner party, but as she mounted to the veranda and came within the range of the light from the doorway, Melanie could see that the pleasure of the evening had vanished for the woman. Her face was pale, her eyes red rimmed from weeping, and she clutched her hands together at her waist. She paused as she saw Melanie, and her eyes widened; then she came on.

"Melanie, I—I apologize for coming so late, but I have got to speak to you. It is about Dom, and Roland."

"Very well," Melanie said, stepping back. "Come inside." She indicated the parlor, then closed the front door and followed the other woman into the room.

"Melanie," Chloe began.

"Come and sit down by the fire," Melanie said. "You must be chilled after your long drive."

"I would rather stand," the woman said, though she moved with an air of distraction to hold her hands out to the flames under the mantel. "I had to see you, Melanie, because of what happened tonight. You know—you know Roland issued a challenge to Dom over this business. They are to meet at dawn in the morning on the sandbar."

Melanie turned away, reaching out her hand to grip the corner of the mantel. "I was not sure," she answered, "but I thought it might come to this."

"You can't let them go through with it!" Chloe cried. "You have got to stop them!"

"I?" Melanie swung back to face Chloe. "How could I stop them? They won't listen to me."

"Why wouldn't they?" Chloe demanded, straightening. "It is you they are fighting over."

"That isn't true. It is Dom's behavior toward me, a different thing entirely."

"Oh, yes, I know what he did was wrong. But I also know it was you who drove him to it. He hasn't been the same man since you married Roland. Ever since that day,

I have watched my brother sink slowly into drunkenness and an all-consuming obsession with you, the woman who was supposed to have been his wife. He doesn't sleep, he hardly eats, he just sits and drinks and stares. The worst of it is, he knows what he has become. Sometimes he blames you, sometimes Roland, but most of all, he blames himself."

"It is distressing, I know," Melanie answered. "Still, why come to me? Why not speak to Dom yourself?"

"He pays no attention to me; it has gone too far for that. Now, after tonight, his one thought is to kill Roland or to be killed himself. For him, it is one or the other, nothing in between, and I am not certain he truly cares which. You needn't suggest I speak to Roland, either. I have just come from him."

"I see," Melanie said.

"No, you don't see at all, no more than I did. Oh, yes, I thought, foolish simpleton that I am, that the trouble tonight was over my flirtation with Roland. I didn't know you had been abducted. I thought Dom might have called out Roland, instead of the other way around. No one at Monmouth had the least idea what had occurred, though they realized something was amiss. Most of the guests left and went home out of sheer good manners. I was about to drive on home myself when the men, Dom, Roland, and Governor Quitman, returned and retired at once to the library, followed by the few gentlemen still present. They were arranging the details of the duel, of course, though the ladies were not permitted to know what was taking place. It was impossible to keep at least the bare bones of the matter from us, however. We knew who was involved, who the seconds were. John Quitman agreed to act for Roland, and it was thought best, in order to keep the contest equal, for Roland to stay the night in the Quitmans' bachelor guest house. That way he would not have such a long and tiring ride back and forth to Cottonwood after a late night. When Roland left the library, he did not return to the company but went straight out to the bachelor's house. I followed him."

Melanie stepped away from the mantel and took a seat on the settee. Folding her hands, she sat waiting for Chloe to continue.

Chloe stared down at her; then her lips twisted in a wry smile. "Roland was not happy to see me; he was angry, in fact. When I tried to talk to him about Dom, he made it clear that his quarrel with my brother had nothing to do with me. He begged my pardon for leading me to think that he had an interest in me. Without putting it into words, he gave me to understand that the purpose of the attention I had received was, first of all, to arouse your jealousy, and second, to goad Dom into calling him out. In the end, what Dom had tried to do to you had given Roland the excuse he needed to be the challenging party himself."

Staring at the other girl, Melanie said, "You mean that all this time, ever since he came back from Cuba, Roland has been laying plans to force Dom into a meeting?"

"Yes, and that is exactly what is going to take place. So you see, if he kills Dom, it will be murder. You have got to stop it. You are the only one who can."

Melanie made a helpless gesture with one hand. "What makes you think Roland will take any heed of what I say?"

"Why wouldn't he? He must love you exceedingly, or he would not do this."

Did Roland love her? He felt something for her, she knew, though whether it was an abiding lust, or some more tender emotion, she could not tell. Of one thing she was certain, however. There was more to this meeting between the two men than Chloe had said. Roland had hinted on that day at Cottonwood, when he had returned from the dead, that he suspected Dom's involvement in the defeat of the expedition. Did Dom's sister know nothing of that episode, or was she merely putting the best face on things in order to persuade Melanie to do as she wished?

"Even if he does love me," Melanie said finally, "that is no guarantee he will hear what I have to say."

"Maybe not, but you have got to try," Chloe cried. "Dom is all I have. If anything happens to him, I don't know what I will do."

Melanie passed her hand over her eyes. "You will survive, like all women."

"Don't be so heartless," Chloe flung at her. "It may not be Dom who is killed. Don't you care what happens to Roland?"

"Yes—yes, of course, I care."

"Then do something! You can't just stand by and let them try to kill each other. Unless you want Roland to kill Dom? Unless you bear him such a grudge for tonight, and because he would not marry you months ago, that you would like to see him dead?"

"That isn't so!"

"No? Then prove it. Admit what you know is true, that you are to blame for what Dom has become, by going to Roland and telling him so. Oh, I know it may do no good, the duel may still go on, but at least Roland may be persuaded to shoot to wound, not to kill."

That argument was a telling one. Melanie caught her bottom lip between her teeth. She looked up at the other girl, her violet blue eyes clouded with doubt as she met Chloe's hazel gaze. "And what of Dom?" she asked. "If I pledge myself to speak to Roland, will you do the same with Dom? Will you make certain his aim is not lethal either?"

"Oh, yes, Melanie, I will, truly, I will."

Melanie turned her mount into the drive of Monmouth. It was not her purpose to arouse the house; a few yards farther on she took to the sound-deadening grass of the lawn, skirting the columned fortress of a building shining silver white in the moonlight.

The guest house reserved for bachelors was a tradition in the south where the lavish hospitality encouraged house parties lasting months on end. With the young gentlemen out of the way, their elders would not be disturbed by their comings and goings at odd hours, and the mothers or chaperones of nubile young ladies of marriageable age could relax their vigilance at night. The guest house at Monmouth was located in a small grove of trees at the rear of the big house. A commodious, dormered cottage, it boasted two bedchambers upstairs and four down, with a parlor and a dining room.

Melanie swung down from her horse and looped the reins through the iron ring on the hitching post. Considering the party the Quitmans had given that evening, she could not be certain of finding Roland alone, but there was only one lamp burning inside the house. Its light came from the windows of the front room, which Melanie took to be the parlor. Looping her riding skirt over her arm, she climbed the steps, crossed the long front porch, and knocked on the door.

The panel swung wide. Roland stood silhouetted in the opening, edged with a golden nimbus from the lamplight behind him. Melanie could not see his face or read his features, though she knew she stood revealed to him as a woman uncertain of her welcome.

"You didn't come home to Greenlea," she said quietly.

"It was late. I thought you would be resting after what happened, and I didn't want to disturb you."

It was plausible. "As you can see, I am not in need of rest."

He inclined his head in ironic acknowledgment.

"May I come in?" she asked.

For an answer, he stepped back. The lamplight glancing along the planes of his face showed a tightly controlled mask. He closed the door quietly, then turned toward her as she stepped into the parlor. Aware of his scrutiny, she did not turn but stood staring about her, noting the masculine heaviness of the furniture, the practical brown and red shades of the carpet, and the pigeonhole desk in one corner. The lamp was placed on one corner of the desk to illuminate the clutter of papers on its writing surface, along with an open inkwell and a pen. Self-conscious under his steady gaze, she moved closer to the

382

desk. The writing on the top sheet seemed to leap up at her.

I, Roland Donavan, being of sound mind . . .

She went still. His will. He was writing a will. Slowly, she turned to face him. "So Chloe was right. You did call Dom out?"

"Yes," he answered, his voice quiet and even.

"Why? Because of me? Because of what happened this evening?"

"Yes."

"No," she contradicted him. "I have Chloe's word that you have been planning this for some time, and I am inclined to think what she says is true."

"And if it is?" he asked, moving into the room, approaching the square directoire settee to stand with his hands braced on its back.

"If it is, then I would like to know why."

"I think you know the reason for it."

"Do you mean because you suspect he may have had something to do with the betrayal of the expedition to Cuba? If so, then there is something else you should know about the events that led up to that act." Sparing herself nothing, she went on to tell him precisely how the thing had come about, how she had been approached by the Spanish ambassador, how she had overheard the news of when the expedition was leaving and had later relayed it to Dom, how she had discovered his treachery, and finally, of her attempts to stop the sailing of the *Pampero*.

His face grew hard as she spoke. When she came to a faltering stop, he stared at her with a frown. "And is that all?"

"All? Don't you see it is my fault? If it had not been for me, Dom would not have had the information, nor would he have known what to do with it."

"Don't be so certain. There is reason to believe you were far from the only person contacted by the Spanish ambassador. In addition, though the information you placed in Dom's hands may have helped serve to confirm the movements of the expedition, you can be certain the Spanish officials in New Orleans did not rely on the word of one person. The trap for the expedition had been carefully baited with tales of revolutionary activities in Cuba, with reports of the weakness of the Cuban government and the army of Spain stationed there, and with lies of how the Cubans were ready to welcome Lopez as a saint and savior. After the setting of such lures by the canny governor-general of Cuba, no official of the consul of Spain would have dared risk ruining so elaborately planned an operation by sending information that had not been carefully checked. I am afraid that if you have been taking the blame for the downfall of Lopez's filibuster campaign, you have been giving yourself too much credit."

Melanie took a quick step forward. "Do you really think so?" she asked, a look of mingled hope and doubt in her eyes.

"I know it," he answered.

"But Roland," she said, moving to the settee, placing her knee on the seat and leaning toward him. "If you can absolve me of guilt, then—"

"Then why not Dom? Because you meant no harm in what you did. Though it might have crossed your mind once or twice that throwing me to the Spaniards would be a just recompense for what I had done to you, you could never have brought yourself to the point of actually lodging the information. Dom, on the other hand, had no such finer feelings. He not only passed the information, he did his best to see that you took any consequences that might come of it. Oh, I know, he was supposed to be goaded by his love for you. That was also his excuse for attacking you tonight. I consider it no more than doing what he had to in order to get what he wanted. But that isn't all that is between Dom and me, it isn't all by far."

"No. I have often thought there was something else," Melanie said, easing back until she was sitting on the settee, one hand resting on the back. "It has something to

384

do with my grandfather, doesn't it? And with Mexico? Won't you tell me what it is? I have wanted so many times to ask you what happened down there. I think I will go mad if I don't know."

A grim smile curved his mouth. "And you think this is your last chance to find out?"

"No," she whispered with a quick shake of her head. "I didn't say that."

"Never mind. It may be true enough. Since you had the courage to tell me what you had done, I suppose I can always hope that you will believe that what I have to say is the truth."

The look in his eyes was reflective, measuring. Melanie said nothing for fear of breaking the tenuous link she had forged between them. She settled back still more into the corner of the settee, watching Roland as he prowled around the other end as though he were disturbed by the thoughts passing through his mind.

His back was turned to her when he began to speak. "The long march overland to Mexico was a strain on Colonel Johnston. At his age, he could not shrug off the heat and dust and long hours in the saddle as he had when he was younger. His age also made him rigid in his thinking, unable to compromise or adapt to new situations. He resented suggestions from his subordinates on the minor details of camp life. As for the strategy of the campaign, he did not agree with General Zachary Taylor's objectives, nor his means of attaining them. He wanted to charge forward at full gallop, overrunning the reportedly weak Mexican army, taking the capital, and finishing the business. We could all be back in Natchez within six weeks, he said, if only the officials in Washington would listen to him."

Pausing, he swung toward her, a thoughtful look on his face. With a shake of his head, he went on. "In many ways, the colonel and General Lopez were alike. They both believed in the hard-charging frontal attack and were so convinced of their own superiority that they consistently underestimated their enemies. The colonel was correct about one thing. General Taylor lacked the enthusiasm to mount an effective invasion of the heart of Mexico. It was the means your grandfather took to rectify this situation that was at fault. It was after Buena Vista. We were all disappointed that we were not ordered to press on into the Mexican countryside. Instead, we fought a series of skirmishes, always drawing back rather than pursuing the enemy. Finally, Colonel Johnston had had enough. He thought that if he and his troop led a charge after the scurrying Mexicans, the rest of the army would follow out of sheer exuberance, even against orders. He was wrong."

"Yes," Melanie said, a faraway look in her eyes. "I can believe he would have done just that."

Roland nodded. "Our troop was alone when the Mexicans turned back, cut us off, and slaughtered the command. Those of us still alive when the flag fell were taken into the interior. As you know, the captives were the colonel, Dom, myself, and three others. Our horses had been shot out from under us or taken. We were marched for miles. We were given little water, and less food. The prison camp, when we reached it, was nothing more than a cactus-fence enclosure around an adobe hut. It had to accommodate nearly fifty men, the rest captured at intervals during the earlier months of the war. There were no sanitation facilities; the hut was infested with fleas and rats and infernally hot during the day. Diseases, fevers, the heat, all took a toll. The number of men in the stockade when we reached it was not a fraction of the number that had been held prisoner there. The rest had died."

Roland glanced at Melanie who nodded her comprehension, recognizing that the bare words he used did not convey more than a portion of the horror the imprisoned men had undergone.

"The colonel collapsed as soon as we arrived. After a day or two, he slipped into unconsciousness and delirium. It was easy to see he wasn't going to last long. All during the overland march, your grandfather had refused to admit he was responsible in any way for the death of his men, but he had gotten it into his head that we all thought so. We did, in a way, but we also admired what he had tried to do, and the gumption and grit that had led him to order it. There was not a man who followed the colonel who could not have turned back with honor by simply obeying when the bugle sounded retreat. At any rate, we, the five of us remaining from the troop, saw that something had to be done. We decided to drop hints to the Mexicans in authority concerning the colonel's influence with various congressmen. He claimed that he was sympathetic to the Mexican cause, though naturally he must pretend otherwise. We made it known that it would be in the best interests of Mexico if Colonel Johnston were not only given medical treatment so he could recover, but it would also be a good idea if he were exchanged as soon as possible."

"Oh," Melanie whispered. "I think I begin to see."

Roland ran his hand over his hair, clasping the back of his neck. "Yes. Well, it worked. The colonel was taken to better quarters, and we heard that his health improved. A little later, he was released, sent back to the United States. Such preferential treament was too unusual for it to be overlooked by the other prisoners. They placed the only possible construction on it. To tell the other men what we had done, however, might have meant that it would leak out to the commandant of the prison stockade and his officers. At first, we had to consider the colonel's safety and well-being. Later, when he was gone, Dom and I were still strong enough to take whatever punishment we might have coming, but two of the men who had been captured with us were not. They were sick with fevers, dying, though we did not know it at the time. The other man was already dead, shot while trying to escape. After a time, it did not seem to matter. It began to look as if we would all die where we were."

Yes, Melanie thought, watching the play of emotions across Roland's sun-bronzed face. It was not difficult to understand how in the filth, misery, and hopelessness something like that could be overlooked.

"After the fall of Mexico City, we were released. Only

387

Dom and I were left. Our enlistment was up, and it looked like a treaty would be signed any day. There was nothing for me in Natchez, and there was a group of veterans of the Mexican campaign heading for California. I decided to go with them. Dom headed back home to Natchez. I had a bit of luck, made a little money when gold was discovered, and then after two years of wandering, I came home."

"You came home," Melanie said, her eyes dark with pain, "and found that the rumors had also come home to roost with the other prisoners, most of them men from Louisiana and Mississippi."

"That is right," he admitted, "and my dear friend and fellow prisoner, Dominic Clements, had done nothing to clear up the situation. He had simply kept quiet and let the colonel work it out for himself. The answer your grandfather came up with was logical. He and I had managed to get along well enough in a working situation, and I had great respect for him, but there were quite a few things we didn't see eye to eye on. I don't know. Maybe by then Dom had met you and was wary of ruining his chances, or maybe he was afraid the colonel would call him to account for it. Maybe Dom even thought I deserved it, because the original idea had been mine to blacken the colonel's character for the sake of his life. Whatever the reason, he made me the scapegoat, and I rode right into the role from California."

"When my grandfather accused you at Monmouth, you made no attempt to defend yourself," Melanie said quietly.

"It was the first I had heard of it. I was too surprised to think the thing through in those first few seconds, but it seemed impossible to blurt out the truth there in front of all those people. It could not help but humiliate the colonel to learn in such a public manner that his life had been bought for him, and at so high a price. I thought I might talk to him in private during the negotiations for the meeting, but he would not agree to it."

"So you met him on the dueling field, and you de-loped."

"I had already wronged him, caused him the kind of suffering that you pointed out to me so strongly that night at Monmouth. How could I exchange shots with him? But the colonel wasn't satisfied with a show of blood."

"No," Melanie said. "I don't think in his last days that he knew what he was doing or saying. He was a man possessed by the thought of your death. And so, all the rest of it."

"Yes, so all the rest. I regret my part in the tarnishing of the colonel's good name, but there is not much of what happened that I would have otherwise."

Melanie raised her violet blue eyes to meet his gaze. It held such a burning emerald light that she felt her heartbeat surge up into her throat. Still, she could not explore that intriguing statement. Not yet. She ran her tongue over her lips. "In the end, the meeting between you and my grandfather solved nothing. Do you really believe that exchanging shots with Dom will settle what lies between you? And if you draw blood, will you be satisfied? You took his fiancée and ruined the tidy plans he had made for his life. Wasn't that enough?"

"Yes, I took his fiancée and made her my wife, at least in body," Roland said, his tone grim. "I never meant it to happen that way, but since it did, I was ready to consider us, Dom and myself, even. Dom was not. He would not let it be. He did his best to have me killed in Cuba, and he tried to take my wife from me. Am I to let that kind of dangerous and brutal treachery go? Or maybe you would have preferred that I had not come home from Cuba? Despite the vicious way Dom meant to use you, maybe you would rather that I not have come to your rescue this evening?"

"No, that is not true at all," Melanie declared, springing to her feet.

"Isn't it? Then why are you here, pleading for him?"

"I am not," she said wildly. "I am pleading for you. It is you I want to live." Taking the few steps that would

389

bring her close to him, she put her hand on his arm. "You have got to believe me."

He put his hands on her arms, brushing gently up to her shoulders where his grip tightened. "I would like to believe you."

"Oh, Roland," she said, searching the lean lines of his face, a tight ache closing her throat, preventing the words that might prove what she had said to be true.

"I would like to believe you more than life itself," he murmured, his green gaze resting on the pure lines of her trembling lips. "I think it is possible you might convince me, if you tried. Will you try to convince me, sweet Melanie, if only for tonight?"

Chapter 21

WITH TEARS blurring her eyes, Melanie went into his arms. Smoothing her hands upward behind his neck, she lifted her soft, parted lips to his. He caught her to him with the fierce grasp of a man holding a prize he fears will be taken from him. His mouth crushed hers with burning force as his kiss deepened. His tongue touched hers, and she met it, hesitantly at first, then with boldness. Her arms tightened, and she strained against him on the tips of her toes, uncaring for the ache of her ribs or the pressure of her breasts flattened against the board hardness of his chest.

The sputter of the flame on the lamp's wick roused them. Roland sighed and relaxed his hold, then with one arm about her waist, moved toward the door.

The dark of the bedchamber was relieved only by the brightness of the harvest moon coming through the window. In its ripe yellow light the bed stood forth in monastic starkness without tester or hangings. The plainness of the room, the placement of the bed, the light through the window, the lateness of the hour, and the fact that she was in her riding clothes combined to give her the feeling that she had been there before. It was as if in some strange way they were being given a second chance, she and Roland. At the same time, she felt the oppressive weight of gentle melancholy, as though in the autumn night stillness there hung the essence of endings and aching farewells.

Melanie swung to Roland in sudden fear. He stared down at her for a somber moment, then with gentle competence, began to unbutton her riding habit. He undressed her with the slow care of a man performing a rite, something to be held in memory for eternity, if need be. Drawing the pins from her hair, he let it cascade in shimmering waves over his hands, gathering the silken curtain and draping it around her, smoothing it down her back.

"Beautiful Melanie," he whispered, cupping her face in his hands. His warm lips brushed her forehead, her eyes, tasted the corners of her mouth, then took the honey nectar of her lips. Lifting his head, he breathed deep of the yellow rose fragrance that was a part of her. Letting his hands fall, he divested himself of his clothing in a few quick moves, then drew her down upon the bed.

As he held her close against the long length of his body without moving, Melanie felt the ache of a fearful enchantment in the region of her heart. Raising one hand, she touched the crisp texture of his hair, trailed her fingers along the firm line of his cheekbone, and then down his jaw. She brushed across his shoulder, taking a deep, unreasoning pleasure in the tactile sensation and the feel of the smooth muscles of his skin, and continued lower to the hard length of his flank. His breathing quickened, and she was made aware of the rise of his ardor. Shifting slightly, he joined her in the tender exploration, his touch ravishingly gentle. Their warm breath mingled as their lips met and clung. There was no need for haste in the velvet heaviness of the night. If anything, they felt the compulsion to go slowly, to stretch the inflaming rapture to the edge of endurance. Melanie felt the full blossoming of abandon. With her full heart swelling in her chest, she gave herself without reserve, holding nothing back. When she thought she could stand no more without sliding into madness, Roland raised himself above her. She guided his entry, and he pressed deep into her. She caught her breath in sensuous delight as her body accepted the heat and pulsing pressure of his. He was still, holding her in that profound, almost mystical union, until she stirred with a small sound in her throat. He began to move. Pleasure coursed over her in waves, tingling over the surface of her skin as by degrees the rhythm increased. Her senses expanded, drowning in the warm male scent of his body overlaid with the spice tang of bay rum. She turned her head from side to side in wanton response to his thrusts. In the soaring, engrossing transport they shared it seemed as if the world and morning could be held at bay, that they could transcend the threat of death by holding fast to each other. To have ecstasy come to its bursting end and fall away, to feel the ebb of passion was, then, a loss to be mourned. Still, they did not let each other go but with bodies fitted close, lay staring into the dark until sleep overcame them.

Melanie awoke when Roland disentangled himself from her arms and rose from the bed. The moon had set, and the room was in darkness, though there was a faint light beyond the window that indicated the dawn could not be more than an hour away. Through slitted eyes, she watched as he gathered up his clothing, took his coat and cravat from where they hung over a chair, and let himself out of the bedchamber.

He was going. Nothing she had said had made any impression. She was not surprised. She had known from the beginning it was unlikely she could influence him. Hearing the full catalog of sins he had laid at Dom's door, she had been sure of it. In spite of her failure, she did not regret coming. She had found the strength to tell him of her part in the Lopez affair and been absolved of her guilt by his scathing words. She had learned the bittersweet truth about her grandfather and the rumors that had marred his last days, and though she was not certain he believed her, she had told Roland that she cared for him. More than that, she had not let him go without saying good-bye. True enough, it had been a wordless farewell, edged with a passionate sadness; yet both had known full well its meaning. There had been no need for the last lingering kiss before he left her. Rather than wake her for it and extend the time of her dread, he had gone thinking she slept, thinking that when she woke it would be over. It was a fine and generous gesture. It was not his fault that it would be wasted.

Melanie waited until she heard the front door close behind him, heard his footsteps cross the porch and become muffled in the grass as he strode away toward Monmouth. She slid out of bed and hurried into her clothing. Snatching up her skirt, she ran from the bedchamber. In the parlor, she sped to a window. At the big white house, a lamp burned and a pair of saddled horses were being walked slowly up and down the drive in front by a stable boy. Her own mount was still tied before the door of the bachelor house. He had slipped his bit and was mildly, patiently, cropping at the sparse grass near the hitching post.

She could not go yet. She would have to wait. No thoughts of propriety troubled her, however. Her purpose was to reach the place appointed for the dawn meeting without being stopped. If Roland and Governor Quitman saw her, they would undoubtedly forbid her to be present. She would have to keep enough distance behind them so there was no chance of being seen.

Melanie had put up her hair in such a hurry it was straggling down her back again. Though she lacked a brush, she decided to use the time while she waited to make a neater job of it. She began to pull the pins from her hair. Looking around her for a place to put them down, she stepped toward the writing surface of the pigeonhole desk. The paper Roland had been working on the night before was finished, she saw. It lay neatly folded, weighted by the inkwell. The name inscribed across the front was that of Jackson Turnbull, the man who had been lawyer to both Roland's father and her grandfather. Putting down her pins, bundling her hair into a knot on the nape of her neck, she stared at it. When the last pin was in place, she reached slowly for the inkwell and set it aside. She picked up the stiffly folded parchment, then after a moment's hesitation, opened it out. It was a simple document. Except for that portion of his es-

394

tate which must go to his mother, Roland had left his share of Cottonwood and everything else he possessed to her. To his beloved wife, Melanie Johnston Donavan.

The sandbar in the Mississippi River below Natchez was a favorite dueling ground, had been for a number of years. Neutral ground for both parties, it was near enough to town to be convenient, yet distant enough to discourage the curious who might hear of a meeting. That it was also out of the jurisdiction of the town sheriff, who might be concerned since dueling was against the law, did much to enhance the reputation of that isolated spot surrounded by water. Willows and young cypress trees hung with Spanish moss grew on its verge in the rich river silt, but in the center was a clear space of waving grass large enough to accommodate the deadly purpose of the men who gathered there.

The only way to reach the sandbar was by boat. There were men along the edge of the riverbank who turned a nice profit with a leaky scow and a paddle taking men back and forth. They were the same kind of men who rowed out and searched the eddies of the river for the bodies of the dead disposed of by Natchez-Under-The-Hill every night. Sometimes a wounded duelist did not return from the sandbar, though he might have set out for town. Sometimes the injured man might be lifeless when he reached the bank and his valuables mysteriously missing. Though there were honest men among the boatmen, the trick was to find one.

Rather than trust to luck, Melanie asked the opinion of the man tending the river ferry. He directed her to a soft-spoken older man with the glum look of a Scotsman. He heard what she wanted in silence, looked her up and down, spat mightily, then gave a slow nod when she told him she would pay his fee only when she was safely back in Natchez.

His boat was a trim craft with a look of a New England dinghy complete with long, heavy oars set in oarlocks. It had been many years since it had last had a coat of paint, but the oarlocks were well oiled and there was no sign of water in the bottom. The boatman gave her no name, nor did he talk as he sent the heavy boat skimming over the waves. It did not matter. There was about him a look of dependability. Besides, Melanie had not mentioned her own name, nor did she feel inclined toward pointless conversation.

The water that lapped and swirled around the boat was gray, reflecting the color of the predawn sky. They cut through it with precision, keeping to the quieter water near the bank. The air was cool and dank, making Melanie wish she had some wrap to go over the jacket of her habit, and the river smelled of fish and mud and decaying vegetation. The rhythmic sound of the oarlocks and the splash of the oars were loud in the stillness. Overhead came the honking of a wedge of geese pointing south, a sign that the weather was due for a change, but today was going to be fair. Already there was a pink cast to the sky on the eastern horizon.

Around the bend, the sandbar appeared, a long, dark bulk in the water made hazy by the river mists. As they drew nearer, Melanie saw other boats beached on a stretch of sand. There were more of them than she had expected. It seemed they were to have a crowd of spectators after all, though from this angle she could not see the dueling ground for the massed growth of willows.

The man she had hired ran the dinghy up onto the sand, then jumped out and pulled the bow higher before handing Melanie out. Her face grave and a little pale, she stared up at him.

"You will wait for me?" she asked.

"Yep," he replied, spitting to one side, "though I may sashay over to see what is going on to bring a lady like you out here."

Melanie nodded, and the two of them swung toward the damp and well-trodden trail that snaked through the willows.

There were three groups of men standing on the cleared area of the dueling ground. The spectators, who stood well back out of range; Dom and his second at the near edge of the grassy plot; Roland and Governor Quitman at the far end. To one side, with his black bag at his feet and his hands clasped before him in a waiting pose, was the doctor.

Roland was conferring quietly with John Quitman. At the other end of the field, Dom was complaining in loud tones about the quality of the pistol that had been offered to him. His voice was overloud, with a rough edge that indicated plainly that he had resorted to the bottle to fortify himself for the meeting.

Melanie hesitated at the edge of the willows. Now that she was here, she was uncertain of how to proceed. Roland had not heeded her when they were alone; he was even less likely to do so here in public. Dom she might have swayed, but he was not the challenging party. He could not refuse to go on with the affair without appearing a coward. She had known these things when she left the guest house at Monmouth, and in truth, she had no real expectations of affecting the outcome one way or another. It was just that she had felt compelled to see for herself. She had to know what was taking place. She could not bear the thought of waiting for someone to come and tell her whether Roland lived or died. Even so, she felt an overwhelming urge to turn and flee now. She was no longer sure she could bear to watch, that she would not as soon delay knowing as long as possible if the final results should be contrary to her most fervent prayers.

Suddenly Dom turned his head and stared straight at her. "Melanie," he said, a tone of wonder in his voice. "Melanie!"

She stood rooted to the spot as all eyes turned toward her. To run, or to brave it out and stay, there was the choice. With her head held high, Melanie moved forward.

"Have you come to watch me make you a widow?" Dom called, giving a reckless laugh that seemed to have in it the soaring uncontrol of madness. "It is about time you were free. It is about time you were able to leave the bed and board of the man who killed your grandfather with his sneaking lies. You know I did not mean to hurt you last night. You know I love you. Give me your favor and I will be your knight. I will slay the monster that holds you prisoner and set you free, and we shall live happily ever after."

Melanie did not answer until she was close enough that she would not have to shout. Then when she spoke, her voice was hard and clear. "I have no favor to give you, Dom, for all I have belongs to my husband. It is you who lies, for you know that the stories told to the Mexican authorities, told by you and Roland and the other members of Johnston's Volunteers were beneficent lies designed to protect an aging, sick man. It was not the fault of any of you that those stories lived to haunt my grandfather's last days. But the fault is yours, Dom, that you did not explain when the time came, that you let the rumors grow and become blacker until they ate like a canker into my grandfather's heart, that you let Roland take the blame for the monstrous tale that had begun as an act of mercy."

"So Roland told you about that, did he? Now he is a hero in your eyes, noble and upstanding, a hero who took the woman who was going to be my wife."

Melanie ignored the stirring of the group of men who stood to one side, and Roland's white-faced stillness at the far end of the field. "I don't think I need remind you that you could have married me, and did not. But what you don't seem to understand is this, even if I should be a widow after today, I will not marry you. I will never, ever, be your wife. Do you understand me?" She swung to face Roland. "Do both of you understand me? I realize there are other matters besides myself between you, but if either of you feel anything for me, you will stop this here and now. I want no man's blood on my hands."

Quiet fell as both men stared at her, and then Governor Quitman came forward and put his arms around her. "There now, Melanie. Come back out of the way. It has

398

gone too far now to stop, you know, and you are distract-ing Roland."

"Oh, Governor," she said, with tears rising in her eyes. "Make them stop."

"I can't do that. I guess nobody can. It's a bad business sometimes, but there it is."

The pistols were primed and ready. The two men re-moved their coats and waistcoats, then advanced to the center of the field to stand with their backs together. At ten paces they would turn and fire. The count began. Five, six, seven, eight—

Abruptly, Dom whirled. "If I can't have her, I'll make sure you don't!" he shouted. Hard on his words, he fired.

Melanie screamed. The men around her erupted into shouts. The count had not been complete. Roland's back had still been to Dom. Though he had started to turn at Dom's shout, the ball of the dueling pistol took him low in the side, spattering his shirt bright red. He spun around as he was pitched forward to fall full length in the grass.

Dom's second stood stunned, though it was his duty to restrain his man under such circumstances. Before a man among them could move, Dom leaped for his waistcoat, took out his derringer, and started at a staggering run for the fallen man. "I'll kill you!" he shouted. "This time I'll make sure. It won't be like Cuba. This time you'll stay dead!"

Melanie had started toward Roland as he fell, as had the doctor and John Quitman. The moment took on the quality of a nightmare as it seemed that no one would stop Dom, that none could reach Roland in time to shield him. Roland was moving, levering himself to his elbow, his fact twisted with pain, but it did not seem possible that he could steady the pistol he still held in his hand and bring it to bear in time.

"No," Melanie cried. "No!"

At her scream, Dom wavered, a tortured look passing over his features before they hardened once more.

Melanie did not stop. She had outdistanced the others. Covering the last few feet, she flung herself down beside her husband. Blood was pouring from his wound, staining the grass where he lay. The barrel of the pistol shook as his arm trembled with strain. There was no time to take the weapon from him. She placed one hand on Roland's shoulders to support him, and with the other she reached out, curling her slim fingers around his hard, brown fist, steadying, aiming.

"Now," she whispered on a sobbing breath, and the pistol roared.

Dom, almost directly above them, flung up his arms and crashed backward to lie unmoving. There was an enormous hole in his chest from which the blood poured, soaking into the ground. His hazel eyes were open, staring at the sky, and there was on his thin face a look of sudden peace. A stray breeze ruffled his sandy blond hair and swirled the acrid, gray blue powder smoke away, out over the river.

Melanie swallowed hard and looked down at Roland. The pistol had fallen from his grasp, and he had slumped forward with his eyes closed.

"Here, now, let me see," the doctor said.

"Is he—?" Melanie could not say the word.

"No, just unconscious, but he is losing blood at a tremendous rate. I'll patch him up a bit, and then we will have to get him home. Too bad Cottonwood is so far out."

"I'll take him to Greenlea," Melanie said.

"Are you sure? He's going to be a sick man for quite a while. He'll need a lot of care."

"I'm sure," Melanie answered, one hand lying protectively upon the shoulder of her husband.

Willing hands picked Roland up and carried him toward the landing. The doctor tarried a moment to examine Dom for signs of life. It did not take him long to determine that there were none. Before they could put Roland in the boat—the craft Melanie had hired, since it was the largest—the doctor had rejoined them to see that the patient he still might be able to help was settled with

400

the least amount of jarring and pulling about. That done, he took his place beside Roland on the stern seat.

The tall and dour boatman spat over the side, then settled himself to the oars. Melanie seated herself in the prow, and they were pushed off.

Bending his back to his work, the boatman turned his craft, swinging it upriver. The first golden light of day lifted above the trees then, glinting toward them, growing brighter as it cut through the river mist to strike across the water. Here the river made a wide eastward curve. The prow of the boat swung into the brilliant burning path of the sun, and they began the long, hard pull to Natchez.

Chapter 22

THE LAMP burned low, an island of light in the darkness of the bedchamber. Melanie sat beside it, bending over her needlework, her hair catching the light like a fiery halo around her head. Now and then her hands would grow still, and she would look up, her watchful gaze going to the man who lay so still beneath the sheets of the bed on the other side of the room. Roland, his sun-bronzed arms and chest a strong contrast to the snowy white linen of his nightshirt, one of her grandfather's, lay there. He was not awake, she was certain of that much, and yet, he was so restless. She thought his fever was rising. It was not to be wondered at, of course. The doctor had warned her it probably would. Still it disturbed her, because it made her feel so helpless.

The doctor had gone hours ago. He had removed the bullet and thrown it down in triumph, declaring that it had touched no vital organs. Roland was a strong and healthy man, he said. He should recover nicely, barring complications, but it would not happen overnight. The human body, not unreasonably, resented injuries of this sort. It was far from unusual for the patient to be thrown into a fever as his tissues rushed to heal themselves. Many doctors still recommended bleeding to bring down such fevers, and while the method was effective in most cases, he was of the opinion it weakened the patient unnecessarily. The best thing to be done was to leave well enough alone. Give her husband broth and liquids, laudanum for pain, and food when he asked for it; then let him get about the business of healing himself.

The doctor's words were welcome news, and reassuring so long as he was in the house. But when he had gone and the midnight hours came, when Roland's skin burned to the touch and he thrashed about on the bed, they did not help.

"Melanie?"

She looked up once more at the sound of her name. Roland, his eyes bright with fever, was calling her. She came to her feet in a rush and moved swiftly to the side of the bed.

"Yes, Roland?" she said, placing her cool fingers on his hand. It was scorchingly hot.

"Melanie?" he said again, such questioning surprise in his low voice that she felt the press of tears against her throat.

"Yes, I am here."

His fingers turned to clasp hers. His dark green gaze drifted over the pure oval of her face, touching on her mouth, returning to the violet blue of her eyes. "Stay with me," he whispered.

"I will," Melanie answered.

"I want you with me always."

"I will be, always," she said, her voice soft, sure.

The shadow of a smile curved his mouth. His eyelids fell, and the grip of his hand relaxed. Still, it was a long time before Melanie released her grasp and moved away from the bed.

As she resumed her seat and picked up her needle, his weakness was like an ache inside her. He had always been so unassailable in his strength. His lack of it now was what made her sit watching him with dry, stinging eyes, caught in a painful vigil of fear.

His fever raged for three days more. Colleen, Elena, and Cicero took their turns staying in the room with him, keeping alert for any change. But only Melanie could quiet him with a touch, penetrating with the quiet sound of her voice the heated discomfort that tormented him. It

403

was she who was with him when perspiration began to pour from his hot skin, wetting his hair, soaking the sheets and his nightshirt. When he was made comfortable again, he fell into an easy, natural slumber.

Colleen had been called to help with the changing of linens and nightwear. As his chest began the steady rise and fall of sleep, she reached out to touch his cool, damp forehead.

"Thank God," the older woman breathed.

"Yes," Melanie said, and tears of weary gratitude rose into her eyes, creeping slowly down her cheeks.

"He will be all right now," Colleen said.

"I know," Melanie answered, but she could not stop crying.

"It is you I am beginning to be worried about. You are exhausted. Go to bed now and rest. I will sit with him."

"I couldn't rest."

"Yes, you could," Colleen insisted. "Go on with you. I promise to call you if anything happens."

"You promise?" Melanie said anxiously.

"On my word of honor!"

There was no need for a call. Roland slept the clock around. It was longer before Melanie woke again.

The patient improved steadily after that. At first he slept most of the time, helped by the laudanum administered for his pain. Later, he lay quietly, watching the movement of the sunlight on the wall as the days advanced and retreated, resting his gaze on Melanie's face as she read the news sheets to him, or leaned over him to hold a water glass or a spoon to his lips. But before many days had passed, he began to grow restless. His mood turned surly and brooding. He refused the laudanum drops and on one memorable morning, worked himself into such a temper that he shied the china invalid's cup with its molded spout at Cicero's head when he tried to give him his chicken broth, and threatened to fling the basin of shaving water across the room if the butler didn't hand him the razor and let him shave himself.

Colleen, hearing the uproar, sailed into the room in

time to catch the nightshirt Roland sent flying. At the sight of her, Cicero, sighing with relief, took the offending garment, and with a thankful look on his countenance, went from the room to find the upstairs maid and send her to clean up the mess.

Precisely what Colleen said to her son was not known, but he apologized to Cicero, and the incident was not repeated. Still, his black depression did not lift. He ate what was put before him but seemed to have little appetite. He curtly dismissed the idea of being entertained with cards or reading, spending long hours staring at the ceiling. He progressed from sitting up in bed to wrapping the dressing gown that had belonged to Colonel Johnston about himself and moving stiffly to a chair beside the window. And then one morning, he demanded his clothes.

Melanie and Colleen were in the parlor when Cicero brought the request. A strained smile moved over Melanie's face, and she glanced at Colleen before turning back to the butler.

"Do you think he is strong enough, Cicero?" she asked.

"He thinks he is, Miss Melanie."

"I know, but that isn't the same thing, is it?" she said. "I wonder, do you know why he wants them?"

"I'm not sure, Miss Melanie, but I think he means to go back to Cottonwood. He was asking about the horses in the stable and who takes care of them, and saying how he had to leave here."

Melanie avoided the unspoken sympathy in the soft brown eyes of the butler. "I thought it might be that. Tell him—tell him he can have his clothes in the morning. I will bring them to him then."

"Are you sure, Miss Melanie? I'll tell him, but I wish I didn't have to do it. He's not going to like having to wait that long."

Colleen got to her feet. "Never mind, Cicero," she said. "I will do it. It is time I was taking my own leave, and I will see if I can distract him by saying my goodbyes."

When the butler had made his gratitude known and bowed himself from the room, Melanie turned to the

405

actress. "You aren't serious, are you? About going, I mean?"

"Yes, I think so, my dear. Though I would not have missed knowing you for the world, or having these weeks with you to improve our knowledge of each other, I feel it is time I went back to my own life. My face has healed as much as it is going to, except for some of the redness which will fade eventually. It is time I revealed it under the stage lights, for I am afraid that if I don't do so soon, my fears will defeat me and I will shirk the ordeal indefinitely, even forever."

"I had thought you might stay with us, with me, and make your home here. I would love to have you, and I am sure Roland would be happy."

The actress shook her head. "That is sweet of you, but my place is in the theater. If I did not have that outlet for my energies, I would become as restless and hard to live with as Roland is these days."

"Are you quite certain I cannot persuade you to change your mind?"

"Quite certain. If my own feelings were not enough to tell me, I would have known beyond a doubt when I received a letter, as I did yesterday, from Jean-Claude. He has discovered a play that he wants to see produced, a modern version of *The Taming of the Shrew*. He has been kind enough to say I will make a perfect Katherine. I am quite excited about it and anxious to see Jean-Claude. Scoundrels, sometimes, make the best friends. Knowing their own faults too well, they are ready to overlook any you might have."

"I am glad for you then, if that is what you want, though we will be sorry to lose you. I suppose you will take Elena with you?"

"I offered her the position as my maid and stage dresser, but she refused. She wants to return to New Orleans, to a convent there where the nuns are women like herself, an order of Negresses and women of mixed blood. They devote themselves to nursing, something Elena has discovered she enjoys. I have promised to make arrangements for her steamboat passage before I go."

Melanie nodded. "It may be a wise choice. The veil will be an adequate protection for her from prosecution for the death of Henri."

And she will find peace by doing penance for it in helping the sick and injured," Colleen agreed.

Melanie got to her feet and moved to the window. "About Roland. Do you think it is merely having to lie still in bed that has made him so withdrawn and ill tempered lately?"

"No, I think not," his mother answered, a relieved look on her face. "I am so glad you asked, for I have been wondering how to open the subject with you without laying myself open to a charge of interference, or putting myself forward in something that is none of my business."

Melanie managed a smile for the wry tone of the other woman's words. "What is it?" she asked. "Why has he turned against me? When he was so ill, he gave me his trust and, I thought, his love. Now that he is better, he can hardly bear to have me in the room. He seldom speaks to me or even looks in my direction. Now he wants to leave here and go back to Cottonwood. It is as though he does not need or want me anymore, now that he is nearly well."

"That isn't so. It isn't so at all," Colleen declared. "His love for you is a deep and abiding thing, but he cannot bring himself to believe you care. If what you told me at White Sulphur Springs is true, the reasons are not hard to find. What surprises me is that you do not hate each other."

"But I don't hate him. I love him."

"Have you told him so?" Colleen asked.

"No, not in so many words, but I have tried to show him."

"I am afraid he has learned to question your motives for turning to him, to search for any reason other than what you may feel toward him."

407

Melanie lowered her lashes. "I suppose he cannot be blamed for that."

"I think you may look on his wariness and his need to escape from you as a sign of the depth of his feelings. If he did not love you, you would have no power to hurt him. He could stay and take what you have to give without danger to himself, without wondering if you are coming to him out of some feeling of debt you might have because you misjudged him over the matter of your grandfather and Dominic Clements, or if it is because you are dependent on him, having no money to keep yourself or to run this house."

"But it's nothing like that, nothing at all."

"I think you will have to take drastic measures to make Roland believe it; but if you can, I think you will find that you are loved as few women have ever been loved."

"And if I don't succeed?" Melanie whispered.

"It will be a great pity—for Roland as well as you."

A message sent to the steamboat landing produced the information that a packet was scheduled to call in at Natchez on its way upriver that afternoon. With characteristic decision, Colleen made plans to be on it. Packing on short notice was no problem for her. By luncheon time, the house was swept clean of her belongings, and her trunks were loaded on the carriage.

Directly after the noon meal, Colleen went up to make her final farewell to Roland. When she came down again, there was a mist of tears in her eyes, but she was smiling. Melanie walked with her out onto the veranda.

"You know you are welcome to return at any time," Melanie said.

"Yes, I know, and I don't need to tell you, I think, that if you ever need me, you have only to send for me. A message may take a while to catch up to me, but I promise I will come the minute it arrives."

"I will remember," Melanie said.

Colleen gave a nod and began to pull on her gloves. "I would wish you happiness," she said, "but I believe you are intelligent and resourceful enough to arrange that for yourself."

Smiling, Melanie said, "At least I intend to try."

The two women embraced. Cicero came forward to help Colleen into the carriage and then with Jim Coachman on the box, the vehicle pulled away down the drive. As Colleen looked back, Melanie waved. Then with a lift of her chin she turned back into the house.

She did not go near Roland's bedchamber for the rest of the afternoon. Taking Cicero to one side, she gave him careful instructions. Certain he understood, she retired to her own room, ordering a bath to be brought to her. She lay soaking in the warm, scented water for a long time, a look of quiet contemplation in her eyes. Rousing herself at last, she worked lather, scented with the perfume of yellow roses, into her hair, then rang for more water to rinse away the last trace of soap. The day was cool, and she donned a wrapper before she drew close to the fire in the fireplace to comb the tangles from her hair and dry the silken skein. Frowning a little, she rang once more for the maid to be certain a fire was kindled in the bedchamber where Roland lay. At the same time, she sent a request to the kitchen for a dinner tray for two to be served upstairs before that fire.

The early dusk of autumn was drawing in when Melanie took from her wardrobe a dressing gown of lavender blue satin, a parting gift from Colleen. Removing her comfortable wrapper, she stood naked for an instant. Then taking a deep breath, she slipped into the dressing gown.

The heavy satin clung like a second skin, emphasizing the proud thrust of her breasts as the deeply cut neckline revealed their enticing curves. The bell-shaped sleeves cupped her elbows, giving her arms and hands a look of graceful perfection. A wide sash spanned her narrow waist, the trailing ends blending with the fullness of the skirt that draped over her hips, falling in heavy folds to her feet. She left her hair loose about her shoulders in a shining auburn cape shot with copper. With it swinging around her, she searched out a pair of slippers and stepped into them, then stopped in front of the mirror for one last inspection.

She was more than a little pale, but that was not a bad thing, for it made her eyes look enormous and gave her an air of appealing vulnerability. Turning away, she moved to the door, drew it open, and stepped out into the hallway.

The great house was quiet and empty around her. The servants had gone to their quarters, with the exception of Cicero. Melanie stopped for an instant at the stairwell to make certain that the butler was on duty. He was there, sitting on a bench near the foot of the stairs. He glanced up at her and nodded. Lifting a hand, she moved away from the bannister and continued along the hall.

She did not let herself hesitate outside Roland's door but entered swiftly and closed the panel behind her. He lay propped on pillows with his hands clasped behind his head as he stared into the fire. There was a closed-in look about his features as he turned slowly to face her. His green eyes rested for a moment on her face, then traveled slowly over her hair and the dressing gown shaped to the exquisite lines of her form. The affecting paleness of her face was replaced by a flush at the sardonic expression that crept into his eyes. She refused to let it upset her, however. Head high, she came to stand at the foot of the bed, resting her hands lightly on the footboard.

"So you decided to pay me a visit?" he said.

Summoning a smile, Melanie answered, "Yes. Have you missed me?"

He made no reply to her question, but neither did his gaze waver. "Did you by any chance bring my clothes with you?"

"No," she answered, her voice steady. "I have decided that you will not need them."

"You what?" he demanded, his brows snapping together.

"I have decided that you have no use for them. It was my understanding that when you were dressed you meant

410

to leave Greenlea. This is something I cannot allow. I do not mean for you to leave me again, ever."

She did not trust herself to wait for his reaction. Stepping around the foot of the bed, she moved to the bell pull and gave it a tug. Almost immediately, there came the grate of a key in the lock of the door. Hearing it, she gave a small sigh of relief. For better or worse, the deed was done.

"What is this?" Roland asked, rolling to one elbow, hard suspicion in his face as he stared at her.

Melanie glanced at him, then stepped to the side of the bed, placed one foot on the railing, and jumped up to seat herself at his feet. The dressing gown parted to reveal one knee and a length of thigh, but she made no move to cover herself. In that position, leaning against the post that held the tester, she was close enough to speak in a natural tone, yet tantalizingly out of reach.

"What is it?" she repeated softly. "Precisely what I said. I have taken steps to see that you do not leave here. Cicero has locked us in, and I have instructed him to open the door only on my orders. Oh, I know you informed me once that my property is yours now, since we are husband and wife. Cicero does not recognize that fact, I am afraid. He considers himself my servant and will do as I say. You might try to break the door down, but in that case he will summon help from the stables. I do not think," she said judiciously, "that you will be up to such a feat of strength for some days yet, but I ordered that precaution against it anyway."

"I may not be strong enough to break the door down," he said quietly, "but I feel sure I would have no trouble closing my hands around your lovely throat."

She raised an eyebrow. "Possibly, but you would have to catch me first, and before then, you will have to listen to what I have to say."

He stared at her, watching the gleam of firelight on her hair and the gradually widening opening in her dressing gown where the sheen of naked skin hinted that she wore nothing under that garment of shining satin. "All right," he drawled, easing back on his pillows. "I will play your game. Tell me whatever you please."

Melanie did not quite trust the look she saw in his eyes. Still there might not be a better opening. Oblivious of the effect upon her dressing gown, she lifted her knee and clasped her hands around it. Swallowing hard, she looked away to the deepening darkness beyond the window.

"Our marriage has never been an easy one," she began. "It would never have taken place at all were it not for the conventions that require a man and a woman who have enjoyed carnal knowledge of each other to sanctify that union. I think we both recognize that. But there was another reason for my decision to marry you. I meant to be revenged for what you had done to my grandfather and to me. Not to put too fine a point on it, I hated you and I felt trapped by what you had done. I meant to see that you paid for the position in which I found myself. I have thought once or twice that you were well aware of my feelings."

A stillness had descended upon him as she spoke. Now with his eyes fastened on her face, he answered, "I guessed something of the sort from the beginning."

She nodded. "Yes, but what I don't think you realize is that it is no longer true. It is easy to hate someone you don't know, but when you begin to understand him, to share a part of his life, the feelings you hold begin to change, and vengeance becomes a petty thing. I think—I think that if we could have stayed together, if there had not been the Lopez expedition and the separations it brought, this change might not have taken so long. As it was, the time came for you to go to war, to leave me yet again, before I knew I was in love with you. I wanted to tell you the night you left for Cuba, but you did not come to me then, and in the morning, you were gone."

"Melanie," he said, sitting up straighter. "What did you say?"

She turned her head to look at him, and she did not flinch from his hard green gaze. "I said I love you. I am so sorry for the time we have wasted, for the mistakes

412

and twisted reasoning that has kept us apart. This time, if you will stay with me, perhaps we can find not only love, but joy together."

"Stay with you? I would never have left you if it had not hurt too much to be with you. I have loved you, Melanie, since I watched you come down the stairs at Monmouth on the night we met. You asked me then to go away. Do you remember?"

"Oh, Roland," Melanie said. Releasing her knee, she stretched her leg out along the bed, bracing on one arm as she leaned toward him.

"I joined the Lopez expedition because I realized after only a week of marriage that the longer I stayed with you, the stronger what I felt for you would grow, and the harder it would be to lose you when you finally decided, as I thought you must, that revenge was not worth what it cost you to be the wife of a man you despised. It didn't work. Did you never wonder why I was able to reach you so quickly when you set out for New Orleans. It was because when John Quitman told me you were on your way, I was packed, and I had in my pocket permission from General Lopez to return to Natchez and escort my wife downriver. For a time after that, I thought I had won, that you were beginning to care, and then I realized that you had just changed your tactics. I told myself I didn't care, but later, when the business with Colleen came up, and you turned cold toward me again, I knew I did care, that taking you against your will left the taste of ashes in my mouth."

"So you left for Texas with Governor Quitman and then went to Mobile."

"And came back again to find you with Dom. When I saw there was a chance of losing you to another man, I knew the prospect of being forever without you was a thousand times worse than having to force my way into your bed."

"Dom never meant anything to me," Melanie said with vehemence.

"How could I believe it, when he was always near you?"

"I have explained that."

"Yes, I know. Before that, I heard it from Colleen. Still, I could not let myself believe it until that moment on the dueling field when you guided my hand and helped me to fire."

"I don't think I have been so afraid in my life as I was at that moment."

"Colleen also told me of how you saved her life, of how you cried when you lost your child, and of how you called my name when you were so ill. I have wished more times than you can imagine that I had not left you then. If I had stayed with you it would not have happened."

Melanie shook her head. "There is no end to that kind of reasoning. If I had not come to the sandbar that morning, Dom might not have been goaded into firing too soon, and you might not have been hurt. You see? But I had to come. I had grown tired of you making love to me and then leaving me alone."

He shook his head, his voice low as he answered, "I never wanted to leave you, but it seemed the only thing I could do so long as the situation with Dom remained unsettled. I died a thousand small deaths wondering if each time would be the last."

"You came close to a final end on the sandbar, closer than I care to bring to mind. But I warn you that death was your last chance of getting away from me. Even beyond the lock that is on that door, Roland Donavan, I will never let you go again."

He reached out to touch her ankle, his fingers warm as they closed around it, caressing the smooth skin of her instep with his thumb. "I would like to believe what you say," he said, "but there is something stubborn inside me that demands that there be no doubt. Are you certain that you are not saying these things as a recompense for believing me guilty of wronging your grandfather?"

"No, I swear it is not so," she said.

414

"Or does your sudden excess of affection have anything to do with the fact that it is my money that feeds and clothes you?"

Gratitude to Colleen for having warned her of these very points flowed over Melanie as she shook her hair back, her expression clear and smiling. "Is the fact that my grandfather's heart might not have failed him if he had not faced you on the dueling field the only reason you married me?" she asked.

"Of course not," he answered.

"Have you fed and clothed me these months merely for the purpose of keeping me under an obligation to you that would let you come and make love to me when you pleased?"

"No," he growled.

"But I can be no more certain that you are telling me the truth than you can of what I say."

"No," he said slowly, "but we can always put it to the test."

Before she could guess his intention, his fingers clamped down on her ankle and he dragged her toward him. The dressing gown was swept up to her waist, exposing the porcelain whiteness of her hip. His hand smoothed over that rounded surface as he gathered her close across his lap and set his mouth to hers in a deep and bruising kiss. She returned it with all the pent-up fervor of the long, anxious days. As she felt the give of the belt at her waist and his hands moving over the length of her body, caressing, arousing, it was as though some long-held fear dissolved inside her, and she gave herself with trembling gladness to his touch.

At last he raised his head and stared down at her. "Melanie, my sweet love," he whispered. "If I dare to believe you, never tell me I am wrong."

"Never," she answered, "so long as you will promise the same."

He brushed his mouth across her eyelids and down her cheek to the tender curve of her neck, moving in gentle,

415

fiery progression toward the rose-crested mound of her breast.

Abruptly Melanie gasped, "Roland, your wound—you should not have strained it."

"Since you came into the room my wound has not pained me as much as another portion of my body. To see you reclining like some ancient temptress, so near and yet so far away, was more than I could stand. But I was not meant to resist, was I?"

A smile twitched the corner of her mouth. "I hoped you would not," she answered softly.

Once more his mouth descended in warm and devouring passion. She clung to him, freeing herself of the folds of her satin dressing gown, moving closer so he need not exert himself to reach him.

A knock fell on the locked door. "The dinner tray you ordered, Miss Melanie," Cicero called.

Roland breathed a soft curse. "I would tell him to go away," he whispered, "but he doesn't obey my orders."

Melanie smiled with the slow rise of happiness in her violet blue eyes. "Cicero," she called over her shoulder, "take the tray away and bring it back again later—a great deal later."

Beyond the door, the butler was heard to give a quiet chuckle, and then came the sound of a cheerful, whistling tune as his footsteps faded away down the hall of Greenlea.